TAKE A CHANCE ON ME

BOOK 2 OF THE MARC AND MEG DUET

EMILIA FINN

bee*lieve*

PUBLISHING, Pty Ltd.

TAKE A CHANCE ON ME: book 2 of the Marc and Meg duet

By: Emilia Finn

Copyright 2018. Emilia Finn

Publisher: Beelieve Publishing, Pty Ltd.

Cover Design: Amy Queue

Editing: Brandi Bumstead

ISBN: 978 172 397 1778

www.emiliafinn.com

The best way to stay in touch is to subscribe to Emilia's newsletter: www.emiliafinn.com/signup

If you don't hear from her regularly, please check your junk/spam folder and set her emails to safe/not spam, that way, you won't miss new books, chances to win amazing prizes, or possible appearances in your area.

Kindle readers: follow Emilia on **Amazon** to be notified of new releases as they become available.

Bookbub readers: follow Emilia on **Bookbub** to be notified of new releases as they become available.

ALSO BY EMILIA FINN

(in reading order)

The Rollin On Series

Finding Home

Finding Victory

Finding Forever

Finding Peace

Finding Redemption

Finding Hope

The Survivor Series

Because of You

Surviving You

Without You

Rewriting You

Always You

Take A Chance On Me

The Checkmate Series

Pawns In The Bishop's Game

Till The Sun Dies

Castling The Rook

Playing For Keeps

Rise Of The King

Sacrifice The Knight

Winner Takes All

Checkmate

Stacked Deck - Rollin On Next Gen

Wildcard

Reshuffle

Game of Hearts

Full House

No Limits

Bluff

Seven Card Stud

Crazy Eights

Eleusis

Dynamite

Busted

Gilded Knights (Rosa Brothers)

Redeeming The Rose

Chasing Fire

Animal Instincts

Inamorata

The Fiera Princess

The Fiera Ruins

The Fiera Reign

Rollin On Novellas

(Do not read before finishing the Rollin On Series)

Begin Again – A Short Story

Written in the Stars – A Short Story

Full Circle – A Short Story

Worth Fighting For – A Bobby & Kit Novella

LOOKING TO CONNECT?

Website
Facebook
Newsletter
Email
The Crew

Did you know you can get a FREE book? Go to emiliafinn.com/signup
to get your free copy sent direct to your inbox.

TAKE A CHANCE ON ME

THE SURVIVOR SERIES, # 6

Emilia Finn

1

MEG

BEGIN AGAIN

There might be an earthquake somewhere on the west coast. Or the Earth's core is finally imploding. Maybe Frodo destroyed the ring, or Dumbledore is falling from the tower. *Something* is causing the room to shake, and I'm positive it isn't my nerves.

Denial; my best friend.

"Say it. Do it quickly." I glance between Sammy, my best friend, and Kari, my boyfriend's sister. She's also my nurse. "I'm begging you, Macchio, please put me out of my misery."

She swallows and glances between me and Sammy. "You're pregnant, Meg."

You're pregnant, Meg.

I make the nervous 'pffft' noise. "Um. No. I'm not." I stand from the hospital bed in protest, like I'm going to storm out in a rage. I'm not. I'm frozen in this room until she puts my world back on its axis. "No, Kari. I'm not. It's impossible."

She lets out a deep breath and passes her notes to me. "Yes, you are. Look here." She points to a list of numbers. Rows and rows and lots and lots of numbers. My name. My date of birth. The address of Sammy's apartment, which is now my apartment. I'm in the middle of a divorce, and this–

"Nope. No way. I have no friggin clue what these papers say, but this shit isn't funny." I meet her eyes angrily. "Tasteless joke, Kari. I'm not fucking impressed."

She's shaking, too. I feel it as she stands close and shows off stupid papers that make no sense to anyone without a medical degree. "Trust me, this is my brother's life. I'm not kidding."

Her brother. "Your brother… No. It's not possible."

"Of course it's possible! You have sex, it's possible."

"We use condoms *and* the pill. Every single time. I don't *want* kids, Kari! Which means we didn't forget one condom and I didn't miss one pill. Not once."

"Meg, your HCG levels are through the damn roof. This isn't a false alarm."

"I don't know what HCG means!" I stomp away from her and stare desperately into Sammy's eyes. *Help me.* "I'm not pregnant." *Help me!* I look at baby Lily in Sammy's arms. "Oh God! I'm not pregnant. There's no way."

"This is happening, Meg. Your HCG levels aren't normal."

I spin back angrily. "What. Does. That. Mean?"

"It means you're a cat with seven babies in there, or you're a lot further along than someone getting these tests usually are."

"I… what?"

She takes my shoulders and pushes me back until I sit on the bed. Pulling up a rolling chair and sitting between my legs, she takes my right hand between hers and squeezes. "Lots of moms come in here–"

"Don't call me a mom! Don't do it."

Taking in a deep breath and holding it, she stares at me in silence. Releasing it on a heavy gust, she nods. "Fine. Lots of *women* come in here when they're, say, three, four, five weeks pregnant. HCG," she pauses at my glare. *Stop saying things I don't fucking know!* "HCG, or Human chorionic gona– *HCG* is a hormone produced in your body, but only *after* a baby begins growing. We have a standard table of numbers we refer to, and though the groups can swing wildly, HCG in your body means there *is* a fetus." She clears her throat awkwardly. "There are other things that could produce this hormone, but–"

"Like what?"

"Meg, it's not likely, so don't wor–"

"Like what?!"

"Cancer. Cancer could also produce HCG, but I'm telling you not to worry about that for right now. We need more tests, and I'll be doing a couple things in here myself. I've got you, Meg. I promise." She points back down at her papers. "Early pregnancy, say, three, four, five weeks, means your numbers should be somewhere around four hundreds."

"Okay…"

She turns my papers. "Two hundred *thousand*, Meg. That makes you the next octo-mom, or you're two or three *months* pregnant."

"No."

"Yes. I'll order up an ultrasound. Figure it out. If you lay down, I can literally feel around your tummy…" She pauses. "Snitch, if you're as far along as I suspect, can't you feel it? You've had no symptoms? No sickness? No tiredness?"

"I'm always tired!" I grab her hand as she tries to push me back on the bed. "You're telling me my options today are cancer, or pregnancy? Those are the only options I have?"

"I'm saying, I think it's very, *very* unlikely you have cancer." Her large green eyes, just like Marc's, look deep into mine. "I think you're pregnant, and I think you're several months along." She attempts to push me back. "Please lie back, Meg. I swear, I can literally poke around your belly for thirty seconds and have more answers than we have now."

Tears cloud my vision as I lie back. Sammy remains where she first sat when we came in, and with pure shock painted over her features, she watches me struggle to keep my shit locked up tight.

Cancer or pregnancy. Those are my options. They both fucking suck!

"I don't want a baby, Kari. I never wanted a baby." I don't want cancer, either. I just shook Drew off. I'm finally working towards something for me. A career. Something real and good.

I clutch at her arm, but she refuses to acknowledge my comment. She simply helps me lift my legs until I'm flat. "I'm going to touch your belly, okay?" She rubs her hands together to warm them, but I don't miss the tremble. "Are you ready?"

I turn away and stare at the wall. I'm mad at her. I shouldn't be, but I am. She's ruining my life.

"Meg. Are you ready? I need you to say the words."

"Yeah. Whatever."

She lifts my shirt and pops the button on my twenty-dollar jeans. Sliding the zipper open and lowering the denim an inch down my hips, she starts poking. Strong hands, fingers like steel, she starts high near my sternum and starts pressing in deep. She moves down inch by inch, and when her fingers pass my belly button, I turn smug that there's nothing there – until I remember the alternative is cancer.

Another inch down and everything changes. Soft belly turns to something hard. And round. Unforgiving.

She lets out a deep breath. "There it is."

"There *what* is, Kari?"

"Your uterus." Her fingers rest about an inch above my hip bone. Just above where my jeans dig in and make me uncomfortable. She pokes some more. "It's moving up. This is good news, Meg."

"Good? Are you fucking crazy?"

"If you were only a couple weeks pregnant, I wouldn't be able to feel that. The uterus tends to move up out of the pelvis and into the belly around twelve weeks. That means your HCG levels are high – not because there are multiples in there, and not because you have cancer – but because you're a few months along."

"How far along?"

She steps to a drawer in her desk and pulls out a small measuring tape. Poking around my sternum, she pokes, pokes, pokes down until she finds the solid mass deep inside, then with her other hand, she pokes lower. When she anchors her hand to my pelvic bone, she measures from hand to hand. "This isn't particularly accurate. We need an ultrasound, but…" She studies her tape and counts off the numbers. "I'm going to say three months." Her eyes meet mine. "You're three-ish months pregnant."

Oh my God.

I jump from gaze to gaze. Sammy's. Kari's.

Sammy wears a small smile. Hopeful. To most people, I'm sure this is good news. Kari watches me warily. Part medical professional. Part aunty.

Oh my God, aunty.

Or not.

"We need to know exactly what day this…" I bite off my words. "This… *thing* was conceived."

She removes the tape and refastens the button on my jeans. "What do you mean?"

I look between Sammy's eyes and Kari's.

Best friends. Sisters. Confidants. Family.

Bile rises in my throat at the thoughts that ricochet around in my brain. I count dates. "Two-ish months, Marc. Four-ish months," I swallow heavily, "*not* Marc. I need to know the exact date, because I slept with my husband this year, too."

2

MARC

WORST CASE SCENARIO

I've had Megan Montgomery in my home for a whole week, and funnily, when it's just the two of us, we don't fight. It's like our feuding is only a show we put on for everyone else. A fun game we play.

The winner; the one who can fling around the most attitude.

The prize; glory and bragging rights.

It's fun, and I don't even dislike the competition, but when you take us down to basics, remove the excess, remove the noise, remove the audience, when it's just me and Meg in a room with nothing else around, no distractions, no demands, when we aren't putting on a show for our friends, we're actually really fucking happy.

I'm in love with a girl I met when I was fifteen years old.

She walked in full of sass. She hit on my best friend, and in retaliation – because I'm nothing if not proud – I was mean to her. That day begun a fifteen-year war, and though I've called truce a million times, I'm pretty sure she gets off on fighting with me.

But under it all, under the bullshit, I fell in love with a girl who went off and married someone else. For fifteen years, she was in someone else's bed, someone else's home. Not my bed, not my home.

But now she is.

I look up when the front door opens and three chattering women walk in. Tossing the remote aside, I jump up off the couch to intercept with a smile. "Hey."

My sister stops just past the threshold with wide eyes. "Marc. You're not with the guys?"

"Nope." Odd nerves swarm around in my gut. I'm giddy like a nervous teenage punk waiting outside the classroom for his girlfriend.

Ironically, we did this in high school. Scotch was always waiting for Sammy, and where Sammy was, Meg was. And where they were...

I step toward the girls and stop in front of *my* girl. There are three women here, three beautiful women, plus a toddler, but only one of them has all of my attention, and that's something else for me entirely.

Ever since my baby sister came home from the hospital in a fluffy pale-yellow blanket and pink knitted booties, my life has revolved around her. I played daddy to that baby from day one, and that role was only solidified when our parents died in a not-so-botched home invasion when I was twelve.

She's been my little girl and sole focus our whole lives, and now Meg sashays through my door and suddenly my eyes are at war in an attempt to look in two different directions at once.

"I was waiting for Meg to get home." I throw my arm out to catch her as she walks by, but using her years of dance training and the uncanny ability to dodge me since the day we met, she slides out of reach and moves into the kitchen.

I frown and watch her go, but then I remember that we're not 'happy Meg and Marc' around others – *apparently*. I wish we were. I wish I got to keep the perfect version of us always. "I wanted to talk to you about something."

"Hm...?" She avoids my eyes and takes out a carton of orange juice. She pours a tall glass, turns her back to us, and drinks the whole thing dry.

I turn back to my visitors, instead. "Are you guys hanging around here for a bit?" I love them, I truly do, but I want Meg time.

They look around me slowly. Following their worried gazes, I watch Meg shake her head softly. With a frown, I turn back to my sister. "Okay. What's going on?"

"Nothing." She steps into my arms and rests her face on my chest. "We're heading out. We have plans for this afternoon. I'll be around, you know, if you wanna call or whatever, but we were just dropping Meg off. Gotta head out now."

"Alright, well…" I drop a kiss on the crown of Kari's head, and when she steps back, I move in and lay a noisy kiss on baby Lily's cheek. She's the only person here who looks happy to see me. "Love you, Lily girl. I'll come over later to play." I step in and pull Sammy into a side hug. "See ya, Soda. I'll be over this afternoon before the club."

I watch the girls move outside, and I don't close my front door until they've secured the baby in her seat, pulled their own seatbelts on, and driven to the end of my long driveway and onto the asphalt road.

With a pep to my step and a heart galloping with excitement, I slam the front door and walk across the kitchen. "Hey, beautiful." I trap her body between mine and the still open fridge, drop my lips to her neck, and nibble. "I have a question for you. It's super important and can't wait."

Her body tenses, but putting the carton of juice back on the shelf and angling her neck like I knew she would – she's powerless to that spot – she groans and relaxes into my chest. "What question?"

"Do you wanna go out on a date with me?"

She closes the fridge at her back and turns to face me with a frown. "What?"

"A date." I lean in and continue my assault on her neck. I brush aside her long blonde hair and gently bite her earlobe. "I'm asking you out on a real, actual date. Like how grown-ups do it. We've never truly done that, and I know you're not keen on an official *us*, but I really want to take you to dinner."

"Um…" Shaking out of her stupor, she steps back and dances out of my grip. "Marc. I have to work this afternoon."

"I know." Like we're dancing without touching, every step she takes in retreat, I fill with a step forward. "You're off Monday night. I made a reservation at a cute little place – Bella *Lela*. It's new and I've never been, but Luc said it's good. They have this Russian roulette thing–"

"Actually," she skirts around the edge of the couch until it sits firmly between us, "I have to work Monday, too. Katrina called me earlier… While we were out. We had coffee and cake and–"

I frown at her defensive hands. "Okay, you had brunch. Cool story." I take another step forward until my thighs touch the back of the couch. "Are you okay? Are you still feeling weird?"

Her hand snaps to her belly and her eyes grow wide. "Um, yeah. Tummy bug, maybe."

I step around the couch and snag her hand before she bolts. "What did Kari say?" With a pale face and shaking hands, her eyes well up with emotion. "Woah." I half carry, half walk her to the couch and force her to sit down. She was sick like this last night, too, and it's getting beyond a mild annoyance. She's been sick for too long. Tired for too long. "What's going on, Meg?" I brush hair out of her face. "Talk to me, baby. What did Kari say?" I angle my hips and feel around my pockets in search of my phone. "Do you want me to call her back? Are you dizzy?"

"No." Her hand comes down on my knee and pats weakly. "No. Don't call her back, I'm not dizzy."

I press my lips to her brow to test her temperature – like I've done every day for the last week; like I've done so many times over the last two months when she looked out of it – but like every other time, she's not warm. Not sickly warm, anyway.

"I'm worried about you, Meg." I place my hand under her jaw and drag her eyes up to mine. Hers glisten with tears and sadness. "Did you get really bad news? Is that why Kari was being weird?"

I unlock my phone screen, but Meg snatches it and shakes her head. "No. Don't call. I'm fine. Not sick."

"Tell me something, Meg. You're not a crier. Tell me why you look like you're about to lose it."

"I'm not." Taking a deep breath, she shakes my arm off and scoots along the couch. I scoot right along with her, and when she's sandwiched at the end, she stands with a huff and steps around the coffee table. "I have to work in a little while, Marc. I'm fine. I promise I'm healthy. Cancer free," she deadpans.

I narrow my eyes. "That's not funny."

"Really? You'd prefer I had cancer?"

"No, smartass. It's not funny that you're even joking about it. Those shitty words shouldn't be on your lips. The universe is fucked up, and joking about cancer is a sure way to ask for it."

She steps around the back of the couch, her steely spine a direct contrast to the shaking and weakness from a moment ago. Bending low where she dropped her handbag on the way in, she picks it up and turns back to me. "You're right. The universe really is fucked up. It's not my turn to be happy yet, though I swear I worked for it."

I stand slowly and move toward her. "What's going on, Meg? You need to give me some words right now."

"Okay. I have to go home and get ready for work."

"Megan! What the fuck?"

She spins like a rocket. Grabbing a half empty plastic water bottle off the kitchen counter, she cocks her arm back and pegs it at my head. "Don't call me Megan! I'm sick of saying the same damn thing a hundred times."

I stand tall after dodging the bottle, and with adrenaline zinging through my body, I look her up and down with new eyes. "Is this it for us, Meg? Good times, bad times. Are you fucking bipolar, because this rollercoaster is making me dizzy. We were happy just a couple hours ago. What the fuck changed?"

"Nothing changed. Everything changed." She digs keys out of her handbag and turns back to face me. "I need space. Give me space, Macchio."

"Like last time? You need another month? Two? More?"

"Yup!" She swings the door wide with a flourish. "Don't follow me. Don't call me. I'll be back when I'm ready."

"No! That shit's not gonna fly anymore, Poot. I'm over here freaking out and worrying about your health, and you're over there deciding on a whim you need space. I don't want a one week on, one month off relationship anymore!"

"We don't have *any* relationship, Marcus! We fuck, obviously. We fuck too damn much. But what we don't have is a relationship."

"Coulda fooled me! What was it we shared this week? What about when you slept in my arms every single night this week? Casual fuckers don't do that." *I want her to love me back. Why the fuck won't she sit still and love me back?*

"Obviously casual people do cuddle sometimes." Her eyes switch from fiery anger to devastation in one heartbeat. "I'm asking for space. If I've ever needed it, it's now. Today. This week. I need it so bad I feel like my head's going to explode. Don't follow me." She swings out the door a million times faster than when she came in. The silence she leaves behind is deafening.

"What the fuck just happened?"

I storm to my front door and swing it wide just in time to watch her wheels skid from the gravel and dirt of my driveway until they grip the asphalt road. My cow looks between me and her namesake like we're crazy. She isn't wrong.

Don't follow me.

I need space.

We have no relationship.

I swear, my life was normal an hour ago. I was ready to take her out to dinner, tell her I love her, make shit official. I know her life is complicated. I know she has a mess on her hands with her soon-to-be ex-husband, but I can ride that wave with her. I can help her.

"What the fuck just happened?!" I spin and slam my door shut so hard, my entire A-frame house rattles on its foundations.

Don't follow her, my ass.

I sit down on the edge of my couch, stare at the clock, and count down each excruciatingly long minute one at a time. She can have space. She can have an hour, then she's straightening her moody ass out and she's talking.

Then she's bringing her ass back here where she belongs.

I haven't wanted a whole lot in my life. I've never once asked for anything from Santa or my parents. I never asked for a birthday present. They'd ask – my mom and dad would sit me down each year and they'd try and talk me into asking for something.

'A new bike, honey? I bet you'd love a shiny red bike to ride with your friends.'

I didn't ask. I didn't want. Even at twelve, I had this weights and scales image in my head. The more I'd ask for, the more the weights would stack on my side, until eventually, it would all fall over.

Even at eight and nine and ten years old, the concept battered at the back of my mind. I had a baby sister to be a role model for, to look after, to love on. Then when my parents died merely three weeks after my twelfth birthday, a birthday that I was spoiled with gifts I didn't ask for and a chocolate mud cake that I excitedly blew the candles out on, my theory was cemented.

I would never again ask for something that isn't mine. If I wanted something from that day forward, I worked for it. If Kari wanted something, I'd work my ass off for that, too. I'd provide for her every whimsical request, but nothing came to me free.

But now, for the first time in my life, I'm asking for something. And when she says no, which after her little display just now, I'm positive she will, I'll turn around and demand.

It's *my* turn. Damn straight it's my turn.

Fifty-three minutes after her tires touched the road and she thinks she got away unscathed, I jump up from my couch and ignore my ringing phone. Tucking it into the back pocket of my jeans and snatching up the keys to my bike, I sprint out my front door and ignore the chickens that peck at my weeds.

Throwing my leg over the bike, a heady mixture of adrenaline, excitement, and dread swirl dangerously in my gut. I'm flying toward the sun. I'm bringing those scales crashing down and I'm demanding what's mine.

No way am I walking away.

How can she not see that I love her?

How can she not see the words I scream in my head every time I look at her?

I switch the old bike on and rev the engine. I let go of the brakes and race along the gravel driveway at a fast clip, and when I hit the asphalt road and my wheels gain traction, I increase speed.

Maybe I should've sung for her that time she asked.

I've been singing for her for years. Writing songs for her for years.

It's hard to see straight when you have two of the world's most stubborn individuals in the same room. I could be less stubborn if she needed that from me. I could be less proud. Less...

Just... less.

I pull into the parking lot at the back of the garage a few minutes after leaving home, and climbing off my bike, I step past her old and shitty car and head toward the stairs. Several cars I recognize litter the space, but most of the guys are probably in Ang's garage, not upstairs. I'll send the girls downstairs so Meg and I can have some privacy, then we're straightening this shit out.

Today.

I'm either walking out of here with the woman I love and an understanding with where our relationship stands, or I'll be walking out empty handed and broken hearted.

It won't matter, though.

I've been broken hearted since I was twelve. I can handle a little pain. I'll be back next week. And the week after. And the week after that.

I stomp up the stairs loudly, because it's what I'd want when I'm being a stubborn prick. Don't ambush me, give me a minute to pull my head out of my ass privately.

I test the doorknob, though I have keys to this place. I've had keys since Scotch moved in straight out of high school. I tap the door twice, and that's it. That's all the notice she gets.

Swinging the door wide, I step into the small kitchen and stop in my tracks at the sight of Luc holding her sobbing body.

Kari stands nearby with shimmering eyes, and Angelo stands against the wall with his ankles lazily crossed.

"He'll be okay, Snitch. He'll come aro–" Sammy stops and stares wide eyed when her gaze locks on mine. With shaking hands, she holds a blue and white rice bag that we use to warm sore muscles in one hand, and a bottle of water in the other. "Shit."

Luc's horrified eyes meet mine, but I don't think the worst. A small part of me rebels at the sight of him holding her the way he does. So fucking intimately, it does something to my heart – like a small pinch. Teeny tiny, not deathly, not even all that painful, but a small pinch nonetheless.

I cock my head to the side, but I'm not thinking the worst. He's holding her because we're family, not for any sinister reason that might make me want to crush his skull against a wall. "Everything okay?"

Like my soft murmur was as loud as a gunshot, she jumps in his arms and spins around to face me. Tears soak her cheeks. Her hair sticks to the moisture, and her lips, normally so plump and sensual, simply look plump and swollen.

I step forward as that pinch turns to something a little more painful. Tantrums forgotten, I reach out for her hand. "I need you to talk to me. Why are you crying, baby?"

She swipes the tears away angrily and again, her eyes switch from sad to pissed. "I told you not to follow me, Marcus. I told you with words that I know you couldn't have mistaken for something else."

Pinch.

"Why are you being mean? What did I do wrong?"

"You didn't listen to me!" She stomps forward and pushes me back a step. "I need you to leave. I need time to think. Space. Alone time."

I look around the crowded room, and as expected, right after Sammy stepped into the room, Scotch was but a step behind her. "You wanted alone time? You and six of your closest friends?"

Everyone except me.

"Yup! I don't understand what's confusing to you."

"Speak to me, Meg!" I step back and take a deep breath when Ang steps forward. He's readying to shut me the fuck up. I lift my hands to show him I'm fine, but I keep my eyes locked on hers. "Speak to me. We were fine this morning. We were happy, then boom!" I clap my hands and make her jump. "What the fuck happened between happy and not happy? What did I do? I can't fix it if I don't know."

"What happened is I asked for space and you refuse to listen to me!" She shoves me back another step. "Leave. I'm asking you to leave right now. I'm begging you to leave before I say something that I can't take back."

She holds her stomach as though jolted with pain, but instead of leaving, I swing back fast as a snake and pin her to the wall. "I will *not* leave until you speak to me. Use your big words, Megan Montgomery. I *refuse* to leave until you pull your head out of your ass and speak to me."

She bucks against me, but I retaliate by pressing my weight against hers. I pin her from thigh to chest, and though Angelo's hand slams down on my shoulder so hard I know I'll still feel it next week, it's not until I pin her that Meg's dam bursts and she sobs in my arms. Her taut body turns weak as she buries her face against my chest and releases whatever poison is hurting her.

Finally. *Finally*, a breakthrough.

I brush her hair aside and drag her gaze up to meet mine. "Meg, I know this is a really shitty time to tell you this, but I love you. I love you like Scotch loves Sammy, and you running out isn't an *inconvenience* for me. It hurts deep inside in a way I can't put into words."

She sobs and squeezes my shirt between her fingers.

"I'm not mad at you for leaving. I promise I'm not. I just need us to find a better way to communicate. This on and off stuff guts me every time you walk. I want more for us. I want you to love me back."

Big, fat tears slide along her cheeks as she looks up at me. Her lips tremble and her hands shake. "I do love you, Marc."

Soaring. My heart soars with more happiness than anything I've ever felt in my life. "That's good, baby. That's a reason to stay, not run away. You don't have to be scared of loving somebody. I'll make it easy for you, I promise."

She shakes her head. "No. Not easy… I'm pregnant."

Like she pistol whipped me, my head snaps back with shock. I feel the *pinch, pinch, pinch,* and yet, my heart doesn't crash to the ground. Maybe not soaring, but I can adjust. I can climb altitude again as soon as I adjust. "Oh… Um. Wow. Okay."

"It wasn't supposed to happen. We were careful. There were no accidents."

"I mean…" My heart missed a few beats, but it's not so bad now. In fact, tiny little wings sprout. I can do this. "It's not ideal timing, but we can make this work. I'd have a baby with you, Meg. It was my end goal, anyway. We got there sooner than I'd planned, but it's not a deal breaker."

She looks desperately into my eyes. "No."

"Yeah. I mean, it's not the end of the world. I'll start renovations on the house this weekend. Get development applications in. Add a few bedrooms. It's not a big deal. I won't make you climb a ladder with a baby, I swear." I look over her shoulder to my brothers. "The guys will help. We'll add the extra space straight away, and it won't look DIY, I promise." I look back to her. "We built that house with our own hands. It'll look like the house was originally built that way. We could get married. I know that's probably not how you wanted to be asked, but it's there, anyway. We could make a life together." Fuck that rule about not asking for things. I'm asking for it all. "We could make a happy life together, Meg." I brush more tears from her cheeks. "I'll make you happy. I promise."

She fights my hold on her face. Tears dribble freely and slash me every time a new line marks her beautiful face. "No."

"Yes!"

"I never wanted kids, Marc. You knew that. Everyone knew that!"

"But plans change. Plans are allowed to change!"

"No…" She takes a long, cleansing breath, and the way her lungs fill brings her stomach out to press against mine. My baby. My baby's in there. My family. She's the mother to my baby.

Double down. Ask for it all.

"We can be a family, Meg. I'll make you happy."

"No…" She turns her face away in protest. She can't look me in the eye. "I'm going to have an abortion."

Weights and scales. They all come toppling down eventually.

3

MEG
GOING HOME

I watch through the crack between the blinds as he stumbles out like a wounded soldier. A wounded soldier missing some important limbs. Maybe a gushing head wound. A heart riddled with bullets, and maybe he hasn't eaten in a few days, either.

I broke his heart.

I literally watched the way his face screwed up in pain. I'm pretty sure I watched his heart through his eyes. Through his soul. I watched it metaphorically crumble and dry out like an old prune. I watched it explode into dust.

That's why I needed space. That's why he needed to leave me be for now. I needed to think through my plans, I needed to think through what I would tell him.

"Can someone follow him, please?" I turn back to my stunned friends. "Angelo? Would you mind? You know he's not doing well right now."

I swipe tears from my cheek and lock in every single bone and muscle I possess. If I let it go, if I relax, I might just melt into a puddle of despair on the floor.

I can't break yet. I still have friends to get out of my home.

Then I can melt.

Angelo steps up to me instead of out the front door. Bending his neck low, his eyes bore into mine. "An abortion? Really, Snitch?"

I look away as shame washes over me. "I have to."

"You made that decision in the three hours since you found out you were pregnant? Three hours is all you're giving it? Didn't think to sleep on it?"

"No." I swallow nervously. "Yes." I cowardly shrug. "I'm not having babies, Ang. Everybody knew that already. This wasn't a rash decision."

He shrugs casually and turns away in dismissal. Collecting his keys, he steps out the door and turns back with sad eyes. "Whatever. Your body, your life. I'll be with Marc." The door slams at his back and his boots stomp down the stairs.

He didn't say he disapproves. He didn't say he was mad or sad or disappointed, but the slammed door has fresh tears spilling over and dribbling onto my lips.

I get why I've been so emotional lately. I get the mood swings. Even the dizziness when I thought I was hungover.

"Oh my God." My eyes meet Sammy's. "I was pregnant and drinking. A lot."

Unclasping her hand from Scotch's, she scoots around Luc and Kari, and stops in front of me.

She takes my shaking hands in hers, and it's not until her steady and warm hands hold mine that I realize how violently I'm shaking. "Abortion, Meg? You didn't mention that before now. You kinda just dropped a bomb on everyone. That's probably something you should've done with him in private."

"I told him I needed space! I told him to leave me alone."

"So you punish his inability to stay away from the woman he loves by threatening abortion?"

"No! I'm not threatening him. I'm... He doesn't love me, Sammy. I needed space. I asked him for space." I plead with my eyes. "I never wanted babies. I've said it a million times."

"You should think about this." Scotch steps forward. "I'm not judging you. Trust me – I've learned my lesson. We're family and we'll support whatever choice you make, but give it time. You have time to choose." He looks me up and down. "What are you, a few weeks along? You have time."

"I think she's about three months," Kari murmurs. "It's hard to see. She has no belly, but the timing, HCG, placenta placement; we need an ultrasound to check, but I think she's already stepping into second trimester."

His face screws up. "Three months already. Ouch. Can you feel it moving?"

"Don't put that on me!" I step forward and poke his chest. "I know what you're doing. You're making it a person instead of a fetus. I know what you're doing, Samuel, and it's not fair."

"We need to book a scan."

I glare at Kari. "You want me to see the baby. To hear it's heart-beat." I look from one set of eyes to the next as I scan my friends. "She *thinks* it's three months. I'm still married to my husband, guys. I was still having sex while with my husband." Luc's face pales. He gets it. "This could be Drew's baby!"

"Drew's baby or not, you don't have to abort. It's still your baby, Snitch. Marc will love it no matter what. He'll love *you* no matter what."

"You're not listening to me!" I snatch up my discarded handbag. "This isn't about Drew or Marc. This is about *me*. I'm not having babies!"

"They get no choice?" Scotch's eyes plead just like mine. "I get it. Women's rights. I'm not judging you. I'll support your decisions till my dying breath – even at the expense of my brother's heart – I'm just asking that you think it through. This is a life changing decision, Meg. You can never undo it."

"I know what this is, Samuel. And I know what my choices are." I turn and swing the door open. "I appreciate your support, I really do, but this isn't a decision by committee. This isn't a vote. This is *my* choice, and I made it a long time ago. *That's* why it was easy to marry a piece of shit, because I knew I'd never have his babies. I'll under-stand if you don't agree with me. I'll even understand if you hate me.

But this is *my* choice and not up for discussion." I step outside before I break down.

Before I admit my fears.

"I don't want a scan, Kari. I want an abortion. If you can't help organize that for me, I'll understand. I know you're caught in the middle of this and your brother. I know I hurt him. I can find medical care elsewhere." With a final sob and fresh tears when Kari's face screws up *exactly* the way Marc's did, I slam the door shut and jog down my stairs.

I came home to have space. Alone time. To come to terms with my choices and try to beat back my fears.

I can't have babies – this isn't a choice for me.

I jump into my beat-up car, pull out of the lot, and begin the process of undoing a lot of hiding I've done the last few months.

Years, even.

For the first time in well over a decade, I drive toward my old home. Toward the estate side of town.

The Turners live on Maple Tree Hill. That's where Scotch grew up. Where Marc lived in high school. I still don't even know why he lived there. They're brothers by choice, but not by blood, and it never occurred to me to ask why he lived there.

Because I'm a self-absorbed and selfish bitch.

On the very opposite side of town, not so far from Marc's new home, is Sera Grove Estate. I pull up at the large, wrought iron gates, press in a fifteen-year-old code, and when the gates slide open, I burst into tears.

He never changed the codes in all this time.

He's been waiting for me to come home.

I drive my old car up the hedge-lined driveway until I pull up beside the eighteen-car climate-controlled garage. I climb out and hold my stomach when the movement twinges with pain.

I've managed to go months with no clue something was growing in there, but now that I know, I can't *not* focus on it.

Every move I make reminds me of the softball in my belly. Every time I turn, I feel the pressure deep inside my stomach. Every grumble of hunger reminds me why I've been so hungry lately; because someone else is feeding off of me. Taking my food for itself.

My baby. Marc's baby.

If I have to accept the fact I'm carrying a baby, then it's Marc's. I refuse to entertain any other option.

But if I own the fact it's Marc's, then my choices burn hotter from inside.

I'm going to abort Marc's baby.

I climb the front stairs weakly, as though I've run a fifty-mile marathon and barely have the strength for fifty more steps. Using the keys I've kept since high school, I insert the right one in the lock and sob when the barrel snicks and the door unlocks. I step into the silent home that I always loathed for its museum-like feel. It was always so cold. So impersonal.

I spent my entire childhood mostly alone. We didn't have a live-in housekeeper once I was old enough to order takeout on my own. We had no nanny once I was old enough to wipe my own ass. My daddy had a demanding career and a shattered heart after the death of my mom. He spent his time sitting alone in his study talking to my mom's framed photograph, and I spent my time in my room wishing I had more friends and a daddy who loved me more than he loved a ghost.

I feel his presence long before his words, and when I look up to find my elderly father standing at the entrance to the front foyer, I swallow down the dread and nerves.

He's aged so much.

In his seventies already, my mom and dad were older when they decided to have kids. His hair has thinned and lightened. His jowls hang where they never did before.

We have so much to talk about. So much to make up for.

My hand flutters to my belly. "I'm pregnant, Daddy. I'm so scared."

"Megan."

We both step forward, neither one of us stopping until we slam together, our tears merging and our breath clashing.

I have to bend my neck to rest against his shoulder. He's almost two whole feet shorter than Marc, and though I came here to escape Marc, I realize now I really want him to hold me. I sob harder, not because my estranged father holds me, but at the memory of Marc stumbling away after I fired my death shot at his heart.

Why am I this person? Why do I have to hurt him?

"Come inside, sweetheart." Daddy pulls me through the foyer until we step into the large reception room. Nothing has changed. In all these years, nothing has changed. He helps me sit on the dark-brown club lounge that I wasn't allowed to sit on before I was ten, because God forbid I mess it up.

Reburying my face in his soft neck, his shaking hands brush my hair aside and his scent, musk and brandy, envelopes me in the hug I never received when I was a child yearning for one. "I'm so happy to see you, honey."

"I'm sorry, Daddy. I'm sorry I haven't been around."

"You're here now. You came home when you needed to."

"I love you." A brand-new bout of tears soak my cheeks. "I'm sorry I haven't told you that in so long. I'm sorry I've been so mad at you." I was so mad he named me after my mom. I was so mad he essentially tried to make me my mom's clone instead of my own *me*. I spent my entire childhood trying to live up to her memory, and no matter how hard I tried, he still retired to his room for hours every night to talk to her photo instead of me. "I get it now. I get why you chose her."

"What are you talking about?" His thick hands swipe away my tears. His eyes are the same as mine. Speckled green and watering with heartbreak. "Chose who, sweetheart?"

"Mama. I'd choose Marc, too. If he died, I'd talk to his photo. I'd miss him with my whole heart." His face screws up in pain and confusion, and probably a million other things. I'm hurting everyone today. I'm reminding my daddy of the death of his one true love.

I killed her.

Of course he chose her over me. Of course he never came looking for me all these years I've dodged him.

"I'm so sorry, Daddy. I get it now."

~

FOR HOURS, my phone goes ignored. My bag, stuffed under the couch and out of sight. I sent Katrina a deeply apologetic text requesting the night off work about an hour ago. After that, I set my phone to silent, packed it away, then sat back and let my daddy take care of me.

I need to be that precious spoiled princess again. Just for a little while until I go back to reality. Just another hour until I make decisions that will set me on a course for the rest of my life.

It's not the course I ever expected for myself, but it's the way my life is now.

"So you're expecting a baby?" Daddy passes a delicate pink and white china teacup, and pours from the matching pot. "That's exciting news, sweetheart."

"I'm getting a divorce." I look up shyly when I feel his gaze snap sharp. I have so much to admit to. "I left Drew several months ago. I was so stupid. He was cheating on me, stealing from me. Stealing from us. He had me sign the deeds to the house over to him."

My daddy's a lawyer. That's his life's work, so when he finishes pouring his own tea and sits down, he sits as Arthur Montgomery – lawyer, not father. He leans over the side of the couch, where he has a conveniently stashed yellow legal pad, turns back to me with a pen poised and ready, and a shrewd brow lifted. "Please explain, Megan. Go back to the start."

Of course.

I warm my hands on the teacup and rub my thighs together to create friction. I'm cold. Shivering cold. Nervous and nauseous. "I trusted him. He was my husband, and stupidly, I blindly trusted him. I didn't pay attention to anything he did. Said. Didn't say or do." I brush loose tendrils of hair from my face and tuck them behind my ears. "I don't ever remember signing, and if he'd been upfront about it, had been honest, then I never would have, but he has the deeds to the house now. With my signature. It's not a forgery, I did sign, Daddy. But I never meant to. He snuck them in somewhere, I wasn't paying attention to what I was signing. He stole more than seven million dollars from my account." I meet his eyes nervously. "I know that's your money. He stole, and because it came so easily to me, I didn't look after it the way I should have. I'm sorry I let him have your money."

Daddy pats my knee gently. "Money isn't a big deal to me, sweetheart. I have more than I can ever use in my lifetime. I have more than *you* could spend or Drew could steal in this lifetime. But that's not the point here. If he stole from you, then we make him pay. There are criminal charges to consider–"

"It's already happening," I interrupt him. "I spoke to a lawyer months ago. The criminal case is already with the DA and they're sorting through the paperwork now." I dial down my naiveté and don't stutter over the long legal words Jules has been feeding me the last few months. "The criminal stuff is being taken care of, but my lawyer did suggest finding a separate divorce lawyer… you know, if you wanted to do it. I know you're good at it."

With fire in his eyes, he nods and squeezes my knee. "I'll do it, honey."

"I wasn't gonna ask you. I didn't want to run back to Daddy, you know?"

"This isn't you running back to your daddy. This is you hiring the best divorce lawyer this country has. It'll be the last full case I take before retirement."

"I didn't want you to save me."

He sits back on the couch and pulls me into his arms. I haven't been hugged by him like this in… maybe ever. "I'll always want to save you, Megan. Always. You're my baby girl, and no matter what, no matter how long you're gone, I'll never stop treating you as such."

"Can you call me Meg? Please?"

His soft arms turn taut. "Your name's Megan, Megan. That's the name your mother and I gave you."

"No." I sit up and break the hug that I so desperately want. *"Her* name was Megan, and when she died, you gave me her name." I hiccup and rest a hand on my belly. I would never call this baby Megan. Never ever. "What name had you guys picked out for me? Before she died? I'm not my mom, Daddy, and I'm not Megan. I'm just Meg. I'm just me. I want you to acknowledge that, and I need you to know that calling me Megan hurts me."

"Sweetheart..."

"You named me after a woman I never knew. I don't miss her, because I never knew her. I don't love her, because I never knew her. But her legacy haunts me. It haunted me every day of my life because you tried to pigeonhole me into being her, and she still haunts me now while I sit here with this baby in my belly."

Like he forgot my announcement, his eyes turn soft and his hand covers mine. "I'm going to be a grandpa? You're not seventeen anymore, Mega–" He catches himself and cuts off his word.

Hope swells in my heart. In all my life, he's never been open to change. If we'd had this conversation back in high school, he simply would've shut me down and called my request nonsense.

"*Meg*. Sweetheart, I'm not sad or mad that you're pregnant. You're not a baby anymore. You're a grown woman, and I'm an old man. It's not ideal – what with Drew and whatnot, but I'm thrilled for you. A baby is a blessing, and up until today, I had no clue I'd ever get to be a grandpa. You could've had children already and I'd have no way of knowing. You haven't returned my calls in years–"

"I don't know who the father is." I close my eyes in shame when his grow wide. *'I don't know who the father is'* – exactly what every dad wants to hear his daughter say. "I think it's probably Marc, the man I've been seeing recently, but Kari, my... doctor... has yet to confirm dates. She said I could be three or four months along, and if that's the truth, then it could be Drew's."

"I can help you make an appointment for scans. If you're already four months, then you need to get everything straightened out, sweetheart. You need prenatal supplements, medical care. You could know if that's a boy or a girl. You need to shop and set up a nursery. Lamaze classes. The baby will be here soon, and you need to be ready. You can come back home, since your life is in flux right now. There's room here and I'd love to have you. You can put the baby in your old room, it shares a door with the next bedroom. You can have an entire wing to yourselves, and–"

"No, Daddy." I clasp his hand in mine and prepare to hurt another person I love. "No nursery, no scans, no Lamaze. I'm going to have an abortion."

"You– What?"

I take a deep breath and beg the world to forgive me. And if not the whole world, then just Marc. His is the only forgiveness I truly want. "An abortion. I can't have this baby."

"Why not? Why would you abort? I might have been... *lacking* as a father. I know I could've done better, but I never regretted you. I love you with my whole heart, sweetheart, and that's nothing you can know until you hold your own baby in your arms."

"Did you hold me, Daddy? Right after I was born?"

"Of course I–"

"You held me? Really?" I study his deceitful eyes. "My mom died in that birthing suite, and you held me while she was lying there dead?"

His face pales. "I mean–"

"How long after she died before you actually held me, Daddy? How long was it until you could see past the grief? How long did it take before you discharged me from the neonatal ward, named me, fed me?"

"It was a hard time for me–"

"I know it was." I squeeze his sun-spotted hand. "I get it now. I'm not mad at you anymore, but I can't keep this baby. I just can't."

He's getting frustrated, his voice turning sharper. "Why not, Megan? Abortion shouldn't be your first option. There are a hundred other choices that should come before it."

"Why? Because I'm scared!"

"Of what? There's nothing to be scared of. You and the baby can live here. Drew will be taken care of legally. If it's his baby, he'll be relieved of responsibility. If it's this Marc fellow's, then we relieve him, too. Everything will be fine. What's there to be scared of?"

"Of dying! I'm scared to die. I'm scared of restarting the cycle. If I was keeping the baby, you would *not* be 'relieving' Marc of custody, because he's a good man! A wonderful, caring, loving, stable and perfect man, but I'm not keeping it. I'm scared of dying, and of Marc becoming you – bitter and sad and lonely – and mostly I'm scared my baby will live in my shadow. I won't do that again."

"So you give the baby no chance at all? I don't understand your choice!"

"I'm not asking you to understand, Daddy. I came here because I needed shelter from the world. Everything I know, every*one* I know is a damn hurricane right now. A hurricane I created, but it's there, nonetheless. For the first time since I moved out after high school, in fact, for the first time in my *life*, I came home looking for a damn hug. I know my choice fucking sucks. I know it, and I know this makes me a coward, but I don't want to die." He pulls me into his arms when fresh tears spill over. "I know I'm a coward. I know I hurt people. I know I'm a terrible, terrible person, and I know I'll go to hell for this, but I'm scared to die."

4

MARC
IT HURTS

Hot, salty, pussy bitch tears slide along my cheeks and dribble off the end of my nose. I pick up a six-by-four timber beam that was slated to become some rich mother-fucker's new kitchen hutch, and throw it as hard as I can. My muscles sing as it slams against the side of my barn and splinters like shrapnel spray. I pick up an old axe, and with a roar of something that feels like actual death, I send it flying after the beam. It slams against the wall and sticks in blade first.

I can't do this. I can't live knowing my baby's in her belly and she's on the way to kill it.

I turn and charge as soon as Angelo walks through the barn door. Eyes wary, instantly lifting his fists, he skips out of my way when I swing.

I don't know why I'm swinging at him. I can't control myself. It's better than hitting her. "She's just going to kill it!"

Ang skips out of my way when I turn back and charge again. "Calm down, Marc. Just take a breath."

"I love her and she's going to kill my baby?" I pick up another beam of wood, smaller than the last one, and as though it were that prized slugger Meg kept boasting about, I grip it tightly and slam it down on my drop saw. The entire metal structure crashes to the floor and the cord tears from the socket and whips around. The metal prongs of the plug glance off the side of my face, and though I can feel the blood trickle along my jaw, I don't feel the pain.

"I have nothing, Angelo. I've never had anything in life but family. *Family*!" I roar. "To a man who has nothing, can afford nothing, was never given a damn thing, family is pretty fucking important, and she's going to kill mine?" I feel like my brain's going to explode. I just can't compute. My heart won't accept it. "I have to be able to fix this! There has to be a way."

He steps around the mess I made and approaches slowly. I'm the wild boar and he's the foolish animal tamer. "I don't know, man. I don't know. I don't know your rights. I don't know hers. It's only been a few hours since she found out. Nothing's gonna happen overnight, so we all need to just calm down."

"Fuck you and your calm bullshit. You calm down!" I lift a heavy sledge hammer and slam it down over my shitty old tractor. Steel slides on steel, and the hammer dents the front grille, but the mark blends in with the billion other dents and marks already on the old pile of shit. "Because I'm not rich? Is that what this is?" I spin and face him with the hammer cocked over my shoulder. His eyes snap between mine and my weapon. "She doesn't want my broke ass babies in her body?" I swing again and smash the headlights out of the tractor. "I knew she was a spoiled brat, I knew she was a pain in my ass, but this? Really?" Tears – tears I don't remember ever crying – slide over the edge of my jaw. "Has she been planning to break me all along? Where's the mercy? Where are my choices?"

He warily steps forward and reaches out for the hammer, but I cock my shoulder back out of his reach.

"It all happened just hours ago." He stops his forward movement and raises his hands. "She found out just hours ago. Nothing bad has happened yet."

"She already said what she's gonna do. Something already happened! She already broke me."

"Nothing's permanent until it is. Let's just relax, sit down. She's with Luc and Scotch. Nothing will happen without you knowing about it, so just… just calm down, man."

"I can't." My heart throbs to the same beat as my brain. Tears burn the backs of my eyes and my throat aches from shouting. "I can't relax. I need to see her. I need to stop her, beg her."

"Not today." He steps forward and takes my hammer. "Tomorrow. We'll talk to the guys tomorrow. We'll talk to her. You don't get to tell her what she'll do with her body, but you can at least talk it out."

"There's not enough alcohol in the world to fix this, to make me forget what she told me today." I turn away as angry tears fall over my chin. "I love her, Ang. I love a selfish fucking whore, and when I promise to take care of her, of the baby, she'd rather abort. She'd rather kill a human being than live her life with me. What the fuck is that? What's so wrong with me that abortion is the option she chooses?"

"We know her." He sets the hammer down and presses his hand to my shoulder. "She's our friend, so there's probably more to it–"

"What *more*, Angelo? This isn't third hand information! She told me to my face she's going to kill my baby."

"There could be a million reasons. She hasn't explained herself yet. Give her time."

"There's no time!" I throw his hand off and stomp toward the axe wedged in the wall. "There's no time! How far along is she? How long into it is she allowed to abort?" I spin and pat my pockets in search of my keys and wallet. "How long do those places take to give out an appointment? Fuck! What place does she have to go to? The hospital?" I swing past him and evade his arm when he tries to stop me. "Let's go to the hospital, stand the fuck in her way when she tries to go through with it."

"Dude." He shakes his head and steps in front of the barn door. With arms crossed and sad eyes, he denies my exit. "No. You cannot stand in her way. I love you, Marc. I really do. We've been brothers for as long as I can remember, but I will not stand with you so you can force a woman into medical decisions she doesn't want."

"What about what *I* want? What about me? Why don't I get a choice?"

He lets out a deep sigh. "This is one of those things in life, man. It's not always fair, but you cannot force a woman to have a baby she doesn't want."

"But she can't just abort a baby that's wanted! There has to be a middle ground. There *has* to be."

He steps out of my way, but only so he can maneuver me toward the house. I haven't been inside since I left with intentions to ask Meg for more. I got a hell of a lot *more* out of that visit. And then it was stolen away within two seconds.

"Come inside and sit." He pushes me forward. "I'll text the guys, we'll see what's going on, but we're staying here. We aren't going to find her. We aren't going to the clinic with picket signs to stop her."

"I wanna get drunk."

He nods and claps a hand to my shoulder. "Yeah, let's do that. I'm not going anywhere. Let's get drunk, we'll stay up and bitch about women. Just like old times."

I laugh as we walk into my house, though there's no humor. It's more of a sob disguised as a laugh so as not to show Angelo how truly broken I am.

I don't want to laugh and drink and bitch. I want to go beg her for my life. I want to beg for my baby's life. There's nothing in this world I wouldn't give if she'd just stop and listen to me. Just two minutes, that's all I'm asking. Two minutes for her to stop and let me speak, let me plead.

I step through my kitchen to the cabinet beside my microwave, and pull out a bottle of cheap scotch. "Is the garage closed?"

"Nah, but I'll text Scotch and tell him to do it. The guys will have it under control until closing time, then Scotch has keys to shut it all down. I'll stay here with you as long as you want me."

I turn back to the counter with a couple of glass tumblers and the liquor, and a strange mixture of hate and love swirl inside my belly. It won't join and mix. I can't make the two feelings live in harmony. I hate her, then I remember I fucking love her, and my heart loses a brand-new chunk of life. "Where is she, Ang?" I hate the bitch. I fucking loathe her. "Is she at her place? Is she safe?" I love her. I hate that I love her.

"She was there with the others when she asked me to follow you."

I stop halfway through unscrewing the cap on the bottle. "You're here because she told you to? You don't wanna be here?"

"I'm here because you're my brother and I love you. She just so happened to ask me to follow. She cares, Marc. No matter what you're feeling in your heart right now, she cares."

"Yeah, she cares; about money, about status, about getting her way. What she doesn't care about is anyone but herself."

He sighs and watches the floor. "Give it a day or two before you condemn her. You love her, we all heard you. That shit doesn't just switch off because she hurt you."

"Wanna bet?" She can rot in hell. "Is this how it's going down, then? Scotch and Luc are siding with her? It all comes down to this?"

"There are no sides, Marc. Kari's with them, too. That's your baby sister – she's not choosing sides, and neither are the others. They're simply there right now, and we're here." He pulls out a stool and sits down as I slide a glass over my countertop.

This is one way to take a trip down memory lane.

Let's get smashed on scotch while thinking about Megan Montgomery.

Just like old times.

"Can you text them?"

He spins the glass in front of him, and though I down my first quickly and pour another, he just holds his and takes out his cell. He taps at the screen for a minute. "There. I asked where she is."

"Good. Take a drink, Ang. I need to drink enough to make my brain forget the last twelve hours."

He shakes his head, but picks up the glass and shoots it back until he wheezes from the burn. "I'm not drinking enough to forget, but I'll have a few with you."

Shrugging, I pour his second and my third. "Whatever floats your boat, Alesi. You were always solid. Always there for us."

"Don't get sappy now. Things will work out."

I shoot back my third and let the liquid slide down my throat into my gut. "I was going there today to ask her for more. I love her."

He nods and continues to spin his glass. "I know you love her. We all see it."

"Instead, I got what I got and now I'm sitting here with you instead of her."

He laughs under his breath. "You're lucky I'm not sensitive. I might be offended that you don't want me here."

"I wish it was her." I look up and meet his gaze. "I love you, Ang. But I love her more, and I wish it was her in my kitchen right now. We don't fight when it's just us. Did you know that?" When he softly shakes his head, I shoot back my next drink and pour another. "We still talk shit at each other. We pretend to fight, but that's our flirting, I think. She likes to piss me off, because it's not *real* pissing me off. It's just a battle of attitude."

"Yeah, Macchio. We know." He laughs and drinks his shot. "We've been watching this show for years." His phone dings. Looking down, he reads aloud, "Says she's not there. She went for a drive an hour or so ago."

I nod and look down at my watch. "Probably at work. She had to work tonight."

He locks his phone screen and watches me. "Leave her alone for now. Don't go there."

I tip the bottle up to my lips and take two heavy swallows. Swiping my arm across my lips, I nod and refill his glass. "Yeah, I won't go there today. I can't have the conversation we need to have with her boss around. Or Mac. He'd probably beat me up for yelling at her."

"So maybe don't yell at her." His dark eyes come up to mine. "You know it's coming, so prepare a *different* speech."

Dropping my elbows to the cold counter, I press my face into my hands and noisily breathe through the pain. So much pain. It hurts so fucking much. "I asked her to marry me and she said no."

"Don't take that personally. I don't think any chick wants to be proposed to because she's knocked up. Ask her again some other day, when you're both less angry and emotional. She might give a different answer."

I laugh bitterly into my hands. Giving up on the silent deal I made with myself a minute ago, I pick up the bottle and take another mouthful. "There's no coming back from this, Ang." I lick the cheap liquor from my lips and scan my house. This wasn't enough for her. I built this house with my own hands, but it's not enough for her. "She's aborting my baby, man. I can't love her enough to get over that. This has been coming since high school. Hooking up was inevitable. Breaking up was inevitable. Too bad she has to break me in the process."

5

MEG

TAKING THOSE STEPS

For the whole week following my pregnancy announcement, I sleep in the bed I slept in during high school. I live, for the first time in my life, under the care of an attentive and loving daddy. He takes off work and assures me his young new partner is perfectly capable of running the office without him.

Of course she is. Jules could run a multi-trillion dollar merger between a tire factory and a fast food joint, and there would be zero hiccups or ripples. She's *that* good. And according to her, my father's out of the office more than he's in these days. His calling in would hardly interrupt her flow.

I have to tell him soon that she's his contact for the criminal case. I haven't given him the information he needs yet. It's not urgent, and I just don't feel like it. I'll do it soon.

I sit at my daddy's kitchen counter with a bowl of soggy cereal fermenting in front of me, and scroll through my text messages with dread. They've been coming in regularly all week. But they've all gone unanswered.

Kari: You need to find a doctor, but please, don't cut me out.

Kari: I love you, no matter your choices. That won't change.

Kari: Be safe. Text me when you're ready. I'll come with you to the clinic.

Kari: Are you still feeling dizzy?

Kari: Drink lots of water, eat good food. I love you.

And then from *Luc: You're freaking my girlfriend out, Snitch. Answer our damn calls!*

Luc: You can trust us to be there for you. No guilt. No judgement.

Luc: We can love you and Marc at the same time. I promise. Call any time of the day or night. I'll come.

Then *Marc: Please call me, baby. I'm begging you to call me.*

Marc: I love you. We can work through this. We can work through anything as long as we talk.

Marc: Don't make any rash decisions. That's my family, too.

Marc: I fucking hate you for doing this to us.

My daddy walks into the kitchen on Thursday morning in pleated slacks and a black T-shirt. Stopping at the industrially fancy coffee machine, he starts grinding beans and frothing milk. I simply hold onto my mug of instant coffee – my one single allotted serving of caffeine per day. Studying the delicate white ceramic, I wish for the brown chipped mug Marc's cow licked.

"What are your plans for today, sweetheart?"

I'm going to the clinic. I'm starting the process. "I'm going to work. I'll be heading out in an hour or so." I wait for him to finish making his coffee and turn back to lean on the counter. "I'm going back home tonight. It's time to go back to real life."

"You don't have to go." He pushes off the counter with pleading eyes. "You can stay. I thought you were staying."

"No, Daddy. But I'll be around, I promise." I stand and walk around the wide island counter. I stop in front of him and smile as bravely as I can manage. "I promise to come back. To visit often. I won't be a stranger anymore."

"I thought we'd been doing better…"

"We have. You've given me a week to come home, to recoup, to be a little girl while I sort out my life."

"You've still been working."

I laugh softly. "I still have a job to do. I can't afford to get fired. And I still have that wedding to organize. I won't let them down."

"Your work ethic, honey, it's—"

"Surprising?" I lean back against the opposite counter. "Bet you didn't expect me to be working class one day."

"Honey…"

"I like it, Daddy. I don't want you to save me. I don't want you to buy me out of trouble. I want to be independent and…" I search for the word. "And free. I want to buy my own freedom."

"Who's handling your case, honey? The criminal case. I don't know what's happening. I'd like to offer my help."

He'd like to take over. To fix everything. "Client confidentiality forbids me from telling you his or her name."

He glares with barely concealed frustration. "That's not how that works."

I let out a frustrated sigh. Frustration at myself, not him. "I'll make an appointment through your PA in a week or so. I need time to rest, then I'll make an appointment and we'll get the ball rolling. I promise."

"Stay one more night," he bargains. "I didn't realize last night was your last. I would've done something special. Something more than watching movies."

"Die Hard is an epic movie marathon, and I don't regret our choices one bit. It was nice doing it with you, Daddy. It was nice to chill out, eat bad food, and watch movies with you."

Thick brows shadow his light eyes. "I'm sorry we never did that before. We should've been doing that all along, but instead, I—"

"Why did mom die? The actual medical reason."

His features change. It's only subtle, but I see the way his eyes change. The way they darken. "Your mom got sick a few years before you were born, sweetheart. It put strain on her heart, and sometimes when that happens, your blood can clot. We didn't know this at the time, though. Her sickness was years before and we basically forgot about it. Apparently, without us realizing, her blood had clotted, and it wasn't until giving birth – the strain of it, I guess – that the clot in her brain hurt her. She had a stroke on the table, and she… well," his voice shakes, "she never recovered."

I study my feet as nerves and anxiety swarm in my belly. I'm so terrified of dying while giving birth. I'm terrified of having a baby that I'll never know. "Do you think maybe I have the same sickness? The same issue?"

"No, I don't." He places his coffee on the counter and steps forward to take my hand. "What she had, what happened to her wasn't hereditary. It just… was." He looks down at the floor and shakes his head. "It was just bad luck. But it won't hurt you, too. I promise."

As soon as I can escape the kitchen without hurting Daddy's feelings, I move toward my old bedroom, take my cell out of my pocket, and lay back on my bed with a hand over my belly.

Like a cruel joke that just won't go away, the universe decided now that the cat's out of the bag and the whole world knows my shame, it's time to make my belly pop.

A special announcement for those who missed the big news.

It's not huge. I don't look super pregnant, but if anyone cared to look, you can definitely see a small bump. In the time between Kari's measuring tape last week and now, the fetus has risen out of my pelvis and firmly into my stomach area, and that softball only she as a medical professional could feel last week, is now obvious to even me.

Lying on my back like this makes it more obvious. The placenta is sitting right there. Taunting me. Daring me to chicken out of my plans.

Before I lose my nerve, I dial Kari's number and wait for her to pick up.

"Meg?"

"Hey." And just like that, my voice breaks. Kari's barely a handful of miles away, but it feels like thousands and like I'm calling home. It feels like my life with them is too far away to touch.

"Are you okay? What's going on?"

"Yeah." I cough and clear my throat. "Yeah, I'm okay. Sorry about the radio silence. I've been lying low. Getting my bearings."

Almost like she's moving through her house and closing doors on the way, I can hear the silence around her change. "That's okay. Bearings are good. Laying low is fine. So… did you, um…"

"Not yet." I run my spare hand over the solid ball inside my belly. "Um… I was wondering if you could help me."

"I can help you. Anything you want."

"Can you refer me…? Um. I'm not sure where I need to go to get this done."

"Oh." She clears her throat nervously. "You're going ahead with it. Okay," she adds with fake cheer. "I'll help you. I promise."

"Just tell me where to go. You don't have to come with me. You don't have to get involved."

"Meg, no. It's okay. I'd rather be there for you than not. It's important to me that I support you in this."

"But, it's your–" I close my eyes. Taking a deep breath through my nose and out my mouth, I add, "I guess I need to see my regular doctor first. To get dating scans and such."

"Yeah," she answers softly. "That's the first step. Um. You can do that at the clinic appointment. They'll want to scan before they do anything."

"The clinic?" I mentally plan my course of action. "The clinic on Cedar Hill?"

"Yeah. I know a girl who does rotations there, so I'll help you hook it up. It'll be comforting having someone we know."

"Kari?" My voice cracks as a single tear slides from the corner of my eye and down over my temple. "How is he? Is he okay?"

"He's… coping. He's angry right now, but he's alive and well, and right now, that's all I need."

"You don't think he'd… You– He'll be okay, right?"

"He's not going anywhere. For once, I'm glad he's ridiculously overprotective of me. It keeps him close so I'm able to watch over him."

"Thank you, Kari. Thank you for watching over him. Thank you for not condemning me."

"S'okay. I'll call my friend and find out how to get you an appointment. When do you wanna go in?"

"Today. Tomorrow. Whenever we can. I need to do this now. I need to stop living in limbo."

"Alright. I'll call now, then I'll call you back. I promise." She's silent for almost a whole minute. "Meg? Thank you for trusting me. Thank you for calling me."

I swallow down the choking lump in my throat. Turning to my side on the bed, I tuck my legs up as high as they go until my thighs touch my barely protruding belly. "Thanks for taking my call. I know you have reason not to."

"I'll always take your call. Give me twenty, I'll talk to Shanna, then I'll call you back. Do you have to work today?"

"Tentatively." I swipe away the traitorous tears that balance on the edge of my nose. "Katrina knows everything, so at the moment, I'm on shift, but she knows that I'm making this call today. She's playing it by ear and will pick up the slack if I need to call in sick."

"Alright. Did you work all week?"

"Yeah. Gotta pay rent somehow." My voice cracks pathetically. "I didn't see Marc all week."

"Yeah. He's staying away. The guys made him promise to give you the space you asked for. And he doesn't trust what he'd say or do if he did see you. He's mad, but he doesn't wanna hurt you, either. So, he's staying away."

I nod, though she can't see me. After hanging up, I lie in exactly the same position until she calls back fifteen minutes later with an appointment time.

Even in abortion clinics, I guess it's good to know people in high places, because my appointment is less than two hours away.

Rip the Band-Aid off. Get it done before I chicken out.

KARI, Sammy, and I are led into treatment room three at eleven on the dot. Following us in, a young woman not a whole lot older than us sits on a roller stool with a clipboard in her hands and an impassive smile on her face. "Ladies." She looks at all three of us in turn, as though she's unsure which of us are knocked up. "My name is Leanne and I'm the physician's assistant. I'm here to help answer any questions you might have, and get the ball rolling."

I shyly raise my hand like an idiot, and when her kind smile stops on my face, I swallow nervously. "My name's Megan Montgomery. I'm the pregnant one."

She smiles and flips a page on her clipboard. "Yes, Mrs. Montgomery. Shall we start?"

I nod and look at the floor, and for the next hour, we discuss my medical history, my birth control plans for the future to avoid the same thing happening twice, and she asks about a hundred times in a hundred creatively different ways if I know what I'm doing.

I say yes out loud, but inside, my stomach hurts.

No. I don't know what I'm doing, but the unknown has me paralyzed with fear. I don't know what else to do. I just don't know what to do, and after everything I've done to him, I'm thoroughly ashamed of myself because right this second, while discussing aborting his baby, I really want Marc to come to me.

I want his arms to envelope me and his voice to whisper into my hair that everything will be okay.

Mostly, I want him to tell me he forgives me.

6

MARC

NOT A BABY ANYMORE

She was with my sister.

I know she was, because Sammy told Scotch, and Scotch accidentally opened his mouth. He didn't set out to let me know, it was simply a slip of the tongue, but now I know.

Meg made contact.

She's been AWOL for more than a week, and though I promised to stay away, I actually haven't. I drove past her apartment every day since the last time I was inside, but every single night, the lights were out. Nothing changed. The place was deserted, and if it wasn't for the fact Mac told me he sees her at work, I would've lit the world on fire looking for her.

But AWOL or not, she made contact. She's okay, and as far as I know at this point, she hasn't gone through with it.

My sister shares an apartment across town with the twins – Luc's twin sisters – so it's not odd that I find his bike parked out front on a weekday morning. I don't stop to think it through, I simply thank the universe that my sister's small car is parked out front, too. That means I don't have to go searching for her. I don't feel like going out in public. I just want to stay home and work, or in town at my friends' houses.

Letting myself in the front door without knocking, I come to a dead stop at the sight of creamy white flesh, back dimples, and long golden-brown hair fisted in a man's hands.

My disbelieving eyes meet his over her shoulder, and I watch as he tosses her to the side so quickly, my baby sister crashes to the hard floor with a boom.

Luc's eyes grow wide and his hands shoot up in defense. "Marc... Man, we can explain."

In shock, and stupid with it, my eyes go back to my sister for confirmation. Light blue jeans and a pastel pink bra... that's it. Her top, the same top she wore to Oz's that time, the top that was too damn small for her and showed off her belly button, now sits covering my former best friend's bulging jeans.

She watches me with petrified eyes, but scrambles to her feet at the same moment a red tinge blinds me and I dive toward Luc. "Marc, no!"

He's dead to me now, and soon, he'll be dead to everyone else.

I slam my fist down on his jaw with a sickening crack, and blood spurts across the cream tiled floor. I don't know if it was my hand that broke, or his jaw, but the sound is music to my ears when he drops like a sack of shit and his head cracks against the tiles.

For the first time in ten days, I'm mellowed the fuck out.

Except I'm not.

"I'll kill you, motherfucker." My arm sings with pain, but my fists rain down, anyway. Slamming again and again over his stupid pretty fucking face, I let him wear every single moment of hurt, frustration, terror, and uncertainty I've had to endure since the day my parents were stolen from us. "She's mine!" I scream in his face. "Mine!" I let him wear every second of heartbreak that Meg inflicted on me from *before* the abortion thing, and then I let him wear everything from *after*.

The after is the most potent anger of all.

He keeps his arms up to protect his face. My knuckles crack when I slam my right hand down on his elbow. But I don't stop. I can't. Blood coats my fists and arms, and with racing breath and a hammering heart, I don't even hear my sister screaming at me to stop.

It feels like an hour, but only a second at the same time. I'm on him, then strong hands pick me up and toss me off. I kick my legs out and kick Luc's slack jaw, but the strong arms refuse to let me free.

I fight my captor's hold, but I'm not released until I'm in Kari's kitchen and my heart ricochets and lodges in my throat. "Calm the fuck down," he shouts in my face. "Cool it now, or I'll call X."

"He touched my baby sister!" Spit flies between us, but Jack Reilly doesn't let me loose. He doesn't shy away from my screaming and he doesn't back down when instead of fighting to get away from him, I turn my fists on him. "I'll kill him. I'll kill that motherfucker!"

"I think you already did, you fuckin' idiot." He pulls a cell from his pocket and dials with one hand. He speaks into the phone so calmly, like my life isn't teetering on the edge of insanity. "X, you need to come to Kari's place. Now. It's Luc. He might need an ambulance or something. No." He pauses to listen. "Marc. Beat the piss outta him. Okay, catch you in a bit."

"Marc..." Red flames inside my brain at the sound of Luc's slurred words. Spinning back to the entrance, I dive at the same time Jack does, and he pulls me back.

"Cool it, man!"

"I thought we were brothers!" I fight Jack's hold as Kari steps up behind Luc with teary eyes. She rests her hand on his forearm, not in restraint, but as though she's showing who she's standing with.

Pinch, pinch, pinch.

Luc's face is messed up bad. Blood smears his cheeks, his split lip, his arms. He holds one arm close to his body as though injured, his left eye, already swelling shut. "Kari and I... It's not as bad as it looks, brother, I swear."

"Don't call me brother! You're no brother to me." His eyes shutter, his Adam's apple bobs. He's hurt more by my words than my fists, but I don't give a fuck. "I thought we were family, Luca! I thought you had my back, but you do this? She's not like Sassy. She's not like those girls."

"Marc, I swear, it's not like that. If you'd just listen to us–"

"Us? *Us!*" I look between them and swallow down the bile that rises in my throat. "There's no *us* for you two. I trusted you, Luc! I trusted you. I'd send my sister home with you. You were her safe ride when I couldn't do it. You're her brother. Not her fuck buddy!"

"Marc." She steps forward hesitantly, and when he shoots his arm out to stop her, to protect her, to keep her from me, I roar and fight against Jack's hold.

"You don't stop her from coming to me, you motherfucker!"

"Marc." Kari slips around Luc's hold. Stopping in front of me, she looks up into my eyes with tears in hers. "It's not so bad, I promise. We're in love. If you take a breath, I can explain it."

"In love? He's a fucking whore, and you're my baby sister."

"I'm not a damn baby anymore, Marcus!" Angrily, she pushes me back against Jack. "You need to get that through your thick head. I'm grown now! I'm not a baby, and I don't have to ask your permission to date someone."

"You don't get to date *him!* You need to put a fucking shirt on, then he's leaving and never coming back. You'll never see him again, Kari!"

"Oh, for fuck's sake. You don't get to make that call. I'm in love with him. Do you hear me?" She taps her fingers on the side of my pounding head. "We've been seeing each other for a long time, but you don't know that because you refuse to see me as a woman instead of a scared eight-year-old girl."

"Seems he has no problem seeing you as a woman!" I push past her when Jack's hold slackens. Slamming my fist down on his tender jaw, he whips around until the side of his head slams onto the kitchen counter. Dropping to the floor like a sack of potatoes, his body slides lifelessly onto the tile.

Jack roughly drags me from the room, and through my red tinged vision, I watch Kari dive onto Luc in panic. Jack drags me past Britt, and with the memory of a dinner from so long ago, I spin in his arms. "He fucked Britt, too. Don't you remember that? Let me get in there and finish him so he doesn't get to touch what doesn't belong to him anymore."

"You remind me of that ever again, and I'll kill *you!*" He shoves me onto the same couch Luc and Kari were sitting on only minutes ago, and when I try to jump up and move away, he slams his meaty fist into my chest and pushes me back down.

I can't breathe past the panic, past the horror, the sickness, the hurt. I can't breathe.

I came here looking for information on Meg, and instead, I got a front row seat to the final scene of my sanity.

This is what happens to me. Scales and weights. I ask for one thing, and I get something entirely different.

Alex and Oz rush through Kari's living room at some point in the afternoon, though I couldn't honestly say whether it was a minute after Jack dragged me away from Luc, or one hour, or six. EMT's rush through shortly after, and though they carry big scary med-bags, I can't find it in my heart to give a flying fuck about his well-being.

This is too much. I'm done. I'm out.

Alex walks out a long time after he walked into the kitchen. Sitting on the coffee table in front of me, his deep blue eyes watch me with an expression he's never used when looking at me before. Ever. "You could have killed him, Macchio."

"I hope I did."

Shaking his head, he takes out a notebook and half a pencil. "You don't mean that. He could press serious charges, Marc. That wasn't a tap. You messed him the fuck up. That's jail time, and not just a night or thirty. That's serious time. And let's not forget he's employed by the state, emergency services. That'll add time to your sentence."

I sit forward and press the heels of my palms into my eyes. "I don't care. I'll do it."

"You will?" His brow arches skeptically. Looking over to Oz as he enters the room, his gaze comes back to mine. "You'll do time?"

"Yup. No reason not to. Got nothing else to do."

"What about your sister? Who'll look out for her then? Luc?"

"Motherfucker."

Alex leans forward with concerned eyes. "I heard rumors, Macchio. Pretty serious rumors. We're supposed to be brothers, but I hear this shit on the grapevine instead of from your mouth? You want to go to prison and leave your kid out here?"

I shrug carelessly, but inside, I'm sobbing like a little bitch. "She's aborting, anyway. Don't care."

"You better fucking care!" He stands from the table and leans over me. "You just beat the fucking crap out of your brother. Your sister told me he slammed his head on the cabinets. His eyesight's wonky because you smashed his head. That's not okay, Marc. In no universe is that okay."

"He's fucking Kari."

"I…" He swallows heavily. "I get that hurts, man, but what you did is worse. Way worse."

"How the fuck is that worse?" I jump up from my seat and stand toe to toe with the chief. One of us has a gun and authority. The other is just a fucking pussy who's always getting fucked over.

"How is it worse? You could have killed him, Marcus!" He shoves me back down into the chair. "You're pissed today, I get that, but tomorrow, he'd still be dead. Then what? You can't undo that shit." He leans forward and drags me out of my seat. Spinning me, he drags my hands behind my back and slams the cuffs down over my tender wrists.

"You're under arrest, Marcus Macchio, for assault and battery resulting in grievous bodily harm. I'm doing this for your own good, I promise you that. You have the right to remain silent. I don't want you to say shit, because anything you say can be used against you. You have the right to an attorney, but you do *not* have the right to ask my wife to rep you. If you do ask her, I'll shoot you in the face."

He shoves me past a silent and crying Kari toward the front door. I turn my eyes away with shame. She's choosing him. She's not standing with me.

It's all over.

I lost Meg.

I lost the baby.

I lost my sister.

I even lost my brother.

I lost everything that means something to me.

I'm done. I'm tapping out.

~

LIKE I'M fifteen years into a thirty year sentence, I sit against the wall of my cell – though my cell is simply the drunk tank at the local station, not at the State Penitentiary. I tap my sore knuckles against the concrete floor and hum under my breath. If I stop humming, I'll start thinking about my life. If I start thinking about my life, I might break.

Can't break.

I honestly don't know what will happen if I do, and the fact I'm so close scares the shit out of me.

Never in my life have I been as scared of anything as I am of my slippery hold on sanity.

I feel like Rocky Balboa, the scene after Apollo beat the shit out of him. Not because I've been hit. I haven't. Luc didn't throw a single jab. He didn't touch me, he simply did his best to protect his own face, but he let me have at it without complaint.

No, I feel like Rocky, because he took a billion punches to the head, and stumbling around, he was losing his marbles all while looking for his girl in the crowd.

I feel like I've taken a million hits. I feel like I'm stumbling around. I feel like I should just curl into a fucking ball and die. I don't want this anymore.

I've lived every day of my life for as long as I remember for Kari.

I only ever wanted to raise her, make a good life for her, make her happy. But I'm out now. She doesn't need me. She's choosing someone else, and I'm just a boat floating in the water with no anchor and no sails.

This whole time, I thought I was Kari's anchor. Kari's sails.

But I realize in their absence, she was mine. Now, without her, without my life's mission of taking care of her, I realize I have nothing else. Like a couple of married folks who devoted a hundred percent of themselves to raising their kids, then when the kids grow and move out, they have nothing left. They don't know what to do with their marriage, because for the last couple decades, their marriage was wrapped around their kids.

My kid's gone now.

And where I might fill that hole with my new life, my new relationship – I don't have that anymore, either. Meg's gone, too. I'm just me, sitting alone in a cold and shitty cell, and I'm having an epic pity party for one.

Heavy footsteps move down the hallway to my left. Two sets of footsteps. When they stop at my enclosure and look down at me, I don't bother looking higher than their knees.

Alex and Luc.

"Fuck off, Luc."

"I wanna talk."

"There's no talking. You're nobody to me." I look up into his eyes and work to not feel bad about his messed-up face.

I fucked him up bad, and if anyone else did that to him, I'd tear them apart. "We're done. Don't come around me anymore. I don't wanna know you." His cheeks are still marred with blood, his bottom lip swollen to triple its size with a gnarly split stretching from top to bottom.

I bet that bitch stings a million times more than my knuckles.

His eyes are swollen, though his left is way worse than his right. I make a mental note to do better with my left jabs in the future. I could've done so much more to even him up.

Blood stains his work shirt, and the front pocket lies ripped and limp against his chest. His arms, visible from beneath his rolled-up sleeves, are bruised and mottled with easily recognizable knuckle shaped bruises. Blood from my cracked knuckles. His blood from his face. Mixed together in a sickening concoction.

It's probably a good thing I trust that he's healthy and clean, because we have each other's blood mixing within us right now.

"It doesn't have to be like that, Marc." His voice slurs, his hands clench. "I love you. I do. You're my brother. It doesn't have to go down this way."

"It already did. The day you touched what wasn't yours was the day we were done. I just didn't know it yet." I meet his stare. "But you knew it, which is why you didn't man up and tell me."

"Man up and tell you?" His brow lifts over a swollen eye. "This wasn't about manning up. An ass kicking, I can take, but this *'you're dead to me'* bullshit, that's not okay! That's why I didn't tell you."

"It's the way it is. Don't come around me anymore, Lenaghan. I'd say don't go around my sister, too, but it looks like she's standing on your side of the divide."

"She's not standing on any side, idiot! She's stuck in the middle and you're the one hurting her right now."

I jump to my feet and grip the solid bars between my hands. Alex steps forward, but I'm literally in a cage. I can't escape. "I'm not hurting her, you fucking asshole! I've never hurt her. She's mine, not yours! You're stealing from me and you know it. You know she's not yours to touch."

"She's not a *thing*, Marcus. She's a human being. She's beautiful and smart and caring, and I'm so fucking in love with her, I was willing to risk you and me. I don't want to lose you." His voice turns quieter. "I don't wanna lose you, and I won't make it easy for you to walk away, but I won't lose her just to keep you. Just like Scotch would choose Sammy, and you'd choose Meg, I choose Kari. That's the way it's supposed to be."

"Get the fuck outta here, Lenaghan. Don't say her name in front of me. Don't say Meg's, either."

"I'm going with her." He steps in close to the bars to murmur through bleeding lips. "To the clinic. She has no one, so I'll be standing with her, and when she needs someone to tell her what she's doing is okay, I'll be that man."

"But it's not okay!" I attempt to rattle the bars. I'm so fucking angry, I feel like I could tear them down and get to him. "What she's doing is not okay! And you standing with her is not okay." My voice cracks with emotion. "Why are you doing this to me, Luc? Why are you hurting me? What did I ever do to you?"

"I'm not trying to hurt you, Marc. These are two completely separate issues that both exploded at the same time. I love your sister, and I have for as long as I remember. We've had ups and downs, but those are between me and her. She's finally willing to take a chance on me, so whether you like it or not, I'm not wasting it. And Meg... I don't agree with her choice, but I won't condemn her for it. She needs support, too, and I won't be vilifying her when she needs love the most."

"But what about what I want?" My anger turns to despair. I'll beg at this point. I've yet to see her. Somehow, I'm begging Luc for my baby's life, instead of Meg, the one person on this planet who has all the control. "Just let me talk to her before she does anything. Ask her to speak to me. Five minutes."

"No." He steps away from the bars. His eyes are cold, his jaw set. "You can't talk to her beforehand, Marc. I love you, and if I could, I'd fix this for you, but this is her choice, and you don't get to talk her out of it or make her feel bad. You obviously can't keep your shit under control when you're pissed. I get it, I do, this shit ain't fair, but screaming in her face is not what's best for her."

"Luc..."

"I'm just trying to do the right thing by her. I hope you'll forgive me some day. I hope you'll forgive me for Bear, too. Neither of these things can be changed. I won't give her up, but I hope one day you can see I'm trying to do the right thing. I'm sorry, brother."

His voice is so final. His tone non-negotiable. He's so set. So cold.

I drop my head and turn away. "You're not my brother. You're nothing. Go away. Never come back."

"Marc... It doesn't have to–"

"Go. Alex, get him out. I don't wanna see him."

"I'm not pressing charges," Luc rumbles at my back. "We're here to let you out."

I slump down onto the metal bench on the opposite wall. Dropping my head low and letting my shoulders droop, I think about the baby I'll never meet, and the baby I did meet that's now been stolen from me. "Remove him from this station before you let me out, X. I can't promise I won't finish what I started."

"I hope you come to see me soon," Luc murmurs. "I want to talk about it. I want you to hear me out. You'll understand one day that she and I are meant to be together. You want her to be happy, and that's me. I make her happy."

"Leave." I lay back on the bench and turn toward the wall. My hands shake so violently, I know I won't be able to stop if he and I weren't separated by iron bars. "I'm staying here all night, X. Don't let me out. It'd hurt my sister if I killed him. Don't let me out."

"It doesn't have to be like that!"

"Whatever, man. I'm done with you." I let out a sigh and thank God I'm facing the wall when a single tear slides over the bridge of my nose. "For the rest of my life, we're done. You're nobody to me now."

7

MEG
TODAY'S THE DAY

The sound of stomping on my outside stairs is the first indication that today's really happening.

It's Monday.

Just a regular Monday for everyone else.

Work for the average Joe.

School for the average Mac.

I haven't seen Marc in more than two weeks – since I broke his heart and stomped any last remnants of life from it. I promptly ditched civilization, went missing and hid out at my daddy's place. And though I've been back home for more than a week, though I've had a fairly steady stream of visitors, I've yet to see *him*.

Hell, I've yet to hear of him.

No one's saying his name. No one dares even whisper the name that begins with M, for fear of making me cry, so I sit here all alone in my apartment – also known as a sensory deprivation tank.

I see Sammy, I see Scotch. I even see Angelo when he wanders upstairs from work most days with a bag of Chinese food, or pizza, or even just ice cream, and a silent shoulder to lean against, but everyone else has gone incognito. Luc texts me every day to check in, but I haven't seen him in a week. Kari calls me, though she's not all that talkative lately.

But none of my friends can distract me from him. It's like I can *feel* him around, I know he's near, but my friends are forcing this space between us. They're protecting me from someone that deserves the protection. I'm hurting him, I know I am, but he's asking me to choose him and the baby over me.

And I should.

I should choose them over me.

In all the heroic stories and legends, the mother would always choose them over her. Legends have mothers finding superhuman strength in the face of their child being in danger. The stories are of mothers literally dying to save their offspring, but this is real life, *my* real life, and death is the scariest thing I've ever considered.

Death by explosive brain is terrifying.

It's not so easy to be brave when you're staring death in the eye. It's not easy being that fictional hero when this is real life and your options are to drop down and cower, or to literally walk into death's hands.

Death is scary. Death is horrifying and has me walking around with hot flushes half the time, and bone aching chills the rest.

Or maybe that's the pregnancy.

Once the stomping feet stop at the top of the stairs, after a long silent pause, Sammy knocks softly on the door and forces my stomach to perform a sickening somersault. Opening it silently and poking her head in, she smiles warily when she finds me sitting at the kitchen table.

If you could take a side by side picture of the me from a year ago – high class, expensive clothes that were made for *my* body, expensive shoes that were considered painful enough to be stylish; and the me of now – plain black tank top, dark blue jeans, bra with no underwire – everything about me now is about comfort over style.

The teeny tiny baby that hid so well for three months has since decided to pop out and scream its presence to the world. It's here, and just like Marc's silent but still very much *there* demands, his baby demands attention. She or he, I don't know which, won't go down without letting its wishes known.

"Hey, Snitch..." She steps into the kitchen quietly. "Are you ready?"

I frown when Kari and Luc follow her in. Luc looks messed up. Bad. Painfully bad.

I stand and move toward him, and fingering the brim of his navy-blue hat aside, I reveal his black eyes and split lip. "Jesus, Luc. What the hell happened?"

"Nothing." He smiles charmingly, though his painful wince proves it hurts. "Fell into a doorknob...?"

"Luca!"

"I don't wanna talk about it right now." His usually sparkling blue eyes are sad, but his lips turn up in a painful smirk. "You ready to go? We've got your back."

"No!" I tear my wrist from his hold. "I'm not ready to go. Tell me what happened to your face, Luca. If you want to walk around in public with me, then I want to know what happened. I *demand* to know."

"Marc found out about us," Kari quietly interjects. "He didn't take it well."

"So he ran you down with his truck?"

Luc smiles painfully, and his poor split lip tugs at the scab that's trying to heal the cut. "No trucks were involved. Don't worry about it, Snitch."

"No, I *will* worry about it! You let him beat on you? What the hell is his problem? He has anger issues that he needs to work the hell out!"

"He didn't beat on me. We took it to the yard and now it's done."

"So you've both worked it out of your system? You're friends again?"

His lips twitch. "Ah, no. Not yet, but we'll be okay. He's asking me to choose between him and Bear. Eventually, he'll understand that I can have both."

I look at Kari's pale face. "Are you okay?"

Misty eyes, steely spine, she stubbornly juts her chin forward. "It sucked that he got so mad, but we knew it was coming. It's exactly why we didn't tell him. When he found out..." She clears the croak from her throat. "It was the first time in my life he looked at me like... well... *disappointed*. That's how he looked. And hurt. But he'll be fine. He has a lot going on right now, he'll process in his own time, then everything will be fine and he'll love me again."

Luc frowns and pulls her under his arm. He drops a sweet kiss on the crown of her head. "He loves you, Bear. You're his whole world, which is precisely the reason he took it so badly. But he'll be fine, I promise."

"How'd he find out?"

Again, with the nervous throat clearing. "He, ah... he walked in on us at my place." Her face flames red. This isn't the same girl who so confidently stuck me with a needle not so long ago. This is a shy young woman who doesn't know who to look at in the eye. "Luc was at my place. The twins were working, and Luc and I were on night shifts... so last week, mid-morning, I guess Marc was coming over to see me. He walked in without knocking and I might've been missing my top."

"Were you..." I can't stop staring at them wide eyed. "Were you, like..." I push my hands together in the only way I can say sex without saying sex.

Chuckling softly, Luc shakes his head. "Nope. Everyone was wearing their pants."

"Thank God," Kari murmurs. "It was already bad. My brother saw my little pink bra. It was mortifying, then it wasn't mortifying anymore, it was dangerous, because Marc lost his damn mind and Luc got hurt."

"I'm okay, Bear." He squeezes her close. "Nothing that hasn't happened before. We fight," his voice cracks when I know he didn't mean it to, "but everything will be fine. He'll come around. I'll make sure of it." He nods back toward the door. "Can we go?"

I move back to the kitchen chair. Dropping my eyes to the tabletop, I bite my lip. "You guys don't have to come with me if you don't want to. I'll understand."

Luc scoffs and steps closer. Kneeling down in front of me, his gaze burns the side of my head. "We're gonna be with you the whole time. This is your choice, Meg, and though we wish it could all go down differently, we don't judge you."

"But you shouldn't come with me, Luc. Especially not now."

"Why not now?"

"Because, look at you! Look at your face. You and he are already kinda fucked. Your relationship needs to be fixed. You taking me to an abortion clinic isn't exactly going to endear you to him. It might be the straw that breaks his back, Luc, and I don't want to be the person that finishes it for you guys."

"Yeah? Well, I refuse to stand by and let him tell a woman what she can and can't do with her body. I have sisters too, Meg. And if any man thinks he can force her to carry and birth a baby she doesn't want, then he'll be getting messed up a million times worse than what Marc gave to me. I feel like I *should* be telling you to keep that baby, but as my sisters' big brother, I can't. I can't get on board with being a prick to you about this, and then turn around and expect different behavior and opinions if we swap you out for Laine or Jess. I can't be a hypocrite. So, are you ready to go?" He reaches out and takes my hand.

Pulling me back to my feet, we come eye to eye. He *wants* to be the hypocrite. He wants to not go through with this. "Just remember that nothing's final until it's final. You can change your mind and I'll support that, too. But no matter what happens, we're here for you."

"You think I'm making the wrong choice…"

He shrugs and turns away. "It doesn't matter what I think, what matters is your body, your autonomy, and the fact that it's your choice and yours alone. We'll support you and it'll never be fodder for future judgment. I promise. Come on." He gestures me and Sammy ahead. Following behind, he and Kari step out onto the stair landing and pull the door closed. "We can't be late for the appointment. You've got everything you need?"

I pat my handbag and move down the stairs. Clutching at Sammy's hand for support, I wait until Luc and Kari meet my gaze. My heart thunders with nerves and sickness. "Is this going to hurt? The actual procedure."

"This isn't my–" He stops and swallows. "This isn't *our* area, Snitch. We don't know–"

"Don't bullshit a bullshitter, Luc. You always tell the truth. Don't disrespect me now."

"I think it'll be like a painful period – after it's done," Kari says. "You'll go home and be crampy, you'll bleed. It'll be like the worst period of your life – that's what I've read, anyway."

"What about during?"

"You'll have a local anesthetic," Luc interjects. "You won't feel a thing."

"They said I could be fully sedated. Asleep."

We step to Sammy's car and slowly slide in. My belly tweaks with what I now know is called ligament pain. I've been Googling. I shouldn't have done that.

"Why didn't you choose that?" Luc asks when he climbs in behind the wheel. "Why stay awake?"

I shrug and look everywhere but into his eyes. Pulling on my seatbelt and maneuvering it below my small bump, I sit back with a huff of breath. "Dunno. Feels important that I stay awake for it."

Kari fastens her seatbelt in the front passenger seat, and turns back to me with wary eyes as Luc pulls out of the parking lot. "Remember the protesters from last week. It's not personal, they're not there for you personally. They're always there. Keep your head down, move forward. Don't engage with them. Don't talk to them. Don't do anything but walk."

"They're not bad people."

"No," she agrees quietly. "They're not. They're just on a different side of this issue. But *they* don't get to choose what you do with *your* body. Head down, move forward."

"Okay." Dry mouth. Dry like the desert, and metallic, my tongue feels thick and annoys me. Three months of having no clue, and as a final rebellion, now everything makes itself known. Nausea. Cravings.

Every little thing I experienced before but brushed off as a hangover – dizziness, upset tummy, hunger – it's all amplified tenfold. "Won't talk to them. Won't look at them."

"When we get inside, I'll find another way to leave," Luc adds. "We have to go in the front when we get there, because I don't know any other way, but I promise I'll find another way out. We'll get it done, then you can go home and rest."

"Okay."

Sammy rhythmically strokes the back of my hand with her thumb. She's silent, she's here, she's strong where I'm starting to fall apart.

"It's Marc's baby," I add on a whisper. "I did the math."

Luc's ocean blue eyes meet mine in the rearview mirror. He's so sad. So lonely. So conflicted. "I know, Snitch." That's all he says.

I don't know why I felt the need to clarify one way or the other. I don't even know why I did the math. Like aborting Drew's baby would be easier, or carrying Marc's would be easier, because either way, the result is the same. No baby at the end of the day.

"Will he be there?"

Kari's shoulders come up defensively. Biting her bottom lip, she turns so her cheek rests on the shoulder section of the seat. "I don't know. He didn't say."

"You talked to him recently?"

"Yeah. I went over last night. He's still mad at me, so he wasn't chatty. You don't want him there, though. That won't make this easier."

"Is Angelo with him?"

"Yeah," she whispers. "And Scotch, too."

The tears choke me. The nerves swallow me whole. "I've split the group. I'm so sorry, guys."

"Hey, it'll be okay. He's my brother, and whether he's mad at me or not, I'll make sure he's okay. Don't let his feelings sway you on this."

I nod as we pull up at the curb in front of the clinic across town. Instantly, the protesters move toward us with their signs and shouts. Their bibles tap our windows and their pleas penetrate the closed glass. I've barely 'popped' yet, nothing a loose top can't hide, and with three women in the car, they can't know which of us is here to sin, so they converge on us all as we climb out.

Maybe this was the girls' plan all along. A distraction. A decoy.

The four of us move around the car as Luc beeps it closed, and as he takes Kari under his arm like he's naturally inclined to do, it makes the protesters think she's the one here that needs protecting.

They circle her, shout at her, press pamphlets and books at her. Signs dance in the sky and crosses on necklaces are pressed into our hands. Luc pushes Kari through the front door and turns back to bring me and Sammy in front of him, but Scotch emerges from the crowd and pushes us under his arms. He helps us through the last of the protesters and into the silent foyer of the clinic.

Like day and night. Like dark and light. The outside is noisy, and scary, and mean, and inside is clean, and silent, and sterile. Emotionless.

Maybe even more terrifying than the outside.

Luc spins and pins Scotch with a glare. "What are you doing here? You're supposed to be on Marc!"

"He's with Ang."

I turn and clutch at Scotch's arm. "How is he? He's safe? He's okay?"

"Yeah, he's fine. He, ah… he told me he forgives you."

"He… What?" My stomach jumps as my heart does a deadly *thump-thump*. "You're lying."

He takes a deep cleansing breath, and though it rattles, though he's scared to be here, scared to leave his brother, scared to leave his wife, he still smiles the smallest, most painful smile I've ever seen in my life. "He did. He said I could come here to you."

"You mean to Sammy."

His smile grows fractionally. "Yeah, to Ricci. But he said I could come here, and he told me he forgives you."

"He told you to tell me that?"

"No." He looks away to avoid my gaze. "He didn't ask me to pass anything on. He just said he's okay, that I can leave, and when I asked if he's truly okay, he said yes, and that he forgives you. Then he took a shot of whiskey."

Ouch.

"Mrs. Montgomery? If you'll follow us, please."

I release Scotch and cling to Sammy. This is it. These are the actions that can never be undone. A spindly, middle-aged woman with dark hair and light eyes steps up to us with a kind, non-judgmental smile. This is just a regular work day to her. It's the biggest day of my life. Possibly the one and only day I'll truly regret for the rest of my life. But to her, it's just Monday.

Dark hair and light eyes – just like Marc. He's everywhere. He haunts me right until the end. "I'll need you to fill out these forms," she passes me a clipboard and pen as she leads us down a stark hall. "Step into this room. You can have one support person," she looks at my entourage, "just one of you, I'm sorry. Fill out these forms. Take off your pants and put on this gown. You can sit on the bed once you're done, and we'll be ready for you shortly."

She steps out of the room just as quickly as she brought us in, and when I turn back to the guys, Luc and Scotch look everywhere but at me. The girls watch me with moist eyes and wobbling lips.

"You can all go."

"Snitch, no–"

"You don't have to be here for this, guys. I know what I'm doing, and I know it hurts you. You've supported me. I appreciate it, I really do, but you can go. Kari, honey," I take her hand and squeeze, "especially you. I get it. This choice I'm making affects you directly. It's your family."

"But–"

"Please leave. I'd rather not look into this baby's aunt's eyes when I do this."

Big fat tears dribble over her cheeks, but turning on her heels, she releases my hand and brushes hers over Luc's strong arm. I turn to Sammy. "And you, too. Both of you." I meet Scotch's devastated eyes. "I know about your past. I know you lived this already. I don't want to do this to you. Please leave. I love you guys, I truly do, but you can go."

They argue. They plead, but it's easy to see they want to leave as much as I want them gone. I don't want an audience for this.

I'm scared I'm going to pull out at the last second.

I'm terrified I won't.

"Just me and you then, Snitch?" Luc steps forward and takes my hand in his. He was always the joker, the flirt, the crazy and wild one, but today, he stands in his work uniform and smiles down at me.

So tall, so grown up, so handsome and sweet.

And serious.

I choke on a sob and look at the floor. "I was going to ask you to leave too, but I don't think I can. I can't be in here alone. I'm scared I won't go through with it."

"I'll stay with you, honey. I won't let you go."

"You should go be with Kari."

"I'll be with her in an hour. She understands. Take your pants off, Snitch. I've been waiting forever to see this show."

I choke on a sobbing laugh and release his hand. "I've figured you out, Luc Lenaghan. You're a lot more like me than I ever realized."

He steps to the counter lining the wall, leans back, and cocks his head to the side. "Yeah? How do you suppose?"

"We both think we're a lot funnier than we actually are."

"Excuse you very much. I *am* funny."

"And we use humor when we're uncomfortable. You don't want to see my ass, because you're hopelessly and stupidly in love with your best friend's baby sister. But you joke, because inside, your heart's running a million miles an hour and your stomach's twisted up in knots. Just like me. You don't want to be here, but you wouldn't be you if you left me here alone when I asked you to stay."

"You think you know so much." He scoffs and looks away. "I'm here because I get to see your Poot."

I burst out in desperately sad laughter. "Oh my God, that is *not* why he calls me Poot."

"No?"

"No! He hasn't told you guys?"

He chuckles and relaxes back against the counter. "Nope. And trust me, I tried. I got him so fucking drunk one time with the express intention of getting it out of him. Marc couldn't walk. He literally couldn't feel his fingers when he pressed them together."

"And he still didn't tell you?"

"No, but he told me you smell like flowers and that he liked you."

"He... What? When was this? Recently?"

"Nah, a few weeks after prom."

"Prom?"

He laughs under his breath. "I've hinted at that conversation so many times over the years, but he's never admitted to it. And he doesn't let me pour his drinks anymore, either. That young Jedi learns his lessons, he does."

"Obviously he doesn't," I admit bitterly. "I was an asshole to him every day since we met. Then we slept together. Then I was mean again. Then we slept together again. Do you see a pattern of him coming back for more?

"It's different when it's for the right person, Snitch." His serious eyes come up to meet mine. "Everything's different when it's for our other person."

I tilt my head to the side. His conversation eases my racing heart, which, I suppose, is exactly his intention. "Other person?"

He nods, and maybe even blushes a little. "Bear's been my other person since long before I should've even been looking at her."

"She forced your hand, didn't she?"

He looks up through long lashes with a smile. "How do you mean?"

"I mean, she was too young for you. Marc's little sister. She was *way* off limits. I know you would've been doing the right thing for a long ass time, and I know that's why we all thought you were a flirty whore. I said I figured you out, didn't I? Humor and flirting to cover the real."

He shrugs, but his smile creeps up. "So what?"

"So, I know you would've kept saying no. What did she do to push you over the edge? What was the thing that made you decide to give it a go?"

"She showed me her boobs...?"

"Ha-ha." I roll my eyes, and though I continue to finger the button of my jeans, I can't bring myself to pop it open. "See, there's that humor again. What was the defining moment? When did your loyalty to Marc come second to Kari?"

His smile dissipates in an instant. "It's not like that, Snitch. He's my brother, and I've fucking hurt him. Possibly irreparably. Maybe I've hurt me and Bear, too, because even if we were always meant to be together, she idolizes Marc. She won't be able to hold out forever. She won't be with a man her brother hates. That's not who she is."

"Hey, I didn't mean to imply you betrayed Marc."

"But I have!"

"You love his sister, and deep down beneath it all, just like a daddy, all he wants is for her to be happy. To find someone who'll love her as much as he does. He'll be fine when he sees that, just give him time." Twenty minutes ago, it was him that was sure they'd be okay, and now it's me telling him, when really, beneath it all, neither of us have any clue what the future will bring. "When did it all change, though? When did the scales tip?"

"Would you believe me if I told you we kissed back in the summer after she turned eighteen? That was the first time we stepped over that line. But then she went off to college and ignored me. For four years, she ignored me."

"Why'd she ignore you?"

"Because I told her to," he admits. "I said the kiss was wrong. That it was bad and we shouldn't do it. That she was too young and not for me. I told her to go to school and not kiss me again. I hurt her feelings with my rejection."

"And then?"

"Well," he lets out a gust of breath, "then she went to school and started kissing other people, instead. Longest four years of my life."

"You missed her."

"With my whole fucking soul, Snitch. What we did wasn't wrong, it just wasn't right, either. She left town when she was just a girl, a teenager, and in her absence, Marc and I continued our lives as brothers. I sure as shit didn't tell him what I did. I pretended I wasn't a traitor asshole and did my best to be an awesome friend. But then she came back a woman. Twenty-two years old and all grown-up.

She was so beautiful, it was like looking into the sun. I was sunk then."

That feeling of first love swirls in my belly. "She's your other person…"

"She was always my other person…" His eyes meet mine. "And Marc was always yours. He told me so one blurry night after prom."

I swallow painfully through a desert dry throat. "This thing I'm doing today – it's killing him."

He watches his feet and nods. "Yeah, but he's had worse. He'll be okay, we'll make sure of it."

"But?"

"But…" He takes in a long breath through his nose. "It's probably best if you stay away for a while."

I nod and finally pop my jeans. He's right. I'm destroying Marc today, and if I expect to be able to just hang around like it never happened, then I'm fooling myself. It did happen. I made the choices I made, and in the process, I'm breaking Marcus. The blame lands squarely in my lap, and no matter how much I plead for forgiveness, no matter how scared I am, these are my choices.

I need to live with the consequences.

No more Marc.

The same woman from before steps back into the room after a soft *tap-tap-tap* at the door. Carrying a bigger, fatter clipboard, a broad, older man steps in behind her. "Mrs. Montgomery." His voice is deep and commanding. Stretching out his hand, he takes mine in a firm grip. "Hello. I'm Doctor Marks."

Marks. "Of course you are."

"Take a seat, please. We'll have a small chat before we get started." He smiles at Luc. "You can sit with your wife, if you–"

"He's not my husband."

"I'll sit with you anyway, Snitch." Luc shuffles me along the bed and jumps up so his thick thigh runs the length of mine. Clasping my hand in his, he takes a deep breath and nods. "Okay. Go ahead, doc."

"Ah… Okay. Mrs. Montgomery. It's my duty to talk to you about this today before we proceed. I need to ask that you've truly considered your options."

"I've considered my options." My answer is short, concise, and brooks no argument. I don't have the emotional energy to keep going back and forth about this.

He watches me with brown eyes that remind me of dark chocolate, but with a succinct nod, flips the page in his folder. "Alright. I have a few medical history questions."

"Shoot."

"Smoker?"

"No."

He ticks it off on the sheet in front of him. "Never?"

"Maybe two cigarettes in my life. Back when I was a teen and didn't care about cancer. None since then."

"Drinker?"

"Casual, social. And yes, I've been drunk during this pregnancy. Obviously this was a surprise. I didn't realize it when I was drinking."

"History of blood pressure issues? High or low."

"No. Always normal."

"Allergies?"

"Just to bees. And dust."

"Everyone's allergic to dust." Luc bumps me with his shoulder. I love him for trying to be funny while I shake like a leaf.

"Have you eaten today?"

"No. They told me not to. Not after midnight."

He nods and makes notes. "Good. Do you understand the procedure today? What will happen? Who'll be in the OR? How long it will take?"

"Yes. They spoke about it at my last appointment. And I Googled it."

He chuckles softly. "Don't ever Google medical stuff. Did you input your symptoms?"

"Yes, sir."

"What are you dying from?"

"Cancer," I admit on a nervous laugh. "It said I'll be gone within six months to ten years. It couldn't be more specific than that."

"Would you like me to get oncology in here?"

This man is good. He has me smiling in a ridiculously non-smiling time. "No, thank you. I concluded that Google may not always know what it's talking about. I doubt I have cancer."

"Atta girl." He sets the folder down and nods to the woman. "We'll need to do a sonogram before we continue. I know that will be distressing for you, but it's procedure. You don't have to look, though I suggest you at least consider it. You hardly have a belly, so I suspect the fetus is still low in your pelvis. You didn't get into your gown yet, but that's okay. If you could just lower your zipper, lower your jeans a couple inches, and lie back on the bed, we can start."

"In here?"

"Yes." He stands from his chair and nods at a large machine on the opposite side of the bed. The woman from earlier fusses with buttons and preps bottles of what looks like liquid jelly. "Just lie back – oh, before I forget." He pulls out a small silver packet from a drawer, and turning, he moves to a small bar fridge and pulls out a bottle of water. "It's just Tylenol. We'll get this sonogram done, then we'll get started."

I accept the packet of two pills and look at Luc, who's been my lifeline, as he scrutinizes the foil packet over my shoulder. Satisfied the doctor hasn't tried to slip me something sinister, he nods and opens the water bottle for me.

Like the sonogram machine is a fully functional space shuttle instead of just a baby machine, the lights power up, the beeps beep differently from the *beep!* at the checkout at Jonah's store, the power surges through the machine, and my heart tumbles in my chest.

"You want me to turn around, Snitch? Want me to leave?"

"No." I lower the zipper and push my jeans a couple inches down my hips. Climbing onto the bed and lifting my shirt, I lay back with a huff and meet his eyes. "It's just my belly button. If you can't handle that sexiness, then feel free to look away."

He smirks and takes my hand. "I see you in there, trying to be funny because you're scared."

I squeeze his hand when a traitorous tear slides down the side of my face. "I'm so scared, Luc. Don't leave me."

"You have my word." He crouches down beside my head. Resting his chin on my bed, his sparkling blue eyes shimmer with the heartbreak he's trying his best to hide. "I won't leave you, honey. Whatever you need, I've got your back."

"I love you, Luc. Not like how Sammy loves Scotch, but how I would love my brother if I ever had one."

He smiles, and for the first time ever, I watch a tear slide along his cheek. "You do have one, honey. You have three of us. And you have Marc, too. We're in the storm, it's messy right now, but we're all family. This'll work out fine."

"This might be cold," the doctor interrupts us. Luc sidesteps less than a foot, and stopping again, his eyes meet mine. That's it, that's as far as he's moving for the doctor. That's as far as he'll go from me. And I don't miss the way I have to bend my neck to keep him in my sight, in the opposite direction of the sonograph screen. "Applying the gel now."

I jump when the cold liquid hits my belly. Clasping Luc's hand tighter, a second tear slides into the hair at the side of my head. "I'm so sorry, Luc. I'm so sorry this is happening."

"You'll be okay, honey. I promise I support your decisions."

Whoosh whoosh, whoosh whoosh.

My heart clogs my throat, my stomach threatens to explode, and my head snaps up dangerously fast when the sound cuts out conspicuously. The doctor smiles ruefully. "Sorry."

"What was that? Was that the heartbeat?"

He slides the probe around on my stomach, and as though he's purposely avoiding my gaze, he acts as though the screen behind me is the most interesting thing he's ever seen in his life. "Not the heartbeat. That's the placenta."

"So, the heartbeat?"

"That's *your* blood feeding the placenta. *Your* heartbeat."

I nod and go back to Luc. His thumb strokes my palm in rhythmic circles while the doctor slides the probe around on my belly. "Are you gonna marry Kari?"

He chuckles softly and swipes at an annoying tear. "Yeah, I am."

"When?" A sob works its way up my throat as the doctor silently presses the probe low near my hipbone. He pushes so hard, I worry for my baby's safety, then I realize how ridiculous I sound, considering the very reason I'm here. "When will you marry her?"

"When Marc says it's okay."

"Really?" I bend my torso so I can hold Luc's hands with both of mine. I'm fidgety. I want to get up and run. I want to get this over and done with. I want today to be over already. "You'll wait for Marc?"

He nods and relaxes against the bed. "I'll wait a lifetime. I get to keep her with or without the wedding, so I'll wait for him to agree to walk her to me. I doubt she'll do it without him, and I don't want to take her from him. I want her given to me. We can't do it without him."

"I'm pregnant, Luc. Don't say emotional shit like that." I sniffle inelegantly and swipe the back of my hand over my nose. "He'll come around." I use my thumb to gently probe his split lip. "He didn't mean to do that."

He chuckles sarcastically. "He meant it, alright. He meant every single punch he threw. And probably a hundred more he didn't get to before he was pulled off me."

"He'll come around."

"Yeah. He will, one day."

"Do you want to look at the screen, Mrs. Montgomery?"

My breath comes out on a weak shudder.

I do.

I don't.

I shake my head at Luc, which has him looking up to the doctor. "She doesn't wanna look. Let's move this along. She's suffering."

Accepting a wad of paper towel from the woman, the doctor roughly wipes it over my stomach to collect leftover gel. He packs the sonogram probe aside and switches the screen off. "Alright. Let's get ready for surgery. The fetus is where it needs to be. This will all be over quickly."

"Wait. Can you tell me the date of conception?"

He watches me curiously as he wipes gel off the probe. "It's not perfect, Mrs. Montgom–"

"Your best guess, then. It's really important that I know."

He looks back down to his notes for a long moment. "Well, as long as you understand it's not exact, I have the baby measuring at fourteen weeks and four days."

Luc studies me. "Marc?"

I nod and hold my breath. Marc's baby. I'm both elated and heart-broken at my confirmed knowledge. I don't know why I insist on knowing this, but I feel like I must know it's his.

I must know that the baby that took root in my belly is his.

Somehow that makes this better, though of course, it should make it worse. So much worse.

The doctor turns to the woman when I refuse to say more. "Please page the anesthetist. Send him to OR three. We'll be there in a couple minutes and we can start."

My head snaps around. "Anesthetist? I thought I was staying awake?"

He flips through his notes. "Ah, no. That's not what I have here. Due to the fetus' age–"

"No, it's okay." *It's not okay.* "It's fine. Can we get it done now? Luc…?"

"I'm here, Snitch." He clasps my shaking hands between his and squeezes them to minimize the tremors. "I won't leave you. You have my word."

"Let's go, Mrs. Montgomery. I need to scrub up, you need to dress down."

Sitting up and pulling my top down, I hang my legs over the edge of the bed and let the emotions free. I sob into my hands and I pray to whoever's up there that I'll be forgiven for what I'm about to do.

8

MARC

IT'S DONE

I sit on a small two-foot red-brick fence at the back of the clinic and stare at the back entrance, though it feels like I'm watching for a ghost. I watched my family walk out of that door an hour ago, though I didn't make myself known.

I don't want to see them.

I don't want to talk to them.

I'm here because I couldn't stay away.

I can't let her go through this alone. She might never know I was here, but *I* know I was here. She might be in there right now disposing of my baby, but it took the both of us to put that baby in there, and I've lumped her with all of the blame, all of the responsibility.

I'm a coward and a bully. I'm the exact kind of person I despise.

My phone buzzes for the hundredth time on the bricks beside me. Picking it up, I sigh at Angelo's name flashing angrily. "What?"

"Where are you?"

"Around." I sound so chill. So unaffected. "Where are you?"

"Leave her alone, Macchio! You need to leave her be. Are you at the clinic? I went there looking, but I couldn't find you."

Yeah. Because I'm hiding. "She's in there right now, Ang. It's happening right now."

"Get away from there!" His shout wars with the sound of his car in the background and the wind whistling through the phone. He really is looking for me. "Leave, Macchio. Nothing good can come of this. You're only hurting yourself by being there, and if she sees you, you'll hurt her, too."

"She can't see me. She's inside doing it. I'm out here."

"Where are you?"

I look up at the blue sky, but the warmth from the sun fails to penetrate my skin. I feel numb. I feel drunk – though I'm not. One single shot doesn't make for a drunk Marc anymore.

I've matured since high school.

"It's been more than an hour now, Ang. What do you think's happening? Do you think it hurts? What she's doing... do you think it hurts *her*?" I don't want her to feel any pain.

"Don't do this, man. Just leave."

"She said she loves me, so maybe after this, maybe we can go back to being happy. I won't knock her up again, we can be together. I'll get her a puppy or something. Or me. I'll get the puppy for me and I won't make her look after it."

"You can't replace a baby with a puppy, Marc! You need to just leave. Step out into the street where I can see you. I'm driving down the clinic street now. Where are you?"

"Hiding. Watching over her."

"Marcus! Where are you?"

I bring my bruised and sore hand up to my face. Fingering my lip, I think about how Luc must be feeling today.

He's in there with her. Right now, he's with her. The funny group-whore now holds all the power. He has my girl, and he has my sister. "Did you know about Luc and Kari?"

"Umm... What?"

"You did." I nod and look down at my shoes. "I think maybe everyone knew except me. I hurt him really bad."

"He deserved it."

"You shouldn't sleep with your friend's sister. It's a rule, right? Especially not Kari. She's special. There's a rule, right?"

"Yeah." He clears his throat uncomfortably. I lengthen my neck and watch past the cars in the lot as Ang slowly drives past. "There's definitely a rule."

"I think I lost all of my family this past week. All I ever wanted was family, but now I have none left. I was broke as fuck when I was twelve, but at least I had family. Now, I have money, but it's useless if I don't have a family to support. Kari's all grown up, she doesn't need me."

"We're right here, man. You didn't lose anyone. Where are you?"

"I lost Meg. I lost the baby. I hurt Luc, and Kari loves him. He told me so, so she'll leave me, too."

"She won't choose a man over you, so you need to relax."

"I'd pick Meg over you guys." I grip the back of my neck. I'm so tired. I don't think I've slept in days. "I would. Maybe you don't understand it yet, but Scotch would understand. He'd pick Soda over us."

"I do get it, okay? I get it. Maybe one day you'll find that again. With someone else, or maybe one day you and Snitch can talk and find some version of happiness, but that day ain't today. You need to leave that clinic right now. Being there will hurt her. You love her, right? You don't wanna hurt her."

"I do love her." The fog suffocating my brain begins to lift. The bland blue of the sky turns bright and blinding. The noise from the picketers out front finally reaches my eardrums. "I wish she'd choose us. I could make her happy. I'd stop calling her Poot, and I'd never be grumpy again."

"Oh, thank God." I look up when his voice comes from beside me rather than over the phone. He slides his thumb over the screen and pockets it. Sitting down with a grunt, his knee touches mine and his eyes scan my face.

"I didn't hear you stop the car."

"You look awful, Macchio."

"Thanks. I even brushed my hair before coming here."

He looks out into the lot. Towards the clinic she's in right now. "Where's everyone?"

I shrug and let my shoulders droop. I'm on the edge of crying. I'm ready to break down and let go. "Soda and Kari walked out that door about an hour ago."

"And Scotch?"

"He came out a few minutes later and called them back in." I look up. "The girls were crying."

He bites off a swear, and with his elbows on his knees, looks between his open legs. "Fuck."

"They're crying for a reason, Ang. She already did it."

He nods and continues to study his shoes. "And Luc?"

"He didn't come out at all. I guess he's with her. Doesn't surprise me."

"You should take it easy on him. He's your brother. Give it time before you make decisions."

I laugh bitterly. "Everyone's saying that a lot lately."

"Marc–"

"And yet, they still make these decisions that can't be undone."

"Marc… It'll get better over time. Eventually, it'll stop hurting so much."

The back door slams open with a building-shaking boom. Sprinting through the space, Luc stops with frantic eyes and a heaving chest. "Oh my God." His broad shoulders fold in on themselves. This is it. This is where he tells me it's done. This is where he tells me the baby's gone.

But he doesn't.

Instead, his hand comes around and he slingshots a sobbing Meg across the lot toward me.

I jump up and drop my phone to the concrete. Sprinting toward her, she throws herself into my arms halfway across the lot.

Wrapping her legs around my hips and her arms around my neck, she presses her lips to my neck over and over and over again. "I'm sorry." She sobs into my neck, her wailing sobs so loud, my eardrums turn tinny. "I'm sorry, Marc. I didn't do it. I couldn't do it."

I feel like I'm going to be sick. My legs shake and my arms turn weak. My heart pounds against hers and my stomach revolts at what I think may be my official slide into insanity. "What's going on? What happened?"

"I couldn't do it." She leans back and cups my face with shaking hands. "I couldn't go through with it."

"It's still in there?" My eyes snap between hers and where our bellies meet. "Baby's okay?"

Her lips quiver, her eyes spill over. She nods and presses her face to my neck. "Baby's still in there. It's fine." Relief washes through me as heavily as a tidal wave. Crossing my ankles, I simply drop to the ground and sit before I fall. She adjusts in my lap and cinches her legs around my waist. "I'm sorry, Marc. I'm so sorry for everything. I'm sorry for hurting you."

"You're keeping the baby?" I brush hair from her eyes, and though they're pink and puffy, they're smiling. They're happy.

"I couldn't go through with it. They asked me to get changed into the gown, and when I bent to take off my shoes, the baby moved in my belly."

"The baby moved?" I'm gonna be sick. "It moved inside you?"

She hiccups and scrunches her eyes closed. "Like tiny little popping bubbles, it moved inside me."

"Has that happened before?"

She shakes her head. "Never. Baby moved because it knew this was his last chance. He knew what was coming, so he moved to let me know he didn't wanna go."

I'm not a crier. Never in my life have I been a crier, but today I am. Tears slide over my cheeks and mingle with hers. "The baby moved?"

"I'm sorry," she sobs. "Please forgive me. I was scared. I'm still so scared, but I choose you. I choose the baby."

"I choose you, too." I brush her hair away with frantic hands and press my lips to hers. The kiss is noisy, but dry. It's not passion, it's relief and a cry of desperation. "I choose you, Meg. I forgive you. I just want us to be happy together."

She slumps in my lap and rewraps her arms around my neck. "I'm so sorry. I couldn't do it, Marc. It's your baby in me. He was conceived the first time we ever made love. You had me tied up and blindfolded and all sorts of filthy shit, but the universe still decided to give us a baby."

"I'll take care of you both." I drag her hair back until her soaked eyes look into mine. For the first time in more than two weeks, I finally get to see the golden specks. The tiny freckles that dot the tops of her cheeks. She hides those with makeup, but not today. Today it's just her. Just the girl who emerged after I washed her in my shower. "I love you, Meg. I truly do. I'll take care of you both."

She nods against my neck. "Okay."

"You can come live with me. Move in, make a family with me. I know it's not traditional. I know it's all rushed, but we were going in this direction, anyway. It was gonna happen one day."

"Okay."

"I'll add rooms right away. I'll move the bed to the ground floor today, you won't have to climb a ladder. Then we'll build the extra rooms and everything will be okay."

"This won't be an easy transition, Marc. I haven't adjusted to this new reality."

My heart throbs painfully in my chest. "We'll make it work."

"I don't want you to become like my daddy."

I look back and hold her face. "What do you mean?"

"If I die." She chokes on her tears. "If I die, I want you to try harder than my daddy did. I know that's not fair and I know it'll be hard work, but you need to do better than he did."

"What? Why would you die, baby?"

"You need to not name the baby Megan. If it's a girl, I refuse to let you name her Megan. When it's just you two, you need to promise to do better. Don't ignore her because you're talking to a ghost."

"Wait." I hold her fussing hands still. "What the hell are you talking about? Why would you die?"

"I might," she chokes. "I might die like my mom did. You need to do better."

"Come on, guys." Angelo stands over us with an extended hand. "Let's take this out of the parking lot. You need to take her home, rest up, talk."

She nods and swipes at her runny nose. Climbing out of my lap with Ang's help, she stands in front of me and watches me shakily climb to my own feet. "We need to talk." She swipes at her nose as fat tears dribble over her lips. "There's a lot to plan between now and then."

～

TWENTY MINUTES LATER, without a single word spoken to the rest of our friends – especially not Luc – Meg and I step through my front door as Angelo leaves with a look that says 'talk your shit out. Now.'

She wanders to the couch on weak legs. Looking for a single minute of extra distraction, I move to the fridge. "Water?"

She nods, though she remains facing forward so I only see the back of her head. "Yes, please."

I grab two bottles out, set my keys and wallet on the counter, and move to the couch, though I leave about a foot of space between us.

I have no fucking clue where we're at. An emotional hug in a parking lot doesn't answer anything. "Here." I pass the opened bottle. "Talk to me, Meg. I've just lived through the worst few weeks of my life and I don't know what my reality is right now."

She nods and avoids my eyes. She looks down at my hands with a small frown. "You hurt Luc. Really bad."

"Did he snitch like a little bitch?"

She shakes her head. Any other day, that would get a smile from her. "He didn't have to snitch. His left eye still barely looks human. Of course that damage came from you."

Damn straight it did. I'd do it again, too. "Did you know about him and Kari?"

She nods, though her eyes go back to the floor. "Yeah, it wasn't so hard to figure out. It's like," she raises her hands, "he looks at everyone *this* way, then he looks at her... *that* way."

"I don't wanna talk about how the guy I thought was my best friend looks at my sister."

"He loves her." She looks up at me. "He loves her the way a man loves a woman. Don't be so hard on him."

"Fuck him." I brush it off like he's less important than a bug. "I wanna talk about you. Talk to me, Meg–" Her whole name almost slips past my lips.

I don't call her Megan to piss her off. It's just her whole name, the same way I use everyone else's full name when they piss me off. But I'm walking a tightrope now.

A rope I refuse to stumble off.

Luc had all the power an hour ago, but now it's shifted. Meg has it. She didn't go through with it today, but I still don't know what's going to happen tomorrow, or next week, next month. "Please talk to me. I'm begging you to help me see straight."

She watches the floor and swallows heavily. "I couldn't go through with it. I couldn't abort your baby."

Thank God. "I'm sorry you had to deal with the last few weeks alone."

"Scotch said you forgive me… When the plan was to abort, he told me you forgive me."

That was a lie I was trying to force myself to believe. "I was trying really hard to see things from your side. It hurt really fucking bad, but there was also this other part of my heart that loves you without the baby. It was hard trying to reconcile the two parts."

She turns on the couch to face me, but instead of love, or happiness, or even boredom, her features crumble. "You didn't tell me you loved me till after the baby news."

"That's not true. I told you a bunch of times before that day. You were too asleep to hear me."

"Too asleep?" She forces a wobbly smile. "You told me while I slept?"

I nod and scoot a foot closer so our legs touch. Taking her shaking hand in mine, I bring them to my lap. "About a million times. Then a million more in the last couple weeks. I also told you that day at the apartment. Before you told me about the baby. You were crying, but I didn't know why yet. I told you I loved you *before* the baby news."

"Would you really have been able to be with me if I aborted?"

I shrug my shoulders, though my instinctive answer is *fuck no!* "I would've tried really hard."

"Why?"

"Why what?"

"Why try? If I aborted the baby, why stick around?"

"Because I'd still love you." I press her palm over my heart. "I'd have to actively work at falling *out* of love with you, and maybe I could have done it, eventually, but I'm not there yet."

She nods and watches me play with her dainty fingers; fingers bare of jewelry. "I don't want to get married." I look up and watch her eyes sparkle with sadness. "Not yet, anyway," she continues. "I don't want a proposal because I got knocked up. Plus, I'm still married to Drew. I need to keep the two things separate. Shake him off, put him away. I need to do it all before the baby's due."

"Though I want that done as soon as possible too, trust me, there's no one on this planet who hates him more than I do, but why before the baby's due?"

She shrugs and turns her eyes away. "Just in case. I'm not leaving that thread untied. I have a lot to do between now and then."

I watch a fat tear spill from her eye, dribble along her cheek, and drip off her chin into her lap. Pulling her into my lap, she doesn't even fight me when I rearrange her so she resembles a tiny child resting against my broad chest. "Does this hurt the baby?"

She shakes her head. "I can feel pressure on my tummy, so that probably means I won't be able to sit like this next week, but today's fine."

"Baby's growing fast?"

"So fast." She burrows into my chest. "It feels like a giant ticking time bomb in my uterus."

"Talk to me about this dying stuff, Meg. I have no clue what you're talking about, but I promise you, I won't let anything hurt you. You know me. The only person on this planet more stubborn than me is you. Between us, we won't let anything go wrong."

"My mom died from an undiagnosed aneurysm. When she was

giving birth to me, something went pop in her brain and that was that. She never got to hold me, because I murdered her on the way out."

I pull back with a frown. "You didn't murder her, baby. That was just a really tragic accident, but it wasn't your fault."

"Just like Megan the cow, huh? That was tragic, too."

"Meg–"

"Well, all I'm saying is if something *tragic* were to happen, I need to put some plans into place. At least I know it's coming."

"You don't *know* it's coming." I turn her face so our eyes meet. "Medicine has advanced more than thirty years since you were born. If you have worries, then we make sure the doctors know and make it better. I'm not just gonna walk you into that hospital in nine months and play a game of Russian roulette and hope for the best."

"Six months."

"I–" pause. "Huh?"

"I'm fourteen weeks. Nearly fifteen. Forty weeks to a standard pregnancy. Twenty-six weeks to go. That's six months, give or take. I Googled."

She just wiped away three months I didn't even realize I was clinging to. "Okay, so six months. I have money saved, Meg. I pay for really good health insurance. If you look past the not wanting to get married thing for now, we can get you linked up, too."

"Oh good." She rolls her eyes and looks away. "First, a proposal because I'm pregnant. Now a proposal so I can mooch your health insurance."

"It's not like that. I'm just trying to take care of you."

"If you want to take care of me, then you need to add a room to your house for the baby, then you need to make good with Kari and Luc. Just in case it doesn't work out. Just in case I'm not here in six month's time, I need you to show me you can do better than my daddy. I need you to raise the baby differently. I want it to never wonder if it's loved."

"She'll never wonder, baby. She'll be told every single day, from both of us."

"Marc–"

"I want you to stop with the doomsday stuff. We go to the doctors and we make them help us. Figure out if we should worry. I'm not walking away from this couch with the *ifs* and *maybes* bullshit. Attract what you want from the universe. You *will* be fine. You *will* still be here next Christmas."

"And you *will* talk to Luc."

"No." Now it's my turn to look away. "It's not that easy."

"It really is that friggin easy. He held my hand today and he cried for your baby. He cried for your friendship. Make it better, Marcus Macchio. You *will* make it better."

"Babe, it's not—"

She gasps and jumps in my lap. Her hands shoot to her stomach, and I swear, has my heart pinging dangerously in my chest and threatening to die. She's got me jumpy with the dying bullshit. "What? What is it?"

"The bubbles. I can feel the baby moving..."

I pick her up and lay her out flat on the couch. Kneeling on the floor beside her, I lay my ear over the teeniest, tiniest pudge at the bottom of her stomach and listen for the bubbles. "I can only hear your stomach grumbling."

She smirks and looks down the line of her body. She'd die if she knew about her double chin from this angle. "I haven't eaten since yesterday."

"Can you still feel the bubbles?"

She nods and bites her bottom lip. "Uh huh. You can't hear it? It's only super light."

I don't dare move my head, I just lie as still as possible and close my eyes. "I don't hear anything."

"She's saying *'go talk to Uncle Luc.'*"

I sit up with narrowed eyes. "Really? That was all a lie? You're a jerk, Poot."

She snickers, though I know she's still shaken to her core from today. She's trying to pretend everything is fine. "The next six months are gonna end up with one of us dead, is all I'm saying."

"Can you stop saying shit like that? It pisses me off."

"Which means… we're back to normal."

I drop my face back down to her belly. "The whole fucking world changed the last couple weeks, Meg. But it's still kinda the same; you're still actively trying to annoy me." I turn my head so my ear presses to her belly. "I'm gonna be a daddy?"

She sighs thoughtfully. "Looks like it."

"Are you okay? Are you happy?"

"Yeah. But I'm scared. I'm terrified to my bones."

"If I promise to make you safe, if we exclude that from the equation right now, are you happy? Are you happy to be having a baby with me?"

She watches me for a long minute. Her flecked eyes flip between mine. "Yeah. There's no one on this planet I'd rather do it with."

Her words make me giddy, happy beyond anything I've ever experienced. She soothes me, and finally, after weeks of always running on heartbreak and overdrive, I can breathe again.

"Except maybe John Cena. He's hot, too."

Breathe. Bite my tongue. Don't react; that's what she wants. "You're an asshole, Poot."

She wins.

And that's okay.

9

MEG
LIFE GOES ON

Marc didn't end up tossing his bed over the side of the loft last night. He would have. He started to, but seeing as I barely even have a belly yet, I convinced him he was being ridiculous, and that *yes*, I can climb a ladder. *No*, I wouldn't fall, and *fine*, he could climb behind me if it would make him feel better.

Though, I realized my mistake around eleven p.m. when I had to get up to pee. And then again at three. Then at six. But, no matter how tired he was, no matter how annoying I felt, he got up each time without complaint, turned on every light in the house to avoid me tripping on a stray shoe, escorted me up and down the ladder, and tucked me back into bed when I was done.

This sweetly protective version of Marc is exciting and new, and I can't deny the butterflies that flutter in my belly when he does these things. Or maybe the butterfly is his baby, and the flutters are the bubbles tickling me from inside.

My sweet butterfly baby that refused to be ignored.

Marc and I didn't have sex last night.

We just... I don't know why. It didn't feel quite right.

Everything's so out of whack, it's almost like we're shipwreck survivors that are just happy to be holding hands, happy to be alive.

Making love didn't enter my mind, and if it entered his, he didn't bring it up.

"Marc?" I step to the edge of the loft and call out softly. Poking his head out from behind the fridge door, he looks at me inquisitively with his bed messed hair and bare chest.

It's going on eight in the morning, and despite the fact he works for himself, he's officially late to start the day. "Mm?"

"I'm ready to come down."

He slams the fridge door and races across the open plan living space. Scrambling up the ladder like he's in a fight for his life, he stops at the top rung with a lopsided grin and dancing eyes. "Let's go."

I roll my eyes. "We can't keep doing this. I can get down myself."

"Which makes me eternally grateful that despite the fact you think this is dumb, you're still humoring me."

"Whatever."

I turn and present my jeaned ass to climb down, but tapping my back pocket, he rumbles, "Wait. Turn around?"

I turn and cock my head to the side. "Why?"

He hooks his arm around my hips and pulls me forward until I'm an inch in front of his face. He lifts my polo shirt and presses his lips to my belly fat. "I'll love you for the rest of my life, Meg. But this, the baby, I'll love you forever for this, too."

"Marc…"

He taps my hips and slowly spins me. Pulling me back slowly, I step onto the top rung and start climbing down with him two rungs below. Slowly, way slower than I ever climbed prior to the pregnancy bomb, Marc allows me to move down the ladder unhurried, like a two-legged turtle, and once we reach the floor, he spins me and drops a gentle kiss on my cheek. "You hungry?"

My stomach grumbles noisily. "Yeah, I'm starving."

Taking my hand in his, he leads us across the living space to the kitchen. "What are you hungry for?"

I stop at the counter and pull out a stool. Climbing up and grunting at the pinch of my jeans, I mentally sob at the fact they won't fit for much longer. "Cereal's fine. You don't have to cook for me. You don't have to serve me."

"I want to." He moves to the large corner pantry and rummages around until he pulls out two separate cereal boxes. "Which one?"

I nod toward the less sugar loaded cereal. I want the sugar, but I need real energy.

Protein and fiber – adulting sucks.

He tosses the other box back in haphazardly and places the chosen box on the counter. Pulling out a bowl, spoon, and stepping to the fridge, he pulls out a gallon of milk and sets about preparing it for me.

I can't say I dislike watching a half naked, tanned, muscular and shirtless man prepare my food. It might be the sexiest thing I've ever seen. "What are you doing today?"

"Ang and Scotch are coming over. We're getting started on the renovation."

"Just like that?"

"Just like that." He stops what he's doing. "Um... if you don't mind, once we get started, if we could go to your apartment for the time it takes to tear out walls and build it all back up to the lockup stage, that would be easiest for you."

"You want me to go back to my apartment?"

"Both of us." He coughs nervously and slides my bowl across the sleek counter. "If I was living alone, I'd make do, camp out, stay here and work from dark to dark, but I'm not alone, and you're not sleeping in a house that's missing an external wall. So, your apartment. It'll only be a few days–"

"A few days to renovate?" I pick up my spoon. "I didn't realize it happens so quickly."

"Not to finish, but to get the frame up and the house lockable again. We can stay at the apartment the whole time and you'll never see or hear the messy build, or once the wall's back up, we can come back and just sheet off the space until its done. Your choice."

I stir my cereal and frown with thought. "Are you mad your house has to be changed for this?"

He stops pouring his own cereal and looks at me questioningly.

"Mad? No. You've made me happier than you'll ever know. It's just a house, and we're making it better. We're making it into a home."

"But… What if we don't work out?"

He sits the gallon of milk down, slow and deliberate, and though his chest and shoulders tense and turn rigid, his voice remains smooth and calm. "We *will* work out. I get that you're scared, babe. I get that this is happening fast, but I also know this will work. We're happy together. You know that and so do I. The last few weeks don't count, so stop with the doubts. I'm taking care of business and you're gonna be fuckin' happy about it."

I look down into my cereal with a smirk. I know he added the last sentence to make me smile. It worked. I hate that I'm kind of crazy about him. I hate even more that despite his constant reassurances, I'm still scared of the floor falling out beneath me.

"Hey." He steps around the counter and pulls my face up with a finger under my jaw. "It'll be okay. I promise."

"You love me, right? Like, real, actual love."

His plump lips pull up into a sweet grin. "I might be bordering on insanity, because I'm setting myself up for a life-time of bickering with you, but my heart won't let me switch it off. I love you, Meg. I've been crushing on you since I was fifteen. I remembered what you ordered every time at the club because I remember *everything* about you. I paid attention to every move you made. I lost you for more than a decade when Scotch lost Sammy, but you're back, and I'm not letting you go again. Everything else is the gray that we don't pay attention to, remember?"

"But…" I let out a deep sigh. "We're okay."

He nods. "We're safe. You're safe. My sister is safe."

"The rest is gray."

"Exactly." He leans down until my neck is no longer bending. "Can I kiss you, Meg? It's been way too long. It's like you literally reached into my throat, tore out my heart, and took it with you. I'd really like to seal this with a kiss."

Ugh, he kills me with the sweetness. Insecure Marc is not a man

I've met before. "Yeah, you can kiss me. I'm all in. No more worrying about us."

"I can kiss you anytime I want?"

I nod.

"What about your ass? Can I touch it anytime I want?"

"I mean…" I laugh softly and remember the conversation we had right here forever ago. "If you're set on the ass thing, then sure, but be gentle."

He chuckles and closes the final couple inches separating us. His lips press down on mine and his tongue darts out to swipe along my lips. It's like coming home from a long trip away, and the stupid baby hormones have me feeling all weepy.

Pulling back slowly, his emerald green eyes stare into mine. "I promise it'll be okay. I won't let anything happen to you. I won't let anything happen to us."

I clear my throat and attempt to look away. "It's just the hormones. I'm a mess lately."

He smirks. "You're allowed to be hormonal. You're growing a human inside you.

"Ha. Let me hear you say that again in a month or two when my hormones are sending you crazy."

"Only crazy in the best way. Eat your breakfast. Make my son strong."

"Your son?" I look at him incredulously. "What do you know that I don't?"

He shrugs and pulls out the stool beside mine. "I'm sick to death of women. They're everywhere, and they're pains in my ass. Give me a son, Poot, and let him be big and strong."

There he is.

Surprisingly, that's the Marc I love.

I turn back and pick up my spoon. I'm starving, and I have a big day ahead of me. I already had a long to-do list for today – things that I could've done while sitting on the couch crying about the 'worst period pain of my life', but now I also have to go grocery shopping for my apartment. I've been living on cereal or diner food for weeks because I didn't have the energy or enthusiasm to do better, but I don't think Marc will let me eat processed cereal on his watch.

Wouldn't want to stunt his strong son's growth.

"You'll be here all day with the guys?"

He nods and spoons cereal into his mouth. "Uh-huh."

"No other jobs that you need to finish off first?"

He shrugs and swallows his mouthful. "Nothing that can't wait. I book my projects really well so I always have a bunch of cushion room."

"Why?"

He shrugs. "What I do isn't only physical work. I need inspiration to strike sometimes. Like, for designs and stuff. Deadlines cripple my creativity. So, I give myself huge cushions."

"Makes sense…" Talking about Marc's creativity has Oz's wedding on my mind. I have to get that done before the baby arrives, too. The rest of my life was on hold for the last two and a half weeks, but wedding planning was not. Technology is amazing, and despite having cried myself to sleep every day for weeks, it hasn't stopped me from getting on the phone or internet each day and getting shit done. No one will ever know I had a huge personal crisis in the middle of planning that wedding.

"What are you doing today?"

It's like he can read my mind. "I have to talk to some vendors. Clean my apartment. Go shopping."

He turns to me with a frown. "For what?"

"Um… Milk. Bread. Probably some form of protein. Do you have any of that jumbo pack of toilet paper left?"

"No, not the shopping. The vendors."

"Oz's wedding. I have to talk to florists today. Oh, and you guys have been booked as the band. Well, it's not official yet, asking was also on my to-do list. Which is another reason you and Luc need to kiss and make up. If you ruin that wedding because you brained your brother with your bass guitar, I'll kill you. You have to promise not to ruin this for me." It might actually be easier to book the Rolling Stones.

"He's not my brother."

"Well that sure is a problem for your shitty-named band. A problem you *need* to fix or I'll make your life a living hell. Trust me, you don't want that. Then tonight I'll go into the diner for a short shift. I owe Katrina for picking up my slack lately."

His head snaps up as dribbled milk sits on the curve of his chin. "Woah up. You're not working tonight. In fact, you don't have to go back at all."

I make the pfft sound. "Give yourself an uppercut, Marcus. I'll be going back every day between now and... forever. Maybe not the day of the wedding, because that'll be a busy day, but every other day."

"You don't have to sling dishes when you're pregnant, Meg. I've worked nearly every single day since I was a kid for this exact reason."

"Why? So your one night stand can quit her job at Franky's diner?"

"No! So the woman I love doesn't have to bust her ass at a job she doesn't like. Especially not when she's carrying my baby."

"I can see the rest of our lives is gonna be peachy fricken fun." I drop my spoon into the cream ceramic bowl with a loud 'ting!' "I'm not quitting my job, Marcus. Shove your money up your butt crack. I don't want it, and I didn't ask for it. I'm a grown ass woman, and I've literally only just stumbled into some pathetic version of independence. I'm not giving it up now."

"But–"

"But nothing. Hush your face and get over it. I'm not quitting my job until the baby literally slips out of my cooch and slides along the diner floor."

His poor face turns ghostly white. "Meg. You're gonna kill me."

"Yeah, well, I warned you." I turn in my seat and place my hands on his muscular forearms. Wielding a saw all day never looked so good on a man until him. "I'm not quitting. I'm trying to do something with my life, Marc. I'm trying to springboard Oz's wedding into something huge. If I'm lucky and survive the whole baby thing, then I intend to make a career of this. I have tens of thousands of dollars riding on this event. Several tens. Then when it's done and I pull if off, I'll be able to charge anything I want."

"If you mention the 'surviving the baby thing' one more time, I might go buy that paddle you wanted, but you won't like it."

I lean forward with a smirk and drop a kiss on the ball of his shoulder. "You really do care. That makes my stomach flutter."

He shakes his head with frustration. "I really do care, Meg. It's important to me you *do* survive, so stop daring the universe with that shit."

I SLIDE out of my car at three in the afternoon with my phone tucked against my ear and my keys in my hands. Locking the car and listening to the dial tone, I dig through my handbag in search of a dry cracker to help ease my stomach. The butterfly in my tummy is quickly transforming from cute flutters to plain nausea.

All the internet searches call it morning sickness, but mine seems to hover around the middle of the afternoon. It's definitely a boy in there, and it's definitely like Marc – stubborn and refuses to conform.

"Megan."

"Lucky! Finally. I've been trying to reach you."

"Sorry, honey. I've had a stomach flu, but I'm back on deck and everything's running smooth."

"What's Jase up to?"

"He's got servers signing contracts as we speak. Everyone's being vetted and if anyone mentions their love of professional fighting on social media, they're nixed. No fans, no fangirls, no messy shit."

"Good. Guest list is coming in at around two hundred people. You guys can handle that?"

She scoffs. "Two hundred is like a baby wedding for us. I did a fifteen hundred last weekend – which, by the way, is where I think I was exposed to yucky stomach germs."

"Careful you're not pregnant. It's a damn epidemic."

"Ew." I know her face is scrunching up. I haven't even told her about my situation yet. "Have you heard from Hannah recently?"

I make the gagging sound. My soon-to-be ex-husband's pregnant whore. And the irony doesn't escape me that I'm now pregnant, to someone that's not my husband. Fuck, I'm fairly certain I'm a whore, too. "No. Hannah and I aren't pen pals. I hope to never see her again."

"What about Drew? Have you talked to him?"

"Nah, that's what lawyers are for." It's time to catch my daddy up to speed. Add that to my to-do list. Not to mention, Jules said they're getting ready to send out his summons for the initial hearing. That's the first time he'll know he's in trouble, then at that hearing, he'll either plead guilty... or not. *Probably not.* Drew would never make it so easy for me.

After that, the DA that was assigned to my case starts working on burying him. I look forward to it, though I don't tell any of that to my cake caterer. Some things are better left private.

I munch on my cracker and walk around the block from the diner parking lot. There's a back entry, but the sun's out and I have time.

"So, you and Jase are all settled, then? What do you need from me?"

"Just the usual," she murmurs distractedly. "Rough numbers for now. Final numbers a week out. Dietary needs – vegetarian, nuts, that sorta shit. What's on the menu? Jase didn't tell me."

"I don't know yet. He said he was preparing 'a culinary master-piece.' He'll be coming here sometime between now and then. In a month or two, I guess, and I get to taste everything." Actually, I should turn that into a family dinner. He can feed us all.

Add *that* to my to-do list, too.

I step into the diner and smile at Mac. He might be my new best friend. It doesn't matter that he's only twelve. "Alright, Lucky. I gotta go. Text me if you need anything. Anything at all. This wedding will *not* have speedbumps. Talk to you soon."

"Alrighty. Kiss, kiss, darling."

I laugh and stop in front of Mac's booth. "Not with those germy lips, lady. Feel better. Talk to you later." I hang up and bump Mac with my hip. "Scoot over, handsome. I wanna sit down."

He scoots so fast you'd think his ass was on fire. Turning to the side to face me, his eyes flip between my belly and my face. My new best friend is twelve, and best friend status or not, I didn't tell the kid I was heading out to get an abortion yesterday. That's just not something you tell a pre-teen. All he knows is that there's a baby in there – which isn't something I told him. He just happened to pay attention to the atmosphere around here, noticed me turning green a time too many with that stupid three p.m. sickness, then he put two and two together.

And since he saw Marc and me sitting together far too often for it to be platonic, Mac was *this* close to throwing a baby shower in my honor.

"How's it going, baby mama?"

I don't think he understands what he's calling me. I laugh and steal a fry from his plate. "All good here. Marc thinks it's a boy."

He nods and chews his lip thoughtfully. "Probably is. Marc's rarely wrong."

Thick as thieves. I roll my eyes and look down at his leg. No longer in the cast, though he definitely walks with a limp. "How does it feel to be free?"

"Feels amazing. I don't have to cut my jeans anymore. It was breaking mom's heart every time we had to do that."

"Are you still grounded?"

He snorts and picks up his soda. "I'm grounded for the rest of my life."

"Well, maybe you'll have learned your lesson. Sneaking out and throwing yourself off a gantry crane to show off for the pretty ladies isn't the smartest thing you ever did."

He rolls his eyes. "I didn't throw myself off. I fell. And I wasn't showing off for anyone. It was just an accident."

He was totally showing off for girls. "Was the sneaking out an accident, too?"

"Shut your pie hole, preggo. Nobody asked you."

The bell dings over the diner door. Looking up, we both smile when Mac's *real* best friend saunters through. Ben Conner is one of two best men in the wedding I'm planning, but at only sixteen years old, he looks like a man already. He's older than Mac, but familial relations have the boys pushed together so often, it's not surprising they've bonded, and now that he's here, Mac's kicking my 'preggo' ass to the curb.

I slide out of the booth and look *up* at Ben as he walks by. He's learning to fight, just like Mac was before he threw himself off a crane, and sixteen or twenty-six, that training has Ben bulking up.

"Hey, Miss Meg."

"Hey Benny. How's it going?"

"All good. How's the baby?"

I look down at my small belly. "Does everyone know my business? Because I sure as hell didn't announce this yet."

He grins handsomely and pats my stomach. "This is a small town. No secrets around here. Plus, Marc's our pal. That makes Mac and me soon-to-be uncles."

Jesus. I shake my head and step away. "You people need to mind your own business. Did you write your speech yet, Ben?"

He slides into the booth and sneaks Mac's fries. "For the baby shower?"

"No! For the wedding, dummy."

He scoffs arrogantly. "No. That's forever away. You don't get to give me homework, woman. I have school teachers doing that."

I lift my hands and step back. "I'm just saying, Alex's speech might be better than yours. That'd be embarrassing."

His brows pull low. "Have you read it? What's it say?"

I highly doubt Alex has done his homework, either. "I'm not telling. Just saying you better bring your A game."

"Don't worry about me. Take care of that baby, give my mom a beautiful wedding. I'll take care of me."

"Mmhmm." I turn and dance under Katrina's arm as she brings plates to waiting diners. "Your son and his friend swore."

Without missing a single step or spilling her trays, she smacks them on the back of the head as she passes. Katrina's a pro, and though she's several years younger than me, I hope I grow up to be like her one day.

She's badass. And she's done a badass job of raising her son.

10

MARC
DOWNWARD DOG

I walk into the diner at eight that night – not too late to eat dinner with my girl, not too early so I can wait around for her shift to end. I slide into the booth next to Mac's and toss my phone and keys onto the table. My muscles ache from a hard day's work, my knuckles ache for a whole other reason.

"Marcus Macchio! What the hell happened to you?"

Beauty and grace stops at my table with a mean scowl painted across her face and a dangerously popped hip.

Her right hand reaches out and yanks my face toward hers, and her left hand balances a bowl of piping hot soup.

"Please don't spill that on me."

Her eyes turn to slits. "I should. I'll be back. Don't move."

She dances away and plops the bowl down in front of a customer. Practically sprinting around, she refills jugs and replaces dropped cutlery, swipes up a bill and cash, and runs it through the register, then grabs a basket of bread and speaks to Stefan briefly through the divider between the dining room and the kitchen. Turning back in my direction, she saunters over – though I don't think she means to *saunter*. I think she's charging slowly, like a seductive warrior that's about to slit my throat.

She tosses the bread down on my table with a loud crack. "What happened to your face, Marcus?"

"Fell into a door?"

Silence. Hands on hips. *I'm in big trouble.* "Fell into a door... Funny you mention that. Luc said something similar, too."

Smile. Everything's fine. She doesn't scare you. "Coincidence?"

"What did you do, Macchio?"

Run away! She terrifies you!

I shrug as casually as I can manage and avoid her gaze. Picking up the bread and taking a large bite, my stomach rumbles with hunger, since I haven't eaten since lunch. "Don't get mad, beautiful. It's bad for the baby."

"Don't you even think about starting that shit with me. And don't call me beautiful when you're in trouble. Why'd you hit him?"

"Pssht," Mac snickers from behind us. "He's deep in the shit."

She turns her glare on him and has him shrinking back into the booth.

I look up to her as innocently as I can manage. "I'm the one with a split lip, baby. Why do you assume I'm the bad guy?"

"Because your knuckles are freshly split, and because he loves you and wants to make it better. Smacking you around unprovoked ain't gonna do that."

"So maybe he's a dummy. Maybe he thought hitting me was exactly what would make me forget how bad he fucked me over." *Fuckin' asshole.* Just thinking about him and my sister within arm's reach sends my blood boiling. "He deserves more than what he got."

"You aren't teenagers anymore, Marcus. You're grown ass men. He has a really important job, and if you keep messing up his pretty face, it won't bode well for his career. You want the man seeing your sister to be unemployed?"

"No! I want him to not see her!"

She shakes her head ominously. She thinks I'm overreacting. She thinks I'm wrong. "You're a dumbass if you think he isn't the best man on this planet for her."

I cross my arms and look back to my bread. "He's not. He's not even close."

"So, who is?"

"Nobody!"

Yep, she really thinks I'm wrong. "You're an idiot, Marcus Macchio. I love your guts, but I'm not blind to the fact you're dumb as a rock about this. They're in love and they don't need your permission. Make peace with your brother, because he'll be around for a long time. Now, answer my first question, and don't lie."

"I hit him."

"Why?"

"Because he came over to the house to help with the renovations."

"And…" Her perfectly styled brow pops up. "And what? He egged your house? He called you ugly? He kicked Helen and now she's so traumatized she'll never lay another egg again? What? What did he do to provoke your wrath?"

"He came over to the house! That's it. He disrespected me by coming to my house. I told him I didn't wanna see him."

"He came over to the house you want to share with me and the baby, he came over to help renovate the house that would shelter your family, and that pissed you off?"

"Yup."

"Stefan!" She turns on her heel, and thankfully, doesn't notice the way both Mac and I jump in our seats. She holds my world in her angry little hands, and frankly, scares the shit out of me.

Stefan pokes his head through the gap. Smiling like he was listening this whole time, he turns his gaze to Meg. "Yeah, darlin'?"

"Cancel the first order. Send soup, instead. He doesn't deserve a juicy burger and fries. Cancel the shake, too. He doesn't deserve shit."

"Poot!"

"And definitely no pie. No way does he get pie that I helped make."

"Gotcha, darlin'." He winks and ducks away as she turns.

"Don't Poot me, you stubborn mule. Your life ain't gonna be pretty until you make up with Luc. That's my final decision."

"I'm never giving him permission to date my sister, so looks like our life is gonna be kinda miserable."

"Suits me." She turns away when the bell dings. Collecting my shitty soup and a roll of cutlery, she drops it at my table with a snarl. "I hope it tastes like crap." She steps away, but stops again with a glare. "Mac! Eyes down, do your homework. Don't make me cancel your pie, too."

"Yes'm." We watch her walk away, and it's not until she steps into the kitchen that his eyes come back to mine. "She's scary, man."

I turn on him incredulously. "You say that like I don't know. Shit, Mac. Shut up and do your damn homework."

I WALK into the apartment living room days after the no-pie fiasco. Last night was a restless night for Meg, up a handful of times with heart-burn and bathroom breaks. I know she's getting so tired with broken sleep. But we both know that's nothing on what life will be like after the baby arrives. This is nature's way of preparing us for half a decade of no sleep.

I intend to make her coffee and breakfast. I intend to rub her feet while she eats before we both have to go our separate ways and work.

The house won't take that long to get back to lockup stage – less time if I allowed the extra set of hands Luc's offering. And Meg has a wedding to plan, a meal plan to discuss, seating plans to map. She's working her ass off at the diner, then she's working her ass off times a thousand on this wedding that isn't even hers.

I'd be tempted to tell her to slow down, if she wasn't smiling the whole time she's working. It's not work if you love what you're doing, and Meg sure as hell enjoys coordinating that wedding.

She gets on the phone and tears a new asshole for anyone who dares defy her. She's coordinating a wedding that *looks* like it cost upwards of a hundred thousand dollars, and she's using her cute looks to get it all for free.

Can't say I blame those people for saying yes. I'd tell her yes on anything she asked, too.

But despite all my best laid plans and intentions for breakfast and coffee and foot massages, I stop at the threshold of the living room with a hungry smirk and a throbbing... heart. I cock my head to the side and stare.

And stare.

And stare some more.

I fucking love whoever invented yoga.

I especially love whoever invented downward dog.

Tight black yoga pants with zero visible panty lines – which means my girl's wearing a thong, or even better, nothing at all. Standing with her feet together, her hands on the ground, her ass at the exact right height for me to just walk on in and use her in the best way I know how. She hums under her breath a song I know by heart – Of course I know it.

I wrote it.

For her.

Way back in senior year.

She'd already moved away by that point. She was two grades above me, and when Sammy ditched town, Meg wasn't far behind, but whether I saw her daily or not didn't stop me from thinking about her.

She doesn't know that song was written for her. Nobody knows. But it was, and I can't say I'm unhappy that she likes it enough to sing it to herself.

Meg hums and stretches and groans as her joints pop and her muscles warm. Like a hot pretzel on a warm day in Venice, she bends and moves and transitions into what I have zero clue the technical yoga name, but I'd like to call it 'this is how I'd like to fuck my future wife.'

She makes a bridge with her body so my baby pops high into the sky. Arched back, toned thighs, strong arms, and long blond hair hanging loose and curtaining the back of her head.

I walk forward and move between her open legs. "Can I fuck you like that?" She startles at my words, but I take the weight off her hips and press my cock against her core. "Sorry, didn't mean to scare you."

She makes a rumbling noise in the back of her throat when I rub my solid length against her. Lifting her legs off the ground, I hold her weight and slowly lower her to the ground. Her back straightens, her arms release their hold, her neck straightens, and finally, her smile blinds when our eyes meet.

"Hey, beautiful." I lean over her, but I see my baby in there now. I see that bump. So I lay over her side and hold my weight up on my elbows. Leaning forward, I drop a kiss on her lips.

"Morning, Marcus."

I love how she says my name. So much conviction. So much intent. Even when she's mad at me, it's like she knows I love hearing it. "You rested?"

She stretches her neck the way only she ever has for me, and when I begin nibbling, her rumbles turn to purrs. "Mmhmm. You?"

"Nuh-uh. You snore."

I smile when her body turns taut and her neck escapes my lips. "S'cuse me very much?"

"It's okay. I looked it up. The internet says it's normal."

"Um, no!" She pushes me back until I sit on my haunches. She painfully pokes my chest. "I do not snore!"

"You do." I attempt to move forward in search of her neck. "It's not a big deal. I think it's cute."

"It's not cute!" She shoves me back and scrambles lithely to her feet. "I don't wanna be a cute snorer! I'm just cute... full stop. Not a snorer."

"Okay, fine." I climb to my feet and drag her against my chest. I bury my face in her hair and my lips in her neck. "I'm sorry. You don't snore."

She totally does.

"Do I really? Tell me the truth."

"You do."

"Goddamit, Marcus!" She shoves me back and spins away.

"Come back, Meg!" She spins and twirls and escapes my grasp. She's small and slippery, talented on her feet, and not scared of fucking up her footing and falling down. "Come back, baby." I pull her into me so her back presses against my chest and her ass against my cock. "Don't run away."

"You messed up my exercise."

I nibble on her neck and run my hands along her ribs. "I wanna fuck you. Don't hate on a man for walking in on what I did today and wanting to finish what you started."

"I didn't start anything. I was stretching."

"Yeah you were."

"I don't wanna fuck. I'm hungry for breakfast. You should be making sure I'm eating."

"You can eat my sausage if you want."

She snickers and relaxes against me. "You're such a pig. I hate you."

"Mmm." I bite down on the soft skin behind her ear. "You don't mean that. But I love you, and I *do* mean that."

She grunts in mock exasperation. We're playing hard to get today, obviously. "Okay. One fuck. Really quick."

Or not.

I slide my right hand over her ribs, over the bump of her belly, and into her pants, past the non-existent panties. Every second I nibble on her neck sends her body heavier and heavier against mine. Her head drops forward, and when I dip my fingers into her pussy, her hair follows and hides her from me.

She lets out a sexy groan. "Marcus."

"Mmhmm." I probe two fingers deep inside her. My own orgasm builds just from the feel of her clenching around my fingers, from the sounds she makes, the way her body shakes in my arms. "Do that other one again." I press the small of her back with my left hand until she's bent over in front of me.

Legs splayed wide. Hands on the floor.

I have to bend to keep my fingers seated deep inside her, but giving up after a minute, I pull out, help her remove her yoga pants completely, then my fingers move back in to work.

I pump them in roughly. In and out, her breath races and her thighs shake. "I love you, and you love me, right?"

"Mmm." Her voice comes out in breathy cries. "Yeah. Oh... Marcus."

"Let me in without a condom this time. Can't get you *more* pregnant than you already are."

Her hair slides along the floor as she nods. "Okay. Do it quick."

I unsnap the buttons on my jeans with one hand and tear the belt from the loops. I watch her ass shake barely a foot from my face, the tiny puckered hole that dares me to intrude, the strong thighs that beg to ride me.

My cock springs free. Liquid seeps from the tip, and when I remove my fingers, she lets out a cry that has my cock jumping in reaction. "Is this gonna hurt you?"

"I hope so. Do it."

My eyes snap shut and my dick twitches with pleasure. "Meg." I line up and rub the head of my dick around her asshole. Lubricating the entrance just for fun, she lets out a whiny cry of pleasure and pushes back against me.

I don't enter. I'm too desperate to go slow, too ready to be careful.

Lowering my dick and pressing it to her more conventional opening, my heart gallops at the fiery inferno that transfers from her flesh to mine. I intend to savor. I intend to enjoy her bare skin, inch by delectable inch, but with a grunt of frustration, she lifts to her tiptoes and slams back onto me so my balls touch her clit and my dick touches something deep inside her.

She cries out on a moan, but I simply close my eyes and hold my breath. "Holy shit." *Don't blow it, Marc. Don't fucking blow it.* "You feel so good." My heart gallops painfully against the wall of my chest. My dick, squeezed in her tight, hot pussy. Opening one eye experimentally, I hold her narrow hips in my hands. Sliding out slowly, a bead of sweat dribbles down my spine in my attempt to pleasure her. With every inch I take, I drag myself closer to the brink of ecstasy. "Fuck, Meg."

"Mmm." She opens her legs wider and leans further forward onto her arms. "Feels so good."

I lean forward and press my fingers to her clit. She needs to catch the fuck up. The first time a man goes bare with a woman, especially *this* woman, he should be forgiven for sprinting to the finish line.

She cries out from the combination of my fingers and my cock slamming into her from behind. Turning her head to the side, her teeth latch onto her own bicep and her eyes squeeze shut.

Her walls flutter around me, tightening and releasing. Tight, so fucking tight, release. My release strangles my balls. My fingers tease her relentlessly. My hips slam against hers and her body jolts forward every time we meet. I catch her with my hand on her hip, then I pull her back and slam again.

"Marc…"

"Go, Meg. Come on my cock. Let me feel you cream."

"It's too much."

"No, it's not." *Yes, it is.* I circle her clit and tap, slam, pull her back, circle, tap. "Come on my cock, baby. Squeeze me."

She cries out and squeezes. Her breath is a sob. Her teeth painfully clamp the skin on her bicep. She's going to give herself a hickey.

I take my fingers from her clit and bring them to her ass. Her cry of displeasure turns to a loud mewling when I push my thumb against her asshole. Her body bucks, her spine arches upwards, her limbs shake, and dragging me to an almost standstill, she milks my cock on a violent cry.

Thank God. It's my turn.

My thighs can barely hold my weight, but my hot cum gleefully spurts deep inside her. The breath is robbed from my body, and if I was less of a man, I might just let her catch herself while I slide to the floor.

I can't catch my breath. I can't do anything but stand here and pray I don't fall on her. "Fuck me, Poot."

She snickers and leans heavily against me. "Pretty sure you just fucked me."

"Did we just make twins?"

Every time she laughs, she squeezes my dick, which sends a bolt of electricity through my groin, into my stomach and up into my chest.

It's like she electrocutes me. Gives me life. Reinvigorates me.

"No," she laughs. "That's not how that works, dummy. Let me

down." She slides forward until my softening cock falls free. Lowering herself to her knees, she groans and stretches her back. "I think you hurt me a little bit."

I drop to my knees and pull her into the cradle my body makes. "What hurts, baby?"

"My vag," she snickers. "Relax. I'm okay."

"Did we hurt, the ah…"

She lays her head back and looks up at me with a lazy smile. "I doubt we're the only people in the world who have sex while pregnant."

"We're probably the only ones who do it like that. Upside down probably isn't healthy."

"Doubt it." She looks at her arm lazily, traces her fingers over the bite marks she left behind. "We should do that more. You're onto something with the yoga sex."

I groan and sit back on my still jeaned ass. I tuck my dick back in, despite our mixed and smeared fluids, then pull her back onto her ass, forcing her to pull her legs out from beneath her and sit with them bent in front.

Lying back lazily against my chest, she hums under her breath and draws designs into my thigh with her fingertip.

"Thank you… for trusting me."

Her finger pauses briefly, but when she resumes, she asks, "Trust you with what?"

"Well, the no condom, for starters."

She shrugs, though I can feel her smile in the air around us. "I can't get any *more* pregnant. So, whatevs."

"Meg."

"Love you…" she sing-songs.

I chuckle and press a heavy kiss to the side of her head. "Thank you for trusting me with everything. Renovations, moving in, giving us a go."

"Didn't give me much choice. You told me you loved me, your baby wiggled right on cue. Now you've got me emotionally invested."

I want to shake my head at her easy words, but I know she does that to cover the real. Wild and loud Meg is actually painfully shy, and I bet almost no one else in the world knows that about her. Only those truly closest to her.

"Marc?"

"Hmm?"

"Thank you, too. For everything."

I smile and hold her half naked body tight against my chest. "We're a team."

"Uh-huh."

"Always. There's no need to be scared anymore. I promise."

"Okay."

11

MEG
KEEP ON SWIMMING

I climb out of my car out front of Kari's small home, and though my twenty-weeks baby bump now officially precedes me everywhere I go, I can still manage to sit behind my steering wheel comfortably – for now.

Something tells me Marcus Macchio would never dare create a small baby. Fifteen-pound football head, no doubt. He promises he'll make me safe with the blood clotting thing, we'll do tests, see doctors and whatnot, but not once did he promise to make a dainty six-pound baby.

I'll be the mom who makes international news headlines: *Baby stuck halfway out of cooch. Baby and mother learn to live in harmony. Mother walks like a duck for the rest of her life while baby continues to grow and thrive half in, half out.*

Mother never has sex again.

I walk up the path out front of the home Kari shares with Luc's twin sisters – I mean, obviously Luc would be around a lot; how did Marc not see this coming? – and knock on the front door.

It's a weekday, mid-morning. Laine's a school teacher at the same school Britt teaches at, and Jess works in Jules' – and my dad's – law office.

That just leaves the lovebirds who work on rotating shifts at the local hospital – and I sure as hell noticed how their shifts line up so often.

Seriously, Marcus! How did he not see this?

After a solid minute of clothes rustling, hopping on tile floors, whispers and giggles, Kari swings the door wide.

Her flushed cheeks and smile are the first things I notice.

The second is the fact her shirt's on inside out.

And if that weren't enough, the third – and only *after* Kari says 'it's only Snitch' – is Luc stepping into view with no shirt, and a cheeky smile.

"Put your clothes on, horn bag." I step into the living room and swipe up a little black bra from the arm of the couch. I turn with it dangling from the tip of my finger. "Really, nympho?"

"Shut up." With a huff, Kari closes the front door and snatches her bra from my grasp. Luc steps forward and snatches it, folds it up, and shoves it into the back pocket of his jeans with a silly smirk.

I shake my head. "Marc finds his sister's bra in your pocket, shit's gonna get messy again."

Luc rolls his eyes and collects his shirt from the coffee table, pulling it on over his tanned skin. "Shit's already messy as hell. I don't know what to do."

"Maybe stop fucking his sister in the living room, for a start."

"We were in the bedroom," Kari huffs. She walks back into the living room from her kitchen clutching two tall glasses of lemonade. Passing one to me, she blushes. "We just started in here."

I take the glass and exaggeratedly inspect it. "I hope you washed your hands before pouring this. Do the girls not get mad you two are worse than rabbits? They sit on that couch, too."

"Laine's never here," Luc grumbles. "And Jess is at the office more often than not. In fact, I see her less than I see you."

"And now I see even less of you. Take your shirt off again, big boy."

He scrunches his nose playfully. "I'll send you pics. You know, for when you're lonely."

I walk to the couch with a laugh and slump down lazily. "Jesus, can you imagine how messy it would get if Marc found you texting me half naked pictures of yourself?"

"Fuck." Luc's large hands come up and his fingers probe at a still sore lip. "I can't take anymore beatings, Snitch. I'm developing a nervous tic. Every minute of every day, I'm tense and waiting for him to come out and smack me down some more."

"He'll come around, just give it time. And *don't* touch her in front of him."

"I *can't* touch her in front of him! I literally never see him at the same time she's in the room, and when I do see him, it's only for two seconds while he hits me."

I laugh and lift my feet onto their coffee table like a total slob. "How much longer do I have to do this, guys?"

Kari purses her lips and stares me down. "Really? You're twenty weeks. That means you're halfway, dumbass. Twenty more to go."

"Crap. My skin's already stretching." I look up and meet her eyes. "How big were you born?"

"Nine pounds, ten ounces."

"Fuck."

She laughs and flops down onto the couch beside me, while Luc sits on the arm of the chair on her side. "Marc was eleven and a half pounds, I think."

"You're lying."

"I'm actually not. You should see our baby pictures. We were big fat roly-poly obese babies. I think my mom was making pure cream in her boobs."

I groan and throw my head back. "Oh my God. Boobs! I'm gonna have to feed this baby off my boobs!"

She snickers and places her hand on my belly. She's hoping for the first kick that can be felt on the outside. I don't bemoan her trying, but I truly hope Marc gets to feel it first. I feel the baby rolling around in there a lot now, but nothing that can be felt on the outside – yet.

"Yes, you have to feed the baby from your boobs. Well, you don't *have* to. You don't live in a third-world country, we have formula nowadays, but it's very likely a baby will be latched onto you at least once this year."

"I didn't sign up for this shit." I turn my head lazily. "My boobs won't sit up nice and perky anymore after this."

"They might."

"Don't patronize me."

"If you ask really nicely, my brother might buy you new boobs. Better boobs."

"You're a jerk. And you two better be careful. Getting pregnant is super friggin easy, apparently."

Luc's smile turns to a visible shudder. "It's not that I don't want a family with you, Bear. I really do, but maybe after Marc's old and dead. I can't handle the *'I got your sister pregnant'* talk. I just can't do it. Not this year."

She pats his knee with her other hand. "You'll be okay. I'll protect you."

"Anywho…" I regain their attention. "I need medical advice."

"We're not doctors, Snitch. Seriously. Call a damn OBGYN!"

"I have one of those, so stop freaking out. I have an appointment this week, but that's why I want to talk to you guys first. I don't know that OB. She's a stranger to me. She might be going with the whole 'up-sell' thing like at fast food places. I just want to know what I should do about the whole…" My heart thunders in my chest at the same time my hands turn clammy. I act cool, adjusted, okay with everything, but I'm so terrified of dying, it paralyzes me. "What can I do to make sure I'm not gonna die while giving birth?"

"Aww, honey." Kari turns into me and rests her head on my shoulder. "It won't happen. Your dad said it wasn't hereditary. Just super shitty luck."

"But I'm still scared. I don't want to die, and I especially don't want to leave Marc here all alone with a newborn baby. He'll handle it. Hell, he'll handle it way better than Daddy, plus he has all of you to help, but I still don't wanna die. I just want to know what I can do between now and then that could give me some kind of assurances."

"I mean…" Luc rubs his hands over the light stubble on his jaw. He looks to Kari. "CT scan?"

She scoffs immediately. "No way in hell a *competent* medical provider is gonna give out CT's like they're candy. No way. Way too much radiation – they wouldn't risk that unless they had actual concerns."

"I'm *actually* concerned!"

Eyes full of pity, she takes my hand. "I get it, Snitch, I really do. You're worried with your heart and emotions, but doctors don't work like that. There's logically no medical reason to worry. You're no more likely to die of an aneurysm than anyone else, including me."

"MRI? MRA?" Luc suggests thoughtfully. He stares at the front window as though the answers are written in the sky outside.

"Nah. No one will do that just because."

"D-Dimers?"

"Guys! Speak English!"

"D-Dimers tend to be elevated during pregnancy," Kari rolls right over me. "She'll get a false positive, which will result with an unnecessary CT. I don't like the idea of exposing her to that radiation just for shits and giggles. It's not worth it."

"So…?"

"I vote DNA test."

I frown. "I already know who my parents are."

She snickers and rubs circles into my belly. "It's a blood test…"

"Ewwie."

"…where they'll test for genetic clotting disorders," she continues with an eyeroll. "Maybe prescribe you medication if you're high-risk." She looks into my eyes with determination. "Which you won't be."

"A needle?"

"*One* needle. You'll be fine. You'll have a human clawing it's way out of your body in a few months. A needle is cake."

"Wow. Thanks for that visual, you asshole. Now I see that movie Alien, you know, where the chest opened up and…" I shiver from top to toe. I can't believe I was complaining about a half in, half out baby and no sex. That's better than an alien clawing its way out of my chest.

"You'll be fine. It's one single needle, five minutes, all done. Want me to come with you?"

"Can you do my testing?"

"No, honey, I can't. I'm not your doctor, this isn't a backyard clinic, and you need to do this properly. But I *can* come with you. I'll hold your hand, make sure they're using clean needles."

"Jerk!" I push her head off my shoulder, though she only laughs. "No, it's fine. I'll take Marc. I'd rather look at his pretty eyes while they stick me with stupid needles."

"He and I have the same eyes!"

"I know, baby girl, which is why I understand how Luc loves you. I feel a little lesbionic sometimes when I look at you."

Her nose scrunches. "One, gross. Two, lesbionic's not a real word."

"But when I feel myself getting a little *too* attracted to you, I go home and fuck your brother. I kinda like him. He's cute and not nearly as mean as I led you guys to believe."

She shakes her head. "So gross. Do you have an appointment?"

I huff out a breath and sip at my lemonade. It's fresh and sweet. A little tangy, icy cold, and so refreshing, I literally feel the cool liquid work its way down my throat and into my stomach. The baby will start doing backflips soon. "Mmm. Did you make this?"

"Uh-huh."

"It's so good." I close my eyes and savor. "Yeah," I answer her question. "We have an appointment, but I was hoping to talk you into doing it."

"Well, I won't, but I am curious about the results. Let me know when you get them back?"

"Sure. How long will they take?"

"Two to four weeks from today," Alicia, my vampire nurse with cute hair and a nice smile, informs us. Wearing a bland blue outfit just like those you see on all the hospital dramas on TV, she pushes the needle into my arm like she's simply out for a Sunday stroll.

So fucking casual, stabbing people.

As soon as the steel needle pierces my skin, my body breaks out in a cold sweat, and Marc – my sweet, understanding… *Boyfriend? That sounds too high school. Spouse…? That just sounds plain weird. Significant other? Jesus, that sounds like I'm eighty years old. Okay, baby daddy. We're rolling with baby daddy* – baby daddy pulls my un-stabbed hand into his lap and clasps it between his. "Hey." His voice is strong, sure, deep and comforting when I want to peel the skin from my bones and run out of here all naked skeleton. "Look at me, Poot."

"Don't call me Poot."

Alicia smiles at us, but she doesn't make comment on our exchange.

"I call you Poot in my head every single time." He smirks, and those eyes, barely inches from mine, twinkle with fun. "Even when I call you beautiful out loud, inside I'm saying Poot. It gives me a sick thrill playing with fire."

"You're too scared to say it out loud? Good. Be scared."

Alicia does something with her needle, tugging on my vein and yanking it from beneath my skin. Well, not really. But still, it brings tears to my eyes and sweat to my spine.

"I'm definitely scared." He takes my chin in his hand and turns me from Alicia. "I'm waiting for the day I never wake again. I'll go to sleep to the sweet sounds of your hog snoring, then boom, I'm flying with the angels."

"You'll be flying with the angels if you ever say 'hog snoring' in reference to me again. I'm not playing, Marcus."

His eyes twinkle. "Do you wanna go out on a date with me, beautiful?"

I'm pregnant with his baby and essentially living with him now, yet he still feels the need to formally ask. I never could have guessed that this man could make me swoon, but here we are. "Did you just call me Poot in your head?"

Alicia snickers and hurriedly covers it with a cough.

"I did." He brushes the tip of his nose against mine. "You're Poot to me. It's a term of endearment. I already told you that."

"Marcus…"

"It's not my fault you farted that time."

Alicia chokes on a laugh and hurriedly turns away to collect herself – and a Band-Aid. "I'm sorry," she croaks with a red face. "Allergies."

I turn back to Marc with a glare. "I hate your guts."

His large hand gently presses over my stomach. "I love yours. Go on a date with me."

"Is that a question or a demand?"

He shrugs. "Little bit of A, little bit of B."

"Do I have to sleep with you on the first date?"

"Of course not. That wouldn't be proper."

"Will you still treat me like a lady tomorrow?"

"Yeah." Finally, as Alicia removes the needle from my arm and presses a wad of cotton to my elbow to stem the bleeding, Marc presses a dry kiss to my lips. "For the rest of my life, beautiful."

12

MARC
DATE NIGHT

I move up the stairs to her apartment the next night with a bouquet of wildflowers in my left hand and a Snickers bar in my coat pocket. I tried to dress up for her. I really, really tried, but the pants felt weird and the tie was too tight. So instead, I arrive at the apartment above Ang's garage in jeans, a white dress shirt – top two buttons undone – and a suit coat. If you ignore the buttons, I look fancy as hell from the waist up.

I lift my spare hand and *tap-tap-tap,* and when the sound of heels *click-click-click* on the floor inside, I smile so big my cheeks squish near my eyes.

She stops at the closed door and the heels silence. "Who's out there?"

She's such a good girl. Careful, just like I begged her to be. No peep hole in this door means she could be ambushed.

Not on my fucking watch.

"Just me, babe."

The door swings wide and a flurry of red moves away distractedly. "I was wondering where you were." She lets out an unladylike scoff without looking back. "And you say that I'm high maintenance. We're gonna be late if you don't get dressed."

"Hey." I snag her wrist and spin her back, and her eyes, all smoky and beautiful, meet mine with confusion. "I'm ready. I'm here to pick you up. Like a gentleman."

Her eyes scan me from shoes to hair until her distracted gaze turns to a sexy smirk. When she backtracks to the flowers, her softening gaze comes back to mine. "You got me flowers?"

"No, these are for Ang. Is he here?"

She purses her lips. "You're such a jerk." But she studies them with a soft smile. "Do you wanna know a secret?"

"Sure." I play with her fingers and thrill in the way her breath turns fast as I step into her space.

"I've never been given flowers before."

"Never?"

"Never. Drew wasn't exactly George Jetson, and I never dated anyone before or after him, so..." She turns away and takes down a vase from above the fridge. Filling it at the sink and setting it on the counter, she takes the bouquet from my hands as gently as though she were holding a bomb. Or a newborn baby.

"I have so much to say about that, but first, what about George Jetson?"

She shrugs shyly and nibbles on her fire engine red lips. "He seems like the type who'd bring Mrs. Jetson flowers every now and then."

"That cartoon hasn't been on TV in... how long?"

Another shrug. "I dunno. Twenty. Thirty years?"

"And you're using them in reference now, because...?"

She laughs softly. "Dunno. I saw the flowers. The Jetsons popped into my head. Why the hell are you nitpicking?"

I chuckle lightly. Stepping toward her, I pull her in close until the only thing separating us is our baby. "My dad used to bring my mom flowers every single Tuesday."

"Every Tues–" She watches me with wide eyes. "Every single week?"

"Yep, every single week. Sometimes he bought them from the florists, sometimes he stole them from someone's yard. If he was desperate, he wasn't above buying a wilted flower from the gas station, but yeah, for as long as I can remember, every week on Tuesdays…"

Her brows crinkle adorably. "That's really sweet. Your daddy will make me cry with these baby hormones."

I drop a kiss on her lips – easier to reach, since she's wearing sexy heels. "Come on, beautiful. Let's go to dinner. Are you hungry?"

"So hungry I could eat the crotch out of a ragdoll."

I stop when she turns toward the door. "Wow, really? The crotch? Do you enjoy speaking to me with that filthy mouth?"

"Sure I do. And I think you enjoy it, too."

Yeah, I do. "Wanna suck my dick before we go?"

She bursts out in laughter and sends the ironed curls in her hair bouncing. "You're such a pig, Marcus, it's *almost* cute. No, I don't wanna suck your dick, but if you play your cards right, you might get a blowjob when we get home."

"Because sleeping together on the first date is cheap, but a blowy in the parking lot…"

She steps back in and presses her hand to my chest. "Sleeping together on the first date got me pregnant, Macchio. I don't know what you did to get those swimmers through the pill *and* the cock socks–"

"Cock socks?" I flash a dirty grin. "Are they the same as love gloves?"

She grins. "Shut up. Also, yes."

"We should call mine Magnums. Ya know, 'cause of my donkey dick."

She rolls her eyes. "That's what you think, but–"

"Hey!"

"But now I know what you're capable of," she continues with her sassy smile. Never mind my wilted manhood. "Swallowing never got any girl pregnant before."

"I told you you should've sucked me off that night. That'll teach you."

"I did!"

"Oh, yeah." I smirk and drop a kiss on her jaw. "You did. I liked that."

"I hate you."

Another kiss. "You don't mean that. Let's go. You look beautiful, by the way." Her amazing baby bump is the only difference to her body – well, and bigger boobs. The rest of her is as slim as she always was. She's in a skin tight, halter neck, bright red dress that stops just below her knee, and has a slit that moves up to the middle of her left thigh. Strappy golden heels give her a few inches, and though I worry for her and the baby if she stumbles in them, instead of suggesting she change, I silently vow to have a hand on her at all times tonight. I'll catch her. "So beautiful. I love your shoes."

"They're Sammy's."

We've played this game before. "I love your hair like that."

She smiles and turns back to the door. Pulling it open and collecting her purse from the table nearby, she looks back to me over her shoulder like a stunning succubus ready to eat my soul. As long as she continues to smile at me like that, I wouldn't even mind. "Thank you."

I sit the Snickers bar on the counter where her bag was, pull the door closed behind us, and lead her to our first ever official date.

WE FOLLOW the hostess to our booth in the back corner. This restaurant is dark and cozy, new to town, and Italian. Delicious. She leads us past an already seated couple that I've met a million times before – of the *Roller* variety – but they don't notice us as we walk by. They're too busy making googly eyes at each other and pretending not to fondle each other under the table.

Not my place to judge, seeing as I intend to fondle in three, two, one...

"Your table, Mr. Macchio."

I hold Meg's hand and help her slide in, and when her belly literally skims along the edge of the table, I make a mental note to ask for a regular table next time we come back. She'll be pissed if she can't fit, and I don't ever intend to make her feel self-conscious about growing my baby.

I slide in after her and move until we're touching from shoulder to knee. Accepting the menu's *Tricia* – according to her name tag – offers us, I place one in front of Meg and a kiss to her temple.

"Thanks." Crass Meg has stepped out, and in her place is the oddly shy girl.

"Can I offer you both a drink?"

"I'll just have a coke," Meg says. "Please."

"We have Pepsi, is that okay?"

And Shy Meg leaves again. "How is it in this day and age that restaurants don't carry both? Seriously! What's up with that?"

"She'll have a Pepsi," I interrupt before she goes Hulk smash on the place and ruins my plans for the evening. "And I will, too. Thank you."

"Alright. I'll be back soon." Tricia collects the wine glasses that we won't use, turns with a kind smile, and leaves us alone.

"Is it weird that I want to get up and bus that table?"

I look toward a table that a couple literally just stood up from and tossed down some cash. I smile and turn back into her. "I think you're finally one of us."

"One of who?"

"The working-class citizens," I tease. "It's kinda fun, right?"

"I mean, if you call working forty hours a week to barely cover rent, then, sure."

I chuckle and run circles on her thigh with my fingertips. "I guess that's what I meant. Oz's wedding coming along?"

"Mmhmm. We have a date. We have a cake. We have a band whose bass player still isn't talking to the drummer, so that's becoming a friggin issue."

I poke her leg. "For the love of all that's holy, please don't make me think about him tonight. Just me and you. Not…" *the guy … my sister…* "Ew. No."

"And Oz?"

I laugh and start with the circles again. "Point taken. I just wanna know how it's all going. You run around like crazy with that planner and your phone, and though I see no physical evidence stacking up – no gift registry stuff arriving at the apartment, no caterers camping in our kitchen – I get the feeling that you're planning a siege and it's happening flawlessly."

"I am... A siege," she confirms easily. Arrogantly, even. "Everything except the band."

"Meg! Shut up about the damn band."

She laughs. "Fine! Sorry. Whatever. Actually, I was thinking of calling the King's Chaos guys back." We pause and smile when our drinks are served. Snatching hers up as soon as the server is gone, Meg takes a long sip with a smile on her face and her eyes closed. "Mmm. Icy cold. So good."

"King's Chaos?"

"Mmhmm. They called when they heard I was doing this wedding. They want–"

"Ah, hold the fuck up. Who the hell are they?"

"Oh please! As if you don't know who they are."

I do know. I know exactly who she's talking about. A band made up of four Luc's, basically. Darker features to his blonde, but the whole man-whore, groupie-lover, let's share STD's because it's edgy and cool, shit is spot on. "You're talking about *the* Chaos?"

Another orgasmic sip of soda. Another smile. "Of course."

"Why are you speaking to them? What the hell's wrong with our band? What the fuck, Meg? Sleeping with the enemy, much?"

"The enemy?" She snorts and sets her drink down. "One, you guys aren't even remotely interested in going big. You wanna play 188 on the weekends – you've *never* wanted out of that club. Chaos are looking for huge record deals."

"Um, should we want out of that club? We like it there. Doesn't mean we need to sign onto a huge record deal."

"Nobody said you did. You guys are happy where you are, so no, don't change a thing. But the King's do. They want big, which means you and they aren't even close to enemies. Not even competition.

That's like you racing go-carts on weekends and calling Jeff Gordon your competition."

"Jeff Gordon?"

"Yeah, NASCAR." She makes a face like I'm an embarrassing dad who admits in front of her teeny-bopper friends I don't know who Lady Gaga is. I know who Jeff Gordon is, and for the record, I know who Gaga is, too, but, "You're comparing our band to a broken-down go-kart? Jesus, tell me how you really feel. Don't hold back now."

She rolls her eyes. "I did *not* say that, Marcus. But yes, basically broken down, because the bass player in *your* band is a stubborn ass who refuses to talk to his drummer. The King's talk to each other. You and Luc play shows three nights a week at the club, yet you continue to ignore each other. And when he won't let you ignore him, you hit him!"

"Which shows that we can still work together like professionals." Well, not the hitting, but the still getting the shows in despite the fact I fucking loathe the prick. "There's no reason to kick us out of the wedding, Meg. Oz is my family."

"And finally," she adds on a sigh. "Maybe you guys don't want to work that night. It's your friend's wedding. Maybe you just wanna relax, ever think of that?"

"No. I didn't think of that. We've been playing since I was twelve years old. We can relax *and* play, baby. We have loads of practice. We never once partied at The Shed in high school without also being the band. It never felt like work, it was just what we did. None of us ever actually thought of it as work, or not fun. We were still there, still having fun."

She smirks. "Did girls ever give you their panties? Bands are hot, even in high school. I could see myself fangirling over the band." She brushes me off. "Not *your* band, because the bass player was an asshole. But other bands. Probably the King's."

"One, yes. Two, don't even fucking think about it."

"Yes, girls gave you their panties?" Her eyes twinkle with fun. "Those dirty hoes, though I don't blame them. You're sexy, even when you're an asshole. Actually, maybe even more so." She plays with my hand, strokes my fingers, and twines hers between mine. "You still keep my panties in your pocket, Marcus? You've had them for months... ever take them out and look at them?"

Yes.

My heart thumps in my chest. She's only teasing me with the other band shit. That's what she does, she lives on pissing me off, but I lean in anyway. I take her plump lip between my teeth and nip hard enough to make her gasp. "Do me a favor?"

"What?" Her question comes out on a breathy moan that scorches straight down my throat and into my lungs. I can taste the Pepsi on her lips. The lipstick. Her.

"I love you."

Her clouded gaze snaps into smiling focus. "I love you, too. Little bit."

She just can't let me have it. Luckily, I know this about her now. "Don't love the Chaos more than you love me. Definitely don't give them your panties. I won't like it."

She nibbles on my lip. I'm sure I'm wearing as much lipstick now as she is, but I really don't give a shit. As long as it was hers first. "Jealous Marc is adorable. And a turn on."

"And Smartass Meg makes me hard." I take her hand and lay it over my hardened cock. "Wanna go hang out in the bathrooms with me for ten minutes?"

"Ten minutes is all you need?" She scoffs, but her breath is still part moan. "Not gonna knock a chick up with only ten minutes."

"Lucky I already got that part of the evening done." I drop a kiss on her collarbone and slide my hand along her thigh to the very top of the split in the fabric. "Do what you gotta do with the wedding, babe. I don't mind. This is your circus and I'm your monkey. I'll do whatever makes you happy."

"*You* make me happy."

"Good." I bite down on the soft skin at the base of her neck. "You piss me off more often than not, but strangely, that makes me happy."

"So I should try harder?"

I chuckle and work my lips up her slender neck. "Whatever makes you happy. If you want the other band, that's cool. That just means I get to follow you around and help instead of watching from the stage."

"You're only being so amenable because you don't wanna make up with Luc." She stretches her neck and purrs when I find the soft spot behind her ear. "I really want you to make up with him."

"Not today." *Not this decade.* But that hurts her, so I don't say it out loud. "And no, I'm just agreeing because this wedding is all yours. Your springboard for a career I know excites you. I won't be an obstacle."

Our server awkwardly clears her throat, and when I dislodge my lips from Meg's neck, I look up to find the poor woman with a red face and apologetic eyes. "I'm so sorry. Would you like to order?"

I turn to Meg. "What do you wanna eat, baby?"

She shrugs and smooths a hand over her inflated belly. I can see her definite outie belly button now. It used to be a sort of innie, sort of outie, but the baby has it officially poking through the fabric of her dress – and that belly button alone, the way it pops out, that single feature on her beautiful body has me falling deeper in love with a girl I thought I'd never have a chance with.

"Anything's fine. As long as it has cottage cheese."

I laugh. "Get her a bowl of cottage cheese."

"And sweet and sour sauce," Meg adds. "Do you have any of that?"

The waitress looks at us like we're punking her. "I mean, McDonalds is up the street."

"Good plan. Go steal some of the little sachets." I turn to Meg. "Do you like spicy?"

She shrugs easily.

"Okay." I look back to our waitress. "We'll take the roulette plate, please. And maybe some garlic twists or something. I'm starving."

"Sir, the roulette plate is fun, but it's super spicy."

"It'll be okay. We're tough."

With a casual shrug and a fun smile, she collects our menus and bops away.

Meg turns to me curiously. "What's the roulette plate?"

Twenty minutes later, a large plate is set down in front of us. Waving my arm toward it the way those chicks do in game shows to show off the grand prize, I smile and pick up my newly topped up soda. "The roulette plate is twenty pieces of deep fried... something. I don't even know what. I think it's chicken. But apparently it's delicious."

"Okay...?"

"But one of the twenty is a chilli pepper. Super spicy. Blow your head off spicy. We eat, we take turns, one of us will get the chilli."

Her eyes light up as she studies the plate. "It's like you know my soul. I love this game."

Megan Montgomery is nothing if not a competitive freak. "You say that because you assume I'll lose."

Her elegant brow pops with attitude. And dare. And definitely confidence. "You probably will." She leans forward and carefully studies the plate. "They all look exactly the same. Same size, same shape, same consistency."

"Is that what you say about all the boys?"

She turns her head and smirks. "Not all of them. Those Chaos guys..."

I bark out a laugh and bump her shoulder with mine. "Smartass. How's your cottage cheese?"

She pulls the large bowl toward her, then a small condiments bowl. "I can't believe they actually gave me a dish of cottage cheese."

"And sweet and sour sauce."

"Right?" She dips her pinky finger into the sauce and tastes is slowly. "They didn't steal. This isn't Maccas."

Cower! Find a bunker. Duck for cover.

"It's pretty good, though. Different, but still good."

"Oh, thank God."

She rolls her eyes and picks up a chunk of crumbled cheese. "Mmm. I swear, this and sauce together... it's better than an orgasm."

"Really? Even the orgasms I give you?"

"Mmhmm. Those Chaos guys, though..."

I roll my eyes and pick up a piece of the deep fried maybe-chilli bullet. Taking a brave bite, juicy chicken and spices send my taste buds into their own orgasm that might be better than any real orgasm I've ever had.

I'm such a liar.

"Chicken?"

I turn to her with a smile. "So good. Your turn."

She doesn't hesitate. Doesn't argue. She simply chooses her piece and brings it to her mouth.

"Wait." I grab her wrist and stop her just before she takes a bite. "If you happen to get the chilli, will it hurt the baby? I didn't think of that before I ordered."

"Baby will be fine, because I won't lose. But even if I do, I can handle spicy."

"You promise? Don't be competitive. Be smart."

She rolls her eyes and plops the chicken in her mouth. "I'm always smart, dummy. Well," she chews her chicken and talks around it, she's all elegance and class, "except for the whole marrying Drew thing. And letting him steal all my shit. Getting knocked up on the first date. Getting fired from Jonah's store on my first day. Losing my job at the bowling alley… Wow. I guess I'm not all that smart." She swallows the chicken and grins. "Your turn, handsome."

She's going to wear me out. Before I'm forty, she'll have worn me down to a nub of the man I am now. I'll be a puppy who sits on command, rolls over, plays. Anything she wants.

And I wouldn't even be sorry. I pick up a piece of chicken/possible atomic bomb, inspect it, and start nibbling.

"Can I ask you a question?"

I take a small bite and breathe out in relief. It's just chicken. "Sure, but if it's about Luc, then no. The answer is no." When she rolls her eyes, I sit my half-eaten chicken back on the plate. "What's on your mind, baby?"

"Your mom and dad, actually."

"Mine?"

"Mmhmm." She nervously picks at her bowl of cottage cheese and avoids my gaze.

"You mean my actual folks, or the Turners?"

"Your actual folks. I..." She hesitates for a long moment. "I realized that in all the time I've known you, I was too selfish and self-absorbed to even ask. I knew you lived with the Turners when you were younger. You and Kari were fostered by them... but I never stopped to ask why."

"Oh..."

"But since you've yet to volunteer that information," she rushes on, "then maybe it's not something you wanna talk about. So that's okay, too. You don't have to talk about it. Just tell me it's off limits, and like Ana sneaking into the red room of pain after she was told not to, I'll just ask someone else."

I laugh and relax into the booth. Picking up my chicken, I keep eating. "My mom and dad died when I was twelve."

"Both of them? At the same time?"

"Yeah. Some people snuck into our house. Burglary, I guess. We had a two-story house across town, and though all the bedrooms were upstairs, I guess my folks were still downstairs. I dunno why. I don't remember what time it was, but Kari and I went to bed hours earlier."

"They hurt your parents?"

"Yeah." I watch her carefully select her next piece of chicken. Holding my breath when she bites, I mentally prepare to douse her in water if she needs it. "I heard loud noises. They woke me up. My mom screamed. My dad shouted. I dunno. I didn't even think to run downstairs. I just ran from my room into Kari's and tossed us into the closet to hide. We didn't come out again until Chief Turner opened the door what felt like a billion years later."

"Were you in there long?"

"Long enough to sing Twinkle-Twinkle Little Star about a hundred and forty-three times. That was her favorite song." I look down at Meg, but in my mind, I see my baby sister in her nightgown with her stuffed doll clutched in her arms. Long wavy hair that almost touched her butt, a million freckles even though I made her wear sunblock and a hat in the sun.

"Probably less than an hour. In fact, probably less than half an hour.

My parents weren't quiet. The intruders weren't quiet, so I guess our neighbors called the cops pretty quick." I rub my hand over Meg's belly in contemplation. "That's why I can't forgive Luc. He knows our past. He knows she's my baby girl, and yet…"

"He loves her, Marc." She places her hands over mine and moves them a couple inches to the left. Maybe the baby is kicking, and though we've tried this a hundred times this month, I still feel nothing. "He loves your sister so much. Of all the men in the whole world, you need to trust me when I tell you he's the best one for her. You need to hand over the reins someday, Daddy. It's better that it's to him and not some asshole we don't know."

I concentrate on our hands. I want my baby to kick. Let me know he's in there and listening.

"Maybe one day I'll be able to see it the way you do, but not today. She's still my baby girl, and today's not the day I let her go." She leans forward and takes a piece of chicken. Holding it up to my lips, I take a bite. "I'd almost wonder if you're purposely feeding me the chilli."

"I would never."

She totally would.

She smirks and eats the other half. "I'm really sorry about your parents. Were the intruders ever caught?"

"Yeah. A few days later they were found with my mom's pearls at the local pawn shop. Kari and I were in a temporary foster place for a few nights. She slept in my arms every night." I can see her as clearly as if it was yesterday. "She didn't cry once, because she figured as long as I was there, everything was fine. I don't think she even understood how much her world was flipped, because she thought *I* was her world. I was holding her every night, so in her mind, everything was fine."

"You're still her world, Marc."

I smile nostalgically. "Obviously not. And maybe that's my problem with Luc. I'm mad he's even looking at her that way, but maybe I'm also mad her world doesn't revolve around me anymore."

She dips her finger in the sauce and holds it up for me to taste. It's sweet and sour sauce. We're eating sweet and sour sauce like it's as fancy as caviar. "Did you stop to think maybe she feels the same way about me?" She cocks her head to the side thoughtfully. "You're over here hating on her, hating on Luc. You've shifted her world more than the death of her parents did, *and* you've got a new girlfriend and a baby on the way. I bet that's shaken her. I bet she needs her big brother to smile and let her know she's still loved."

"She is loved. I love her like I love so few people in this world. Nothing will change that."

"Well, I'm just saying, she cried after you found out about her and Luc. You said she didn't cry after your parents, but when you looked at her with disappointment... that cut her."

"Don't tell me this shit." I turn away and pick up the next piece of chicken. I want the chilli this time. Give me a fucking distraction. "I don't wanna know how I hurt her. She hurt me, too."

"Having a loving adult relationship with a good man isn't her trying to hurt you. That's her simply being an adult and falling in love." She squeezes my hand. "It's fun falling in love. This thing you feel." She places her hand on my chest. "What you feel in your heart, it feels good, right? You should be happy she feels that, too."

"I'm not ready."

She rolls her eyes and turns to grab the next piece. "It's not up to you. This is *her* rollercoaster. Her life. You either want to be a part of it, or not. I just want you to keep in mind he was the man who held my hand in that clinic. When I sobbed, he held me. When I was scared, he–"

"Yeah, he was in there with you. What kinda friend does that? He didn't have my back with that."

"No, he had *my* back. But he held my hand and shed a tear for you, Marc, because he knew what I was doing would hurt you. Luc was the man who helped me escape that place when they were getting ready to take me into the OR. He was doing something he strongly, *strongly* disagreed with, but he was doing it because he was doing the right thing by me. Then when I changed my mind, he essentially fought them off and threw me into your arms. He almost collapsed with relief when I told him to get me out. He was with me until the last second, and if he wasn't, maybe I would've gone through with it. Maybe they would've ushered me into that room, and I would've gone, because I was too tired to do anything else. One single word, our silly safe word, and he got me out."

"Silly safe word?"

She nods and snuggles into me. "He was using humor to cover the fact he was freaking the hell out. He told me to say *Popeyes*. As in, he'll take me to Popeyes if I change my mind. *'Just say the word, Snitch.'*" She mimics him with a ridiculously deep voice. *"'Just say the word and I'll untie you from my Saint Andrew's Cross. We can get outta here and eat.'"*

"Saint Andrew's, what?"

She snickers and picks at her cheese. "Don't ask. You're not ready. Just… Maybe if you're not ready to talk to *him* yet, you really should call her. Take her out to lunch like I know you used to do eight times a week. I know you want to."

"Eight times a week is a total exaggeration. As soon as people start exaggerating like that, everything they say becomes less credible. Don't be that person, Poot. It's not cute."

Her red lips turn up in a smile. "Okay, three times a week."

I drop a kiss on the top of her head and breathe her in. "Three times a week is much more accurate."

"Yeah? So, how many times this week…?"

Ouch. I sit up and hold my chest. "That hurt."

"I'm just trying to be the voice of reason. She can be your baby girl *and* have an adult life, too. Don't miss out on the now because you're clinging to the past. She's gonna grow up no matter how much you don't want her to. Don't be such a stubborn mule. It's not worth what you might miss out on."

I pick up the next piece of chicken and avoid her gaze. I *am* stubborn, and I *won't* admit it out loud. "Maybe I'll call her tomorrow."

"Good plan. Now gimme that chicken. Mix it with the cheese, it's delicious."

I dip the chicken into the sauce, then the cheese, and though she opens her mouth in expectation, I take a big bite and keep it for myself. "Ah fuck."

"You got the chilli?" She sits up with a wide smile. "Is it bad? Are you dying?"

"Actually…" I chew thoughtfully as flavors sizzle on my tongue. "It's not so bad." I roll the chilli around. The cheese creates a nice contrast. Hot and cold. And the sauce makes it all deliciously tangy. "It's kinda warming up." Still not too bad. Warming up. Pleasant tingles on my tongue. Warmer. Warmer. Hotter, but doable. Spicy. "Ah, fuck!" I spit the raging inferno pile of fire into my hands as an angel from hell led by Hercules and his mother murders me from within. "It burns!"

She cackles and slides her bowl of cheese out of my reach. "Milk? Cheese?" I literally dribble onto my chin as my mouth burns with pain, so much pain. Tears spring to my eyes and my tongue hangs limp and dead. "It hurts, baby. Make it stop."

13

MEG

MAKING APPOINTMENTS

I knock on the front door and walk into Kari's place the next morning with yet another to-do list as long as my arm and hunger pains so epic, I'm tempted to go straight to their kitchen and pig out.

Fortunately for me, Luc and Kari aren't half naked on the couch, and even luckier, they're in the kitchen anyway.

Score!

I walk straight through their small living room, past the icky sex couch, and into the kitchen. Moving straight past the kissing couple to the fridge, I pull out the jumbo tub of yogurt and drop my bag at my feet. Taking a soup spoon from the silverware drawer, I peel the lid off the tub and lean against the counter. "'Sup, guys?"

"Um." Luc clears his throat awkwardly, until finally, the atmosphere in the room registers in my brain. They're not standing and hugging and making out. They're standing and hugging and she's got the crying sniffles.

I dump the tub on the counter and snatch her around so I can see her face. Puffy eyes, wobbling lips, and reddened cheeks – which only have her freckles standing out more – meet my gaze. "What the hell happened?" I look her up and down from head to toe. "Jesus, seriously.

I can't take more bad news. I can't deliver bad news to your brother. I already fucked him over this year."

"He texted me." She clutches to her phone with white knuckles, and with a shaking hand, unlocks the screen and turns it toward me.

Marc: *I'll love you always. Even when I don't agree with your decisions. Douchebag boyfriends will never change that. Have lunch with me? I wanna hug you.*

"Aww, shit." I look up at her with a goofy smile. "He's so cute. I love your brother so hard."

"Why'd he change his mind?" Her breath catches pathetically. "Why does he wanna see me? Is he gonna yell at me?"

"No, honey." I pull her in for a hug while poor Luc stands mere feet away with a pout like I just stole his prized possession. I kind of did. "He's not going to yell at you." *Probably.* "But he misses you. He was telling me last night." And this morning. And minutes before I got in the car to come here. If I'd known he was going to send that message, I might've stuck around to give him a big stupid hug. "Are you going to reply? Will you have lunch with him?"

She sniffles and swipes her sleeve under her nose. "Of course." She turns to Luc. "I don't think you should come today."

"Ha. No. No Luc, today." His poor eyes darken, but this is for the best. "Give it time. Let him have a date with his baby sister. You and Marc have to sort your shit separately. Not at lunch in the middle of the week. But I'm super glad you're gonna go out with him. I know he's probably waiting anxiously for your reply."

"Where is he right now?"

I finally release her so she can step back to who she really wants. "He was at the apartment when I left, but he said he was heading to the house. He's been going over there every morning and afternoon to deal with the farm animals, collect the eggs, *not* milk the cow, then spending all day there on the build."

"Do you call them farm animals just to piss him off?"

I laugh and turn back to resume my love affair with yogurt. There's no crisis here. Quite the opposite, actually. It's a good day. "Yes, I call them farm animals specifically to piss him off. Pissing him off is my favorite hobby. But seriously, they're chickens and a cow. How are they *not* farm animals?"

"They're just pets, Snitch."

"He has a cow!"

"He named it Megan," Luc snorts. "Weirdest day of my life, meeting that damn cow. He fed her from a baby bottle at first, did you know that?"

"Ah… no. I don't suppose I did." My stomach flips with weird nerves. "I mean, I knew he had it from newborn, so it makes sense."

"It's a weird visual though, right?" Luc steps back from Kari and swings the fridge open. Pulling out a carton of orange juice, he pulls down two glass tumblers, then a third, but I decline with a shake of my head. "On that note. How'd your tests go?"

"They decided to do something called Factor V." I shrug and spoon in more of the high protein and not particularly delicious yogurt. "It was only one needle and the nurse was nice, so…"

"Phlebotomist."

I stop and frown. Cocking my head to the side, I consider if maybe Kari just had a stroke. "Fla-hoo-what? Are you okay?"

She grins and accepts her glass of juice. "Phle-bot-o-mist. That's your nurse's actual title. The chick who took your blood."

"Oh, her. Her name was Alicia, but I called her Morticia in my head. What kinda sicko do you have to be to go to school specifically because you wanna stab people or take their blood? Who does that shit?"

"Ah, Snitch… both of us!"

"My point exactly." I look Luc up and down the way I learned a million years ago could cut a man down. It's always fun to do that. "Weirdos, both of you. Which is precisely the reason you ended up together. Only weirdos attract weirdos."

"You done?" Kari looks me up and down the way I did Luc, but instead of feeling like she just cut me, I simply smile and plop the lid back on the yogurt. "That's the attitude I love about you Macchios. Oh, on that note; do you hate me?"

Her head snaps back like I hit her. "Of course not! Why would I hate you?"

I shrug and drop the spoon into the dishwasher tray. "I realized last night that maybe Marc has a problem with Luc because he stole his baby girl, right? So maybe you're mad at me for doing the same to you. Stealing your big brother. But not only did I steal him, I kinda eclipse his attention, what with the fact I'm now carrying his baby."

"No." She steps forward with a kind smile. Stopping me when I move to put the yogurt away, she takes my hands and doesn't stop until my belly touches hers. "I love you, Snitch. Like, actual family love. That's my niece or nephew in there." Her hands come down to cup my belly. "Family first for us. That's all we care about." She smirks and looks into my eyes. "You should know that by now. You're family, and that baby shares my blood. I could never hate you. You're one of us, now."

"Aww." Real tears prickle my hormonal eyes. Pulling her into an awkward hug around the baby that binds us, I press my face to the gap between her neck and shoulder, and she does the same to mine. "I love you, Kari. Thank you for saying that."

Luc shuffles forward like a creepy uncle, wraps his arms around us, and pulls us into his chest. "I love you both."

"Get off us, Luc." I elbow him, though it's only gentle. "What's worse than Marc finding you on his sister?"

"Finding me on his sister and wifey." He jumps back like we conduct electricity. Making himself busy closing the dishwasher, Kari and I sniffle and hug like a couple of idiot teenagers.

I swipe a thumb under my eye when we separate, and steadying myself on my feet – since my dance training never really prepared me for being front heavy – I take her hand again. "So I actually had a reason for coming here today."

"Tell me."

"Lindsi's kinda new around here, but Oz isn't."

She scoffs. "Oz is like the big brother I never, *ever* wanted. He's a damn pest more often than not."

"Right." I laugh when Luc moves past us and slaps Kari on the ass.

Marc's not going to adjust to these two. Jesus, help us all. "So Oz is all set. He'll have all the guys to organize his bachelor party, but…"

"But Lindsi won't."

"Right. It hasn't come up yet, and I speak to her most days lately. She said she doesn't want much to do with organizing this wedding, but she's sneaking ideas in. She wants to make it perfect for her man."

Luc wanders past again with his shoes. Stopping at the dining table, he sits on the chair and starts pulling them on. "What about Andi?"

"Did you sleep here last night, Luca?"

He looks around the room like I asked something in another language. "Um, yeah."

"Oh my gawd. Marc is *not* gonna adjust. Okay, moving on." I bend low and snatch up my purse. Pulling out my cell, I swipe the screen open and start making notes. "Who's Andi?"

"Andi is Lindsi's cousin. They're kinda best friends that only see each other twice a year. She lives away."

"Right. You know how to contact her?"

"Nah, but I'll ask Oz. He knows how to."

"Could you text me as soon as you have it?"

"Yeah, no worries." He finishes tying one boot and starts on the next. "Can you change my contact in your phone? Change it to Jess or something, so when Marc sees your phone buzzing with my text, he doesn't add a new reason to murder me."

I laugh and continue making notes in my phone. *Andi. Lives away. Best friend/cousin.* "I'll change your name to Popeye or something. That could be fun."

"Suits me. I'll check in with Oz today." He stands and pats his work pants down. Luc Lenaghan. I've known him since he was an immature fifteen-year-old. He's so grown now. So handsome. Nothing has changed except the age on his driver's license. "So you girls are gonna do it up big? Paint the town red?"

"Not too red. I'm already pregnant. I'll be desi and make sure your girl doesn't flash too many guys. Oh!" I spin and face her with excitement. "King's Chaos!"

"They're a cool band," she admits casually. "I have them on my playlists."

"They're gonna play the wedding."

"No way!"

"No fucking way!" Luc snaps. His 'no way' is a hell of a lot different to Kari's. "What the fuck, Snitch? We're playing the wedding."

"No, you're not. You've been kicked off because management aren't talking to each other."

"Huh?"

"When you have a four man band and fifty percent of them aren't talking to each other, then we have a problem. This is my one and only chance to launch something great. I'm not risking it on you and Marc and your PMS."

"We're still playing fine! We play the club just fine, even when he's being a stubborn prick."

They have no clue how similar they are. "Too bad. I already talked to Scotch, told him you're out because you and Marc can't clean your shit up. He agreed. You're out, King's are in."

"Sleeping with the enemy, much? Whose side are you on, *culo?*"

"Estoy de mi parte, tonto." When he looks at me in shock, I nod. "Step down, little boy. Maybe your big brother taught you some swears in Spanish, but I know them *all*. Plus another four or five languages on top of that. I win. I *always* win. So don't test me."

"We can play the wedding, Snitch. Don't kick us out because of personal business. Family, remember?"

"Aww." I actually feel bad for him. "I'm mostly kidding."

"So no King's?"

"No, the King's will be playing the wedding." His eyes flash with hurt. "But not as punishment to you guys. The King's want this, they want it bad. You guys will be at your brother's wedding. You get the night off. Relax, enjoy, give the stink eye to the enemy band, but otherwise, just relax. Get drunk. Fuck in closets, all that sorta stuff."

"I could do all of that stuff and still play the set."

"You're a pig." I smack his arm when he gets too close. "Don't fuck in the closets, for the love of God, please don't. If Marc catches you…"

"Will you be fucking in the closets?"

"No, I'll be working, and pregnant as hell. I'll be so big by then, I doubt he'll even be able to lift me."

He rolls his eyes and snags Kari as she walks by in her scrub pants and bra. She has her shirt thrown over her arm and her shoes in her hands. No shame, I guess. No shyness around here. "Men will always be able to lift their girls." He swings her up into the cradle of his arms. She lets out a squeal at the fast movement, drops her shoes, and her arms wrap around his neck in panic. "You could be carrying multiples and have a diet exclusively made up of chocolate for nine months and he'd still be able to lift you. It's what we do." He drops an arrogant kiss on her lips. "I'd never drop you, Bear." He drops another kiss on her lips.

Longer, softer.

My cue to leave.

"Right, well. Get that chick's number. Text me. Kari, we need to plan. Help me."

"Mmhmm. I'll help." She'll also make out with Luc with tongues right in front of guests.

"Okey dokey, I'll talk to you later." I escape the kitchen at the same time Luc rearranges her in his arms and sits her on the kitchen counter.

Note to self: do not sit on icky couch. Do not eat off icky counter.

I rush out to my car as another cruises around the corner too fast and sends their tires squealing. Smart guy – speeding in a residential street. Dumbass.

I jump into my car and toss my bag onto the passenger seat. I hope Kari replies to Marc's text soon. I know he'll be on edge all day until she does.

Starting the car and heading across town, I walk into a community center just off the side of the hospital five minutes later. My OB suggested I come here to organize Lamaze classes. On top of organizing a wedding and refereeing Marc and Luc's relationship, I also have to learn how to breathe when an alien claws it's way from my body.

My life is so colorful and exciting.

"Hello, ma'am. Welcome to Beautiful Bellies. Your belly is divine!"

"Aw, thanks. Those spicy chicken wings get me every time. Once I start, I just can't stop until…" I point at my stomach. At her blank stare, I close my eyes to avoid rolling them. Try again. "Hello. My name is Meg, and I'm here to book in for classes. I need to learn how to breathe, apparently."

"Of course." She clears her throat and leads me toward a wall of pamphlets. Taking down a couple, she pushes them at me while she recites their practiced speech. "At BB's, we focus on natural and traditional partner supported childbirth techniques. You and your partner will learn how to work in harmony for the duration of your pregnancy to create a strong and beautiful birthing team."

Oh boy.

I don't know if Marc knows those words. Especially not *harmonious*.

"How far along are you, Meg? We recommend starting classes around the beginning of the third trimester."

"Ah, I dunno what trimester I am. But I'm twenty weeks."

"Lovely. We still have time, and since our classes fill up quickly, that's perfect. Let's go book you and your partner in for around eight weeks from now."

Shat. "Okay." And if she calls him my partner again, I might spew. Partner sounds weird. Can't she say baby daddy like the rest of us?

"Our curriculum lasts six weeks. One class a week, sixty minutes per class, and often, the couples like to hang around and get to know each other."

Yeah, hard pass.

"So, would you like me to book you in?"

I drag my feet and wish I'd gone through with my plan to pick Sammy up on the way here. I need her. I need her bad. "Yeah, sure." *I guess.*

14

MEG

TWENTY-FIVE WEEKS

ndi: I'm flying in on the 23rd. Right?

Laying back on my bed and running circles into my belly with my spare hand, I smile at my phone, at my new sort of friend, Andi.

Tapping at the screen, I reply: *Yes. The 23rd. You don't have to worry about anything. It's all organized. It's a surprise party, so don't tell her you're coming. You just need to get yourself on that plane. I'll pick you up. Send me your flight details so I know what time you arrive. Everything else is organized.*

Andi's cool. We've yet to meet in person, but she's Lindsi's maid of (dis)honor – Lindsi's words, not mine – and the senior management in charge of delegation. As in, as maid of (dis)honor, she *should* be planning the bachelorette party, but she expertly delegated it to me. She's young and silly, flighty and funny, but I can't really hate on her for her freedom. She reminds me of me.

She reminds me of me *a lot.*

Andi: Okay. Fly in on the 23rd in the morning. Party that night. Fly home hungover on the 24th in time for work on the 25th. Got it.

Me: And don't forget flight details. If you forget, you're walking from the airport. I don't have time to hold your hand.

Andi: Not forgetting flight details. Promise. What are the plans? Club or BBQ? Hot guys or no? I need to pack accordingly.

I shake my head – she's totally going to forget. She can walk her ass from the airport. It'll teach her a lesson when she arrives in heels and blisters.

Me: Club. Bring a dress. Slut shoes. Makeup.

Andi: Grazie.

I smile in the silence of the apartment I'm sharing with Marc until the house is finished – which should be any day now. I'm nervous about moving back to the house. Like, sharing the apartment is informal, easy to say we're just hanging out and having fun, but moving back makes it all official. That's us actually moving in together like grown-ups.

I'm scared and excited. Giddy and nervous. There are a million and one 'what ifs' that scare the hell out of me. Not to mention the blood tests that came back negative – as in, I'm fine. But they still scare me. I was so sure they'd come back and spell doom, and now that they don't… It feels like a false sense of security.

And I know that's just me being silly, but try telling that to a hormonal chick who can't seem to sort her emotions out. Everything feels so uncertain, and my pregnancy is a heavy freight train cruising at full speed without brakes.

I can't stop that train no matter what I do, and no matter how much I wish I could, nothing changes until I crash into the labor and delivery ward. Then everything's up to the universe.

Do I live?

Do I die?

I understand there's no logical reason why I won't live. I know it's an emotional worry rather than something based on facts, but that doesn't mean I still don't get nervous sweats every time I think about it.

When you're only in your thirties and staring down the barrel of potential death, shit gets real. Everything you see is sharper. Everything you hear is louder. Everything you do is *more*.

I unlock my darkened screen to reply to Andi, but the baby does an odd roll in my stomach until its butt – or foot, or head, or something – moves my hand. "Oh my God." My voice is a whisper, then, "Oh my God! Marc! Marc come here! Run!"

He skids along the hardwood floors and into the bedroom with a ghostly white face and half a sandwich in his hand. "Baby, what's wrong?"

"Lay down, quick."

He stares mutely.

"Marcus, lay down! Come here, quick."

He dive bombs onto the bed beside me, and I snatch his non-sandwich holding hand and place it where mine was a moment ago.

His chest pumps full of adrenaline and energy as we wait. His breath heavy with worry and exhilaration. His hair is growing longer, so now strands hang over his forehead and into his eyes. "What am I waiting for, babe?"

I turn my face to his and stare into his eyes. Emerald green, so pretty. "Shhh. Patience."

His expression softens now that he knows I'm not going into spontaneous labor in the bedroom. We've done this before. The baby has rolled. I've screamed at him to run. We've lain like this in hopes baby would roll again, then when it doesn't, we've gone about our business... or had a nap.

I'm almost twenty-five weeks pregnant, and Marc has yet to feel his baby move.

His large hand makes my big belly feel small and dainty. His plump lips near mine make me feel loved. Special. Cherished. We study each other in the silence, and though I can still feel the baby moving gently, I need it to do the big mega roll again if Marc has any hope of feeling it.

"Marc?"

He takes a bite of his sandwich and watches me. "Mm?"

"Can you stop eating for a sec?" He smirks and chews. I want to make out with my man, but I don't want to eat secondhand sandwich. He watches me with smiling eyes, and swallowing dramatically, opens his mouth to show that he's done. I narrow my eyes. "Really? How old are you? You're worse than a toddler, I swear."

"I know you are, I said you are, so what am I?"

"An immature fool."

"I know you are, I said you—" His eyes turn wide like plates and his words cut off on a choke. "The baby moved?" His eyes can't decide whether to look at me or his hand. "The baby moved! Holy shit." He tosses his sandwich to the side, and I don't even give him a lecture about food in bed. It's gross, not cute. But this one time, I'll look past it, because the wonder in his eyes as he studies my face is something that I hope to see every single day for the rest of my life.

It's like I'm magic. Like I created a miracle because the baby is rolling.

"Oh my shit, Meg…"

"You feel that?"

He nods in quiet shock. "That's my baby."

A pesky tear pools at the corner of my eye. I hate that I've cried so much these last few months. I'm not actually crying. I'm not sad. They're just tears, but not real crying.

"Could be yours. Could be Ken and Ken from the club."

"Hush. Don't ruin this for me."

I lay my head back and stare at the ceiling with a smile. His large hand follows the movements of my belly.

If the baby moves, he moves.

"Talk."

His head pops up. "Huh?"

I smile when the baby kicks again. Right on cue. "Baby likes your voice. When we're silent, baby goes back to sleep. Let him hear your voice."

Swallowing nervously, he turns back to my belly and lowers his head. His lips are within an inch of my skin, like he wants a private conversation and doesn't want me to listen in. "Hey, son."

I snicker. "We literally have no clue if it's a boy or a girl."

Marc makes a 'pssht' sound. "She doesn't know what she's talking about. I've got your back." The baby does cartwheels in my belly, and the catch in Marc's voice tells me he knows. He can feel it, too. "I can't wait to meet you, baby. I bet you're beautiful, just like your mama."

I hate him for making me want to weep.

"Be nice to her. Don't make her worry about the birth, okay? It'll be a day of celebration, not worry."

I turn my face away and stare at the wall. How could he know I was worrying about that barely minutes ago?

"We really should discuss what we're gonna name you soon." His large hand strokes my skin. His lips hum against my belly. "You need a strong name. Something you'll be proud to carry."

"Not Megan."

His head pops up, and his smile, a smirk even, comforts me. "It's a moot point. This is my son. We can't name a boy Megan."

"Why not? You named a cow Megan?"

He's so pretty, the way he turns back to my belly, the way his hair falls over his forehead and his lips turn up in that cute grin.

I'm in love with Marc Macchio.

Not just love, as in, I love him because he's kind, and smart, loyal, a hard worker. He's a million things that make me love him. But I'm *in* love with him. And I feel like that's an important distinction.

True, deep to my bones, heart does a pitter patter, deep in love with him. That's never been more apparent to me as it is right now – while he strokes my belly and chats with our baby.

"Your mommy and I will discuss it, bud. We'll have a strong name ready and waiting for you, and when you arrive, she'll be your pretty princess, too. As men, we take care of her."

"Hey… Marc?"

"Hm?"

"We want a strong name? Loyal? A family name, even?"

"Exactly." He strokes my belly and drops a kiss right over my dramatically *out* belly button. "A name just like that. A strong name for a strong baby."

"Maybe we could call him Luca."

Silence. Tense shoulders. His eyes slide back to mine. "Not today, Poot. Don't ruin this moment for me."

I smile. He called me Poot, which means I'm getting under his skin. I love being under his skin. It's my favorite place to be. "Marc?"

He huffs impatiently. "I'm having a conversation with my child. Can we talk later?"

I roll my eyes and bump him with my belly. The baby rolls are starting to slow. Our voices are having the opposite effect than I'd intended. We're lulling him – *or her* – to sleep. "This is important."

His eyes turn softer. He's not mad. He's never mad these days. "Fine. What's up?"

"You know how Lily's first word was Marc?"

"Of course. She knows who her favorite uncle is. She's such a clever baby."

"Right... so you know what our baby's first word is gonna be, right?"

"It'll be daddy. Not Marc. He can't call me Marc, but daddy..." His voice is whimsical. Soft. Happy. "Someone's gonna call me daddy. Shit, Meg."

"I'll call you daddy if you want. Will you spank me, Daddy?"

He chokes and drops his face to my belly. "Why do you ruin these moments for me?" He looks up, though he's not mad. "Don't ever call me Daddy again. I just went soft all over. Gross."

I snicker. Moment over. The baby's gone to sleep, anyway. "Marc?"

"Yeah, babe?"

"I love you. I just wanted you to know that. I never knew we'd end up here, but we are and I want you to know I don't regret it."

His eyes turn soft – unlike the rest of his body – and straightening beside me, his large hand cups my face as he brings his plump lips over mine. "I love you, too, Meg. I've loved you for a lot longer than I should have. But I don't regret it, either." His tongue darts out, and sandwich or not, I allow him to move in closer and take my mouth however he wants.

My shirt's already missing. My yoga pants stretched to capacity.

My cheap bra cupping my growing boobs. They're still nice, still perky, but they're definitely getting bigger and long blue veins mark me like a map.

I guess my body's preparing me to be a cow…

Oh my God. Megan the cow.

I can't concentrate on my line of ridiculous thought, because Marc's tongue works magic against mine. His hand slides down my ribs until, sliding under the rolled band of fabric around my hips, his fingers walk lower and lower until my body turns to a vibrating cord waiting to be plucked.

His fingers tap at my opening, forcing a rush of breath from my body, and as he presses his lips down onto mine, he slides his fingers in, and swallows my moan. Long, slow strokes spark a fire deep within me. His fingers are gentle, soothing. This isn't hard and fast and passionate. It's slow and comfortable, like sliding into a gentle orgasm instead of racing to the finish line.

I bend my legs and let them fall open. Closing my eyes, I lay my head back and let him play me as skillfully as he plays his guitar. "Marc…" His name is a whisper on my lips. I'm not looking for a reply. Not looking for anything. I simply say his name because the word feels good on my lips.

My heart races in my chest. Like a duck swimming on a pond, I look calm, relaxed, almost in a meditative state as his fingers pleasure me, but underneath the surface, or in my case, in my chest, my heart races erratically.

I want to explode.

I want to hate myself for almost ruining this. For almost ruining what we could have together.

Marc leans forward and presses a kiss to my lips. Like he needs to taste. Even with my eyes closed, even with me floating on a cloud of relaxed bliss, he still needs to taste. "I love you, Meg. For the rest of my life."

I lift my hips from the bed and work to lower my pants. The tight band restricts his hand, and I don't want that. I want ease, freedom, orgasms. Him. "Help me?"

With a nod, he quickly pops up to his knees and forces a whimper of protest from my lips when he removes his fingers and slides my pants down my legs. He tosses them aside and climbs back up beside me. His fingers go back to where he left off, but with a shake of my head, I turn to my side so he's my big spoon. Undoing his belt blindly, I fumble with the zipper of his jeans until he takes a hint and does it for me.

He hurriedly removes his pants and takes up his place behind me. Lifting my top leg and opening myself up to him, he slides in from behind easily. I let out a shudder of breath as he fills me up. Way better than fingers. So much more, so much better. He leans in close, almost on me, almost squishing me, but not. His lips come down to nibble on my neck and shoulder as his hips gently slide against me. In, deliciously deep, and out, slowly dragging along every single nerve ending, sending me into a silent and quivering mass of relaxation.

His breath races in my ear. His tongue slides along my neck, and his large hand holds onto my hip as he makes love to me. I've never felt so much love in my life. Even without words, just simple actions in the silence of mid-afternoon, I've never felt as loved in my life as I do right this second.

MARC'S CELL vibrates in his jean's pocket as we relax in the silence. He's still behind me. His lips still cruise my skin. Our breathing has returned to normal. Our pounding hearts have relaxed. We simply lie in comfortable silence and hold each other.

He presses his lips to the ball of my shoulder, and his breath rumbles out like a satisfied cat. "What are you thinking about?"

"Hmm? Not a whole lot. I'm pretty mellow right now."

He coughs an almost silent laugh into my hair. "Mellow as fuck. You do that to me."

"Mmm." I snuggle into his arms so we touch from head to toe. I want more. More hugs. More synchronized breathing. "I was thinking about the house."

"Yeah?"

"Yeah. I kinda miss your cow. It'll be cool to move back to the farm and get settled in."

He nips at my ear. "It's not a farm."

"It is, Marcus. Let's not do this again."

He chuckles quietly. "We can go home soon. Really soon. The guys are finishing up today or tomorrow."

"Really?" I slowly turn in his arms to face him. "I didn't realize it was that soon. Why are you here lying in bed if they're busy working on the house?"

"Because I'm not stupid. I could be there working, or I could be here getting laid..."

I roll my eyes and dig my balled fist into his stomach, but it's not even half an effort. I don't want to ruin the relaxation floating in the air. "You planned this all along?"

"I plan everything. Always. Which reminds me," he digs around in his jeans pocket until he pulls out his cell. "Ah, exactly as I'd planned. The house is done."

"What?" I bury my face in his chest and laugh. "You couldn't have possibly planned that."

"Okay, no, I didn't. But it is done, look." He turns the phone to face me. Angelo's name is at the top of his messenger screen. His message literally says *'it's done.'*

I roll my eyes at Angelo's verbosity. "You got lucky with the timing. But you did *not* plan that. Just like you didn't plan that sex playlist that time. You're exceptionally lucky with timing." Let's also not forgot his impeccable timing with my ovulation. Not only did his swimmers get past the pill *and* condoms, but I must have been in the height of ovulation for it to take that easily.

Lucky jerk.

His eyes dance with mirth as though he can read my mind, and leaning forward, he drops a kiss on the tip of my nose. "Hush, don't ruin it. Now... Wanna go home, babe?"

My heart does a flip-flop. Nerves. Excitement. The official-ness. *Officiality?* "Today? Now?"

"Sure. If you wanna. We can check out our new digs. Order take-out. Watch The Notebook or some other equally lame chick movie."

I scoff easily. "You call it lame, but you know what it's called. You don't fool me, Macchio. You're crushing on Noah too, aren't you?"

"Crushing on a pretty boy? No. But maybe he and I have something in common."

Laughter forgotten, my eyes narrow in thought. "What do you and Noah Calhoun have in common?"

"The girl." He leans forward with a slow kiss. "Allie was his first. They were kids, she was his, then she went off and found the bacon elsewhere."

"The bacon...?" I snicker in his face. "Really? Do you have an obsession with pigs? Bacon. Salami. Sausage. It's weird. Oh! Maybe you should get a pig for the farm!"

He brings his hand up and pinches my lips closed. "Shush... I'm saying that even if she took off, she came home eventually. Exactly where she belonged."

I watch his eyes in silence. He's getting all serious on me, and me being me, I need to ruin it. I push his hand away gently, and ask, "I'm sorry, but where in that movie did we see Noah and Allie have a dirty one-night stand? I doubt he ever handcuffed her to his bed. And he sure as hell didn't call her a rude nickname to annoy her. Or name live-stock after her."

He smirks at me. "I bet he did all of that and more. We don't see all their dirty secrets, Poot. The chick in that movie was hot. I bet he did loads of filthy shit to her."

"Don't call me Poot."

He barks out a laugh. "You ruined my story, so I get to call you anything I want. The point is, you came home to me."

"I came home to family. I just happened to fall into bed with you."

"Doesn't matter how we got here, the point is, you're here now. Exactly where you belong. So, last chance, do you wanna go home tonight? Or do you wanna stay here and go tomorrow?"

"You'll go over there later anyway, right? To feed the farm animals."

His eyes sparkle with trouble. If he wants to call me Poot, then I'll call it a farm. "Yes," he answers. "I'll go over there either way to feed the *pets* and make sure they're fine."

"Alright, fine. Let's go." I tap his thigh and attempt to sit up, but when I fall back with a huff at my lack of core strength, he laughs and climbs to his feet. Standing at the end of the bed, he leans forward and takes my hands and pulls me up.

"Ugh." I pout like that princess I swore I wouldn't be. "I feel like a whale."

"You don't look like one." He holds me against his body and breathes in my hair. "You still have loads of growing left, so don't start to freak yet. Get dressed, beautiful. Let's go home."

"Home... Or the farm...?"

He narrows his eyes, and before he can retaliate, I flit away and start packing overnight stuff. I was staying at his house enough before the baby bomb that I have stuff there already, and since I never actually officially moved in with him, then I didn't take all my stuff. Which means I basically have everything I need at both houses. I guess it's almost time to pack up the apartment and move for real.

I'm moving in with Marc Macchio. It's just... surreal.

I toss clothes into a bag and pull on a top and maternity jeans that Marc tosses at me. He watches me flit around the room collecting my things, and when I move to the bathroom to apply a light coat of makeup, he follows and stands at my back. He's silent, watchful. He holds my hips and nibbles on my shoulders and neck. His eyes don't leave mine for almost the entire time I'm in here, and because he's watching, I make particular effort to do it up right. Light, natural, but perfect.

I'm pregnant and self-proclaimed fat, but my tits still look good, my hair is better than it's ever been in my life, and my face is smooth.

There are definite perks to being pregnant.

"You look beautiful."

I apply a coat of soft-pink lip gloss that glistens in the overhead lights. Puckering my lips together, I blow him a kiss which only results in his dick growing against my ass. "Really? An air kiss turns you on?"

"No." He goes back to nibbling my bare skin. "Your lips turn me on. Your eyes turn me on." His hands slide up my ribs and cup my boobs. "These definitely turn me on. There's absolutely nothing about you that isn't a turn on."

"I'm pregnant and fat… that's gotta count against me."

"No." He works his way up and nibbles on my earlobe. "You're carrying *my* baby. That might be the sexiest thing of all." He works his way down my neck. "It's hard to explain, but the fact that you and I made love, that your body took something of mine and created something else, a baby. You created my heir, so to speak. The fact I could do that to you, and that your body took the challenge that was never consciously set down, and it's doing an amazing fucking job…" He grunts with manly satisfaction. "I dunno. There's some caveman shit working there, because just thinking about it does something to me." He bites down on the thin skin at the very base of my neck. "Evolution wants to better our species, right? So, it puts the two best options together to create something even better. You and me… we were the two best things for each other. And our baby will be everything awesome about me and you mixed into one. The Meg that I know would tell anyone that mixture is fucking epic."

"Kinda is." I close my eyes and hum when his hands squeeze pleasantly. "Marc and Meg are pretty awesome."

"Yeah, we are." He pulls my earlobe between his teeth, then like he was never there, he slaps my ass and vanishes. "You look pretty. Let's go."

I end up only packing a small bag of things, because I'm more excited about takeout and The Notebook than I expect. Locking up the apartment and taking Marc's hand, he helps me down the stairs like I'm ninety years old and blind. "I can do it myself, you know?"

He looks back at me with a grin. "It takes no extra effort or time on my part. No way am I risking it."

I roll my eyes and allow him to baby me. Stopping at our cars, I look between mine and his truck as a car cruises down the lane nearby. "Let's take the truck," he answers my unspoken question. "I'll bring you back tomorrow to collect your car."

I toss my bag into his back seat, and when he lifts me into the truck, I don't even make a smartass remark.

For a woman trying so damn hard to be grown-up and independent, being babied by him is so sweet, it's like aloe on a burn. "Thank you."

"You're welcome." He slams the door when I tuck my feet in, then taps on the closed window. I manually wind it open and stop when, with twinkling eyes, he leans in and drops a juicy kiss on my lips. "I'm really happy about this, Meg. We're going home, to *our* home. I might even carry you over the threshold."

When my chin wobbles ever so slightly, he chuckles and taps my nose with the tip of his finger. Ducking away and running around the hood of the truck, he climbs in, starts it up, and pulls out.

"What do you wanna eat?" My stomach rumbles with hunger right on cue. "I want sushi."

"You're not allowed sushi, so stop nagging."

I roll my eyes and sit back lazily. "It's only mercury. It's fine. Then we can follow it with ice-cream sundaes from the bitch's parlor."

"No."

"I hate you."

He pulls up at the one and only set of traffic lights in town, and turning to face me, his lips pull up into a filthy smirk. "You don't mean that."

"I do. At least a little bit."

He chuckles. When the light turns green a moment later, he puts the truck into gear and accelerates through the small intersection. "You love me, Poot. My heart does a little happy dance every time I see you because you're so pretty it hurts my eyes. I know you love me, too."

Charming jerk. "Fine. Little bit…"

We drive over the tracks to exit the town proper. Moving slowly along the winding roads that lead to his house, I sit back and enjoy the cool breeze that fans my face. "I miss the bike."

"The motorcycle?"

"Mm. I miss it."

"Can't ride it, baby. It's too dangerous."

"I know that." I rub my hands over my belly. "I wouldn't be comfortable, anyway. But maybe after… can we go for a ride?"

He reaches across to take my hand and rests them both on my belly. "Sure, babe. As soon as you're ready. We'll call in one of the guys to watch the baby for an hour and we'll ride. I promise."

It doesn't escape me that I've just made my first concrete plans for after the birth. I've had this abstract plan all along to create a career for myself, but I've yet to even look into taking on more clients. It's like my diary literally ends on my due date, then the rest is up to the universe.

Even though I've worked hard to push the worry aside, or at the very least, simply pretend it's not there, I've still not made a single plan for after. Until now. "Thank you. I don't hate you, by the way."

He pulls onto his long driveway and we bump along at barely more than fifteen miles per hour. "I know. I love you, too."

Though I look out for her, Meg the cow doesn't come bounding along the fencing to greet us.

Silly fat girl.

We turn the final bend of the driveway, and when the willows separate to unveil our new home, I hold my breath and study the expanse of what was once an A-frame house that now resembles lots of little A's that almost quadruples the original structure size. "Marc…" Tears rush to my eyes – because I'm an emotional idiot – and my lip wobbles at what he's done for us. "You'd never know it was an addition. It's like it was always like this."

He pulls up near the untouched barn and switches off the engine. Sitting back and throwing his arm on the back of the bench seat, he studies it right alongside me.

"It's turned out pretty nice, huh? I impressed myself."

"You guys did this all by yourself?"

"Mmhmm. We did the build. Had trades in for the fit out – plumbing, electrics, that sorta stuff."

"Plumbing?" I turn with a gasp. "You didn't tear out that beehive bathroom, did you?"

He grins and smooths hair away from my face. "No. We added. We didn't take anything away. The loft is now just storage. There are three bedrooms on the ground floor. And a small office. The office is attached to the master bedroom, so I figure it could be the nursery at first, then when we're comfortable, we can move the baby into its own room. That leaves enough room for two more babies – unless we go into bunk beds and sharing and shit. At that point, the options are endless."

"Woah up, speed racer. More kids? Bunk beds? Yeah, hard pass."

He chuckles and unsnaps my seatbelt. "We'll talk about it some other time. But now your beehive bathroom is *our* bathroom; it's attached to the master. Guests use the shitty not fancy bathroom. The nursery's directly attached to our room, but the kids' rooms aren't far away. We all share walls."

"That's fine. You've done an amazing job."

"Thank you." He climbs out of the truck and skips around to my door. Pulling it open and lowering me gently, he lays a quick kiss on the corner of my lips. "I know when people are renovating and planning out rooms, they don't actually plan to share walls. I know it's not ideal, but I don't want to be far from my family. Especially not in the night."

"You've done an amazing job, Marc."

"Our room's at the front, at the top of the hall, I guess you could say. We have the existing living room, the kitchen, then a hallway. The bedrooms are essentially behind the kitchen. Our room first, so anyone who comes in will get to us first…"

"Marc." I stop us as we approach the small front porch, and in a complete role reversal, I turn his face and pull it down so his eyes meet mine. "I get it. No one's getting past you. No one's hurting your family. You're a good daddy, babe, you always have been. No one's hurting what's yours."

He leans down with emotional eyes and presses a long, dry kiss to my lips. "Thank you. I could've done it up bigger, grander, *more*. You deserve more, but this is what I was comfortable with. For the safety of my family, this is what I was comfortable with."

A mile-long driveway and an impenetrable home. Marcus will

stand in front of anyone who tries to hurt his family. "What you've given us is more than enough. It's beautiful." I step back from him only so I can gesture toward the home he provided. I've lived in what were essentially mansions my whole life. Eleven bedrooms, three floors.

Houses, but not homes.

They were cold and held no love. This home is warm and bursting with love. "You built this, Marc. You can live the rest of your life knowing you built a warm safe haven for your family... you built it with your own hands. That's special."

"Well, I didn't do it alone."

"I bet you laid the important foundations. Watched over everything that your children would touch."

He turns his face away. "Maybe..."

"You did something important here. I love you for what you've done for us."

I swear, it's almost as though he's blushing. It's not obvious, but it's there. "Well, me and the guys," he deflects. "Ang and Scotch, and Luc, too."

"Luc?" I cock my head to the side. "He helped?"

"Yeah, he wouldn't fucking leave. I told him he wasn't invited into my home, so what does he do? He comes outside, mixes cement, works the miter saw, carries scraps to the dumpster. He's a stubborn prick."

I don't even do the sassy girl 'mmhmm' thing. We all know who's stubborn. But the fact that Luc got to help makes me giddy. These men won't fight forever, and when they make up, I'm thrilled they'll still have the shared experience of working on Marc's family home together.

"Alright." He looks down at me. "You ready to go in? Check it out?"

I smile as wide as my face will allow. "Uh-huh."

"Want me to carry you over the threshold?"

"That's for newlyweds, dummy."

"Well, soon then. Come on." He twines his fingers with mine, takes out a set of keys, and unlocks the heavy front door so we can step into the darkness.

I'm a little sad he lost some of the natural light the large wall windows used to provide. I know he enjoyed those. I hope he installed skylights into the new rooms. I loved looking at the stars while lying in bed with him.

Reaching out blindly for the light switch, he illuminates a room filled with flowers. A trillion vases of flowers. "One for every Tuesday that I missed," he explains shyly, but I don't get to jump his bones, because people jump from every corner like super sleuth ninjas and scare the crap out of me.

"Surprise!"

15

MARC

SHOWER HER WITH LOVE

I sit out on my new back deck with a beer in my hand and a cow sitting at my feet. She's not a damn dog, but she thinks she is. The back door stands wide open and the women *ooh* and *ahh* over baby shit barely twenty feet from me.

Meg sits at the head of the room in a dining chair, a party crown on her head, a toy pacifier on a chain around her neck, and a bib that chokes her. The girls gave her a baby doll that she's been warned not to put down, because if she forgets it, she 'loses,' so she just sits with that stupid doll clutched in her arms and watches her girlfriends cluck around her with gifts, cake, and games.

"They did good." Angelo sips his beer and nods toward the group of giggling women. Baby showers are supposed to be for chicks only, so they're inside the house squealing like little girls, and the guys have been exiled to the deck to cook the barbeque and not ruin their fun. "She's having fun, and the surprise wasn't ruined."

Angelo, Scotch, and I sit in a circle of chairs with a new dude – Graham – joining our ranks for the night. Even Luc is out here, and though he's keeping to himself, like he promised not to push himself on me tonight, promised not to ruin my night, he's still here and sitting in a chair a mere two feet from mine.

He simply sips and keeps his trap shut.

That's not the Luc we know. He'd normally be louder. The clown of the party. Hell, any other lifetime, he'd likely be sitting in Meg's chair inside and flirting with the girls.

I hope he looks at the preppy looking Graham and sees what I see when I look at Luc; a guy that thinks he gets to be with his sister. A guy who thinks he can touch our family and get away with it.

I hope it fucking hurts. Prick.

"Yeah, everyone did good." I rub my boot along my cow's stomach in soothing circles. Purring in the cow version of bliss, she lies back with a grunt. "She had no clue this was coming, and I didn't know if she'd actually want a party, so this worked out well."

"It's good to see her smile," Luc murmurs without thought, then as though catching himself, his eyes snap up to mine, his mouth snaps closed, his gaze goes back to his shoes, and he pretends he didn't just speak about something else that's mine and *not* his.

I hate that I hate him. I really do.

I've loved my brother for as long as I can remember. The four of us – me, Luc, Ang, and Scotch – have been best friends since forever. Inseparable. But when you cut it down to the core, Ang and Scotch were two grades above us, so naturally, they were closer, shared experiences and all that, and Luc and I were stuck in homeroom together.

It was good like that. As a group, we were best friends, but as individuals, Luc and I definitely gravitated toward each other in school. He's been my closest friend since I moved here, he was literally at the Turners' house the day we were brought there, so his betrayal cuts deeper now.

He knows what he did was wrong. He knows he fucked up bad. And he knows this isn't me playing games. I don't want to be angry, but I can't let it go. I can't allow him to do what he did... What he's still doing.

I know his punk ass arrived here with her today. Her car isn't hidden behind the barn with everyone else's. She didn't drive herself, and it's unlikely someone else brought her here if her... *boyfriend* was available.

It shows his lack of remorse.

Of all places to drive her, he brings her here, to my house. He's not sorry and he won't stop stealing, so he gets no forgiveness.

Kari and I finally had lunch. We talked. I made her cry for an hour straight while she tried to explain why she's dating Luc. Like I want a fucking explanation. Like she can make it better with words.

In the end, for the sake of our relationship, I asked that she drop it. His involvement in her life doesn't affect the relationship I have with my sister – much. It does, but I refuse to let it. I refuse to miss out on her *now* – like Meg said – because of Kari's poor life choices and Luc's inability to be a loyal fucking brother.

I won't give him the pleasure of coming between us, so bringing my beer to my lips, I simply allow him to shut himself up and I pretend he never spoke.

When the awkward silence stretches out, and Alex and Oz bullshit noisily by the barbeque, I stand from my lazy chair and silently duck my head through the door. I pick up the acoustic guitar standing against the wall and bring it back out into the dark.

We haven't turned on any lights out here, it's just the moonlight and the light flooding from the inside. The barbeque sizzles and wafts delicious scents in the breeze, and the bug zapper hung from the rafters provides us with the continuous sounds of electricity and fried protein.

Sitting back in the wooden chair I made back in senior year, I set my beer on the deck and bring the guitar into my lap – a distraction for my hands instead of smashing Luc's face in.

Angelo leans back lazily as I quietly pluck at the strings. Digging a hand into his jean's pocket and tapping his beer with the other, he grins and looks up at the moon. He sees my efforts to keep my fists to myself.

"It's good to see Laine," Scotch says quietly beside the ever-silent Graham. Is he shy or just boring? "It's been too long."

Luc nods and sips, nods and makes extra effort to not look at me. "Yeah, it's good. I've missed her."

Ang lazily turns his head to Graham; Laine's boyfriend. He's about our age – too fucking old for her – and though he looks like he has his shit together – no tear drop facial tattoo, no giant holes in his ears, no wedding ring to imply he's a cheating sack of shit – just like I don't like Luc, I also don't like this dude.

I didn't invite him here tonight, but if the option was seeing them both or not seeing her at all, I guess I can give him a steak sandwich and a beer. "You and Laine living together now?"

He watches his feet and shakes his head. Maybe he knows what I'm thinking. Maybe he knows he's about as liked as Luc is, so he doesn't meet my eyes.

Technically, I should be on Luc's side. I should be grilling the prick and making sure Luc's okay with the fact *his* baby sister is dating. It hurts me that I can't be that for him now.

"Not living together. Though I hope we might soon. We've been together a while now, so it'll make me happy if she makes the move – officially."

My eyes move between him and a jaw-clenching Luc. It hurts my chest that I can't be Luc's wingman on this shit.

"Did you ask her? To move in," I clarify. The day Luc asks Kari to move in with him is the day he dies. I strum my guitar to distract my hands, because I'm ready to kill a motherfucker at just the thought of my sister – or even *his* sister – shacking up with anyone. Just like Luc *was* my brother, his twin sisters are my sisters, too.

"Yeah." Graham looks up and takes a sip of his beer. He's been on the same one all night. Nursing it. At least he's responsible. "I asked her. She's at my place a lot, but hasn't made the move officially."

"Maybe she's not ready," Ang murmurs. "She's young. No need to play happy families yet."

Graham shrugs easily and takes another sip. "We're in love. I'm happy to wait as long as she needs."

Yeah, no shit he is.

She might not have made any official moves, but she's been AWOL from our family functions for the better part of a year. He's already got her hook, line, and sinker. Prick. "What do you do for a living, Graham?"

"Real estate," he answers easily. "I sell houses."

Real estate agents and car salesmen are the bottom fish that feed on the scum at the bottom of a filthy pond. Luc's eyes come to mine, but again, he flicks them away and doesn't say what he wants to say. That he hates the guy, too. That he wants his sister back.

That he knows what I'm thinking.

I nod slowly in reaction to Graham's answer and strum my guitar. Scotch's knuckles tap on the timber chair rhythmically. Angelo and Luc simply sit fisting their beers with white knuckles. "That's cool. Did you grow up around here?"

No. The answer is he didn't. We'd know him if he did, but I'm quickly running out of small talk.

"No," he answers in monotone. Like he's sick of this conversation. Too bad, motherfucker. This is my house. "Transplant about two years ago."

"You must've met our girl just as you crossed the tracks into town. You've been together awhile."

He watches her through the glass doors. Laine sits with her identical twin sister on the couch. Both in jeans. Both with long platinum blonde hair worn loose. Both with a tall flute of sparkling champagne in their hands.

But only one of them smiles at Meg's antics.

"Yeah, met her at the club the first weekend I moved here. Young, single guy in a new town. I moved here for work, so didn't know anyone. No friends here, no family. Decided to go to the only club in town that was hopping."

"188?"

"Yeah, it's a good club. Good music. Met her there. She was dancing with her girlfriends, I asked her to dance, and the rest is history."

Is he dumb, or he just doesn't care?

The good music was us. The girlfriends are our sisters. And we watch the girls every damn night they're out. "You've been here two years, thereabouts. Met her your first weekend you got here. How long have you been seeing each other? *Officially*."

"About eighteen months." He shrugs and watches me over the lip of his beer. "We danced at the club, but that was it for a while. I found her again, bought her flowers. Wooed her," he smirks. "She wasn't an easy sell. Took some negotiating."

"Negotiating? Sell?" Luc sits up tall. "She ain't real estate, *Greg*. My sister isn't a fucking acquisition."

At any other point in our lives, I'd have already said as much, and if I didn't get to it yet, then I'd at the very least be standing on Luc's flanks ready to rip this guy's tongue out.

But not today.

Today I sit and watch the show, and where I don't have my brother's back, Angelo picks up the slack with a simple fisted hand and tight lips. It takes a hell of a lot to get Angelo loud. He's just watching now. Waiting. But that hand says he's ready.

"I didn't mean it like that, man." Graham lifts his hands in mock surrender. His lips turn up into a playful grin, like a toddler who's being a prick because he knows his folks won't do anything about it. "Lainie and I have been together a long time, now. I love her. I meant no disrespect."

With pained eyes and hunched shoulders, Luc glances my way. He gets it now. He says the same thing to me.

I love her.

I respect her.

I don't react. I don't even say *I told you so*. I simply strum my fucking guitar and risk snapping the neck with my firm hold.

Breathe.

Relax.

Don't give away that either of these assholes are pissing me off.

"Well, since you love her so much…" I wait for his eyes to meet mine. "Maybe you and she can make more of an effort to come to family shit again. We didn't nag. We get the whole new relationship honeymoon phase shit, so we didn't pester her when she kept saying she was busy, but it'd mean a whole lot to us." I nod to each of the guys. Even Luc. "It'd mean a lot to us to see her at the dinner table again."

He nods noncommittally. "I'm not her keeper, man. But next time you make the invitation, I'll help nudge her. She's always working. That's the problem."

"Mmhmm." Fuck Luc for making me stand up for him when I vowed I wouldn't.

I stand up with my guitar. With a nod of dismissal, I turn away, set the guitar against the wall of my house, and step inside since I'd rather hang with the girls than either of those pricks.

Together for eighteen months and she only now introduces him to her family. That means she doesn't like him all that much, or he was *nudging* her away from us. Both those options leave the prick out in the cold away from me and those I love.

I step into the group of women and plop down between the twins.

Meg watches me from beneath her lashes as Britt hands her a gift. She unwraps it gently and pulls out teeny tiny onesies, but her eyes, and her smile, are all for me.

I throw my arms over the twins' shoulders and pull them into me. Turning my head with a smile when they both grunt and whine, I press a kiss to Jess' forehead. "Laine." And another to Laine's. "Jess. How are you guys? I've missed your guts."

Jess pushes me off. So much sass. "We've known you since we were barely out of diapers. Your ass knows I'm not Laine."

Of course I know, but I wanna shake off the assholes outside, and since my girl is busy being showered with love and baby socks, I'll step to the side and take some twin love, instead. "My mistake. You guys look so similar, I keep messing it up." I tap her forehead gently. "Maybe we should tattoo your name here. Make it easier on me."

She smacks my forehead with a loud slap. "Maybe we should tatt *'stubborn ass'* on yours. Maybe if you came around again, you'd know who we are. But no, you get mad at my brother because you're a whiny baby, and now Laine and I are out in the cold. Where's your loyalty, Marcus?"

"Don't even." Smile gone, I sit back and watch Meg watch me. "Your brother's the one with loyalty issues, Thing One."

"Oh, he's loyal," Laine adds with a smirk. "It just ain't to you anymore."

I grind my molars together so painfully, I can hear it in my brain. Snatching her champagne, I down the whole glass in one swallow.

I'm not driving anywhere tonight, so I don't have to stay sober enough to get behind the wheel. This shindig might have been my idea, but now I'd like to get everyone out. I want alone time with Meg. I'm done hosting for today. "You aren't helping, brat."

"Just saying," she continues without a care in the world. "His loyalty's as strong as always, but the focus has shifted." She bumps her shoulder to mine. "I'm telling you now, if your little Care Bear *has* to move on some day and grow up, then you bet your ass you want it to be with a man who looks at her the way Luc does."

The three of us look up and watch my sister pass Meg a new gift, then in sync, we turn to the back door to find Luc watching her. His face drains white when he notices our gaze.

Turning away, I go back to watching *my* sister love on *my* girl because of *my* baby.

That's the way it oughtta be.

All mine.

I've shared, or straight up given away everything else in my life. But those three hearts, they belong to me and I'm not sharing. No fucking way.

Luc made his bed, and he fucked me over in it.

16

LUC
MAKING MYSELF SCARCE

As soon as Marc walks inside with the dirty barbeque trays and empty beer bottles, I stop Bear with a hand on her elbow and pull her back. "Hey, I'll go wait in the car, okay?"

"No." Just as I expected, her eyes flash with anger. "Not okay, Luc! Just wait here. Sit down in the deck chairs and have a beer. I'm going to help with the dishes and stuff. I'm still gonna be an hour or so. You're not waiting in the car for an hour."

Marc's eyes snap up and watch us through the glass door. I take a big step back from her. His anger hurts me. Literally, in my gut, hurts me. "This is his house, Bear. His party. I won't hurt him any more than I have to."

"But—"

"I'll be in the car. I'm fine. Don't rush out, okay?" I hate that by trying to stop hurting Marc, I hurt her. But I can't help it. I don't want him to look at me like that anymore. "Don't rush. I don't care if you're an hour, or five. Stay here, hang out. I'll be fifty feet away. I'll work for a bit."

She rolls her eyes. "You have bodies in the car, Luca?"

I reach out with the intention of tapping her nose the way I have a billion times before, but stop midway and swallow as Marc's eyes burn the side of my head. Hands to myself. Eyes to myself. "No. But I have music I can write. Fuckface Graham's got me all kinds of pissed off. I can use it and write something to sell to idiots like the King's."

"I don't want you to sit out there alone." Her freckles almost twinkle as she scrunches her nose. "I feel like a total jerk being inside while you're out there."

"It's just a car, Bear. Now I'm asking you really nicely; don't rush. Give him and Snitch all the time they need. I won't be mad if you clean so long you pass out on the couch. I need to make things better with him; rushing you out to me isn't gonna help." I look at the tray on the table beside the barbeque. "Go. Help. Wash dishes or fold baby clothes. Whatever you need to do. I'll be twenty seconds away if you need anything."

She looks around us; at the mostly deserted party, the dishes left lying around, the baby paraphernalia scattered on every surface. "Alright. I won't rush, but I won't leave you hanging for long. Give me an hour."

"Take two and hug your brother."

She rolls her eyes, but before she can continue to argue, before Marc's eyes can burn a hole right through to the other side of my head, I step back off the porch and onto spongy grass. Hands dug deep in my pockets and my head bowed low, I turn and walk away at the same time Marc calls for her to get inside.

"I'm coming!" she snaps loudly.

I shake my head and walk slowly in the almost pitch blackness. The moonlight leads my way, barely, but as soon as you step off the porch, Marc's entire property is almost all shadow.

For a guy who wants his fortress protected so much, he sure keeps a lot of shadowed pockets around his property. It's like his common sense and inability to waste money war with his need to protect.

I need to buy the guy some flood lights. And cameras. Maybe a giant ass Rottweiler. The cow just sleeps all the time or licks her own ass.

He wants his sister to hang out here, he wants to have a family here, but he has all this shadowed space, every rustle of the willow branches gives me the heebie-jeebies.

I take out my phone and start searching hardware stores and floodlights as I move toward my car. I should be writing hate songs about Graham. I should be finding ways to get my sister back from that prick, but instead, I search the internet and flop down heavily into the front seat of my car as the wind picks up and sends leaves and dirt swirling over the gravel driveway.

Maybe if I help make his home more secure, it'll soften him up a little. I want my best friend back. I want what we had so bad it hurts.

But not nearly as much as losing Kari would hurt.

Thinking of her has me looking up to glance toward the house. Lights shine through all the skylights and windows, which thankfully, even though the renovations took some of the larger windows, there are still plenty left to allow natural light.

I can still see Meg laughing in her living room. Her little belly protruding. Her cute hair flipping back as she tosses a pair of rolled up socks at someone behind the solid section of the wall.

I look to my left at a small flash of light. Like lightning, but not. Darkness. Nothing. I switch off my phone screen and sit in the pitch dark as goosebumps scream along my skin with the rustling wind.

I'm a grown ass man. I don't get spooked often, but shit, the wind tonight is creepy.

Turning my eyes skyward, I look at the stars and smile. My Bear loves the stars. Ever since she was a kid, I'd find her outside counting stars. *'Twinkle, Twinkle, Little Star.'* I smirk and hum. Something I've done a million times over the years with her. She's only three years younger than me, but still. Too young.

When you're thirty-one and she's twenty-eight, three years is fine. Hell, even X is older than Juliette by more than that, but when she's fifteen and you're a horny eighteen-year-old, it's wrong. Sixteen and nineteen. No, because I'm a grown ass man and she's still a girl. Seventeen and twenty. It's not okay. Eighteen and twenty-one... we kissed.

So wrong.

But so right.

Again, as the flash of lightning goes off, my eyes snap to the left. The shadows are so deep, I can't see anything except silhouettes against the moonlight. Maybe Megan the cow is wandering around. Maybe the lightning is actually light flickering off her tags.

Who the fuck puts dog tags on a cow, anyway?

Who the fuck names a cow after the woman they love?

Human Megan must be as batshit about him as he is about her if she forgives that shit.

On the fourth or fifth lightning strike that isn't lightning, I turn with narrowed eyes and silently climb out of the car. The wind is enough that the sounds of my movements are hidden. I push the car door closed most of the way, dig my hands into my pockets to wrap around my phone, just in case, and take a stroll around the perimeter.

I'll protect my family no matter what. Even if he hates me.

I glance toward the house and windows and smile when Kari walks into sight. She's so fucking beautiful, there's no way in hell I can choose anyone over her; including Marc.

But if I tried hard enough, if he'd just stop and see, he'd realize I'm the best man for his sister.

No one will love her like I do.

No one will take care of her as well as I will.

I step across the driveway and keep the window in my line of sight. The wind and moonlight have given me the creeps. I want to keep my family in sight. A touchstone to home, even if I'm not actually welcome in there.

Meg steps in front of the window, then Marc follows. He smiles. When he's with her, he smiles. The lightning flashes again and changes my trajectory a little further to the left.

Dragging her away from the window, Marc and Meg are hidden by the solid wall for a moment. No lightning. They come back into sight, the lightning begins.

What the fuck is going on?

Stepping backwards and moving behind a thick tree trunk, I take out my cell and text Marc.

Me: Call Alex. Now.

I literally watch Marc through the window as he freezes mid dance with his girl, reaches into his pocket, scans the screen and drops the phone back into his pocket without a second thought.

That asshole is so fucking stubborn.

Again, I open the text box. *Come outside, bitch! Call Alex first.*

Meg is oblivious to Marc's furrowing brows. She and Kari laugh in the middle of the living room as he watches. His phone dings in his pocket, he takes it out, he frowns, he tosses his phone down on the couch and goes back to making out with Meg's neck.

Fuck, he's an asshole.

I open the text window and text Alex myself. *You need to come back. Something weird is happening. You're coming as cop, not brother.*

The lightning strikes again, and for the first time, I catch the sight of a silhouette moving between me and the living room lights.

Adrenaline zings through my body and sends me into hypersensitivity. The cool breeze tickles like fingers on every exposed section of my skin. The moonlight is brighter. The lightning is easier to see; not lightning. Camera flashes.

Some motherfucker is sneaking around.

And he's photographing my family.

I slide out from behind the tree and move silently toward the barn. It's locked up tight, the lights are out, and chains fasten the doors closed. But I've spent so much time here on the rebuild, I know where the scraps are hidden behind the barn, because the dumpster was full and we're waiting for it to be emptied.

I pick up a three-foot length of hardwood like it was a baseball bat. Cocking it over my shoulder, I move slowly around the back of the barn, around the far end of the house, and move up behind our visitor in complete silence.

More Marc and Meg in the window. More lightning.

I stand twenty feet away and crouch down in wait. Like a lion readying to pounce, I simply lower myself to a crouch and watch him.

Who is he? What's he photographing? Is it Drew? Is it someone Drew hired?

If it were any other intruder, anyone looking for a quick steal, he wouldn't be hiding out in the dark photographing my family. So it's definitely got something to do with Drew... What the fuck does he want?

Our visitor moves closer to the house, so I move closer.

Like a choreographed dance, he moves closer to the house by ten feet, I move closer to the house by ten feet. He won't be leaving this property tonight with that camera.

The wind dies down, which stops me from reaching back into my pocket to retrieve my phone. I don't know if Alex got my message. I don't know if he's coming. But for as long as our visitor stays where he is, I'll wait.

My blood boils for every snap of 'lightning' that flashes. He takes photos of Marc and Meg. He takes photos of Meg and Kari.

My Kari.

He takes photos of Meg holding her belly and laughing.

Picking up his gear, he moves forward another half a dozen feet. He's within six feet of the front porch.

Too fucking close.

Tightening the bat in my right hand, I move forward another half a dozen feet.

If Marc had just checked his fucking messages, I wouldn't be out here in the dark contemplating knocking this motherfucker out.

The man in front of me looks like Drew. I haven't seen the asshole since high school. But he's built like an unfit linebacker. Tall. Broad. Fat head. His breathing is noisy; he's unfit, and no doubt, his thighs burn from his perpetual squat.

Click, click, click. Flash, flash, flash.

"Come on, you stupid bitch. Come back to the window."

Anger sizzles beneath my skin. Potent rage and the adrenaline that urges me to take him out.

Hold on. Hold it in. Alex is on the way.

Keep this shit legal. Keep it above board.

Use it for her divorce.

He's trespassing. That shit's illegal.

He's photographing them. That's illegal, too.

Meg steps up to the window with a smile and looks out. She can't see us. We're in the dark and she's in the light, but it's almost as though she looks right at me.

With a soft chuckle of pleasure, Drew reaches into his coat and takes out something small and silver. Not the camera. Something else. "There you are, you stupid bitch. Think you can sic your bitch lawyer on me. Not fuckin' likely."

Standing without thinking, I take the final space between us at a sprint, cock the wood over my head and swing. "Marc! Get the fuck outside!"

Meg jumps back from the window at my shout. Drew falls forward like dead weight. The front door swings wide and Marc stands silhouetted against the light. "What the f—"

"Call the cops. Call X." I dive down over the man I just hurt. I'm Meg's brother. Marc's brother. Protector of my family.

But I'm also a protector of the hurt.

I try to save people for a living, not hurt them. So I dive over him and flip him to his back. Eyes closed, blood coats his right temple and dribbles from his nostril.

Kari ducks beneath Marc's arm and sprints outside toward me. Like a million times in the past, she skids down beside me, unknowing and uncaring about who our victim is, and helps me help them. "It's Drew." I look up into her eyes. "I think he was gonna hurt them."

She presses her fingers to his throat at the same time police cruisers come skidding off the road and into Marc's driveway.

Shaking with rage and holding Meg against his chest at the top of the porch, Marc looks down at us helplessly – not something I've ever seen him do before.

He's always the first line of defense. Always the protector. But tonight, his stubbornness won out over sensibility, and he let the team down.

"He's alive," Kari murmurs. "Strong pulse." She probes around the side of his head. "Giant goose egg on the side of his head. Jesus, Luc. You did this?"

I nod and glance toward the wood. With Kari by his side, I crawl forward on the grass and stop in front of the *weapon*.

Not a gun. Not a weapon. But a silver micro recorder.

His chunky camera lies with a cracked screen in front of the porch stairs. Looking up to Marc and Meg, I reach out for it, but Marc steps down and snatches it up first.

The police cruiser comes to a skidding halt twenty feet from where we are, with the blue and red lights illuminating the yard. Alex sprints from the car, and Jules follows at a fast trot behind. A second car skids off the road. Oz is here, too.

Alex stops in front of us with a police issue gun in his hand and his boots still unlaced. "What the fuck is going on?"

I look up to Marc as his eyes narrow. With the camera on and the screen reflecting in his angry eyes, he scrolls through the digital images as Meg steps up behind him.

"He's got hundreds of pictures," Marc seethes. "The party tonight. The renovations. The beehive bathroom. The apartment." His eyes come to mine. Then back to the screen. "Meg at the diner." He reaches behind and pulls her into his side. "He's got pictures of you alone, baby. You and Mac. You and Katrina. The band at the club. The hospital. The clinic." Feral rage radiates from beneath his skin as his eyes come back to mine. "He violated my home, Luc. He was on my property."

I nod. Of all the things someone could do that would hurt him the most, being on Marc's property without an invitation is one of the worst crimes.

He turns to Alex. "I want him charged with trespassing, X. That's three years. I know. I checked. I have '*no trespass*' signs all over my property." His eyes go back down to continue scrolling.

Fuck us all if he finds an image of Meg half naked.

"Who hit him?"

I climb to my feet shakily. The adrenaline flees my body and leaves me weak. "Me."

Alex takes out a notebook and pencil. He looks to Kari. "He's okay?"

"He's fine. Get Oz to call an ambulance. He'll need to be admitted. Probably a CT to make sure he isn't dying." She looks at me. "He's fine."

Alex looks over his shoulder to Oz. "Get a bus here." Then he turns back to me. "Speak, Lenaghan. What happened?"

"I was sitting in my car." I look over his shoulder in the direction of the car and barn. "Chilling out. Waiting for Be–" I stop and glance at Marc. Then back to Alex. "I was waiting for Kari. She was inside packing up. It's dark as fuck out here without all those lights, so I was sitting in the car in the dark, searching Home Depot and stuff. I saw something, like a tiny flash of light. Brushed it off until the second and third. Got out of the car quietly, grabbed the wood, watched him watch them through the window."

Again, my eyes go to Marc. "Tried to text him. Tried to warn him, but he didn't get my messages. I texted you, hunkered down to wait."

"You were just watching and waiting?" Alex's disbelieving eyes come back to mine. "A guy's on your brother's property, and you're just gonna watch and wait?"

I shrug. "I saw it was Drew. Saw it was just a camera. Realized it was actually a good thing that Marc didn't get my texts. Had he known, you might be arresting him right now for killing Drew. I texted you. Hunkered down."

Alex's piercing blue eyes scan the ground around us. "What happened?"

"He kept getting closer and closer. Every time one of them was in the window, he'd take more pictures."

Marc's eyes turn to the window. A window that probably won't be there tomorrow.

"He started out a good thirty feet from the porch. Kept crawling closer. I stayed back, crawled closer as he did." I swallow heavily. "He got too close, pulled something shiny outta his pocket. I got spooked, smacked him."

Alex's brows pull tight. "What did you think it was?"

"I didn't *think*, X. I saw a glint. I panicked. I hit him."

"You thought it was a gun," Marc snaps out grudgingly. He turns to Alex. "He thought it was a weapon. Drew's trespassing. In this state, we have the right to protect our homes, Chief."

"Cool your jets, Macchio. He's not being arrested."

"What about Drew?"

Alex's eyes go back to an already stirring Drew. "He is. He's on private property. He's taking photographs. You say he got photos of your bathroom?"

Marc nods.

"Add break and enter." Our eyes turn to the road as an ambulance turns into the driveway. Alex turns back to me. "You thought it was a gun. It was self-defense. You were protecting your family."

I nod. Because that's what he wants.

But inside, I'm trembling.

I *did* think it was a gun.

❧

ONE HOME DEPOT visit and fifteen hours later, I finalize the last of the wiring for Marc's new security system. The packaging says DIY. But it was expensive enough that it's not shitty.

I pull up the app on my cell and switch everything on. Twelve individual cameras scan his yard and barn. Twelve individual thumbnails sit on my phone screen and show me, Meg the cow, and one truck cruising along the driveway.

Just in time to test.

I get an alert on my phone that someone drove past the initial sensors at the top of the drive, and as Marc comes closer, a second alert when he passes the final gate and enters his actual yard. He pulls up out front of the barn, the same place he always parks. Looking at my phone screen, the digital image matches the view in front of my eyes.

He slams the truck door and stomps toward me. So angry. So fucking angry. "The fuck you doing here, Lenaghan?"

So much hatred.

"Nothing. I was leaving."

"I'm sick to fuckin' death of assholes being on my property when they aren't invited."

He shows me anger. But inside, he's been shaken. His home was violated. His safe space. The space his family will live. I hold out a single folded leaf of paper, which he snatches from my grasp and tears open. "What's this?"

"Those are instructions. Download the security app, enter that password. Your new system is solar powered and wired in for backup. You get alerts every time someone enters your driveway – on foot or in a vehicle. Another when they reach your yard. Another when they approach your front or back door. I didn't set it up for the barn, but you can if you want. It's just an on/off thing. This thing monitors around the clock, but they don't record."

Angrily, his eyes flash and watch me in silence.

"Meg the cow might set it off sometimes as a false alarm, but that's a small price to pay." I shrug. "That's what I think, anyway. You don't have to be here to log in. You can be anywhere and know what's going on in your home. They've got a help center number if you need help with working them or whatever. Or call me." I step past him and slide to the side when he steps in my way. I don't want to slam shoulders with him today. I don't want to fight. "No one will get into your home again, Marc. You're my brother. I've got your back."

Nostrils flaring, eyes sparking, he looks me down and makes me feel five feet tall, though we're both the same height. "I didn't give you permission to be here, asshole."

I shrug. It hurts me. He hurts me. "I did it anyway. One more intrusion to hopefully stop all others. I just wanna know you guys are safe."

He huffs like I've created a giant inconvenience for him. "I'll cut you a check. Wait here."

"No." I walk toward my car. "I don't want your fucking money, Marcus. I want your friendship or nothing."

He stops at the top of the porch with arms folded across his chest. "Nothing, then. You get nothing from me. You forfeited that when you fucked me over."

So fucking stubborn. "That's what I thought. I'll be around. You know where I am."

"I won't come looking. Not until you send my sister home, back where she belongs." His sentence implies that if Bear and I were to break up, everything would go back to normal. It wouldn't. We've already passed that portion of our lives. Now we have to forge on.

I won't toss her away when I know it won't get him back, anyway.

I wouldn't toss her away even if his friendship was guaranteed.

I won't lose her.

"See you around, Macchio. I love you."

"Fuck you."

Before I even close my car door, his front door slams closed and he *doesn't* step to the windows to watch me leave.

17

MARC
SIX HOURS EARLIER

Pulling up at a set of large wrought iron gates – a place I never knew before last night that I'd ever need to visit – I press my thumb down on the buzzer in a long, demanding buzz until his voice crackles through the speaker. "Hello?"

"Marcus Macchio here to see Arthur Montgomery." As an afterthought, I add, "Sir."

Art Montgomery was old as dinosaurs way back when I knew Meg as a spitfire seventeen-year-old. I served his ungrateful ass at the country club several nights a week. And yet, I still know to expect his next question.

"Who? I have nothing ordered for today."

He sees my truck in his cameras. He probably sees the dust and dirt on my clothes. He expects I'm his pool boy or closet renovator.

"Marcus Macchio, sir. I'm, ah, I'm dating your daughter."

"Oh! Oh, of course." The gates swing open like they're on turbo engines. I expected he'd tell me to fuck off, but when the gates stand open in invitation, I put the truck into gear and move forward.

I park at the top of the driveway and try not to stare at the elegance. This place is old; old owner, old money. But it's not worn down. It's as fancy as it was the day it was built – but fancier, since it was built in the older colonial style. Quality build, quality fixtures. Quality stone and tile and marble.

Fuck.

Yesterday, I was feeling all sorts of smug and impressed with the house I brought Meg to. I'd renovated and tripled its size for her. I'd made it into a home and welcomed her in with dozens and dozens of flowers and a party.

Then Drew ruined it all.

I climb out of the truck and move up the dozen granite stairs. I don't get a chance to knock, because the door swings open before I move off the top stair. An old man that I've seen around town a hundred times since I was freed from my servitude at the country club steps out with worried eyes and shaking hands.

I take my hat off and incline my head. "Ah, hello, sir."

He stops and looks up at me. He's shorter than me by a long shot, but he carries power like I carry power tools. "Mr. Macchio. Is everything okay?"

I take a deep breath. "Yes. No. Not really."

"Is Megan safe?"

"Megan..." She fucking hates that name. "Yes, sir, your daughter's safe. She's with friends right now. I was hoping we could talk. I have some important stuff I'd like to discuss with you."

"You said you're dating my daughter?"

"Yes, sir."

"You're new to town?"

I bite back what I really want to say. I bite back the anger and unimportance I feel. "No, sir. Born and raised here. I went to school with Meg a long time ago." I pause thoughtfully. "You didn't look me up after you found out she was having a baby?"

"No." He studies me, but his eyes turn less shrewd. "She didn't give me your name. She knew I'd look you up. She told me I didn't need to know to do my job in going after Drew."

"Drew." I'd kill him with my bare hands. If I was allowed to be alone with him for five minutes, I'd kill him. "I don't know if you know about last night, but that's why I'm here. You're her divorce lawyer, yeah?"

His eyes narrow. "I am. What happened last night?"

"He–"

"Come inside." He steps back and gestures me in. "I get the distinct feeling I need a drink for this."

"Yes, sir. You probably do."

I walk in ahead of him and peek around the home that Meg always shouted she hated.

She said it was cold. It is.

She said it was museum like. It is.

I stop at the end of the hall and wait for him to pass and lead me where he wants to go. I expect a sitting room of sorts, but he walks through a labyrinth of halls and leads me into an office.

Expensive draperies. Expensive mahogany desk. Genuine cow hide chair.

"Take a seat, Marcus. Can I offer you a drink?"

"No, thank you." I've gotta be sharp. "Feel free to have your own, but I'm fine."

With a smirk so much like his daughter's, he sits in his fancy chair and indicates for me to sit in the chair opposite. "Tell me what happened, Marcus."

"Drew was arrested last night. He was trespassing on my property."

Art's eyes turn to narrowed slits in an instant. He grabs a voice recorder and pops it on the desk between us. "Do you mind?" When I hesitate, he clarifies, "It's only for me. You have my word. I don't want to miss anything important."

I study his sharp eyes for a long minute.

He's old. He could even be confused for *too* old. Bordering on senile. But his eyes tell an entirely different story.

I nod my permission for him to record. "I came to you today not to speak to her father, but the best divorce attorney around."

He nods. "You've come to the right place."

"Are you just the best divorce attorney in town? Because this is a small ass town."

He scoffs lightly. "I'm the best attorney money can buy. And I come with an extra edge of passion, since she's my daughter. You don't have to worry about this, Marcus. I'll fix whatever she needs fixin'.""

I take a deep breath and let it out noisily. "Okay. He was on my property last night." I reach into my back pocket and pull out the small memory card that I swiped from Drew's camera. "Does your computer have a small memory card slot?"

He takes it from my hands and studies it like a giant holding an ant. Screwed up eyes, scrunched nose. He pushes his chair back from the desk and takes a peek at the computer tower.

With a huff of breath, he stands from his desk and walks to a small cabinet against the far wall. "My desk computer doesn't. But my laptop does. Give me a second." He opens drawer after drawer until, finding the brand-new, silver and unmarked laptop, he pulls it out and brings it back to his desk.

Powering up and slipping the card into the slot, his lips turn to thin lines as the images pop up. "How'd you get this?"

"I took it."

"Drew took these?"

"Yes, sir. He's got her at the diner, he's got her at my house, at the apartment. He's even got her here."

"Where's he now?"

"Hospital."

His bushy eyebrows pop in surprise. "Hospital? What happened?"

"He was trespassing. We have the right to defend our home."

"I'm not asking for what you'll say in your official statement," he interrupts. "I'm asking what happened."

"My best friend caught him skulking around the yard close to midnight last night. Snuck up on him. Watched him a few minutes. When Drew got a little too close for comfort, Luc smacked him with a piece of cutoff wood. He's in the hospital under police watch."

"Under police watch? How dangerous is he? Did he have a weapon?"

"The police is my brother." I meet his eyes. "So I get special favors. Drew's not taking a shit without my brother wiping his ass. He didn't have a weapon last night. But my best friend thought he did. That was enough."

"Is he dangerous?"

I shrug. "Dunno. Don't think so. He was skulking around on private property in the dark. He didn't have so much as a box cutter on him. I don't think he's dangerous. But I think he's sneaky and slimy. He's looking for ways to trip her up in the divorce. That's why I came to you. That's why I brought you that SD card."

"The police need this card, Marcus."

"The images are on the camera, too. I made sure they were on the internal memory before I swiped the card. The chief has the camera – and the images. And now you have the images, too. I don't know stalking laws. I don't know what needs to be done for a restraining order to be put into place. But I don't want him near her again. I want him off my property, away from the diner, away from here. I don't want to see him ever again; but more than that, I don't want him to see her again."

He watches me in silence. I don't miss the fact he didn't pour a drink for himself. I get the feeling his offer was a test. Drew probably said yes a million times in the past.

"You're keeping my daughter safe, Marcus? She's stubborn, and when she gets an idea in her head, I've never been able to talk her around."

I pull in a deep breath through my nose and out my mouth. "I'm failing at the moment, Mr. Montgomery. I've never, in fifteen years, been able to talk her out of something. I swear she's more stubborn now than before. And last night…" The failure eats me from inside. "I didn't protect her last night. My best friend did. I fucked up."

"And yet she's safe today."

"She's safe today. She'll be safe every day for as long as she's with me. I won't screw it up twice, I promise."

Sitting back against the lush leather, he steeples his fingers and presses his elbows to his knees.

He's the business empire mogul. Rich man looking down on the peasants. "I don't know if we've been formally introduced. I'm Arthur Montgomery."

"Yes, sir."

"And you're Marcus Macchio – the father of my grandchild. A good man. A *wonderful, caring, loving, stable and perfect man...*"

My brows knit. Is this old coot hitting on me? "Come again, sir?"

"That's what she told me." He smiles. "A little while ago, when she first came home and told me she was having a baby. I was nudging her toward moving back home. I'd take care of her and the baby. We didn't need you." He sits forward with a raised hand before I can tear him apart. "It wasn't personal. I didn't even know you. I was just trying to take care of my baby girl. But she said no. She said you were wonderful and caring and all that other shit."

All that other shit. I didn't know snooty aristocrats knew how to swear.

"Okay."

"Are you wonderful and caring and all that other shit a dad doesn't wanna know about the man dating his daughter?"

"I mean..." I shuffle uncomfortably in my seat. "I'm a good man. Loyal to a fault. Protective to the point of a rap sheet."

His brow lifts with smug inquisition.

"Maybe I get a little heated about the people I love." *Luc.* "But for those I love; I'll fight to the death. I'll fall first, every time." *But not for Luc.* "I'll do anything it takes to keep my family safe." *I miss Luc.*

"But what about happy?"

My gaze goes back to his. "Huh?"

"Well, I kept my daughter *safe* for eighteen years. Fed. Clothed. I provided the best fabrics and the best foods for eighteen years. She had the best tutors. The best classes. The best of everything..."

"Okay..."

"But those things didn't make her *happy*. And happiness is what she wanted. That's what she left me to find elsewhere. Will you make my daughter *happy*, Marcus?"

"Yes, sir. I'll try every day for the rest of my life to make her happy."

"Do you make her happy now?"

I flick my thumb and finger together nervously. "I make her laugh every single day, sir. Usually, she's laughing at my expense. She likes to tease. But I don't mind. There aren't many days I've known her that I haven't made her laugh."

His eyes shadow with sadness. "I honestly don't remember the last time she laughed in front of me." With pursed lips and sad eyes, he looks up. "Every day?"

"Yes sir. Almost every single day."

He looks down and studies a speck of dust floating in the sunlight. "That makes me happy. She just wants to laugh. She wants to be loved. She wants those around her to pay attention to her."

"I won't pretend to know what you feel exactly. Everyone has their own story. I'm not a daddy yet – not like you are. But I have a little sister. She was my responsibility since our folks died when I was twelve. I'm not her daddy, but I feel like I am. So I can relate some-what to how you feel. You're a hell of a lot more understanding than I am in your same position."

He shrugs. "My daughter's a grown woman, Marcus. She's an adult. She supports herself. I don't get a say anymore; proven by the decade long silence. We weren't estranged. She just didn't want to come home for Christmas. I lost a lot of years because she's an adult and she gets to choose. She chose her life, and I chose not to listen. Don't do what I did. You don't get to choose for them. You just get on board, or you stay off and miss out. There's no third option."

AFTER VISITING with the father of the woman I want to marry, in a home I'll never be able to afford or buy for her, I drove my ass to Home Depot to buy a security system. I picked out a set that's DIY, but not cheap. The best available, short of hiring a top tier security company to come in and do it up.

I stood in that hardware store for hours reading reviews online. I slapped down my credit card three hours after I walked in, bought the security system, and downloaded the app in preparation for a long night of fucking around.

I will not be sleeping tonight until my home is secure.

I spent hours after speaking with Art thinking about Luc and Kari, about the possibility of losing her for a decade because she decided she was done with me being a prick. I was edging toward a place of *'accept her for who she loves, because it's better than losing her,'* but that came undone when I drove into my driveway to find him waiting.

I thought I was making progress. I thought I was coming to find a new kind of peace, but a single second of looking into his traitorous eyes, eyes that I've laughed with and laughed at for two decades, eyes that I feel in my gut have betrayed me, the anger rises and my acceptance blows up in smoke.

And when I get out of my truck only to find he'd already bought and installed the exact same system I'd just maxed my credit card over, his gesture doesn't make me feel safe.

It makes me feel incompetent.

Twice in twenty-four hours, my asshole best friend has taken care of my family when it should've been me who was getting the job done.

18

MEG
HIS FIANCÉ…?

A ndi sent her flight information just hours ago.

She forgot.

She absolutely, completely forgot to reply to my texts, and no doubt, it wasn't until she was boarding the plane on her side of the country that she stopped and thought *'oh, dang. I better reply to that chick.'*

She's a big girl, she knows how to call a cab just like the rest of us, so I wasn't stressing about her lack of communication. I just went about my plans knowing that she'd be here one way or the other. But seeing as she did finally text me, I find myself standing in the crowded airport in heels and a cute as hell dress that hugs my butterfly baby, because today is about fun and parties. I'm stepping uncomfortably into the third trimester, and the app on my phone tells me it's the size of a large *eggplant*, though I swear, it should say large *basketball*.

Holding a sign in front of my body that simply states *'Twatwaffle'* – because I feel like Andi and I are twins from another mother, and if that's true, then she'll laugh and zoom straight in on my sign. And if she doesn't get it, then I hope she doesn't pen a strongly worded complaint to Oz and get my pregnant ass in trouble.

I watch the ever-changing screens high above the fast-moving people who dart around like ants under a magnifying glass. Flights arrive. Flights leave. Flights are delayed. And twenty minutes after Andi's flight announced its arrival, a blur of creamy white skin and raven hair zips through the crowd with searching eyes.

I've never met Andi before.

I didn't even go searching for her on social media, so I have no clue what she looks like. But I find this woman that bears serious resemblance to the bride that we're celebrating tonight, not to mention the fact she's carting a hell of a lot of luggage, carry-ons, big sunglasses perched on top of her head, and a phone she drops to the dirty floor at least three times before our eyes lock... It's not hard to figure out this is my girl.

I hold the sign in front of me. Watching her curious eyes turn to twinkling fun, she pushes her way through the crowd and dumps her bags in front of me with a huff. "Thank shit you're here!" She leans in and throws her arms around my shoulders for a squishy hug, and when we touch belly to belly, she jumps back like I bit her. Tearing the sign from my hands to reveal my stomach, her eyes grow wide. "Woah, mama! You're Meg, right?"

"I'm Meg."

"You're also pregnant! What the hell? You didn't tell me that!" She steps back and cups my belly in her hands. "Jesus, are you already crowning? You're all the way."

I purse my lips and wait for this chick – who acts as though we're best friends from way back – to finish. "I'm twenty-eight weeks, jerk. I still have a couple months to go. No, I'm not crowning. And three, I didn't realize I *had* to tell you. I don't even know you!"

"Psht. We're girlfriends now. The text relationship I have with you is the longest in my phone. For reals." She turns in her heels and collects her shit. "I don't text Linds. We talk on the phone. And nine times out of ten, I don't give my phone number to rando guys. If I do, because maybe he had a big dong or something, then usually it only takes about forty-eight hours before he annoys me and I block that shit." We start moving through the crowds without verbally agreeing. She just makes things happen.

"Times are changing, Meg. Dating's not how our folks had it. Back in the day they had to actually ask someone out, they had to go in blind – no online stalking for the boomers – then you had to deal with whatever cards you were dealt that night and decide if you actually liked them. Nowadays, swipe left, swipe right, eww he sent a dick pic, swipe, swipe, swipe. If you're on a date that sucks, your friends call and bail you out because Great Aunt Susie had a heart attack on the shitter or something. It's obnoxious."

She's obnoxious. "So…?"

"So you and me are practically best friends. Our text chat is epically long."

"I already have a best friend."

She stops and points at my belly. "You also have a man, so you wouldn't know about all that swiping."

I shake my head. Finding ourselves standing outside the airport on a warm sunny day, I point toward the parking garage where I parked. I'd offer to help carry her things as we start walking again, but she's a big girl and the one who decided she needed a month's worth of clothes for one single overnight trip.

That's on her.

I'm not busting my ass or tripping in my heels because she couldn't decide which dress to cover her perfectly cute little body.

Fifteen minutes later, after loading her luggage into the car, validating my parking and winding our way down the five levels of the parking garage, we pull out onto the main road and head back toward town.

I smile when my phone dings with Marc's ringtone. He's checking in, and every single day I spend with him leaves me swooning and wanting more.

He's taken it upon himself to take care of me. Every single facet of my life is catered by him.

I'm hungry? He jumps up and cooks me something awesome. And not even something small and quick, but a fully thought out, balanced meal that's beneficial for both me and baby. No microwaved bacon in his house anymore.

My feet ache? He spends hours rubbing them with one hand while he draws with the other. Before Marc and I moved in together, I figure he was a work all night, fall into bed, work all of the next day and night, rinse and repeat kind of guy. But now that he has to be a responsible family man, as soon as I clock off at the diner, if he's not playing at the club, we find ourselves on the couch with movies on the TV, but both of us with our respective notebooks in our faces while we work.

When I have to get up in the night to pee, he's awake, waits for me to get back, snuggles back in and reminds me that he loves me and appreciates the pain I'm already going through for his baby. The only pain I feel right now is that of a bursting bladder twice a night and the occasional cramping where my period should be.

Truth be told, I'm pretty damn comfortable.

Today, Marc has to work. The renovations on the house set his schedule back by a lot. He acts cool, he acts like it's not a big deal, but Marc's a typical Type-A kind of guy, and his schedule has been thrown out. He's working his ass off to catch up, and though I assured him it's fine, he's still sad I'm out 'working' today and he can't help me.

I'd hardly call going out with girlfriends *work*, but it's official and Oz sanctioned it, so I guess in the technical sense, it is.

I pull up at the train tracks when the boom gates slide down and block our path. Picking up my phone, I slide it open and smile at his name.

Andi pokes around in all my car pockets just for the sake of snooping. "She's still in the dark, right?"

"Uh-huh. She has no clue." My face warms and my heart flutters at his text.

Marc: Marco, beautiful.

I snicker and quickly reply: *No, you're Marco, I'm Meg.*

I look up after sending the text, but stop at Andi's keen gaze. "Shut up."

"The guy who knocked you up make you blush like that? You still feel the magic, huh? I figured by the point a guy gets the whole cow, he stops flirting."

I snort at her cow reference. She has no clue how close she is.

"He'll never stop making me blush, but he wasn't flirting that time. He was just checking in."

My phone dings again: *Say it back, Poot. I bought that paddle. I'm not scared to use it, and I know it'll be fun to watch your ass turn red.*

"Well, okay," I clear my throat awkwardly. "He did that time. I might get spanked tonight if I play my cards right." I laugh at Andi's filthy smirk and fanning hands.

Looking back to my phone, I simply reply: *Polo.* Then: *love you.* Then: *yes please, donkey dick.*

The train flies past us at high speed, and within moments of the back end leaving my sight, the flashing lights stop and the boom gates lift.

Putting my car into gear, we move forward over the bumps of the tracks and head toward the center of town. "So, the party's at Club 188. I know the owners. In fact, Lindsi's employed by the owners, so they volunteered their place for the night."

"The Rollers, right?"

"Right."

"Do you know them? I hate how sexy they are."

I laugh as we wind our way along the road. We're not in any particular rush. Almost everything is done. Just like the wedding, this party has been a siege I've planned and will pull off seamlessly. "Yes, I know them. Yes, they're sexy. It's gross, really."

She snickers in agreement. "Wait. Are we talking about the guys or the girls?"

"Both. That short one, Tink… do you know her?" When she nods easily, I purse my lips. "I used to have the nicest tits in town. Now she just struts on in and makes mine look so blah. She has kids, too. Two of them. At the same damn time. I think those kids made her boobs better."

Andi stares at my chest for a long minute before finally looking up. "Your boobs are nice." She grabs hers. "I like mine, too. But yours are definitely better."

"Mine are pregnant lady boobs. I hope they stay where they are after the baby."

She shrugs and watches out the window as we move down Main. "Get your man to buy you new tatas after it's done. It's the least he could do."

I laugh. I swear, twins. "That's my plan. He likes my boobs, so if he wants to keep them this way…"

She nods seriously as I pull up at the back of the mostly empty and silent club. Lindsi isn't here yet. We have a couple hours, and I can't drop Andi off at Lindsi's house and tip her off, so to the club we go.

This party will start out as private – just us. We get the club for a couple hours as a private venue, but by nine, it'll open to the public, the band – Marc's band – will start up, and the place will get noisy.

The girls will either be wasted messes by then and ready for home, or they'll be working towards it.

Andi and I climb out of the car – though my movements are a lot less graceful than they used to be.

With a silly giggle, she walks around and takes my hands like we truly are friends from long ago. She pulls me to my feet with a ridiculous grunt. "Let's go, fatty. Keep your legs closed today. I don't wanna get my hands dirty." She holds them up. "Brand new mani."

"You're gross." I turn and slam my door after grabbing my purse. Walking past the band cars, I smile, because I'll be seeing him in three, two, one…

"Wait." She grabs my arm. "When are you due?"

"A little under twelve weeks. Thereabouts."

She eyes me dangerously. "When's the wedding, genius?"

"Eleven weeks. But!" I jump in before she flips out. "Everyone going is everyone I know. They're my family. The wedding's already planned. Everything's in place. Like a game of dominoes, I just have to tip the first, then everything else will fall into place. I don't *have* to be there if I can't be for whatever reason," *like dying.* "Everything's basically automated. As long as Lindsi doesn't fall on her ass on the way down the aisle, we're set."

"And if she does?"

"Then its your job to pick her the hell up!" I push her forward.

"You're the maid of honor. What exactly do you think your job is around here?"

We walk through the club doors, and as if on cue, we both look up at the wolf whistle coming from the stage. I smile at Luc's obnoxiousness, but my eyes automatically go to Marc as he stands in front of the stage and rolls cords in preparation for tonight.

I turn in their direction and drag Andi along. "Come on, I'll introduce you."

"Nuh-uh, no need." She walks ahead and stops me in my tracks when she slides the fuck under Marc's arm and drops a kiss on his cheek. "Hey there, good-lookin'. I've been thinking about you."

I watch them like I'm on the outside and they're inside a TV. Like, what the actual fuck is going on? "'Scuse me? What the fuck, Marcus?"

"Meg, no." He steps away from a still smiling Andi. His face is white as a ghost, and hers transforms from fun to innocent confusion. Marc steps forward, but Luc jumps off the stage and bolts around to stand in front of me.

Marc stops with flaring nostrils and fire in his eyes. "Get the fuck outta my way, Lenaghan."

I peek around Luc. And around Marc, too. My gaze stops on Andi, and without rambling or giving anyone a chance to get their stories straight, I ask, "Who is he?"

She looks between us curiously. "He's Marc."

"Right. And who is he to you?"

She stares for a moment longer. She doesn't know the right answer. She doesn't know whose side to take, but I'll be fucked if I let a man screw me over again.

Fool me once...

Drew can cheat on me and cop hell a'la Louisville slugger. But then it's over, because that's all he's worth.

But if Marc is cheating, then someone's gonna die today. Definitely me, but probably Marc and Andi, too.

She swallows hesitantly. "He was my fiancé for a short time. Lindsi introduced us, but she said he was single. We broke up because we weren't compatible."

Fiancé. Single. My eyes snap to Marc's. Wide, like 'what the fuck,' but when that doesn't feel satisfying enough, I screech, "What the fuck, Macchio?"

"No." Hands up. Submission. Surrender. "She's joking, baby. It was a joke we shared once ages ago."

"He calls you baby?" She steps forward and stands by Marc similarly to how I stand by Luc. The guys were in the same room and not beating the snot out of each other for once, and now, just like that, Luc stands between Marc and I, and undoes any progress he might have made.

"Something you shared once. Ages ago." I stare into Marc's eyes. "You never told me you were seeing Lindsi's cousin. The chick I've been talking to for months! Months, Marcus! Didn't think to tell me?"

Andi stares at my belly. "That's his baby?" She turns to him with angry eyes. "She's six months pregnant. When exactly did we meet, Marcus?"

"Might not be his," I answer before he can. "Might be Ken's. Not sure anymore."

Marc rolls his eyes. With an angry huff, he shoves Luc aside and takes my arm. His head snaps around like a feral dog under attack when Luc charges back.

He shoves me behind his back so our baby touches us both at the same time and sizes Luc up with a snarl. "Don't ever get between me and her again. You think it's bad when you get between me and my sister, watch what the fuck happens next time you think you can block me from my girl and kid. You'll die, Luca. I'm not playing. Get the fuck outta my way." He turns and takes my arms in his hands.

"She's playing about the engagement thing. Oz and Lindsi's engagement party, Andi was there. That was a week after you were arrested for flogging Drew, by the way. I know that because I remember everything about you. Lindsi was drunk and playing matchmaker with her single cousin and me – I was also single, by the way."

He points to Andi. "We walked away together, because neither of

us were gonna ruin Lindsi's buzz. We sat down. We chatted. She literally joked about how it felt like Lindsi sold her to me, like a bride in
exchange for a goat. We joked about wedding gift registries. We fanta-
sized about six slice toasters. That's it."

We turn to her for clarification. She steps forward with a hesitant
nod. "All of that was true. I didn't expect to see him in here, but when
we walked in just now and I saw him, I remembered the funny guy
from the party. I hugged you when I walked off the plane too, remember? I didn't know he was spoken for, and I definitely didn't know he
was *yours*. I was just playing with the fiancé stuff."

I look back to Marc with narrowed eyes. "Have you been in contact
with each other since? Have you been in contact since you and I
have... *reconnected*? I won't be cheated on again, Marc. I won't be
second best."

He takes a cellphone from his back pocket and thrusts it into my
hands. When he rattles off a six-digit password to unlock it, my breath
catches and our eyes meet. "Your birthday, baby. Open my phone.
Check anything you want. I've never had her number. We've never
talked except for an hour at a party before you and I ever caught up
again. You're not second best to anyone. Especially not to me."

Scotch steps into our group like the hostage negotiator late to the
party. "Alright, that was close, but we're all clear. No one's cheating on
anyone. And Andi's just a flirt."

She raises her hand shamelessly. "Truth."

"And I didn't know you were talking to *her*," Marc adds. "I didn't
know you were talking to Lindsi's cousin. If I did, I would've said
something. It would've been something along the lines of *'watch out
for her, baby. She's crazy. She'll probably get you arrested if you party
together.'* Which," he points toward her, "come on, it's true. You get in
all sorts of trouble on your own. I don't know Andi all that well, but
since you remind me of each other, what with the crazy gene, I bet
she's the same. Put you both together and we're facing an apocalyptic
end of the world scenario." He steps closer and pulls my chin up.
"You're not second best to me. You never have been."

"I asked you at the party why you weren't married yet." Andi steps into our space, uncaring that Marc's lips are barely an inch from mine. "You said the right girl married someone else." Her eyes travel between the side of Marc's face and mine. "And *you* told me the other week you're mid divorce. Oh my God. She's the girl who married someone else." She makes a sarcastic aww face. "You found each other."

"Alrighty." Scotch drags her away.

"You're not second best to me, baby." He moves close enough that his stomach brushes mine. Our baby kicks between us like it knows shit's heavy out here, but with the smallest shake of his head, Marc adds, "You never have to worry about me. I promise. I've been looking at you, and *only* you, for as long as I can remember."

"I'm sorry I flipped."

He smirks. "It was fair. She hugged me and called me her fiancé. She's a troublemaker, but she didn't mean any harm. She's not mean."

I shake my head softly. "Just silly."

He nods in agreement. "Kiss me now. Let's make up. I missed you, was waiting to smack your ass, but instead I get yelled at."

"I think–"

"Less thinking." He leans in closer. "More kissing." He presses his lips down on mine, and his darting tongue silences my words and washes away all my doubt and hormonal overreaction.

I want to say sorry for not letting him explain. I want to say sorry for being crazy, but with his large hands caressing my belly, his plump lips playing with mine, I figure we're both forgiven.

He pulls back slowly. Waiting until my eyes clear of lust, his beautiful lips pull up into a soft smirk. "My world's all better now."

"We're all okay. Everyone's safe."

"Mmm." He hums his confirmation and drops a soft kiss on my nose. "It was iffy for a minute there, but the gray's gone, and it's just you and me left standing. Everything's all better."

~

A LITTLE OVER an hour after Andi and I walked into the club, I walk Marc out to the parking lot to see him off. He'll go home, work, rest, whatever, then he'll be back to make sure my party hasn't descended into chaos – and to play his set for the night.

Pre-pregnant Meg would be happy to hang out all night, watch him play, have a few drinks and some fun.

But I'm not her anymore.

Now I'm Third-trimester Meg, wearing heels, I haven't had a nap today, and after this thing is done, I'll be Tired Meg.

I'll be going home and passing out, and when he gets in around three or four a.m., he can climb into bed beside me and snuggle until we wake hours later.

"Have fun. Be good."

I allow him to drop a kiss on my cheek. "You know me, I'm always good."

He grins and rubs my belly. "I do know you. I'm also trusting you not to get yourself arrested."

I scoff. "Oz wouldn't arrest me. We're tight. Not like that sourpuss Hank."

He looks at me with a silly brow quirked, as if to ask 'who's Hank?' but he doesn't. He has more pressing matters to discuss. "Oz won't arrest you, because he's about as irresponsible as you are. He might even be worse."

"Exactly–"

"But Alex will arrest you."

"He wouldn't!"

"He would. In a damn heartbeat. He arrested me. He almost arrested his own sister. If you're on the wrong side of the law, he'll bring you in every time. He does it to save us from ourselves, I think, but still. He does it."

I tilt my head to the side. "Wait. When did he arrest you?"

"Ah," he clears his throat nervously, "when I hit Luc."

"Which time?"

"The first time." He coughs again. "The time I found out about him and Kari."

"He really arrested you? That's intense. He's basically your brother."

"Yeah, and I honestly think he was doing us both a favor. I might've done something really bad that day if he hadn't stopped me."

I hold his shirt and pull him close. It looks like I want another hug – which he obliges – but really, I just want to keep him close while I speak. "About Luc. What he did today–"

"Yeah, about that." His emerald eyes blaze hot. "If he ever tries to block me from you and the baby again, not even Alex will stop me. He's already forfeited all familial loyalty, babe. He's nothing to me now except a man who thinks he can step in my way. If that was any other man in the street, I wouldn't let that shit go."

"But he's not just any other man in the street. It's Luc. I know you know that, Marc. I know you know he's just looking out for me. You guys need to work through your shit, because none of us are comfortable with the drama."

"There's no drama." He runs his knuckles over my cheek in a ridiculous attempt to calm me. "No drama. There's just me. And there's Luc. We're business partners as far as the band goes, but that's it. And since we're on the subject, I wanna see the seating chart for the wedding. I know your ass would happily seat me and him together just to fuck with me."

Oh really, he's gonna pick up an attitude about this? Cool. I'll play. "I'll seat you wherever the hell I need to seat you, Marcus, and if you bitch about it or move and mess up my work, you'll be in trouble." His eyes narrow in protest, but before he can speak, I add, "Not even Alex will stop me. I'm busting my ass for this wedding. I'm just about to start officially waddling because your baby's head is touching my vagina. If you screw up even a single thing – including, but not limited to the seating arrangements – then you'll be in trouble. Trust me, Six-month pregnant Meg is a pussycat compared to Nine-month pregnant Meg. And if you mess with me, any version of Meg will bust your ass and hold out till your dick shrivels up and falls off."

Eyes narrowed, a tick to his handsome jaw, those pesky strands of hair hanging in his eyes. Leaning forward and dropping an obligatory kiss on my lips, he turns and climbs into his truck and backs out.

I watch his truck pause at the corner leading onto Main, and when he sits there for a minute too long, I cock my head to the side in curiosity. Just as I begin to worry and consider running into the street, my phone dings in the pocket of my dress.

Taking it out and reading his name on the screen, I swipe it open and stop on the picture of a single flower. Beneath the pink rose, it says *'I'm sorry. I love you. I'll try harder.'*

Ugh. And now I feel bad.

Pulling my dress forward, I aim the camera down to catch my cleavage. Snapping a picture, I send it to him and wait to see how he reacts. Thankfully, the streets are mostly empty. He's been idling at that corner for minutes now, and not a single car has pulled up behind him until now. Thirty seconds after I sent my boob picture, he honks the horn and pulls out into the street.

We're both sorry.

We'll both try harder to be nice.

I turn to head back inside to find Andi, but come to a screeching stop when I find her behind me with a smirk on her face and her glasses still perched on top of her head. She studies my face and bites her bottom lip. "I saw what you just sent him. Hussy." I swap the weight between my feet. I'm reaching that point in my pregnancy that standing for too long hurts. Standing in heels hurts even more. "I'm really sorry for causing trouble between you guys. I had no clue you were together."

"It's…" Not *okay*. I don't know what it is. But I know it hurt, even if it was all a mistake.

"I truly had no clue," she continues. "He was just a guy I spoke to once. At that time, he *was* single. Though he did mention the girl who married the wrong guy. He was a fun guy to talk to. He was witty, smart, and we can't deny your man is sexy. It was a fun surprise to see him in there so I kinda just dropped my filter and went in for the hug."

"You dropped your filter?" I look up at her with a smile. "So before, when we were driving and you compared me to a cow, that was filters-up?"

She lifts her shoulders in an easy shrug. "Not really. I don't do well with filters, but I'd like to remind you of the sign that says twatasaurous in your car."

"Twatwaffle."

She laughs. "Same thing. But just so you know, that whole no filter thing means I can't lie for shit. And even if I could, I don't. Can't be fucked making up stories, can't be fucked trying to remember who knows what version of whatever bullshit I told. Nobody has time for that. So... when I say Marc's innocent, I want you to believe me. I'm not here to throw doubt into a solid relationship."

I look back to the street that he drove down. "We're okay. Marc and I... have an odd relationship. An odd history. Circumstances have pushed us together now." I rub my belly absentmindedly. "But we're really happy with how it's worked out. I had a minor freak out today, but we're okay, no doubt, and we'll probably have awesome make up sex when he gets home in the morning."

She laughs and presses her hand over my belly. "I'm glad you guys are fine. I nearly had a heart attack in there when I realized what I maybe did. And make up sex is always the bomb diggity. So that's something to look forward to tonight."

"That's true. And he does such good work."

"Bitch." She slaps my arm and pulls us back toward the club entrance. "He was single when I met him. Damn me for not wanting to get married on the first date. I could've had the perfect man."

"He asked you to marry on the first date?"

"It was implied. He handed over a goat, after all."

I laugh as we step into the darker club. "You have no clue. He has a cow. An actual cow named after me."

"Shut up!"

"True. And when he accidentally knocked me up after our first night together, he proposed marriage. Like he owes it to me because I'm pregnant. He's so archaic, I swear."

"Did you say yes?"

"No! It's a long story, but the bullet points are that I said no. I didn't want a pity proposal. Plus, I'm still working through my divorce with Drew. It's illegal to be married to two men at the same time, and my life was already messy. Married to one, pregnant to another, planning a third. I wasn't going to add engaged on top of that."

"Jesus, girl. You're busy."

"You have no clue." We stop when Luc steps up to us with concern etched across his face. "This here is another problem."

Andi cocks her head to the side and looks Luc up and down. "You're not with him too, are you?"

Luc and I smile. "You okay, Snitch?"

"Yeah." I step in quickly and allow a side hug. In the last six months, Luc has changed from the flirty crazy friend of the guy I'm having sex with, and in exchange, I seem to have inherited a brother.

A real brother who genuinely cares about my well-being. That's not to say Scotch and Angelo don't care about me, but, I don't know, it feels different with Luc.

There's a connection there. Purely platonic and non-sexual, but it's there.

"I'm fine. He's fine. He's gone home, he'll be back later." I step back and stand next to Andi. "You need to stop pissing him off. You jumping between us did *not* help anything."

"I'm not gonna just let him stomp around and shout at you."

"He wasn't shouting."

"But he was gonna. I might have jumped prematurely, but it was coming. He wasn't gonna force his way into your face unless you invited him."

"Yeah, well your chivalry is chipping away at shaky foundations. You need to fix that relationship, not continue to smash it down."

"Well, when we've built it up again, at least then I can sleep at night knowing I did the right thing by you even when I was scared of losing my brother."

Andi frowns and looks between us. "I'm lost. Seriously lost. You and Marc are fighting?"

"Luc and Kari are seeing each other."

"The pretty girl with freckles? Long curly hair?"

Luc smiles wide. "Yeah, the pretty girl. You met her at the engagement party?"

"No. I walked in on you guys making out in the bathroom. Backed my ass up out of there and went and got another beer."

Luc's eyes turn wide. "Oops."

"Why's Marc pissed?" She nods at me. "He's with *this* pretty girl. Why's he so worried about the other one?"

"Kari is Marc's baby sister," I explain quietly. It only takes her a second to grit her teeth and understand it all. "Exactly," I finish. I throw my arm over her shoulder to head to the back and collect the final things for Lindsi's bachelorette party. We have shit to do and a bride to surprise in barely over an hour.

19

MEG

A MISSING CHICKEN

Drinks.

Check.

Music; not the guys' band, just an epic playlist on Scotch's iPod.

Check.

Necklaces similar to those I was forced to wear at my party, but instead of pacifiers, Lindsi's have plastic dicks.

Check.

List of games to play.

Check.

Bride?

Missing.

I move around the main section of the club, past our long list of guests and groups of balloons and streamers. Stopping in front of Juliette – normally my lawyer, but tonight, she's my second in charge – I huff with frustration. "Is she on the way?"

"Alex said Oz said they're on the way."

"Alex said Oz said... Really?" I wait for her sassy expression to meet mine. "That's the best you've got?"

"Hey, cranky pregnant lady, what exactly do you expect me to have? Do you want me to text *her?* Because I can. I don't mind."

"No. Don't text her." I rub the heel of my palm into my ribs, because my long-limbed baby is happily kicking them out of alignment. "Do you know where they are?"

With a bored expression, she taps at her phone. The backlight illuminates her cherry red lips and the long blonde hair that hangs over her shoulder. The club lights are out. The sun works its way down in the sky. The club has strobe lights flashing, but it's not really enough to see too much detail. We're ready to party, but the bride is missing, and though Oz and I had planned for her to be here at six, it's now six-twelve and she's fucking with my plans.

"He just replied; *Two-minutes-ETA.*"

"*ETA.* Jesus, are we in an episode of... something! I can't even think of any police TV shows right now."

"CHiPS." Kit stops beside me in a backless silver top and tight lift-your-ass jeans. "Brooklyn 99. CSI?"

Britt steps in behind her. "Police Academy."

"Robo-Cop," Jules adds with a smirk. "21 Jump Street."

"If you don't stop listing off shows, I'm gonna hit you."

"Oh! Miami Vice," Kit adds.

"Hawaii 5-0," Andi adds when she steps up with a drink already in her hand and the straw held between her tongue and teeth. "Why are we naming TV shows? Is this one of the games tonight?"

"Yep," Kit answers before I can. "Now we have to name inspirational movies. Go."

"Flashdance!"

I glare at Kit, but she simply smirks and cocks her head to the side. "What's the problem, yo? Flashdance is a good movie."

"Dirty Dancing," Britt throws in. "Shawshank Redemption."

I shake my head as though to shake away the stupid. "Shawshank Redemption? What the hell is the matter with you?"

She shrugs and sips at Andi's offered drink. "What? That was inspirational as hell. The way Andy– oh, hey. Andy and Andi." When the girls finish grinning at each other, her eyes come back to mine.

"What? The way he dug his way outta there. The way he fucked that warden up. He's my hero."

"Sidekicks," Kit adds easily. "The movie. Chuck Norris. Best movie *ever* made."

"Anything Chuck Norris touched was the best movie ever made."

"Oh, for fuck's sake." I walk away, down the club stairs, across the main dancefloor, and to the exit. I used to be so much fun. I would've been up there drinking with Andi and poking fun at the party warden, too. But this new me is cranky and tired and no fun at all. This party needs to go off without a hitch, and Lindsi better have a good friggin time.

Any hope that the wedding will be fine and easy and automated so I can sit and relax too, has flown out the window in the last hour. I can't even relax at the bachelorette party, so no way in hell will I be able to relax at the wedding.

I silently poke my head out into the early evening just in time to catch sight of Oz's shiny black truck pulling into the parking lot. Slamming the door shut and spinning on my heels, I cup my mouth and shout at my twenty or so guests, "She's here! Get ready."

Heart racing, adrenaline pumping, anyone would think I'm going into battle, when really, I'm simply preparing the same kind of surprise that I was given so recently.

Kit, Tink, Tina, Izzy, and Britt – the *Rollers* – race down the iron staircase with drinks in their hands, and beautiful hair flying with their movements. Sammy and Kari screech like silly girls as they grab their drinks and dart down the staircase next. Juliette moves her ass, too, but she's not nearly as frantic as everyone else.

I stand close to the door in a small alcove shrouded by darkness. I could stand here and Lindsi would walk right by me, so sticking to that plan, I press my back to the wall and watch my party guests giggle and scramble.

I swear, I had no clue about my surprise party, but the guest list is almost identical to tonight's. How did they manage to surprise me without the giggles, but tonight they can't shut up?

Alcohol. That's the damn difference.

"I thought we could come into the club for date night tonight, Angel. Ben promised he'd stop being a dick. He's got Livi's back and he won't let anything go wrong, so we have until eight before the curfew hammer comes down."

Lindsi snickers as Oz opens the door. "I can't believe my son gives you curfews.

"Mm," Oz rumbles. He's distracted. He's also unsure why the hell he lets his sixteen-year-old step-son dictate their curfew.

"And I can't believe you actually listen to him. No doubt we'll be walking back in the door at seven-fifty-nine, because you don't wanna upset your boyfriend."

"Hm." Again, with the self-deprecating rumble.

"Wait." Lindsi stops barely a foot from me. If she simply yawned and stretched, her hand would touch my belly. "Are they not open? It's not a public holiday, is it?" She checks her watch like it can tell her the date.

Actually, it probably can.

I poke my head out behind Lindsi and wonder where the fuck my 'surprise' is, but nothing. Silence.

They suck at this shit!

"They're open, Angel. I talked to Tink when I made the reservation. I don't know what their problem is, but I know someone is here." His voice is a low grumble. He's pissed that they didn't jump out and surprise her yet. He's just about to fire me.

Oh my God, I hate these people.

I step out behind the couple at the same time heels clink casually on the iron staircase across the room.

Lindsi allows Oz to remove her coat, so she doesn't notice Andi on the stairs, but when he turns and tosses the coat over me and shoots a glare, I realize maybe my secret hiding space isn't immune to cops.

Drat.

With her arms in the air like she was a flag girl in the hot lane between two revving cars, Andi moves down the stairs like Miss Universe on her victory lap. "Welcome to the jungle, Twat. I missed your pretty face."

Lindsi's eyes snap to the stairs. Letting out a squeak and mini jig, she leaves Oz in her dust and sprints across the club and up the stairs. The girls meet halfway up the stairs and crash tackle each other until they're a mass of long limbs and squealy giggles on the staircase.

"That was almost a fail, Snitch."

"Jesus, I know." I step out of the shadows with a hand on my heart and Lindsi's coat still in my arm. "They say not to work with kids or animals. They should change that to 'never work with Andi. Ever, ever, ever.' She's a damn menace."

He chuckles, and with folded arms, watches his soon to be wife practically make out with her cousin on the staircase. "They miss each other so much."

"I don't see the draw," I admit on a laugh. "They're nothing alike."

He shrugs and studies the rest of the club. "One guest at this party? That's all you got?"

"No! There are another twenty people here somewhere. I don't know what their game is, but seeing as Lindsi is smiling right now, I figure Andi has a plan. A plan she didn't think to tell me about." I turn and clutch at his muscular arm. "What if she has an alternate plan for the wedding, too? All my planning could be for nothing if Andi decides she wants to run the show."

"Don't worry about it," he rumbles. "She'd never ruin the wedding. Do whatever you've planned. She'll just add her dramatic flair here and there."

"Awesome." Not awesome. Not at all. "Be kind to me if the wedding goes to shit."

He throws his arm over my shoulder and pulls me in for a side hug. "I don't know if you remember, Meg, but not only are you planning my wedding for free, but you're literally delivering for free. I have to pay for the food we eat, that's it. You're not working for me, hon. You're giving me a huge gift."

"But if I screw it up–"

He looks down at me with playful whiskey colored eyes. "Stop. Think. Are you gonna screw it up?"

"No way in hell."

"Exactly. I trust you, and even if it turns out to be a giant disaster, as long as my bride is holding my hand while we watch the shit show, then I call it a win. Relax. It'll be fine."

"Yeah…" He might think it'll be fine, but it's not so simple for me. He'll get the bride, but if it all goes to shit, I can't very well launch a business off of a shit show.

"Speaking of… Have you made alternate plans in case you drop your baby in the aisle?"

I shove him off when he laughs at my scandalized face. "I will not drop my baby in the damn aisle. Jesus, Oz! What's the matter with you?"

"Just checking…"

"Well, don't. I have everything organized, including a hospital bag in the trunk of my car, just in case. But you don't know me very well if you think I'm letting this baby out before I'm damn well ready. Mama ain't playing."

Holy, shitake mushrooms.

That's the first time I've ever referred to myself as Mama.

Shit's getting real. "Everything's planned down to the second. So long as Andi doesn't go off script, it could all work even if I'm not in attendance." As in, in case my baby has killed me. "I'll have this thing worked down to the second, so don't you go off script, either. That'll piss me off. This is my wedding now, not yours."

He chuckles quietly, and when the girls on the stairs finally climb to their feet, he pats his back pocket. "That's my cue. I'll get out of here."

"You'll be back at nine, won't you?"

He flashes an attractive smirk. "You betcha. Club's open to the public at nine, which means my ass will be here to dance with her. But don't think for a second I'll be the only one. I know for a fact Aiden and Bobby Kincaid have plans to be here. Where Bobby goes, Jon goes. Where Izzy goes, Jimmy goes. I know X said he'll *swing by*, which is code for *'I'm eager as fuck, but can't sound eager because that's not cool.'* Jack follows Britt anywhere she goes. Then we know your guys will be here playing. So really, that's everyone."

"What about the kids?"

He shrugs. "My kids are set. Benny promised he'll stay in with Liv. I trust that asshole with my life, so my house is set. The Kincaid kids aren't my problem, but I'd put good money on tonight being grandma's night. I dunno about Squeak and Charlie Bear, but seeing as those girls are yours, I bet you know."

Yeah, I do. Babysitters.

"Tonight's gonna get messy." He bumps my shoulder with his. "Keep it clean, keep it in this club. You have a whole slew of moms here who are getting their first night off in forever. I'm telling you now, you *need* us here at nine."

"I think shit's already messy. The rest of my party literally still haven't even jumped out to surprise Lindsi." We turn and watch Lindsi and Andi move down the stairs arm in arm. They whisper and giggle and sip drinks that appeared out of thin air. "You can stay if you wanna." Please. Pretty please.

He smiles and takes Lindsi under his arm when she reaches us. "Nope. I have shit to do. You three have a fun night planned. Go all out." He brings Lindsi's mouth up to his. It's purely indecent and has my non-prudish self looking away. "Have fun, Angel. I'll see you later."

"You're not staying?"

"No. This is a chick thing, but I'll be back later to check on you. We'll have our own fun then."

She smiles shyly, as though he's a boy she just met, when really, he's a man that cherishes the ground she walks on. "*Te amo,* Oscar."

"*Te amo,* Angel. Don't kiss the other boys. I won't like it."

As Oz lets himself out the way he entered, the three of us turn and head toward the bar. "He told me we were going out to dinner. I had no clue it would be girl's night out. This'll be fun." We stop at the bar. Dropping her clutch on the countertop, Lindsi turns back to study the empty club with a genuine smile on her face. "It's weird being in here when it's empty."

I turn to Andi and glare behind Lindsi's back. "Yeah, it is weird when it's *empty*. I didn't expect to be the only ones here."

She smiles tartly behind Lindsi, and turning back with a sweet smile when Lindsi spins, she adds, "So, you guys wanna smoke some weed?"

"SURPRISE!"

I jump and maybe push half my baby out when our entire party jump up behind the bar with drinks in their hands and send party poppers and streamers flying over our heads. Lindsi squeals and clutches her chest, though all cool bananas, Andi simply shrugs and sips.

Kit and Tink literally climb up onto the bar. Sliding over the other side, they jump forward and sandwich a happy-crying Lindsi in a group hug. Following suit, Izzy and Tina also climb over the bar.

Within thirty-seconds, twenty sets of feet have stood on that bar, and at least half a dozen sets of panties have been flashed as they climb over and down one handed without spilling a single drop of alcohol.

True skill. True class.

I turn to Andi with a hand on my hip. "What the hell? They were supposed to jump out ten minutes ago!"

"That's not on me." She pops her hip back and mirrors my attitude. "I came out when I was supposed to. They had their own plans."

"You did *not* come out when you were supposed to! Nobody did. You made a grand entrance like a damn diva."

"Oh please." She pulls me in for a hug. "You're jealous because normally you're the diva. Baby's cramping your style." She steps back and sips her almost empty vodka and tonic. "I'm the new, single, not pregnant, hotter diva around here, and you're pissed because you have to be all responsible and shit these days." She pops her brow. "Tell me... How do those apples taste?"

"Bitter and yucky."

She laughs at my scrunched lips. "You're hooking up with a sex God on the regular, and you have his offspring in your tummy. You live in this town with all these awesome people. I'm saying you'll be just fine. And seeing as you're already basically overdue, you'll be able to drink and party again soon."

"I'm not almost overdue! I still have months."

Her perky nose scrunches the exact way I know, *I know,* mine would if I was the single hot chick talking to the unfortunate pregnant woman. "You should probably get a second opinion, Meg. I don't think babies are supposed to grow that big."

I narrow my eyes to slits. She's just being a jerk. I'm not even that big. In fact, my belly is cute, perky, like a basketball smuggled under my dress, but, "You're an asshole! I'm glad you live on the other side of the country, because if we saw each other daily, I think we'd clash. Hard. There's not enough room for both of us in this town."

She rolls her eyes and slurps the last of her drink. She rattles the ice cubes around obnoxiously. "You don't mean that. You and I are one and the same; I'm just the single version of you. And who knows; I might be looking to move soon."

"Here? Really?" That got my attention.

"Like I said, who knows. I'm young and single. I can go anywhere I want. Lindsi took my babies away, so maybe I wanna follow them. Ben was my *boi,* even if he was a cranky shithead. And my pregnant friend Meg has a shiny new house with extra rooms. That's what I heard, anyway. I could bunk with you guys. I could be the ham in your sandwich. The cream to your cookie. The milk to your shake."

"Andi!"

"He looks good when he walks into the kitchen every morning for coffee, doesn't he?" She bounces her brows obnoxiously. With a huff, I try to look stern, but now I'm imagining Marc in the mornings.

Shirtless.

Those back dimples.

He always prepares my one and only coffee of the day and has it ready and waiting on the counter for when I come out of the bathroom. When I whine that it's not enough, which I do every single day, he then makes me a cup of hot chocolate or tea to chase the initial boost of caffeine.

She leans down to catch my vacant eyes. "You fantasizing about him right now?"

"Shut up. Yes. But shut up."

She drops her now empty glass on the bar and squeezes my arm.

"I'm kidding, friend. I won't perve on your man. Taken is taken, and there are plenty of other sexy people in this town. I'll be bringing my A game to that wedding, especially since I get to wear that bomb ass dress Lindsi picked." I picked it. Lindsi said she doesn't care. "I might be a white chick, and she might be marrying a Latino man, but that dress makes my ass look Latina." She holds her hands up in a cupping motion. "Makes my ass look awesome. I promise not to mess up your perfectly choreographed plans, but I also plan to maybe make out with someone in the coat closet."

"Who? And I don't care, just don't lose track of time in there when you have work to do."

"Deal. And I don't know who. We'll figure it out on the day, but I wonder if Oz's junior is still interested…"

"Riley?" I hitch my ass up onto a bar stool. My feet are officially screaming at me in protest. "Riley's such a sweetheart. He used to drive me home from work a lot."

"Yeah? So he's as sweet as I figured, then? That's a bit gross. After Marc told me he was unavailable to marry that time, he pushed me toward the sexy Riley. Nice broad chest. Jeans that weren't too tight in the front." She scrunches her nose. "Some chicks might dig that, but I don't. I don't wanna know what he's packing until I get to unwrap it. I don't wanna see his dick because his jeans are squishing his balls into his throat."

I nod seriously. I get what she's saying. Marc wears his jeans exactly right. Tight in the ass, not tight in the groin. Exactly right.

"Riley was a true gentleman that night. Maybe a little *too* nice for me, seeing as he didn't even look at my boobs once." She points at them. "And we've already established they're awesome, but who knows… He might've gotten meaner in the last six months. A dangerous job makes a man harder. Maybe he's seen things." Her voice turns ominously low. "Killed men. Broken kneecaps."

I laugh and walk away when her eyes turn dreamy and she fantasizes about sweet Riley in a gun fight or breaking up a huge drug ring. I haven't heard of any of those going down in town lately, but you never know. Stranger things have happened, and if anyone was going to stumble onto it, Andi's the girl.

I walk through my milling friends. I have games to play and announcements to make, but I don't want to cause a ripple in the already entertained crowd.

Lindsi jumps on me two drinks later, after she's been hugged and given hugs to every person here.

Clutching at my arm, she spins me around in my heels so dangerously, I thank my daddy for paying out the ass for all those lessons on balance. "Thank you, Meg! This is the coolest surprise ever."

I hold her arms to give myself space. I'm kind of sick of people touching me. Marc's hands seem to be the only hands that don't feel claustrophobic lately. "You're welcome." I look her up and down – she's so happy – but with an *'oh!'*, I turn to the bar and take out her decorations.

Just like at my baby shower, Lindsi has her own crown and necklaces, but since this is her wedding, she also gets a sash and a magic fairy wand, too.

Only the best for the bride-to-be.

I check my watch and count down. "We have an hour and a half until the club's opened to the public. I have it on good authority your man will be back then. As will all the guys. The band will be stepping in a little earlier to finish getting their shit ready for their set, so we have an hour left alone to celebrate you." I turn and pull Tink into our group as she attempts to move past. "The fryers are ready to go. Choose anything off the menu that she knows how to cook, and that's your dinner. Eat, drink, have fun, then everyone can enjoy their night."

She cups my face with sparkling eyes. "You've made this entire experience amazing. I want you to know that."

"Aw, it's okay, just my j–"

"Not just your job!" She plops a juicy kiss square on my lips and sends my brows up in surprise.

Lindsi and I aren't friends, exactly.

She's just a friend of my friends. We talk business, but she hasn't told me her secrets. And now she's emotional and kissing me on the lips. "You've taken something that I was terrified to attempt a second time, and you've made it beautiful and easy. You've made me excited for my wedding day when, sure, I was excited to be with Oz for the rest of my life, but the actual day, the prep, it was terrifying for me. You've made it so I can go to my wedding and enjoy myself almost as though I were a guest."

I take her hands with a shy smile. She's most of the way to drunk already, but I understand what she's trying to say. I can relate. "You *are* a guest at that wedding, Linds. The guest of honor. Your only job is to wake up, get pampered, walk twenty yards from your car to your man, and eat and drink until your dress pops open. After that, I figure Oz will have it under control and you can just lie down."

She smacks my arm, but her eyes twinkle. "You're being dirty."

"Maybe. But he'll have the specifics under control. I just want you to relax. Enjoy. That first marriage was your trial run. This time it's the real thing."

Her brows pull in tight like she's ready to cry. "And if your baby is giving you trouble, if you deliver early, if you deliver on the day, I promise not to be upset. You do you, and everything else will be fine."

"I'm not going to have my damn baby at the wedding! Does no one understand the power of thought? Stop telling the universe I should have my baby at the wedding, because now you're willing it to be. Quit it."

She slurps at a fresh drink that Izzy presses into her hand. "Sorry." *Burp.* "Was just trying to say that it's okay if you need medical leave or whatever. We'll deal."

"*You* don't deal with anything." I poke her shoulder. "*You* put on that huge dress and figure out how you'll pee while wearing it. The rest is up to me, and I *won't* be dropping a baby on your reception dance floor."

Izzy's head tips to the side with curiosity. "Why you so cranky, Meg? Hormones wreaking havoc? Baby giving you trouble?"

"No! Jesus, shut up about my hormones. This is supposed to be a bachelorette party! Have some damn fun or I'll be flipping the lights on and sending you all home early."

"No!" Lindsi spins into Izzy and they take off like I'm the warden with all the power. I'm not, I'm just Un-fun Meg who set out to be more responsible and grown-up six months ago, and now look at me.

Pregnant.

Living with a man.

Not drinking.

And I'm the voice of the reason and the supervisor to make sure these fools don't get arrested tonight.

Where did I go wrong?

It wasn't that long ago that I needed the supervision. It wasn't so long ago that cute-man Hank arrested me for going wild on my husband and his whore with a slugger, which reminds me, I should talk to Jules about an update. Last I heard, Drew was submitting his bullshit *not-guilty* plea.

I turn in search of Jules, only to come to a screeching halt when I find her and Andi dancing on the top of the bar. Drinks held above their heads, cute outfits and heels sparkling in the strobe lights.

Tonight's not the night my lawyer gives me a well thought out and educated answer.

20

MARC
LUC'S BABY MAMA

"So what exactly does a Lamaze class do?" I turn to watch Meg nervously fuss with her purse, but seeing as we're driving, I can't watch her freak-out for long. "Baby?" I take her hand in mine and bring them to my lap. "Why are you so nervous?"

She shrugs and watches out the window as we cruise into town. "Not nervous. And I don't know. I guess they teach us what to expect, how to breathe, how to swaddle a baby. That sorta stuff."

"It's one hour?"

"Yeah, but for six weeks. One hour a night, every Wednesday for six weeks. Katrina thinks this shit is funny, so she's not even mad that I rostered Wednesdays off for this."

"You should be backing off of work, anyway. Look at your belly. Aren't you uncomfortable?"

Her eyes snap my way. "Look at *your* belly! Aren't you uncomfortable?"

I chuckle and release her hand so we can turn onto Main street. As soon as I'm in gear and cruising again, I forcefully take her hand and bring it back to my lap – seeing as she's being a stubborn ass. "I'm fine, but thank you for asking, beautiful. And for the record, I wasn't trying to offend you. I just meant that you work so hard, you need to rest. By the time the baby's here, we won't be getting any sleep for a while, so we should be treasuring what we have for now."

She shrugs nonchalantly and goes back to staring out the window. "I have to work, Marc. I can't just dump everything because I feel like it."

"Everyone who knows you cares about you, baby. We just want you rested and happy, including Katrina and the guys."

Again with the shrugs. "I'm okay, I'm already taking Wednesdays off, then by the time these classes end, I'll be thirty-six weeks. Just about time to pop."

"And you'll rest then?"

"Well, I'll still have the wedding, but I can do most of that sitting on my ass." She turns to me with a smile. "I love technology."

There she is. I bring our clasped hands up to my lips and press a kiss to her knuckles. "Love you, beautiful."

She smirks arrogantly. "You're kinda alright too, I guess."

I shake my head and release her hand, downshifting as we pull into the hospital parking lot. "It's weird that the class is being held here."

"Not really." She unclips her seatbelt and collects her things. "I mean, this is where the baby will be born, right? It's not surprising they have us here to familiarize us with where to go and stuff."

"Yeah, I guess." I climb out of the truck and jog around to her side. Just like so long ago – but add a big beautiful belly full of my baby – I open the truck door, take her delicate hips, and let her slide out. Her belly slides along mine and her hands rest on my shoulders. She looks up at me with a sweet smile.

Meg has so many facets of her personality; obviously the loudest is cockiness, but deep inside is this shy little dancer girl, and when she looks up at me with that smile, I see the gooey center she keeps hidden from everyone else in the world.

"I love you." I lean down and drop a kiss on the corner of her lips. "It took a long time and a lot of shit to get here, to get you to me, but I don't regret it." Her eyes turn softer. Her hands hold onto me tighter. "Even though you could break me, even though you did, I'd do it again and again if it meant I could call you mine."

Her jaw wobbles – as predicted. She steps up onto her tiptoes, pulls my head down, and presses a kiss to my lips the same way I did hers. "I love you, too. I might act invincible, but you have that power over me, too. You should know that before you break my heart."

"No. No more broken hearts. There's nothing we can't overcome now."

She pulls back to look into my eyes. "Promise?"

I nod gently and pull her as tightly to my body as we can manage without squishing her belly. "I promise. We're in it for life, now. You're gonna be seventy years old, dancing in our kitchen. My little dancer, you'll have me rocking boners for you when I'm geriatric."

She laughs and presses her face to my chest. "Such a romantic speech, then it turns into you being an old pervert."

"You'll always be two years older than me, Poot. Never forget that I'll always be your boy toy."

She slaps my chest. Spinning away, she takes off and makes me run to catch her. "Wait for me, baby."

"Stop talking about me being old. I'm already imagining tucking my tatas into my jeans."

I reach up and cup her breast. Running my thumb over her sensitive nipple, I watch our surroundings to make sure no one can see us. "I love your titties, Meg. Best I've ever seen, and they taste even better than they look."

She leans heavier into me as her breath comes out on a soft groan. "You can play with my boobies tonight if you wanna."

"You gonna dance for me? Bend over, touch your toes. Plié."

She looks up at me with a wicked smirk. "You want a thirty-week pregnant chick to dance for you?"

"No. I want *you* to dance for me. You have no clue how sexy you are to me, and you carrying my baby doesn't take away from that. If anything, it makes you sexier."

We step through the hospital automatic doors and stop at the front desk. Meg pulls out her ID. "Hello. We have Lamaze classes here at six."

"Montgomery? Sure. Take the elevator to the third floor and follow the pink lines on the floor. They'll take you where you have to go."

We start out again and move toward the elevators, and despite my general happiness, my teeth still gnash together at her last name. *Montgomery*. I mean, at least she didn't take that fucking idiot's name, but still, I wish it was Macchio.

Will my baby be Montgomery, too?

We walk into the elevator and step out again four floors later. Our feet automatically find the pink line, and though there's also a blue line heading in the opposite direction, and a yellow line heading in another direction, we follow the pink until we find the room of chattering parents-to-be.

Nervous energy permeates the air. Moms giggle with other moms they literally just met. Names are flung around in a 'what do you think of this' way, like complete strangers can and should help name your child. Dad's sit silently in their chairs and refuse to make eye contact with the other dads.

It's a veritable cornucopia of anxiety and nerves.

The room is set up with a large plastic mat in the center, unoccupied beanbags litter the mat, then a circle of chairs run a perimeter around it. A large TV on a stand sits idle on the back wall, and a basket of plastic baby dolls sits beneath a chair at the top of the group.

Awesome. We're going to be playing with dolls.

I lead Meg in and find spare seats toward the bottom end of the circle.

As far away from the teacher as possible to avoid having to do or say or help.

I hold onto her as she sits, then taking the seat beside her, I pull her hands into my lap and squeeze. "Nervous?"

Her eyes ping around the room in an attempt to take everything in. With a faux casual shrug, she shakes her head. "Nope. Not nervous."

"No?" I smile. "Really?"

"Terrified," she laughs nervously. "So nervous that I'm cold, and I don't even know why."

I pull her into my side and rub my hand along her arm for warmth.

"It'll be okay. No babies will be born today. We'll just be watching a movie and playing with dolls, then we're going home and you can strip for me."

She barely even notices my solicitation for sex, she's *that* nervous. She looks around at the other chattering parents nervously. "Why aren't I as excited as them, Marc? I heard that chick over there whine five times already that this has been the longest seven months of her life. I think this has been the fastest of mine."

"We don't all have to think the same, baby. Fast or slow, we've lived the exact same amount of time as she has. It's okay to be nervous."

She gives a jerky shrug and goes back to people watching. "I'm just nervous. And so busy. I wouldn't even care if I was pregnant for twelve months. Or thirty."

I continue to warm her arm. "You're busy creating an empire, baby. She's probably sitting at home knitting booties, or she's waiting to flee work for maternity leave. We're allowed to have different journeys. We'll all end up with a family at the end." I pull her in tight and bring her chin up so I can meet her eyes. "We got those blood test results back. You're in the clear, so try not to worry so much, yeah?"

She nods. In her head, she's saying 'shut the hell up', but to give me comfort, she nods and cuddles into me. She's still freaking the hell out, but she's trying not to.

And I don't know how to help her. I can't lift this weight. I can't take it away. I just need to hold her hand and try to talk her through her anxiety.

A few minutes after we walk in and sit down, a not-pregnant woman walks in and starts playing with the TV. She changes the channel from a plain blue screen to a black and white on pause.

Why are we still watching black and white films in this day and age? Have they not filmed a birth in the last decade?

"Oh, shit…"

My eyes snap down to Meg when her body turns tense, then when she doesn't look up at me, I follow her gaze to the door.

Luc stops on the threshold with a super pregnant chick under his arm. "Motherfuck–" His face pales as soon as he registers my murderous expression, though the woman is oblivious.

She's tall and blonde – just like Luc. Tight curls and caramel skin, her arms and legs are long and spindly, but her belly is about ready to pop.

I stand up with boiling blood. He's cheating on my sister. Not only cheating, but he has his own fucking family in the works.

Meg jumps up beside me and snags my hand before I storm across the room and throw his head through the TV. No one else has noticed his entrance. No one has noticed the thick tension in the air.

No one knows about this silent war except me, Luc, and Meg.

"You need to take a breath, Marcus."

"I need you to sit down, baby. Shit's about to get messy."

She clutches my hand between hers as tightly as she can manage. "If you hit him in here, I'll be epically pissed. I'm not playing right now. Take a breath and think it through. We know Luc. He's not hiding a baby mama in his broom closet."

"Seems he is." I pry her fingers away from my hand, but she refuses to sit when I push her back.

"It's not how it looks." Luc steps closer. The chick looks at each of our faces curiously, but when her eyes meet mine, she shies back and turns her eyes away. Luc takes a step forward to shield her from me. "You need to sit your ass down before you tear up this baby place. This is the wrong place, wrong time, and you've got the wrong idea."

"Fuck I do," I spit out almost silently. "Where's my sister?"

"She's at her place. Not working tonight."

"That's convenient. The one time you're in your place of employment without her, you're with someone else. What the fuck, Luca?"

"Stop." Meg grabs my hand and steps in front of me. Her belly almost touches the other chick's. "Marcus, stop. Luca, what the fuck?"

"I'm working, Snitch. This is work. Donna, meet my bes–" He bites off his sentence and reconsiders. "My friend Meg, and her man, Marcus. Guys, this is Donna."

"Donna?" Meg has to look up an inch or so to meet Donna's eyes. "Is that Luc's baby?"

Donna blushes and shrinks back. For such a tall woman, a beautiful woman that could demand attention from a room full of men, she acts as though she's four feet tall. "No, she–"

"Do you know Luc's girlfriend? Do you know he has a girlfriend?"

"Kari? Yes. She took me shopping this week."

"Donna's been having a rough time with her man," Luc grinds out through gritted teeth. "She made a really brave decision and moved out. I'm helping her with these classes, since she asked me to. Bear took her shopping for clothes on Monday, seeing as her clothes weren't returned to her when she asked for them." He rests his arm over her shoulders comfortably. "If you don't mind, please sit down and leave us be. Her case is none of your damn business, and you definitely don't get to question her reasons for being here. We can sit on the opposite end of the room if you prefer. Pretend we aren't here."

He's right. Of course he is, but fuck, seeing him with another woman sends my gut curdling. Seeing him with a *pregnant* woman sets me on fire.

I don't know what I want more; him to stray so my sister gets a clue and leaves him, or for him to stay, so as to not break her heart.

And seeing him with a pregnant woman only reinforces that if he and my sister do stay together, then this might be her future. Not the abusive man thing – especially not that – but the pregnant. The Lamaze classes.

It's like I'm being forced to choose between several really shitty options. Luc would never physically hurt Kari. Despite my prejudices against him, I know he'd never physically hurt her.

But what of her heart?

And if she does leave him, what if she meets a Drew, or a man like Donna's instead? Not all men are pricks, but some are. And one is too many when it comes to my sister.

Meg reaches out and takes Luc's spare hand. "Come sit next to me." My gaze snaps down to hers in a 'what the fuck?' but she ignores me and smiles at Donna. "It's nice to meet you. I'm sorry about these two. They have beef – unrelated to you. But you can sit with me. It'll be a nice distraction. I don't know about you, but I'm nervous as hell being here."

The girls make small chat, though they're both crapping their pants with nerves, but Luc and I continue our standoff.

He watches me with a twitching jaw. I watch him with narrowed eyes.

Both of us stand with flexing fingers like we're readying to draw and shoot.

Meg pulls Donna down beside her, and following, Luc backs up to sit beside her. I sit down next to Meg, and finally looking up, meet the teacher's eyes and realize someone else in this room did, in fact, notice us.

I give her a quick wave as though to say 'carry on,' but with her own set of narrowed eyes, she makes a mental note to call the cops if Luc and I so much as look at each other again.

Alex would *love* that call.

Not.

Meg looks between us with a huff of frustration as the teacher begins announcing what we're all doing here. Like none of us knew.

"Hello, Moms and Dads. My name is Kelly Hewaur and I'll be your instructor for the next six weeks. We're here because you're all in the business end of a pregnancy. For most of you, this is your first time at these classes, though that's not always true. Sometimes we have repeaters coming back for refreshers. We have a curriculum that we'll follow over the next month and a half, and by the time we're done, most of you will be mere weeks out from delivering your baby." She bends down near her seat and picks up a doll.

"I'd like to start by going around the room and introducing ourselves. Give us your name, how many weeks you are, if this is your first baby or not, and anything else you'd like to share. You don't have to be shy; by the time we're done here, a lot of you will be friends with each other. For some of you, this is your first contact with other parents. That's how we create that village that the generations before us like to talk about."

"I'm good without."

Meg elbows me, painfully digging in right between my ribs and snapping my torso straight. I glare down at her. "What?"

"Shush." She's not stupid. She knows who I was talking about. I look over her shoulder to find an equally unexcited Luc staring at the front of the room, but I see his twitching jaw. I see his flexing hands.

"Just saying I don't want some people in my village."

"And I'm just saying that if you don't stop carrying on like a whiny baby, then I won't dance for you. Ever."

Luc smothers a smirk, which only pisses me off more. He shouldn't be listening. He shouldn't be hearing her talk about personal shit like that.

He shouldn't even fucking be here!

It takes almost ten minutes of other new parents yammering on about their pregnancies and how over the moon they are before it gets to Meg and me, but seeing as I might just tell Luc to go fuck himself instead of introducing us, Meg stands before I can.

"Hello. I'm Meg. He's Marc."

"Hello Meg and Marc." Kelly smiles warmly. "How many weeks are you?"

"Thirty weeks," she answers easily. "And we don't know if it's a boy or a girl. Waiting for the surprise."

"Oh, that's nice. And what are you hoping for? What about your husband?"

I think I was supposed to stand and speak.

"I don't really mind which we get," Meg continues to answer for us both. "I don't think he *cares* either, but he seems to think it's a boy. Oh, and he's not my husband." She points at her belly. "This was a one-night stand. I'm actually married to someone else."

And there she is. I should've fucking stood.

Kelly's face pales. She clutches the little doll to her chest and takes a stricken step back as though Meg was holding a puppy over an open fire. "Oh, well…"

"We're not sorry, exactly," Meg continues. "It was a fun night, but damn this is a stubborn baby. Which probably means it's a boy. Stubborn like its father."

"Alright." I stand and yank her until she sits again. The moms-to-be look scared like Kelly, but the dads smirk and look at the floor. "Luc, stand up."

He scoffs, takes Donna's hands and brings her to her feet. "Hi everyone, I'm Luc. This is Donna. I also have a girlfriend at home, Kari." My jaw clenches tight at my sister's name. "This wasn't a one-night stand, but it's not conventional, either. We're thirty-two weeks, first time parents." He looks down at Donna. "Anything else, honey?"

She smiles at the floor. "It's a girl."

"Oh yeah!" Luc turns back to Kelly. "A beautiful baby girl. A girl who, as her pseudo daddy, I'll look after for the rest of my life like a bear and his cubs, but once she's grown and moved out, once she becomes a nurse and not a doody-head with no brainpower or free will, then I'll step back if her perfect man were to come along and promise a lifetime of loyalty and servitude. You know what I mean?" He looks around the group for allies. "I'll be her protector for now, but once her *real* protector comes along, I'll take a step back and not break families up over something that should be good news."

"Um… okay." Kelly turns away in quick dismissal. Flipping off the lights, she presses play on the TV. "Thank you, Luc and Donna. Please take a seat. We have a twenty-minute video to watch, then we have some breathing exercises to work on."

Luc helps his temporary date sit beside Meg, and though both girls smile at my expense, Luc simply goes back to glaring at the TV.

I guess he's past the 'be nice to Marc and beg for forgiveness' phase of this shit, and now he's joining me in pissed territory.

Fine with me!

I'll get in less trouble with Meg next time I hit him if he's being a smartass prick rather than the meek little girl he never used to be before this began.

Meg leans into me and squeezes my leg just above the knee. "If you retaliate, I'll lace your soup. I'm not playing."

My eyes snap down to hers. Her words were just a whisper, but the venom behind them was loud and clear. "I didn't do anything."

"You're thinking about hitting him. I know you better than you

222 | EMILIA FINN

think, Marcus. If you hit him, I'll run you down with your own tractor. This shit isn't funny anymore."

"It was never funny!" I hiss out. "It was never funny to me."

"Quiet in the back, please."

Meg and I look up to Kelly. I have a feeling we won't be welcome back for our final five classes.

Whatever.

Meg already knows how to breathe. She's been doing it her whole damn life.

We watch a show where everyone speaks with a British accent for twenty minutes. It might not be the worst twenty minutes of my life, but it's pretty shit anyway, and as an added bonus, we get to watch some chick give birth to a baby while she swears at her man with that weird accent.

'You did this to me, you bludgering idgit, didn'ya?'

Barely seconds before I pry my eyeballs out and feed them to Luc, the lights flip back on and the TV, off.

"Alright. I'd like everyone to make their way to the mats. Men, help your ladies to the floor, collect whatever pillows you need, then sit behind her and let her lean into your lap."

Meg jumps up quick as a flash despite her heavy belly. Moving to the corner of the room, she grabs pillows and torpedoes them at Luc. He catches them easily and lies them down in two piles.

One pile for him and Donna. One for me and Meg.

I roll my eyes when I notice how close the piles are. If I have to sit within two-feet of him, I might snap his neck.

Meg moves back through the circle of chairs and stops beside Donna. Taking matters into their own hands, they hold hands and lower each other to the floor while Luc and I simply glare at each other.

"Dads, sitting down, please."

I turn with a lifted lip, and lowering myself to the floor, I sit beside Meg, though I notice the other couples sit with the girl between the guy's legs like how a couple might sit together in the bath.

Like how Meg and I *have* sat in the bath.

I tap her arm and begin bringing her closer. "Alright, come on, baby." It could be worse. Sitting with her in my arms isn't a hardship.

"Nah, Donna and I are gonna pair up." She scoots in the opposite direction and sits behind Donna. Bringing her belly to Donna's back and running her straightened legs out beside Donna's, they get awfully fucking comfortable while Luc and I watch on in surprise.

"Baby?"

"We think you and Luc need some snuggle time. Go for it. Donna and I can breathe together, and besides, Luc has a girlfriend, so humping someone else's back isn't a good look while his future brother-in-law watches."

"So, you'd rather we humped each other's back? Get the fuck outta here, Poot."

Kelly coughs frantically at the front of the room. She's like a matron ready to whip us for our indiscretions. "Please be quiet back there. You're upsetting some of the other parents."

"Not upsetting me," one of the other dads laughs. He sits with his wife in his arms, but his eyes are on us. "It's more entertaining than that *bludgerin'* movie."

His wife snickers in his arms, though she's not nearly brave enough to meet my eyes like her man is. Kelly turns back to me with an evil snarl. "Sit, partner up, or leave."

I scoot so fast to Luc's back, my ass feels the friction through my jeans. "Dibs on being the dude."

Luc spasms forward when my legs hug his. "I'm not the bitch!"

"Today you are, bitch. Sit, submit, shut the hell up."

"Absolutely n–" His words cut off at Meg's glare.

"If you two don't shut the hell up, you'll be in trouble. Nobody thinks you're funny. Sit, breathe, have a fucking baby, but shut the hell up."

Luc sits back as though truly terrified by her words. I mean, she's scary, I get it, but she won't actually hurt us.

Probably.

Kelly watches us. She officially hates us. She was coming to work tonight to meet excited new parents, and instead, she got the group of assholes with one-night stands and odd daddy-daddy pairings. "Alright," she starts warily. "Lean back into your partner–"

I lean forward until my lips are barely half a foot from Luc's ear. My skin crawls with how emasculated I feel, but at least I'm not the bitch. "I'll kill you," I whisper. "I'll kill you like that big fucking bear you're scared of. I'll never give her to you."

"Too bad, motherfucker." His words are as quiet as mine. Meg and Donna can probably hear us, but if they can, they don't mention it. They continue to listen to Kelly discuss the importance of breathing. Well duh, it's important.

We'd be dead without it.

"She's already mine," he continues. "She ain't your baby anymore. She's *mine*. She's crazy as shit for it, but make no mistake, she chooses me. And for as long as she chooses me, I'll fight you for her. Brotherhood comes second to her, and it will for the rest of my life. You better adjust, Macchio, because she'll be coming to classes just like this one day. She'll be coming with me, wearing my ring, carrying my baby. You don't get to make those decisions for her."

"Fuck I don't." I send a short and sharp jab into his kidney. "She can't be yours if you're dead. Watch your surroundings, prick. I'll deal with her sads after I get rid of you. This shit with you and her ain't real, so she'll be sad until the ice-cream sundae arrives at lunch, then she'll be good to go."

"You want her to marry Roy instead?"

My head whips back in surprise. "Who the fuck is Roy?"

He nods. "Exactly, asshole. Better the devil you know, right? You know me, but your ass doesn't know him. You better know that if I'm not around, he will be. Remember that next time you wanna get your panties in a twist." He throws his elbow back and lands a jab against my sternum. "She's mine. Not his and not yours. Not anymore. Move over, big daddy. You take care of your new family, and I'll take care of her."

21

MEG
LINDSI'S BIG DAY

I can't believe I've become this person, but I bring the cellphone to my ear, and when the line connects, I murmur almost inaudibly, "The package is en route. ETA twelve minutes."

And after I say that, Alex simply replies, "Copy that. Waiting at the drop point. We're set and on high alert."

And then, just to be even more ridiculous, I reply, "Copy that. Over and out."

I shake my head at my ridiculousness, but then I shake it off, shove Lindsi into the beautiful limousine that drove down from the city for this with the promise of exposure as the only payment, and when I tuck her amazing Lana Twain gown in and climb in after her, I grunt at my thirty-nine-week belly.

The baby's making its presence known today. Tight bands of pain radiate almost from my back, around my ribs and meet at my belly button. Like a progressive circle of pain, then it goes away.

Lana Twain also dressed me for today – as well as Andi and Lindsi's daughter – so, though my knee length peach colored sweetheart neckline dress was literally made to fit me, as in, Lana herself was in our house late last night sewing and adjusting around my rapidly changing shape, I could be walking around in sweatpants and sneakers and I'd still be grunting like a pig.

I will not drop my baby at this wedding.

I will *not!* I refuse.

I sit down beside Livi, across from Andi and Lindsi, and watch Lindsi visibly shake. I lean forward to take her hands, but give up when my baby won't allow it. "Andi. Hold her hand. Lindsi, pretend that's me."

Lindsi laughs nervously, but Andi does as she's told.

"Alright, sister." I poke my finger into the air between us. "You need to breathe. Cool it." I turn to Livi. "Can you pour her a couple fingers of vodka?"

"My twelve-year-old daughter is not pouring me liquor, thank you very much!"

I turn back with a victorious smirk. "There she is. Scared Lindsi is lame. Take Charge Lindsi is badass. You've got this, stop freaking out."

"I'm nervous. I'm going to get married... again."

"I know, but–"

"The last husband I had was... You know. In the head. By me!"

I shrug casually, pull Livi into my side when she smiles nervously, and turn back to Lindsi. "It's fine. You'll be fine. It's Oz, babe. Oscar Franks is waiting for you."

"He'll be there, right?" She brings her perfectly manicured nail up to her lips nervously. "He won't ditch me?"

"Andi?"

Andi slaps Lindsi's hand away from her mouth with perfect precision. We didn't even plan that one, but her ability to read my mind today is super helpful.

"Are you really spiraling that hard right now? Of course he'll be there. That man is obsessed with you!"

She nods as though she's giving herself an epic talking to in her mind. "Yeah, you're right. He will. He'll be there. Can we go over my parts again? I want to know what to expect, when to expect it. I don't want any surprises. I'm feeling a tad jumpy right now."

I wonder if the bride in every wedding I intend to plan in the future will be this nervous. God help me if they're worse. "You've already done a whole bunch, Linds. You woke up after a big restful sleep – no bags under your eyes, exactly as I ordered." I should've brought gold stars to reward her with. "You had your hair and makeup applied professionally. Thank you, Tracey G who was looking to impress rich people. Your dress is on, your shoes are on." I pull Livi closer into my side and use my right hand to cover her ear. "Your *'property of Oz Franks'* underwear are in place. Your garter belt is ready to be chewed off, and you've been waxed in every single place you need to be. For now, all you need to do is enjoy the ride."

We turn a sharp corner that sends Liv's elbow uncomfortably digging into my ribs. Cramps slice through my belly and momentarily steal my breath.

No! I will not drop this baby today. Positive thoughts, people. Don't will this to happen.

"We'll arrive at the church in about…" I check my phone and breathe through the radiating pain. I peek out the limousine window to confirm our position. "Seven minutes. Oz is there at the top of the aisle waiting for you. Ben's with him, and I have first-hand information that he has *not* been arrested once today."

Her eyes narrow, her blood-red lips thin. "Not funny."

"I wasn't being funny! Legit, he didn't get arrested today, so that's a win for team Conner. Once we arrive, Livi goes first. I'll straighten her dress, fix her bouquet, pat her butt and send her walking. She gets to meet her new daddy first."

Lindsi bursts into tears and slaps her hand over her mouth. "Her new daddy. Oh my God, Meg. Livi, baby–"

"It's fine, Mom." Livi leans forward and joins hands with her mom and Andi. "You aren't allowed to ask again if I'm okay with this. I love him, too. I wanna keep him."

Andi leans around Lindsi and wipes the tears from her eyes with precision. No messing up the makeup!

She's uncharacteristically silent today as she lets me do my work without her usual sauciness or smartassery. She definitely brought her A-game.

She looks amazing with her floor length silver gown. It doesn't have as many diamonds as the DonVicci gown I was supposed to wear before my soon-to-be ex-husband screwed me over, but it definitely still has diamonds. And beading. Andi spent most of her evening at my house last night, too, getting her non-Latina ass sewn into the Pippa Middleton inspired gown.

She's flirting with the *'you're not allowed to look better than the bride'* rule, but she looks so good, I don't think Lindsi even minds. The bride and her maid of (dis)honor share several similar physical traits. Add Liv, and three of the four people in this limousine share the same silky straight, midnight black hair and milky white skin. Natural blushes give their faces color. Good genes help them make their gowns stunning.

Livi's gown is only knee length, but where mine follows the line of my body and accentuates my belly, hers flares at the waist and provides an amazing opportunity to spin on the dancefloor tonight so she can watch the skirt twirl.

"Okay, three minutes to go. Take a drink if you need it. Getting back to our plan, Livi goes first. I'll smarten her up, straighten her dress, send her in. Then Andi. Hair, flowers, gown. Make sure she didn't tuck her dress into her undies in the last hour, then she's going in."

Lindsi's eyes dart from window to window as though in search of an escape. Her breathing accelerates until her chest heaves and stretches her dress. "Wait. I changed my mind!"

Andi and I turn in shocked silence. My worst nightmares are coming true. Well, not the worst. The worst is delivering my baby at the reception and promptly dying of an undiagnosed aneurysm. But next to that is Lindsi calling this whole thing off. "Changed your mind about what, exactly?"

"Alex."

"Alex? What the hell about Alex?"

"I'll be walking the aisle alone." Her voice trembles with nerves. "I was gonna be independent and stuff. I don't wanna. I want him to walk me. He's Oz's best friend."

"Okay, that's easy." That's not cancelling the wedding I've lived and breathed for months. "I'll make it happen."

"And Ben, too."

Now I'm starting to get nervous. "Okay. I'll make it happen. You need to calm down."

"No, wait. Just Ben."

"Lindsi! Pull your head out of your ass and make a damn decision!"

She stops shaking and immediately sits up straight. Her blush burns deeper, but her skittish eyes calm and her fidgeting hands slow. "I'm not mad you yelled at me. You did the right thing."

"Make a choice, Conner. You have one minute, then it's happening whether you like it or not."

"Ben. Just get Ben... Please. It's best if Ben gives me to Oz."

"Okay. Ben." I tap at my phone, though I can already see the church through the limousine window. I text Alex: *Get Ben's ass out the front. Now! Not a drill.*

He replies instantly: *Copy that.*

I can't even explain how weird it is for me to be talking Robo-Cop, but hey, I'm also nine months pregnant with a baby I said I'd never have. Stranger things have happened, and my newly learned language is barely registering at a two on my weird-o-shit meter.

The driver pulls into the large round driveway of an even larger white chapel. No cameras – that belong to paparazzi looking for the Rollers, anyway. One of two photographers contracted to this wedding waits out front and snaps images of our car pulling in.

I turn back to the girls. "It's go time. We're being photographed from here on out. These images will be on Lindsi's mantle for the rest of time, so make them exactly how you want them. You guys are beautiful."

"What's wrong with your face?"

I snap my gaze over to Andi. "'Scuse me, jerk?"

"Your face?" She leans forward until our noses are barely two inches apart, and though hers are beautifully made up with expensive – and fake – extra lashes, I still watch the way her eyes narrow. "Is your belly hurting?"

Yes. "No. Baby's rolling around. Doesn't hurt, though."

She watches me for so long, it feels like I'm standing in the west with my hands flexing beside my gun holster.

Who's feeling lucky, punk?

She leans forward another inch and reaches out to place her hand over my belly. Thankfully, my butterfly baby rolls around at that exact moment and kicks her.

It hurts like a bitch, but the timing is perfect.

"You need to pop a squat, you let me know. Don't be crowning and not tell us. I can't handle that kinda turmoil in my life."

"Pop a squat? Really?"

"Really. Stay close to the medical people at this wedding, just in case."

"I'll be fine, so stop willing it to happen. Livi, it's your turn, honey." I tap the window, and at my signal, the driver opens the door closest to me. Thank you, baby Jesus, the driver is old school and holds his hands out to help a woman from a car. I'm not entirely sure I could've managed it by myself. The girls would have had to shove from inside and push me out.

Emerging from the car into the midafternoon sun, I look up when Ben sprints out the doors and skids down the tall staircase four steps at a time. He's going to break his neck, I know he is. He's going to break his neck on my watch, and though I love the kid for rushing to his mama's side, I'll be pissed if he ruins today.

"Mom?"

I step forward and allow him to hold my arm. This standing gig is for suckers. "She's in there. Can't you see all the white? Your sister's drowning in wedding gown, but other than that, everyone's fine." We watch as Livi climbs out after me, then Andi. The photographer snaps picture after picture after picture, and stepping back so Lindsi can emerge all princess-esque, I tell Ben, "She wants you to walk her down the aisle. She wants you to give her away."

He swallows heavily when her heeled feet poke out the door, then the driver leans in to take her hands. I think Lana Twain may have overcompensated with this gown. It must be heavy as hell. Stifling hot.

But when she stands in all her glory and Ben chokes on his tongue, I decide that Lana did exactly right.

I allow Lindsi and Andi time to fix Lindsi's gown and veil before I release Ben. "Everything stays the same, except instead of watching her walk toward you, you walk *with* her. Keep the walk slow. Don't let her trip over anything. If she wants to run – in any direction at all – you don't let her go. She wants to run away to freedom, you lock her down. She wants to run to Oz, you slow her ass down. Match the steps to the piano."

"Yeah, on that note. Do you hear that?"

I stop and listen… to nothing. Silence "No. Hear what?"

"Exactly. Whoever's supposed to be playing that music ain't here."

"Motherf–" I stop when Lindsi looks up at me with a curious stare, so I paste on a fake smile, take out my cell, and shoot off another text to Alex: *Send Angelo out here. Right now!!*

Pretend everything is fine. Everything *is* fine, Goddamit.

Angelo comes skidding out of the church, and damn if he isn't handsome. I'm like a proud mama who wants to pinch his cheeks and tell him how pleased I am that he shone his shoes. His long hair is tied back neatly into a bun. Wearing a white dress shirt, sleeves rolled up to his elbows, and black slacks that fit him so well, I swoon a little for my man's friend.

Why doesn't he have a girl yet?

"What's up?"

"I need you to find the piano. Go and play the damn thing."

"I don't think you're supposed to say damn on holy ground, Snitch. Today's a really shitty day to dare the universe. We have a wedding and a baby on the line."

I want to tear my hair out. I want to tear *his* hair out. "Please go inside and play Pachelbel's Canon. Please."

He looks at me like I just spoke Mandarin. "I don't know that piece, woman! I can't just pull it out of my ass."

"Google it, Alesi! Find the sheet music, it ain't that hard. I need you, man."

"What do you have to do out here? I'll swap you?"

"You wanna be wedding planner? Go for it. I'm exhausted. I need to pace them. Livi first. I need you to get in there and play. Please Ang, I'm begging you."

"I don't know that song!"

"Fuck it!" I dial Marc when I remember a moment we shared from long, long ago, and as soon as he answers with a 'Yeah, baby?' I rush on. "I need you, Marc."

"What do you need? Are you okay?"

"Yup. Baby's still swimming inside me. Piano. I need you to go find it. Bang your fists down like a monkey. Make some magic."

He laughs, but I know he's standing. I know he's looking. "What do you actually want me to play? And why didn't you ask Ang?"

"I did ask him. He's a pussy and scared to break his nails. Do you know Pachelbel's Canon?"

"I do… not."

"What did you people learn in music school? Jesus, Marcus!"

"Um, sorry princess, we didn't go to music school. Unlike you, Miss Fancy Pants, the rest of us just learned in a garage."

"Fine, do you know Canon D?"

"Nope."

"What *do* you know? Play anything you want, but not that one from Twilight. Way too cliché."

"You don't like that song?"

"I do, but I'm not launching my career off a song I stole from a Vampire movie. Pick something else."

"Paradise, by Coldplay? I can play that like a boss."

"Fine, Coldplay." I spin. "Lindsi, you're walking to Coldplay. Embrace the change. Own it." I bring the phone back to my ear. "Catch you on the other side. Make some magic. I'll be listening."

"I'll be playing for you. Love you, baby. You look beautiful."

"You literally haven't seen me yet!"

"No, but I know you're beautiful anyway. Take it easy, okay? Don't stress. It's bad for the baby."

"Play, Marcus. I can't send Livi in until we hear the music."

"Sitting down right now. I'd just like to point out you *didn't* call your boyfriend from the King's to save the day. This is on me. Remember that when you're flirting with him tonight."

"Yep, will do. Catch ya."

"Meg!" His voice cuts down the line mere seconds before I hang up. "Say it. Don't leave me hanging." He starts playing. I can hear it through the phone and as it drifts out the open doors above us. "Tell me what I wanna hear."

"I love you, Marcus."

"Atta girl. Give 'em hell. See you in a minute."

I love him too much. More than I should. So much that I'll be ruined if something ever happens to us. Long gone are the days that I can walk out because I need *space*. Now, I'm a slave to him. I never want to stop serving him.

I spin to find my small audience watching me. "Right. Piano's set. Angelo, go away. Find your seat, we're walking in in a sec." He jogs away after dropping a kiss on Lindsi's cheek. "Livi, honey, you look perfect. Give Uncle Marc a wave on your way in. He's playing special for you." I take her hand in mine, and slower than I'd like, make my way up the stairs that Ang easily jogged two seconds ago.

If I run right now, I've no doubt this still-unnamed-because-we-don't-know-the-sex baby will just fall out. I take pride in the number of Kegels I've done in the last few months, especially since the Lamaze chick told me I should be doing them, 'or else.' I should have Terry Crews-esque biceps in my vagina at this point, but even with all my work, I feel like the baby will be walking out at any moment.

We reach the top of the stairs with the rest of my bridal party only a few steps behind us, and when Marc transitions to Pachelbel's Canon flawlessly, I grit my teeth and vow to thank him later, *not* smack him for being a fibber about what he can and can't play.

"Stand up straight, baby girl. Shoulders back. Big smile. Walk straight to Oz, but not too fast. Time your steps to the music. Uncle Marc won't let you fall."

With a nervous nod, she practices her slow steps even outside the church. Entering the huge double doors as ushers in fancy black suits open them for her, the music blasts out the door for the twenty seconds they stay open for her.

Oz has her in his sight now.

I turn back to Lindsi. "She's fine. How are you doing?"

"Crapping my pants to be perfectly honest."

"Well don't. I spent hours gluing little rhinestones onto those panties. Don't mess them up. Andi..." I take her hand and bring her forward. It's weird that she's not crazy wild Andi. She's behaving herself. "You ready?"

She nods and caresses my belly seriously. "You okay?"

"I'm fine. Baby's fine."

"If you drop your baby at the wedding, can you name her Andi?"

There she is. "Sure. Now go. Shoulders back. Pop your white-girl ass. Riley's on the right side. Midway, close to the aisle. There's a whole list of single men in there. I have an actual list, procured just for you. Make me proud and I'll hand it over at the reception."

Her eyes sparkle with fun, and though she smooths down her dress and pops her ass, she doesn't take her eyes from mine. "Most eligible?"

"Blake. Front man of the King's Chaos, twenty-six years old. No reported secret babies, no reported cocaine addictions. Mostly it's only family inside; from the station, from the gym, but the King's got an invite. He's single and absolutely *not* ready to marry up. If you're looking for hot fun, he's your man. If you're looking to marry, Riley's no doubt looking fine as hell."

Ben's face blanches. "Can you stop? That's my aunt."

"No, Ben." I turn to him seriously. "These are important details." When my internal clock dings, I thrust Andi toward the doors as they silently open again. "Go. Ass out, boobs out. Look good, but leave some of the beauty for the bride."

I turn as soon as she disappears. Taking Ben's hand in my left, and

Lindsi's in my right, I squeeze and smile. "You're both shaking. It's fine, guys. That's your family in there. We literally ate dinner with almost every single one of them at some point this week. Marc will change the music in a sec, that's your cue. Walk slow. Let your adoring fans get an eyeful. Ben, honey, you look so handsome. Your mama did so good. It's your job to give her to Oz. It'll mean a lot to her if you hand her over gracefully. Don't call your step-daddy a motherfucker in church. Save that for the reception."

He chuckles nervously, but it had to be said. It's not like he's never said shit to Oz in the most vulgar ways. "Alright, the music is changing. Are you ready, honey?" When Lindsi nods yes, but her nervous eyes scream no, I keep hold of their hands and drag them to the doors.

Setting them where they have to be, I move around and fluff out her dress and straighten her veil. "Just walk with Ben. You look beautiful. Let him lead you. When you reach Oz, he'll take over. At that point, Benny, you take up your position next to Alex. Everything from there stays as we practiced. Once you're with Oz, everything will become easier. Just follow the instructions, repeat after your priest, marry your man. As soon as you walk in and get halfway down the aisle and take everyone's eyes with you, I'll step in and the doors will close. I'll be standing at the back watching and making it all go to plan. When you're pronounced married and the music starts again, look to me and I'll signal you to go, though at that point, it doesn't matter so much. Do whatever you want."

The photographer flitters around us obnoxiously. I'm not sure the *click-click-clicking* has stopped once in the last ten minutes. He must have a thousand photos already. "Second photographer's inside. Videographer's inside. Pretend they're not there, just be you, be natural. Look at Oz. That's where the goods are. Are you ready?"

She nods nervously. Then she frowns. Then she nods again, minus the nerves. "I'm ready."

"I knew you would be. Give him hell. He's going to swallow his tongue when he sees you." I usher them forward, and when the doors open and Marc's music changes, the sound of standing bodies tells us it's time.

Ben takes the first step, and falling in sync, they step through the doors together. That's her son, but he dwarves her. He's sixteen now, but he looks like a man. Just like Katrina, these single moms are raising amazing young men who will grow to make amazing young women happy one day.

I count it out and wait for them to reach the midway point, then stepping in moments before the ushers seal the doors, I smile at the back of everyone's heads.

Just as planned, everyone follows her like moths to a flame.

I study the room, the flowers, the guests, the wedding party. Alex stands at the front beside Oz, and both men watch Lindsi and Ben move toward them with awe in their eyes and odd grins on their faces.

Both in James Bond-esque three-piece suits just like Ben's. White shirts. Ties that aren't tied as tight as I'd do it, but they look good anyway. Their hair is combed and styled – and it takes me a moment to realize this might be the first time I've ever seen them that way. I can see the actual hair gel holding their hair in the combed lines, when normally these guys just roll out of bed and shove on a hat.

I look around at the guests. At all of the Kincaids sitting on the Bride's side. At the Kincaid kids looking smart as hell. Oz and Alex's coworkers on the Groom's side. Luc and Kari sit side-by-side on Oz's side. Then the twins. Jess. Laine. Angelo. Scotch and Sammy.

I slide my eyes around the room and note the guests' undivided attention on Ben and Lindsi, but when I turn to my left toward the music, my heart melts when I meet his indulgent eyes.

Marc plays flawlessly. He watches me with that pesky lock of hair hanging over his eyes, and he grins when he looks me up and down. "Beautiful," he mouths softly.

Making a heart shape with my hands and fingers, I tap it to my chest and smile when his eyes soften. Yeah, I love him, so friggin what? It's not an 'I told you so' thing. It just happened, and I'm not super sorry about it.

Though he's watching me, as though he has a second set of eyes on Lindsi, his fingers slow on the piano when Lindsi reaches Oz and Ben hands her over with a gruff, *'here.'*

At least he didn't swear.

I don't bother taking a seat when the priest introduces himself with a booming voice. This is my job, so I walk around inconspicuously to make sure everything runs smoothly. Marc doesn't leave his seat, but as though this beautiful wedding is boring to him, his eyes don't stop burning a hole in the back of my head.

The priest talks about love and commitment. He talks about joining families and conflict resolution. I move past the Rollers' side of the room, and when Bobby Kincaid shoots me a kind smile, I take that as an 'awesome job for not alerting the media to this.'

Bobby Kincaid, Jimmy Kincaid, and Jack Reilly, their brother-in-law, are all former champion fighters. This is a small town, and though around here on a day to day basis they enjoy normality, we all know that the media would be all over this wedding if they knew about it. It's the exact reason why every vendor providing their services today tripped over their own feet to rush forward and volunteer.

A perk to being the daughter of a lawyer is that I can get airtight NDA's drawn up. Not one single person providing their services here today would dare blab.

They risk everything they've ever worked for, plus a whole lot more on top.

The ceremony takes about an hour total. Not as long as some full religious ceremonies. Not as short as mine was. Neither of us were really making promises we meant, so as though in unspoken agreement, Drew and I chose the fast track ceremony.

It would be distasteful to lie in church for longer than necessary.

Andi stands at the front holding Lindsi's bouquet in her left hand, and Livi's hand in her right. They sniffle and smile, and they watch Lindsi pledge her life to a very handsome Oscar Franks.

Alex and Ben stand to Oz's left, and though I knew it would be dicey, when Oz finally gets to kiss his bride, Ben bites down on the swear I know tastes like bitter shit on his tongue.

He's a good kid. He's amazing. But watching his mom kiss her brand-new husband isn't at the top of his list of things he wants to do, ever.

Marc begins the wedding march before I have to ask, and turning back to their family, Oz and Lindsi smile wide and throw their hands in the air.

They did it.

No one died, no babies were delivered, and Ben didn't swear at the priest.

So far, this wedding is a complete success.

22

MEG
MAYDAY, MAYDAY!

Alex taps a spoon to his champagne glass and demands two-hundred and thirty-four guests' attention.

Once the bride and groom worked their way back down the aisle toward me – it took almost thirty whole minutes of hugs and back slaps – we set off to Oz's house for photos.

Just the closest friends were invited: the band, Alex and Jules, Britt and Jack. Andi. Just family.

Everyone else invited today had to find something else to do for a couple hours, and though some weddings allow their guests an open bar at the reception venue while they wait, I nixed that idea.

No way was I risking a drunk King's Chaos band. And I wasn't allowing anyone to mess up the room before Lindsi and Oz got to see it.

So, our sort of small group spent a couple hours in the woods behind Oz's home, and our photographers took some of the most magical images I've ever seen in my life. The only thing we were missing was a unicorn, and if I'd thought of it sooner, I would've made it happen.

A part of me wondered if I should be at the reception for last minute caterer questions, but in the end, I decided I'm here for Lindsi.

That's it.

Wherever she is, I am.

If the caterers can't figure out their jobs at this point, then they aren't worthy of bigger and better events in the future.

Marc left my side only when he had to pose in the photos, but when he didn't have his hand on my back, his eyes were on me. Always.

If he's noticed the way my face tightens with pain every now and then, he hasn't mentioned it. The baby isn't coming. We're just hitting that point in pregnancy that the baby has run out of room, and every move he or she makes, dislodges my ribs.

That's what hurts; the almost broken bones.

I take another look around the amazing reception venue, at the crystal chandeliers that were installed specifically for tonight. At the backdrop behind the bridal table, the sheer curtains and fairy lights. The flower arrangements on every table. The centerpieces. The dishes that are mostly eaten. The band who look amazing in their suits – both bands.

I have another hour or so to keep this thing together, then I'm in the clear.

"As Oz's best man, it's my responsibility to say a few words," Alex begins into the provided microphone. His tie has been loosened every hour since he put it on, but I don't mind. He did good at the ceremony. He did amazing with the photos. He could walk around in tighty whities now, and I wouldn't even mind.

Much.

Ben stands beside Alex with his permanent scowl, and like he sucked on a lemon, he leans into Alex's space and adds, "*One* of the best men. *One.* There are two of us."

Alex frowns and gently pushes Ben back. He sways on his feet and sends my stomach plummeting. "Ah, yeah, so, Oz and I have known each other a long ass time. Since around kindergarten. This little *pendejo* walks into class with a swagger like his–" He stops with a choked garble when he realizes where he's going with that.

Oz's Ma is here, and she doesn't need to know what's hanging between Oz's legs.

Thankfully, with an elbow to the ribs from Ben, Alex changes direction. "So, this kid walks around school all cocky like he's the biggest badass that ever lived. Turns out this kid was so messed up with his words, he wasn't even sure when he was speaking Spanish or when he was speaking English. It still happens even today. Big bad Oz gets flustered and he busts out his Spanglish. That's when you know you're winning a fight." Alex pauses with a smirk, and turning, since Oz is sitting at the table to the left and slightly behind Alex, he winks and turns back to the crowd. "He hit me. That's how we officially met. I was talking to this chick in the lunch line; Sally–"

"*Puta*," Lindsi drops quickly.

Alex chuckles into the microphone. "Right. Puta Sally. Turns out Oz was panting after this chick, she was talking to me in the lunch line in kindergarten, like seriously dude," he spins dramatically, "it was kindergarten! What do you think we were talking about? It wasn't about boys and girls and what they might do together. We were talking about the beige crayon. Legit! It's a shitty color." He turns back to us.

I thought I was in the clear. I thought my work was about done, but this speech has potential to ruin everything.

"But he saw me talking to this girl that, I might add, he'd never talked to before. He got it in his head he liked her, but he never talked to her. So he hits me! Took a swing and knocked me flat on my ass."

"You deserved it, and more," Oz adds with an entertained smirk. His arm rests over Lindsi's shoulder and his lips on her temple, but he's having fun. Lindsi's smiling. The guests are smiling. I'm okay. This is salvageable.

"Our lunchroom monitor pulled us apart," Alex continues. "Because you know there's no way in hell I just sat on my ass and let him hit me for no reason. Mr. James pulled us apart, sent us to the principal. That walk to the office felt like we were walking the plank. But I learned my first Spanish swears that day. He's been my best friend ever since."

The guests make the 'awww' sound. That might have been the worst speech ever, but the sentiment remains.

Alex loves his best friend.

Lifting his glass, Alex waits for the crowd to quiet. "So, to my brother, my best friend, my right hand who has literally saved my life in the field, *literally...*" He turns to Oz with emotional eyes. "Seriously, man. I give you shit, but you're my best friend and brother by choice. I wouldn't trade you, not even for Puta Sally."

Oz lifts his glass with a soft smirk. "I love you, X."

"I love you, brother." Waiting for the crowd to copy him, everyone taps glasses and takes a sip, but before the chatter can die down, Ben bullies his way to the microphone and bumps Alex back.

"Hello everyone. My name's Ben Conner and I'm the other best man. The *best* best man, if you will." Alex's eyes narrow and burn holes in the back of Ben's head. "Oz and I didn't get off to the best start... In fact, like he hit that *pendejo* on their first date, well, I swung at Oz on ours. But a friendship bloomed immediately."

"A friendship? Immediately?" Oz barks out a laugh. "What's in your glass, Sasquatch?"

"Shut up, Pig. Let me love on you for a sec." I swear he mumbles *'Mom said I have to'*, but the sound is muffled by the laughing guests. "Anyway. I know Oz had a best friend before I came along—"

Alex's head whips back. "*Had?*"

"But," Ben continues easily, "once we got to know each other, I know I monopolized Oz's time. I'm not sorry about that. We hung out at his place a lot. We ran every day. Still do," he adds in what I'm positive is another shot at Alex. "Oz spars with me at the gym. Too bad you hate that gym, X. It's prime bro bonding time. The day Oz decided my mom was prettier than you, is the day you lost your best friend."

"Lost?" Alex steps forward and snatches the microphone. "I didn't lose shit. He's right there and I'm standing here as best man!"

Ben takes the microphone back with a smartass grin. "First, don't swear like that in front of Ma. Use your Spanglish like a gentleman or shut the hell up. And two, you've had thirty years with him, I've had one, yet we're both best men, so..." He winks obnoxiously. "Which of us was promoted faster? Anywho!" He spins when Alex lurches forward to take the microphone.

I feel like we're in 8 mile, and they're B. Rabbit and Lyckety Splyt in their rap battle.

I don't know which is Rabbit and which is Lyckety, and I don't know which one will lose this showdown, but I turn to Marc with gritted teeth. "This is going to end badly."

He laughs and presses his hand to the small of my back. He knows exactly where to press into my muscles to relax me. "Let them go. This is entertaining as hell. Bets on who throws the first punch?"

"If anyone throws a punch, I'll smash them both. They will not ruin this for me now that I'm almost over the finish line!" My stomach tightens painfully and steals my breath, but Marc doesn't notice when Ben continues on with his speech.

I will not have this baby today. I will not. I refuse.

"So now that Oz and I live together, he and I have become the best of friends. Plus, Mac." Ben nods at his *other* best friend. "Mac gets around, and he finds trouble when left alone for too long, especially when girls are watching him act a fool, so I can't forget him. As a matter of fact, we went fishing last weekend. Just the three of us. Me and my two best friends." Ben turns to Alex with comically apologetic eyes. "Oh, that's rude of me to mention, since you weren't invited. Sorry, forget I mentioned it. Anway," he lifts his glass to the snickering crowd, "Mom and Oz. I love you guys a crap-ton, and though I might've been resistant to this at first, I can't think of anyone else who loves my mom as much as she deserves. You chose well, Oz, and though you don't deserve her, you'll do. I love you."

Despite Ben's mildly insulting backhanded compliment, you'd think he spoke poems with the way Oz smiles and his eyes sparkle with emotion.

Everyone raises their glasses and takes a sip. Ben turns to head back to his seat, but when Alex takes the microphone again, he stops and snaps his spine straight.

"Yo, Oz, remember that first time after we turned twenty-one and we went out together? It wasn't our first time drinking – sorry Momma and Dad… and Ma – but it was our first time out legally."

Oz lifts his hands with a grin. "Don't tell that story, X. My wife can hear you."

Alex waves Oz away and turns back to his audience. "Nah, it's fun. So, we were twenty-one and so drunk we couldn't walk straight – though we damn well tried. Now, if every friendship has a sensible one and an idiot, then that makes Oz our idiot." He turns to Ben. "I don't know which of you and Mac are stupider, but you should probably find a third to keep y'all alive next time you wanna do stupid shit. But for the sake of my story, I'm saying every idiot has his best friend." Alex's chest puffs with pride. "And this particular night, Oz found himself in some hot water 'cause he kissed a girl that didn't belong to him."

"Dude!" Oz snatches up a dinner roll and pegs it at his not-so-best friend's head. "Are you stoned? Can you stop with the girl stories?"

Again, Alex brushes him off. I don't think he's high, but I do think he's six fingers of whiskey past drunk. "Relax, man. She already signed the contracts. She ain't running now."

Ben stomps forward angrily and shoves Alex away. Snatching the microphone, he glares at Oz. "She didn't sign any contracts, *cabrón*. Watch your 'tude."

Oz throws his hands up at Alex. "See! You get me in trouble, I didn't do shit."

"*Mijo!*" Oh, dear lord. I press the ball of my hand to my forehead when Oz's ma stands angrily. "Stop swearing in front of all these people. You make yourself look bad."

"Ma! It's them. Alex and Ben, sit the hell down, both of you. You make me look bad!"

"Nah." Alex snatches the microphone back and turns to the King's Chaos. "A little mood music, guys?" Their drummer starts a low tap-tap-tap. "So, Oz and I, 'cause we were best friends since I was five or six, we went out for the first time with real legit ID's, Oz kissed this girl, Oz got his ass handed to him for kissing this girl."

Again, Oz angrily pushes to his feet. "I did not! Nobody kicks my ass."

Alex dramatically nods at the crowd. "He did. He got knocked on his ass. But we won't tell his secrets. Pissed – figuratively and literally – we rolled our asses out of that gangster club and decided to find fun elsewhere."

"Alex. Stop."

Marcus chuckles beside me. Leaning into him because I'm ready to pass out, I turn my head. "Do you know this story? How does it end?"

He shakes his head quickly, and with a large grin, turns back to the train wreck that plays out ahead of us.

"So, we head to Rhinos and pick up some new girls." Alex sways on his feet and squints to look past the lights shining in his eyes. "Sorry, Jules. Promise I love you the most. You look so pretty, by the way."

She sits back at the table most of the rest of Marc's band sits at. With her arms folded across her chest, her legs crossed one over the other, her perfectly sculpted brow promises him absolutely zero sympathy when he's sick tomorrow. "Go on, Alex. I wanna hear it all."

He smiles like she's the coolest wife on this planet. He just doesn't get it. For tonight only, the responsible one in the Alex and Oz show is sloppy, and tomorrow, he's in a world of trouble. "So we pick up these chicks from Rhinos, but don't worry, they had all the twenties tucked into their chonies, not singles."

Ben's eyes pop wide. "You fuckers picked up whores?"

Alex makes the pshht noise. "No, *tonto*. Not whores. Dancers."

Oz's face drops to his hands.

Ben's eyes light up.

Alex thinks he's telling the best damn story in the whole world. "So we go to this other club, much dirtier than 188." He points at the Kincaid table. "Your club is much nicer. No syphilis warnings anywhere."

Jon Hart – one of the Rollin Gym brothers – lifts his beer with a wicked smirk. "Thanks, bro. Appreciate that."

"No, seriously." Alex is sidetracked from his dancer story. He's on a roll. "I know I'm mean to you guys a lot. And I do go looking for you at night. I get a sick thrill out of arresting you pricks, especially when you got your pants down, but I love you anyway."

"Oh Jesus," Bobby barks out a laugh. "The deputy's smashed."

"No, no, I love you too, B-man. I pretend to be mean, but really, if I went to high school with you lot, I'd wanna sit with you at lunch."

"Thanks, Deputy. We probably wouldn't invite you to sit with us, but only because it's fun messing with you. You're a cool dude, deep, *deep* down."

Alex smiles like he missed the subtle jabs. "Thanks, Bobby. That means a lot to me." He taps a hand to his heart. "I have a best friend already, but if I didn't, or maybe if someone shot him, you'd be a cool replacement." He studies the red-faced table of Kincaids. "But not Jack. He's not shit to me. He texted me the other week. Maybe 'Bambie' is near 'Alex' in his phone, but don't ever ask me about panties again, *cabrón*. You, motherfucker, are dead to me."

"Alex!" Britt shoots daggers from beside her quietly laughing husband. "Take it back. He's not dead to anyone!"

"Ugh!" Alex groans dramatically and makes a big show about turning front on to Jack. "I take it back. Don't die. That'd piss my sister off. Pissing her off would piss me off. And while we're on the subject, don't get her pregnant again. I did *not* like that shit!"

Britt turns her flaming face into Jack's bouncing chest. She groans something that only the people at her table can hear, but squeezing her shoulder, Jack simply meets Alex's eyes. "Tell me you love me, X. Now's as good a time as any; we're at a wedding, man. Tell me you love me like a brother."

He sways dangerously on his feet. "I will *not* say that."

"Say it, X. Do it. Give the people what they want."

How did we end up here?

I step forward with the intention to steal away the microphone, but Marc pulls me back with a, "Nuh-uh. No way are you stopping this. Alex is telling his truths."

"Marc, this is my career."

"It's only family here, baby. Relax. Let it play out."

"Will you support me forever if I can't make a career out of this? I don't wanna be a kept woman anymore, but I will. If your drunk ass brother ruins this for me, I swear, I'll happily let you support me."

He chuckles and squeezes me against his chest. "For the rest of my life, baby. Relax."

"I won't tell you I love you, *Jackhammer*." Alex spits Jack's fight name like it tastes of rotten lemons. "Maybe you and I need a fight like the one you and Bobby did."

"Oh, hell," Marc cracks quietly. "He's challenging heavyweight champions. Alex isn't a champion. He's just a drunk idiot."

Jack smirks. "You want a tiebreaker beatdown? We could organize it. I'll even do it with my left arm tied behind my back."

"Deal!"

Britt slaps Jack's chest. "No!" She turns to Alex. "No. Absolutely not. You're drunk and stupid. Sit down."

He shakes his head like a dramatic Maybelline model. "Not sitting. I was tellin' a story. Oh, the whores!"

"Dancers!" Oz shouts nervously. "Dancers, not whores." He turns to Lindsi pleadingly. "Dancers, Angel."

Alex waves him away. "Whatever they were, they weren't worth the money."

"You paid them, Pig! What the hell?"

Oz drops his head into his hands. "We paid them to *dance*. At the club. To dance! Nothing else."

"Yeah, well." Alex spins dramatically when he realizes the drummer stopped. "Mood music, Luca!" It's not Luc. Jesus Christ. "It was a good time for money for us. We found these," he does the finger air quotes, "*dancers*, and when their shift was over, we decided to head out to Popcorn Palace to get drunk and lucky."

Oz simply shakes his head. He's dying. He's dead. "I'm gonna kill him."

"We stole two bottles of cheap shit vodka, you know the kind that literally burns holes into your esophagus as you drink it. We took these girls and we walked our happy asses across town to the palace. Took us hours, but instead of sobering up, we just drank more and got messier."

"Alex, I'm begging you, man."

Alex snickers and waves Oz off. "Nah, it's a funny story. So at that point, twenty-one, still in the academy, but my daddy was already pulling the plug on his career. Shitty boss, Dad!" Alex pauses and looks at a man in the crowd. "I'm still mad at you about that. You retired to travel with Momma, and fresh outta the academy, we get that fat idiot as chief. Not cool, man. So me and Oz steal these bottles, not that we ever stole any thing else before or after that," he's still looking at his dad, "promise. But this one time we did, we walked our asses across town with these girls on our backs."

I look up at Marc as a similar memory flashes through my mind. Marc didn't piggyback me the night our group walked across town drunk, and at the time, I never would've guessed he'd considered it, but now that I know him better, now that I know more, I wonder if maybe he did want to.

And maybe he would have, had he been given the chance.

I wonder how different my life would be if I'd never met Drew at the party that night. If I'd never invited him to walk back with us. Maybe I would've ended up walking beside Marc instead. Maybe we would've started talking years sooner than we actually did.

He looks down at me with a shy smile, takes my hand with his and twines his fingers between mine. He drops a kiss on my brow.

Yeah, I think things might be a hell of a lot different today had I made different choices that night.

He lays his spare hand over my still tightening belly and whispers into my hair, "You okay?"

I nod. And I definitely don't tell him his baby is hurting me. I have twelve hours to go. Twelve hours to get out of this wedding success-fully, pack up, sleep, then I can *maybe* consider having a baby. "I'm good. Do you remember that time we all walked h–"

"Of course." He nuzzles my neck. "I'll never forget."

"Would you have held my hand that night… if I offered?"

He nods and presses a smiling kiss against my skin. "Yup. In a heartbeat. Even though I was only fifteen and you were scared of going to jail for kissing a minor."

"So we get across town," Alex continues obnoxiously. "I swear, we're walking up to the Palace barely before the sun came up. Legless drunk. Giggling like girls; me and Oz were the gigglers, not the girls. We have these grand plans what we're gonna do to these pretty girls when we get inside."

"Alex Turner!" Oz stands with a pointing finger. "Sit your ass down now. Give the microphone to someone else."

Again with the 'pfft' noise. "Nah. So we get inside this dilapidated house. We think we're hot shit 'cause we brought these girls home with us. We walk in side by side, we fight 'cause the door only fits one man at a time. We trip with these girls on our backs. Our empty bottles smash on the hardwood floor. We face plant, but that's okay, we'd planned to take it horizontal, anyway." Alex stops and frowns. "Different rooms, though. Like, we weren't gonna see each other's asses or anything. The palace was a whole house, so we could do our thing in privacy and still be the OG's."

I smother a laugh and pretend it's a cough. He's never going to live this down.

"But, because this dodo head wouldn't step back and let me in first, we fight, we trip, we land on our faces. My girl gets a twisted ankle. *Next minute,* we're waking up at four in the afternoon, girls are gone, wallets are gone, phones are gone, so we can't call for help. We had to walk our asses back to town again."

The hundreds of people in the room burst out in laughter. Here I was imagining this was turning into some embarrassing orgy story, when in reality, they were fleeced and unlucky.

Oz drops his face into his hands.

Can Latinos blush? I think they can.

"All of that to say," Alex continues easily – he thinks people are laughing *with* him, "Best friends for life, Oz. We go to the academy together. We drink together. We pass out together." He turns on Ben all *Lyckety Splyt.* "He's *my* best friend. You're just an add on. Don't get comfortable."

I swear, the sophisticated wedding I so laboriously planned with diamonds and crystal chandeliers turns to a backyard bonfire. The spectators cup their mouths in mockery and do the 'oohs' and 'burns.'

Ben takes the microphone arrogantly and circles Alex like a predator readying to strike. "He thinks it's bragging to talk about a failed orgy."

Most of the crowd laughs. Most. But not Lindsi. "Benjamin! You shouldn't even know that word! Where did you learn that?"

He shrugs, but I don't miss the smirk he shoots at Mac. Those boys talk grown ass stuff that they absolutely shouldn't. "Read it in a book, I think. Don't worry about it. My point is, Deputy Dawg thinks he's hot shit because he broke a girl's ankle and passed out in his own urine." He looks back to his rapt audience. "I'm only sixteen, but even I know that ain't cool, *and* you probably ended her career that night. Ever think of that? Now, we both know Oz would rather his best friend be cool like me, which is why he chose me as the *best* best man."

"Our job titles are the same, Conner! There's no *best* best."

"You go ahead and keep thinking that, Deputy, and I'll go ahead and know the truth." He flicks his shirt collar arrogantly. "I'm just saying…" He pauses thoughtfully. "Actually, maybe we should put it to a room vote. Hands up if you think I'm cooler than him."

Oz raises his hand first.

Victorious, Ben sweeps invisible dust from his shoulder.

"No," Oz says. "I'm not voting. I'm asking to speak."

"Oh, of course." Ben points the microphone in Oz's direction, though he refuses to loosen his grip. "Go ahead, *best friend.* Tell 'em the truth."

"The truth is you're both idiots. Sit the hell down!"

Stricken, Ben snatches the microphone back and hugs it against his chest. He turns to Alex with fake bravado. "He doesn't know what he's saying. He told me yesterday he only talks to you because he feels sorry for you. 'Cause you wouldn't have friends if it weren't for him."

"That's a damn lie!" Alex snaps. "You think you're cool because you go fishing with him. Get the frig outta here, junior. I've been fishing with him a million times."

"Frig? Do the big-boy swears offend you, ankle breaker?"

"At least I've kissed a girl, and at least her mom didn't beat me up. Whatcha got to say to that?"

"I've–" Ben's eyes wheel around the room. Shit's getting sticky. "Well, at least I never paid a whore and still couldn't seal the deal!"

"She wasn't a whore. She was a dancer! And at least I got Jules pregnant. Whatcha got now, boo?"

Pandemonium.

23

MARC
POPEYE

"So…" Ang smirks playfully, his word almost pure laughter in the afternoon cacophony of tools being thrown around and men swearing. "Last night was fun."

I lean against the side of a 1983 Chevy pick-up truck in his garage, with a soda in one hand and my phone in the other.

The wedding's done, and Meg's officially due. Which means I'm on high alert and waiting for her to call.

She might literally only be twenty feet from me in the garage lunch room, but I'm still clutching to my phone, just in case.

I'm not game enough to leave her alone so I can work. I'm not going back to the house unless she is, and she refuses to for now, because she's fielding calls about the 'wedding of the decade.'

Okay, so it's not the wedding of the decade as far as socialite standards go, but it was the classiest wedding this town has ever seen, and the funniest wedding this family has ever seen.

She's moaning and groaning that it was a flop, meanwhile, the rest of us have sore faces from smiling so hard.

Meg was right about kicking our band out and getting someone else in. There's no way I could have enjoyed that shit show as much if I was playing.

"So, there's a new baby on the way." I take a sip of my Coke and swipe a sleeve over my mouth. I can't stop smiling. "Guess that explains why he got so hammered last night. His own little celebration, I suppose. Drinking for two."

Angelo snorts from under the hood. "It's a good time to be alive, Macchio. Family's growing. First Britt. Scotch. Your baby will be here any day. Then X."

I look up at the sound of boots on the concrete floor, and at the same moment Luc's eyes meet mine, Meg and Sammy come tearing out of the lunchroom to intercept.

His light eyes are dark, his face sunken and sad. The smile I grew up knowing is gone.

"We need to talk." He stops six feet away with his hands up in surrender, but before I get a word out, Meg's back is to my front and she's pushing me back so I'm pinned between her and the Chevy.

"Get outta my way, babe."

"Nope. Nope. Nope."

"I don't wanna fight anymore." Luc takes another step forward. I don't miss the way Angelo grabs Sammy and pushes her behind him. Not that Luc or I would hurt her purposely, but every time I look at his fucking face, I want to smash it up. Now I just have to move Meg. "Just hear me out," Luc adds. "It's been too long."

"You need to leave, man. I don't wanna hit you anymore. It doesn't make me feel better, so leave. Don't talk to me anymore."

"We're brothers! You're letting a girl get between us."

"She's not just a girl! She's my sister. And *you* put her there! Not me. I told all of you fuckers that she's ours to protect, not to covet. What the fuck is the matter with you, Lenaghan? At what point did you stop and think *'oh she looks good. I'll just hit on her. Marc won't mind.'* That's my baby sister!"

"She's not a baby!" he booms back. "She's a grown ass woman. She's smart and funny and loyal and caring."

"Save it, Luc. I don't wanna hear it." I physically lift Meg an inch off the ground and shuffle her aside. "I'm done. I used to love you. We were family." I watch the way his eyes shutter. "But now we're not.

Family doesn't hurt family like that. Family doesn't take advantage of family like that."

"I'm not taking advantage of anything! This is like beating my head against a brick wall; I'm not looking to fuck her over! She's not an overnight fling for me. She's my forever, and your inability to see that hurts everyone. Including yourself!"

"I'm not hurting anyone but you, Luc. And you deserve it. You drove a wedge between me and her, and I let you. I made her cry too many fucking times, but a wise person talked me around. She told me not to waste the *now* just because my sister is having a momentary lapse in common fucking sense. You can talk out your ass all day long, Luca. You can convince yourself and everyone else around here that she's your forever, but you aren't fooling me, and you aren't *hers*. You're her rebellion. Her wild streak before she finds the right guy."

"She's mine!" He steps forward and angrily slams his hands against my chest. "She's mine. This isn't a fucking fling, and just because you *think* you made up with her, just because you buy her lunch once a week doesn't make her sleep better at night."

"Don't fucking talk to me about how she sleeps! If you were a proper fucking brother, you wouldn't have any clue about that!"

"You take her to lunch, you talk about everything except the one thing she wants your approval on, then you send her home and pat yourself on the back for being the bigger person. Bullshit! She's not stupid, Macchio. She knows you're faking it, and it hurts her."

"So walk away!" I push back. "Walk away and let us repair our relationship!"

"I'll never walk away, Macchio. Never!"

"What the hell is going on in here?" Kari storms into the garage. Her long curls are tied up in a ponytail high on her head. "Why are you two still fighting?" She rushes forward and steps between our adrenaline pumped chests. "Why do you insist on pissing a circle around me? Both of you!" She turns on me, and I swear, when he wraps his arm around her hips to pull her back, my brain snaps.

Red tinges my vision. Whooshing fills my ears. Adrenaline zings through my muscles, down my arms, to the soles of my feet and back up through my thighs. My body readies for a fight, and my mood – so fucking happy five minutes ago – now matches and eggs me on.

Smash him.

Kill him.

"Popeyes."

My head whips up at the faint cry. Like a sniffer dog searching for its target, my nose sits high in the air as I search.

"Popeyes. Help me!"

I spin to Angelo, and when I find just him and Sammy, I spin again. "Meg?" I spin a full three-sixty. "Where's Meg?"

"Help me!"

Finally snapping out of our stunned silence, our group break at the same time. "Meg!" I dash into the lunch room only to find it empty. "Meg? Where are you, baby?"

"Out the back!" Luc shouts in panic. I sprint in the direction of his voice, and when I push the door open, I come to a dead stop when I find her on the concrete ground, laid out on her back with her legs bent and her pants wet with blood.

"Oh no. Oh no, no, no, no, baby." I skid down beside her and bring her head into my lap to give Luc and Kari space near her legs. "Meg, what happened?"

"Baby's coming," she cries out. Tears stream down her face, and her hands clutch at the concrete ground in search of something to hold onto. "It hurts."

Luc's serious face snaps around when Sammy and Angelo run out. "Call an ambulance. We need them here, now. You can't have your baby here, Meg. Hold on, honey." Angelo whips his phone out immediately and dials. "What's going on, Meg? How many minutes apart are your contractions?"

She cries out as another takes hold of her body. Luc lifts her left leg, and Kari takes her right. Together, they bring her thighs high until they touch her stomach. "I don't know." She breathes, pants, breathes just like they tried to teach us at Lamaze. Was I listening? No! Because I was too busy hating on Luc. "Few minutes," she pants. "About two."

"Two?" Luc snaps almost angrily. "What the hell, Snitch? What happened to seven minutes? Or five? Or hell, four!"

"I was working through it."

I stroke the blonde hair back from her forehead. She's already sweating. Her face pale. Her knuckles white.

"Units are on the way," Angelo repeats with the phone still at his ear. "She's in labor, I guess. I don't fucking know!"

"Alright, Snitch. We're just gonna wait it out. We don't wanna have this baby here. Wait for the bus, get you to labor and delivery, then you can have it."

She looks up at me with teary eyes. "I know those tests came back fine, but–"

"Nope. Don't even start that bullshit. This isn't make believe, baby. This isn't a drama soap, this is real life, *my* real life. Don't check out on me now."

"I'm just saying, just in case."

"There's no just in case, Megan! Fuck. Concentrate on what you've gotta do and stop with the doomsday shit."

"We need towels." Luc looks around to Sammy. "Towels. Blankets. Something, please."

She sprints away to the stairs leading to the apartment above the garage. Luc's face looks genuinely pained as he watches Meg writhe on the ground. "I haven't washed my hands. I don't have anything. Can you tell me if you're close, Meg? Do you think you're close?"

She pants, breathes, nods, pants. "I feel like I have to poop."

"Fuck!" His eyes wheel around the space around us. His eyes lock with Kari's, like they're having a silent discussion. Then back to Meg. "Can I take your pants down, Snitch?"

My eyes snap to his in shock. "Fucker, you what?"

"Meg, honey. We need to see. I'm sorry. The ambulance is on the way, but if you're ready to push, then I need to take your pants off."

She nods and clutches at the ground so hard, her nails snap. "Yeah. Pants. Go. Whatever." When he leans forward to lower the maternity denim, her body turns taut and she cries out. "Wait," she whimpers.

Pulling her legs into her chest and bearing down, she lets out an animalistic groan, which sends Luc into a tailspin.

"Don't push yet, Meg. No pushing." He whips her jeans down before anyone can object. Pulling her sticky with wet and blood panties down her legs and over her shoes, he drops them to the side and accepts towels that Sammy rushes out to us.

Unfolding them in a rush, he lifts Meg's hips and slides a towel under and shoves the rest of the pile into Kari's lap. "Do we have a med kit?" He's asking Kari, but he's looking at Meg's white face. "Do we have anything?"

"No, but the bus is on the way."

"Can you hold on two minutes, Snitch? That's how long it'll take. Two minutes, then you can move into the ambulance. They'll have sterile equipment. You need to slow this down, try to relax."

"It hurts," she cries out. Her stomach moves and changes. Her legs flex against Luc and Kari. "Like fire."

Luc's eyes snap down between her legs. Slowly glancing back up at me, he stutters out, "She's crowning. We don't have time."

"Get it out," Meg demands. "You have a duty of care to the baby, right? Get it out, make it safe."

"We're making you both safe, Snitch. Don't get all melodramatic on me now."

I want to spew. My heart literally pounds so hard against my chest, I feel like it's going to explode free and run away. I adjust my legs under her head in an attempt to make her more comfortable.

I don't know what else to do.

I don't know how to help.

I don't know what the fuck my life is going to be like an hour from now.

I reach forward and take her mutilated hand in mine and allow her to squeeze me instead of clutching at the ground. "I've got you, baby. You're gonna do amazing."

"I'm so scared." Her watery eyes meet mine upside down. "Don't call me dramatic, just hear me out." Fat tears slide down the side of her face. Her lips quiver with cold, or shock, or pending doom. I don't know which. "I'm so scared. Please don't call her Megan. I'm begging you not to do that."

"I won't." I slide my hand along her face and swipe away tears. "I promise we won't call her Megan."

"Promise you'll do better for her. She'll be your world, even if I'm not around. Don't pine after a dead person."

My throat presses closed and threatens to kill me. "I promise. She'll be my world. She already is. You both are. I love you, baby. It's not time to go yet."

She nods and looks back toward Luc and Kari, and when her body tenses, her eyes screw shut. She lets out a cry of pain and pushes against them when they hold her legs up.

"Count it out, Snitch."

"Push, ten, nine, eight, seven..." Kari counts calmly. My baby sister manages to stay calm and take control of what could be a life or death situation, meanwhile I'm freaking the fuck out.

Luc looks up at me with wonder in his eyes. "I see your baby, Macchio. She's got more hair than you do."

Meg cries out when Kari finishes the count. Letting her body fall heavily against me, her chest rises and falls dramatically, and her breath comes out in choked sobs like she just sprinted a half mile.

I continue to rub my hand over her hair, like I can subconsciously massage away blood clots. It's ridiculous, and I keep telling her she's being dumb, yet I find myself stroking her head anyway. "Stay with me, baby. Don't leave me."

"Can you hear that, Snitch? Sirens. They're coming. Help's nearly here."

"I have to push again. Luc, I have to push."

"Hold on." He lifts her legs and positions himself somewhere I never would have guessed he'd be. Yet I don't care.

"Save my family, Luc." I wait for his eyes to meet mine. "Please save my family. I'll forgive you for anything, just don't let them hurt."

"Not letting anything happen to them." He scoots closer so he's facing between her legs. Sammy moves in closer and takes one leg, and Kari takes the other so Luc's hands are free to catch.

To catch my fucking baby.

Jesus Christ, I think I'm going to have a heart attack before this is done.

"Any problems with your pregnancy until now, Snitch? Blood pressure. Growth. Everything's fine?"

"Everything's fine," I tell him. "Blood pressure was always fine."

Just the whole aneurysm thing.

He nods his silent understanding and moves in closer. If the universe decides to fuck us over like that, there's nothing he can do. Nothing even the most skilled physicians can do in the most equipped hospital. "We're not gonna make it to the hospital, Meg, so we gotta do it here. Couple more pushes, we're almost past the worst of it. Baby's coming down faster than it should."

"It's hurts. It burns so bad."

"I know, honey. That's normal. Relax for a minute." He swipes his sweaty face on his shoulder. "You need to rest between contractions. Save your energy." He turns his torso in search of tools that aren't there. Kari presses a towel to his hands without being asked, and with a quick smile, he turns back to face between her legs. "Another one is coming, are you ready?"

The sirens grow louder, and police sirens join the music in the air around us. The cavalry is coming, but when she starts choking on her cries and her body tenses, I realize we're on our own.

"Ten, nine, eight…"

"Push, baby." I lean down and kiss her forehead.

"Get off me!" She slaps me away. "Get. Off. Me. Marcus." I sit up in shock to find Luc smirking.

My girl is crowning in a parking lot, my brother – who's dating my sister – is sitting between my girl's legs, and he's fucking smirking.

"Four, three, two, one."

Luc leans in close and works with both hands. Meg cries out to the same rhythm Luc's shoulders move, and when he sits back, she screams out in pain.

Every cry she lets out sends daggers of pain through my heart.

"I'm sorry," he murmurs. "Left shoulder was stuck. Just gotta…"

He looks up at me. "Ya know, stretch the skin around. Last push. I promise. Rest for a minute, then when Bear tells you, you push. Count with her. This is the last one. I promise."

Everyone's breath races in and out like we're all having a baby. We're all sweaty, nervous, freaking out, wrecks.

All except Kari. Cool as a fucking cucumber.

Alex's cruiser slides into the parking lot and stops barely twenty feet away. He jumps out and sprints toward us at the same time the space starts filling with garage workers and customers. A second cruiser pulls up, and immediately, Alex and his officer start moving everyone back.

An ambulance slides into the gap between the cruiser and my truck. I watch as EMTs jump out of the ambulance, but Meg starts screaming and my attention is ripped back to her.

"Last one, Meg. This is it. Count it out."

"Ten, nine, eight…" Kari grunts under the pressure of Meg's straining legs, but she continues counting with a perfectly calm voice, and with Luc working frantically between her legs, I know the exact moment my baby slides free.

Meg's body falls limp. Her legs are lowered gently by the girls.

Luc picks up my purple skinned baby, lays it across his arm so it faces the ground with dangling legs, and massages its back rhythmically.

No cries. No fucking cries. "Where are the cries?"

"Gimme a sec," he murmurs without looking up. Meg cries in my lap. I cry watching Luc massage my limp baby. Kari works on covering Meg with towels, and Sammy watches speechless as Luc massages.

He sits up on his knees, like he wants to stand and shake the baby, but he can't. The cord's still attached. EMTs stop in our group with med bags. Looking up, he demands, "Suction."

They pass him a tiny little blue bulb. Shoving it in the baby's nostril, he suctions goo out and wipes it on the towel on Kari's lap. More suction, more goo. As though it were a time lapse video, I watch my naked baby transform from dark purple, lighter through to a dark pink, until finally with a sneeze, the baby lets out a garbled cry.

With a collective sigh from my family, one of the newer EMTs shoves an insulated blanket into Luc's arms, and he uses it to expertly wrap the baby up nice and tight. "She needs to be transported to the hospital. Watch for hemorrhage. That shit was quick. Ten minutes from start to finish. She said she was contracting at two minutes, we didn't know before that." He holds my baby in his arms like a proud papa and turns back to Meg with a smile. "Wanna hold?"

The hand she uses to clutch to me loosens, and with a sob, she nods. "Yes please."

"Hang on, guys. Let's get her onto a stretcher first." EMTs move in and shuffle me aside like I'm invisible. Luc sticks close to Meg, but only because he literally has no choice; the baby's still attached to her.

I stand on shaking legs and watch men I don't know maneuver the love of my life onto a bed. I stumble back into Angelo, and he steadies me while Kari steps into me with a giddy smile and adoring eyes.

With a sharp whistle, Luc has my sluggish attention snapping back to clarity. He lifts his chin as if to say 'come here,' and when Kari releases my hand, I walk forward hesitantly and stand over Meg. Luc places the baby on her chest, and though it feels like we're moving slower than molasses, from pushing the baby out to laying it on her chest, barely more than three minutes have passed.

Luc claps my shoulder and moves along with the stretcher. "Climb in after them. We'll be in the car behind."

I nod and clutch to the side of Meg's bed. I can't speak. I can't thank him. I can't do anything except clutch to her and the baby.

"By the way, you have a son." He smiles shyly, and that same smile since when we were kids shines through. "I caught a glimpse before we wrapped him up. A little boy, Macchio. Congratulations."

"Come on, sir." Some dude in uniform shuffles me away from Luc as the stretcher moves toward the ambulance. They load her up roughly, and though I want to beat their asses for not being careful with her, I'm still walking around in stunned silence.

I'm a daddy.

She's okay.

In fact, she smiles and holds her pinky finger in our baby's mouth to suckle.

Luc helps me climb into the ambulance. Shuffling along so I can sit alongside Meg, an EMT climbs in with us, and another slams the back doors closed. Another minute passes, blood pressure cuffs are slapped around her arm closest to me.

I'm speechless. I'm in awe. I'm shocked stupid.

"Hey." She turns her head on the pillow. She can't reach out. Her arms and hands are busy, but her smile says everything. She's okay. "That hurt more than your paddle."

The EMT chokes on his laughter, but turning it into a cough, he looks away and fusses with tubes and plastic syringes.

It's my turn to break down. My turn to lose my shit.

Big fat tears slide over my cheeks and my lips wobble, totally non-masculine, when I look at my baby suckling in her arms. "You're so amazing, Meg. You just did that." I lean forward and stroke the baby's dark hair. "You made a baby, you grew him, you did magic."

"*We* made a baby," she adds with a smile. "Don't try and ditch out on me now that the sleepless nights are coming."

I laugh, but it comes out like a watery cry. "Not ditching. Not going anywhere. I love you, Meg."

The EMT takes the cuff away, so now that she has a spare hand, she reaches out and pulls my head to her chest.

I go.

And I cry like a bitch.

"Shh, hey, it's okay."

"I'm so in love with you, Meg."

"I love you, too. Lucky, seeing as now there are two of you."

I choke on my weak laugh. "Can you stop trying to be funny right now?" I sit up, though my face remains barely six inches from hers. "You just took my life and smashed it open. You just gave me a family, Meg. I don't know if you know what that means to me."

She slides her hand up to the back of my head. Running her fingers through my hair, she pulls me forward until our foreheads rest together.

"I do know. And I'm so in love with you too, Marc. I'm not going anywhere."

～

MEG and my nameless baby boy are sent to isolation straight out of the gate.

As soon as the ambulance arrives at the hospital bays, they're wheeled in. She's still on the maternity floor, but her and the baby remain in isolation, which means one visitor at a time, gloves, masks, hand washing.

It's just precaution, because the delivery took place on the outside and the hospital can't risk an infection hurting the other babies and moms.

I don't even care.

I know they're healthy. I watched her birth my chunky baby like a pro, and I watched my family help her. She's fine, she's healthy, and my baby can cry harder than any other baby I know.

That's all that matters to me.

A couple hours after being loaded up for transport, Meg and I finally find ourselves in a room alone; just the three of us.

Immediately after arriving here, the craziness continued; the baby was weighed and measured and tested. The poor little thing was given foot pricks to test sugars, and Meg was hooked up to an IV of antibiotics, just in case. They helped her deliver her placenta, and with Meg's permission, I was allowed to cut the cord – and nearly choked to death with how gross those actions truly were.

For future children, I'll be passing on that *pleasure.*

Our now overpaid and underworked OBGYN arrived to check her over, determined that she was 'lucky' there are no tears; he signed her off as healthy and told us he'd be back tomorrow to check on her.

Dude's not getting a Christmas bonus.

"Nine pounds, Marcus." She turns her not-masked face toward me. Masks are for everyone else. "Almost ten. I should be pissed."

I sit on the edge of my chair and lean toward them as Meg attempts to breastfeed on the bed. The baby was cleaned up and wrapped properly, someone plopped a tiny little yellow beanie on his head to keep him warm, then he was handed over and we were told to hit the emergency call bell if we needed help, or when Meg's IV bag ran out – whichever came first.

That's it.

They trust us to look after this human with absolutely zero experience, no resume, no qualifications.

I should've paid more attention in that damn Lamaze class.

"Nine pounds is small, baby. I was bigger than that."

She turns to me with pursed lips, but I don't miss her dancing eyes or the rose blush in her cheeks. "Couldn't give me a dainty little dancer girl?"

I lean forward and lay my head on her pillow so I can watch the baby eat. He looks like me. There's an actual human on this planet that looks just like me. It's surreal.

"Did you really want a girl, Poot? You're ready to share your princess status? Or do you want a second Marcus; handsome, smart, perfect."

"And humble." She laughs softly, though the melodic sound cuts off immediately as she scrunches her face.

I snap my spine straight and reach out to grab... something. "What's wrong, baby? Are you hurting?"

She shakes her head and reaches out to stroke my jaw. "I'm okay, just don't make me laugh. Or cough... Or move."

"Oh... okay." My eyes pop wide with realization. "Ohhh! Okay. No funnies."

"No funnies." She pulls me down to her pillow. My spine is bent at a ninety-degree angle to the side, but I don't give a shit. I'm not moving.

"We need to name him."

She nods gently and fusses with her boob near his mouth. His eyes are closed, his lashes are long and tickle his fat cheeks.

I never thought to ask about baby photos of myself or Kari, but I really want to go through my parents' stuff now just to compare looks.

"He's really perfect. I've never fallen so completely in love with another human being as quickly as I have with him."

She smiles teasingly. "Not even me?"

I laugh. "Took me a few weeks for you. You're an acquired taste."

"A couple weeks? As in, this year?"

"No, baby, as in back in high school."

She watches me with soft eyes. Reaching across, she strokes the soft skin just below my eye, just like she did to the baby. "What about Kari?"

"What about her?"

"Insta-love?"

I breathe out a sigh of contentment. "I remember the day she came home from the hospital. That was the first time my dad said he couldn't play catch with me, because he wanted to snuggle with the new baby." I look up and meet her beautiful eyes. "I hated her stupid guts."

She laughs and clenches her body tight. "Stop. Don't make me laugh."

"Sorry, baby." I turn into her palm and drop a soft kiss. "No, not even Kari. Took me a couple hours to understand the hype. But this baby…" His eyes flutter softly as he sleeps and suckles. His eyes are dark as night, but I see the color. I wonder if he'll get her eyes, or mine. "He's perfect. He came from you, Meg. How can he not be perfect?"

"What do you think about the name Chance?" She looks up at me hesitantly. "I mean, he made it past the pill, and condoms, plus my sheer willpower that I never get pregnant. Then that decision I almost made." She swallows heavily. "He deserves a special name that reflects the odds that he beat. He was coming to this world no matter what."

I nod and study his precious features. "Chance. I love it."

"Yeah?"

"Mmhmm." I kiss her shoulder and will my body to stop shaking. It's now or never. "Meg?"

"Hmm?"

"Will you marry me?" When she stops breathing, I rush on. "It doesn't have to be today. Doesn't even have to be this year. I can wait that other shit out. But eventually, I want to give you both my name. Nothing would make me happier."

I finally look up into her eyes. I'm terrified of the rejection. Terrified she could easily squash all of my hopes and dreams in one simple, single syllable. Or worse, she could make it into a joke. She could try to crack a funny because she's uncomfortable.

But instead of rejection, I find a sweet smile and a small nod. "Yeah. I want to marry you, Marcus. As soon as I can, I promise."

I stand over her and drop a long, closed mouth kiss on her lips. Laying my forehead on hers, I don't even try to hide the crack in my voice. "Thank you. I'll make you happy. I promise."

She nods and swipes away an errant tear. "I love you. I promise to try and make you happy, too."

I sit back down, but I don't release her face. "You already do. You have no idea how happy you make me."

We sit in silence for several minutes as the enormity of today catches up to us.

We're a family. She's okay.

She survived her worst fear and now we get to name our baby together. We get to raise him together.

"What about a middle name?" she murmurs softly. "Chance Macchio needs a middle name."

My heart soars that she named him Macchio. She makes all my dreams come true so easily. "Um," I clear my throat of the emotion that wants to choke me. "Montgomery? Monty for short."

She smiles. "That's sweet of you to suggest. We don't have to, though. Maybe we can save Monty for our next son."

My heart wants to explode with happiness. She didn't want any babies, then she made an exception for me, for this one, but now she's talking more. "I can't explain to you with real words how happy you make me, Meg. You'll never truly understand."

"I will." She runs her hand along the back of my neck. "I do understand, because I feel the same way about you."

"I have a middle name suggestion…" I look up and meet her eyes. "Something that means a lot to me."

~

MY PHONE RINGS another hour or so later with my sister's name flashing on the screen, and with a gentle nod of approval from Meg, I sit back and answer. "Hey, Kar."

"Is everything okay? We don't know anything."

"Everything's fine." Emotion makes its way up my throat and into my voice. "I'm sorry I didn't call. I've been hanging out with my baby."

"It's okay," she laughs nervously. "I was just worried. How's Meg?"

"She's good. Everyone's good. Can you come up and see us?"

"Of course." I listen to her stand and move around, and with a murmured *I'll be back,'* she comes back to the phone. "Where are you guys? What room? Do you want me to bring you anything? Is Snitch hungry?"

"Isolation. Room 404." I look to Meg. "You hungry, baby?" She shakes her head. "Nah, she's fine. Come up. I wanna see you."

"Alright, I'm leaving the waiting room now. I'll be up in a sec."

"Is Luc with you?"

"No." Her voice catches on disappointment. "I told him to wait in the waiting room. I wouldn't bring him up and upset you guys during such a special time."

"Can you go back and get him? Bring him up."

She stops on the spot. I can tell by the noise around her. Not to mention, her squeaky shoes on the hospital floor. "Why? Are you gonna hit him? I don't want you to hurt him, anymore. He doesn't fight back. It's not a fair fight."

I shake my head and take a deep breath. Cleanse. Wash the shit away. "You really like him, huh?"

"Yeah." She laughs nervously. "I really kinda love him. The real kinda love, not the love I had for my Polly-Pocket."

"More than Polly-Pocket?" I make an exaggerated 'woah,' that thankfully brings a smile to Meg *and* Kari's lips. "Bring him up please, Kar. I wanna tell him thank you for today."

"No hitting?"

"I promise. No hitting. I'm too fucking mellow right now. Bring him up, but don't, like, kiss him or anything in front of me."

She snickers and begins moving again. "Okay, we'll be up in a sec."

I hang up and slide my phone back into my pocket. Laying my head down to resume stroking my son's face, Meg drops a kiss on my forehead. "You wanna hold him?"

"Yeah." I sit up instantly and smile. I've held him twice so far, and both times lasted less than two minutes before someone took him away for some reason or another. When they returned him, they always gave him to Meg, and she would whip out her boob.

I watch her gently unlatch his lips from her nipple, and pulling her top up, she carefully passes the tightly wrapped bundle into my arms.

There's a power surge a man feels when he's holding his firstborn child.

I feel like a God.

Like a king.

I feel invincible, and I am, because as long as they're both in my sight, in my arms, as long as they're both okay, nothing can hurt me.

I sit down with him cuddled up against my chest. He has chunky lips with that same bow shape that Meg has. He has my chin. I don't know how to describe my chin. I mean, it's just there, bone and skin, but despite its plainness, it's mine and it's his.

I reach into his blanket and pull out a tiny wrinkled hand. His nails are long, the skin a little flakey. "He's so beautiful. Little baby Chance."

Meg turns slightly onto her side, places a hand under her cheek, and watches us. "You guys look really handsome together."

"Yeah?" I look up and smile. I can't stop smiling. "You did so good, Meg. Can't tell me growing and birthing babies isn't a kind of magic."

"We can never tell him he was conceived while I was bound and blindfolded. That'd scar him for life."

I snort in Chance's face and shake my head. "I promise to never tell him that. No man ever wants to know that much about his mom." I play with his fingers and look up at her seriously. "Can I ask you something really important?"

"Of course." She watches me warily, like I'm about to drop the hammer and give her bad news.

"Do you think… when your–" I hesitate dramatically. "No. Never mind."

"No, what?" I know her better than she thinks. She just can't help herself. "Tell me, Marcus. Ask me the question."

"Okay, it's just, well, I was wondering if maybe your dad had your mom gagged when you were conceived."

She stares at me. Stares. Stops breathing. Silence. Disbelief. Then she bursts out in laughter and smacks my arm. "You're disgusting! And I told you not to make me laugh. It's gross."

"Aww, you guys." We look up when Kari stands at the open door with a mask hanging off her ear. She steps in and moves directly to the sink to wash her hands. Following in much slower, Luc keeps his eyes on the floor and moves to the sink to wash his hands. "It's good to see you guys smiling."

I scoot over on my seat when she walks toward me, and sitting on the arm of the chair, she leans into me and studies the baby. "He's so handsome. Such a good looking baby."

"He looks like us."

She looks at me arrogantly. "I know. So beautiful."

I bump her back with my shoulder, though loosening my grip on my son, I hold him with one arm and pull my sister into me with the other.

I don't miss the way Luc sticks to the closed door.

Leaning against it, he watches us in silence. He's not willing to risk pissing me off.

"What did you name him?"

"Chance." I look up and smile into my sister's eyes. Green and identical to mine. "He was nine pounds, ten ounces, and twenty-two inches long. My big strong son, Chance Macchio."

"Yeah? Macchio…" She smiles and looks at Meg. "That's a super cool last name. Only the elite get to use it."

Meg shrugs easily. "I'm probably gonna be on the elite team some-time soon. It's a coolish name."

I chuckle. "You're already one of the elite, baby. We just get to have a party and invite the King's Chaos to make it official."

"You totally nailed the whole *'not having a baby at the wedding'* thing, huh?" Kari smiles. "Oz and Lindsi are off, by the way. Partying in Barbados or some such thing."

"Barbados… Really?"

Kari pushes Chance's long hair behind his ear. "Nah, they probably just went to work. I dunno. They're happy, though. The wedding was amazing."

"Did anyone film X's rant?" Luc asks. He realizes his mistake when we look up, but with an apologetic smile, he goes back to studying the floor.

"Um, Kari…" I take her hand in mine. "Meg and I were talking. About family. About life." I wait until her cautious eyes meet mine. "We were wondering if you'd be Chance's godmother?"

She chokes on a happy cry. "Really? Of course! What does the job entail? I don't know, but I'll do it anyway. Do I get a wand? A pump-kin? I feel like I should go out and get him a gift now."

I squeeze her hand. "Both of you."

"If he asks to party when he's not supposed to, I'll say no. I won't be the 'cool' aunty. I'll keep him safe and honest and– wait." She stops and looks between Meg and me. "Both of us who, what?"

"You and Luc. Godparents."

Luc's head snaps up in surprise. "What?"

"You delivered my baby. You kept Meg safe." I carefully stand and allow Kari to slide down into my seat. Stepping toward Luc after Meg's nod of approval, he straightens his stance and looks into my eyes. "Luc, I'd like to introduce you to Chance Luca Macchio. Your nephew and godson, if you accept the job."

"You named him for me?" His hands reach out to touch, but he snaps them back. "You want me to be his godfather? Are you sure?"

"Are you sure about my sister?"

He nods instantly.

"Then I'm sure about you. My entire world changed today, and stupid fights about who my sister dates became exactly that; stupid. She helped deliver my baby today. You and Kari did it all by yourselves. You didn't panic. You didn't fuck it up. You had time to smirk and tease me when Meg started hitting. It helped me see a lot of things clearer.

"Things like the fact she's not a baby anymore. She's a grown woman, and as such, she gets to choose which douches she dates. And you're not the young and stupid Luca anymore. You're a grown ass man who saves lives for a living. I let my shit get in the way of seeing that, so I'm sorry. If my sister insists on dating, then there's no man on this earth I'd rather love her. I know you'll treat her right."

"I will." He swallows nervously. "You have my word, for the rest of our lives, I'll treat her well."

"You break her heart and I'll kill you. It's fair that I warn you."

He chokes on a nervous laugh. "Noted."

"I love you, Luc. I'm sorry for hurting you."

He and I both know I'm talking about emotional hurts, not black eyes, and when he leans in and hugs me over the baby between us, he whispers the same back in my ear.

Pulling back, he sniffs awkwardly. I could play on it. I could tease him about being a bitch, but he delivered my son today, so, "Wanna hold him?"

He nods eagerly, so we do the awkward baby shuffle and I move Chance into Uncle Luc's strong arms. I lead him toward the single chair in the room.

Knowing how the fuck this is going to end, I tap Kari's knee. "Get up. You're not allowed to sit with him. Not allowed to sit *on* him. In fact, new rule, just don't look at each other in front of me."

She stands. She steps back. But when he sits, she sits straight back down on his knee and leans in to study the baby.

I want to claw my eyes out.

I want to beat his ass when his spare arm goes around to her opposite hip to hold her close. "I'll kill you, Lenaghan. I will. I'll do it."

Kari rolls her eyes. "Go away, Marcus. We're bonding with our godson. Go talk to your girl."

Ugh. "Fine! But no kissing. Never ever."

She leans down and drops a dry kiss on Luc's shocked lips.

My heart throbs painfully in my chest. My stomach heaves and my universe shifts. But I don't get a chance to beat him with an IV pole, because Meg snags my shirt and pulls me close.

She pulls me down until my face rests on her pillow, and when she's not happy with that, she grunts and scoots over in the bed. "Climb up. I want a hug so bad, you have no clue."

I climb up. Because my instincts to make her happy are stronger than they are for killing Luc.

Today.

I get comfortable on her pillow, and when she half climbs over me to rest her head on my chest and her leg over my thighs, she throws her IV arm over my stomach and snuggles in.

How could I get mad when I have all this in one single room? My son. My soon-to-be-wife. My sister... My best friend.

Life has never been so sweet.

"I love you, Meg."

EPILOGUE

<u>Meg</u>

"**D**o you want the good news or the bad news first?"

I stare across Jules' office desk and consider tossing the stapler at her stupid head. "How's about you just give me the good? Let's pretend the bad doesn't exist. That's a fun game we could play, and seeing as how my nips are sore as hell today, you kinda owe me a happily ever after."

She snorts and sits back in her chair. Tossing her long blonde hair over her shoulder, she smooths her silk shirt down to show off her still small belly. "I don't owe you shit. I'm spewing at least twelve times a day lately."

"That'll teach you for procreating. I told you that shit was gross."

She looks down at baby Chance snuggled up against my chest. He's a few weeks old and sliding into some ridiculous sleep regression.

Not that it matters. I barely wake. Marc jumps up long before I even get the chance. He snatches the baby up from the bassinet, brings him to me, I feed him, then Marc takes him back to his side of the bed to burp and soothe him.

He caters to my every need.

He's the best daddy I've ever met, and that's a tall order, seeing as I've met Scotch Turner.

I was a married woman looking for a divorce. A bitter, broke – *and spoiled* – thirty-four year old who was looking for a little fun. I ended up with the man I'll love for the rest of my life, and the baby I never knew I wanted until he didn't give me a choice.

I'm so happy with the way things worked out for me. I might have fought it all, but I don't regret one single thing.

"Meg, focus! Good news or bad?"

"Okay, fine. Good news first."

She rolls her eyes. "Of course you'd choose that first. Well, too bad, because the good won't make sense until you get the bad. Let me give it to you in steps. You ready?"

"I have places to be, Juliette. Chance and I have a lunch date with my man. Shake your ass."

"Fine. The good news is Drew's trial was a success." When I stare at her, she adds, "For us. A success for us. He was found guilty and charged for financial crimes."

"That's good. He's a sack of shit."

"Right. More good news; he was sentenced to seven years shacking up with Big-Bubba, another year added on for trespassing, and your money was ordered to be returned to you."

"Oh good. That's good. I might even pay for your services after all this."

She purses her lips. "You done?" When I smile, she continues on grudgingly. "The bad news... is you can't get blood out of a stone."

"Come again, Jones?"

Her eyes turn regretful. "Your money's gone. Every single red cent, all gone. I suspect he moved it, and I doubly suspect his girlfriend has it. But for right now, he hasn't a cent to repay you. But before you freak out, I have more good news."

Seven million dollars. Luxury cars. Huge ass house. All gone.

"Go, give me the good."

"He can get a job in prison when he's not being ass-fucked by Bubba."

"So…?"

"So, he can start punching license plates or something. They'll garnish his wage and send that to you."

"Which works out to be…?"

"Probably around twenty-five bucks a month."

I pick up a pen and toss it at her head. Surprisingly, I'm not angry like I expected. I laugh, instead. "That's not good news, you twat. He'll literally never be able to repay me before he dies."

She grits her teeth. "Good news next, then? That'll smooth out the last burn."

"Is it a legit good, or are you being a smartass?"

"*Real* good. I promise." She takes out a white envelope and pulls out documents with little 'sign here' tags stuck all over it. "Wanna get divorced, Meg?"

"Oh. Oh! OH!" I lurch to the side of my chair and startle Chance awake with my movements. I snatch up my purse and pull out my cell-phone. Swiping my phone screen open until I find the music player, I find *Celebration* and blast it loud enough to make Jules bite her lips to keep her smile contained. I dig around in the bottom of my bag until I find the pen I bought specifically for today. Pulling the lid off, I smile at Jules. "Ready."

"What's that?"

"What?" I look around the room. "Gimme those damn papers."

She rolls her eyes and hugs the documents to her chest. "Is that a gold pen?"

I look down to my hand, then back up. "Yup."

"Sparkles?"

"Mmhmm. It's so pretty."

She shakes her head and sets the papers down in front of me. She grabs her own black pen and slaps it down on top. "I don't mean to rain on your parade, but you cannot sign with gold glitter. Use my pen."

I nod solemnly, then going back to my bag a second time, I come out with my backup pen. A jumbo sized ice-cream cone shape with a unicorn head on top and flashing lights coming from his eyes that, though I think they should be fun for kids, is actually scary as hell. "I worried you'd say that, so I have a second option."

She slaps a piece of paper down in front of me with a huff. "Show me your signature on this paper. It better be black, Snitch, or I'll kick your ass."

"Pfft. I'm not pregnant anymore fatty, you are. I know which of us will win."

"Sign it!"

My hand snaps down and awkwardly maneuvers the stupid pen until I laboriously scratch out my long signature.

When she realizes my unicorn pen is, in fact, black, she nods. "Okay, fine, here you go. Sign here." I do. "And here." I do. "And here."

"Fuck it." I toss the hand cramping pen down and pick up Jules' sensible option.

"And here." I do. "And three more."

"Dude! How many times do I have to divorce him? It only took one signature to marry the asshole. Why does it take so much work to shake him off?"

She shrugs and points. "And here." She flips to the final page. "Two more. Then you're free."

"One…" I bite my lip and concentrate. *Don't screw it up now, Meg. Don't misspell.* "Two…" I look up at her when it's done. "Am I divorced?"

She shrugs and collects the papers to check them over. "Pretty much. Your dad has to file them now, but your part's done."

"I'm done?"

"You're done."

"I can get married?"

"Not today. But soon. As soon as they're filed. Is there a wedding you're inviting me to?"

"You? Sure. Alex?" I snort in her face. "Absolutely. I'll hire him on as the entertainment."

She snickers and tidies away her things. "I can't believe he did that."

"He went head to head with a teenager, and his winning blow was the fact he knocked you up." I laugh so hard it turns to piggy snorts. "How exactly did he think that would win? Ben is sixteen! If he knocks anyone up, he's dead meat."

She shakes her head and sits back. "I have no friggin clue what he was thinking."

"Did you agree to make the announcement that night?"

"Nope." She pops the P, though she doesn't sound mad at all. "He was dirty drunk and talking out his ass. I thought I was gonna have to carry him home and clean up vomit."

"You didn't?"

"Hell no! He carried me home like I was one of his whores and banged my brains out."

I wipe my hand over my eyes as tears leak and mess up my mascara. "I swear to God, I've never seen something so funny in my life."

"Funny for you, maybe. It was mortifying for me."

"Well, it's been amazing for me. It might have been my event planning skills that landed me the Trejo wedding, or it might've been Alex, but either way, I'm all set."

"Trejo?" She jerks forward at her desk. "Trejo? Which Trejo?"

"Who cares! They're richer than my daddy."

She sits back with a snicker, but laughter turns to seriousness after a moment. "I'm really sorry about your money, Meg. I tried, I really did. But like I said, I can't get blood out of a stone. He has no money sitting anywhere. No cars. No houses. It's all hidden. I'll keep working it, but for now we're at a dead end."

I sit back and pat Chance to sleep when our excitement continues to startle him. "It doesn't matter about the money. I'd say his whore has it, and seeing as she'd have had her kid by now, she needs it more than me. Let my money support her. Let her live with that knowledge. It won't last forever, but it'll keep her going long enough to get her away from him. Let's consider it my gift to the assholes."

"That's very... gracious of you. What about you? What are you gonna do?"

"Aren't you listening? Trejo, baby. Onwards and upwards from there. I'll diversify. If you hire anyone else to do your baby shower, I'll cut you. I'll be okay without that money, and earning it is a million times better, anyway. I enjoy being of the working class."

She rolls her eyes. "Fine, whatever. I think that's everything. I know where to find you if it's not. Go out, have lunch with your man. Today's a day to celebrate."

I smile and silence my phone. "I think I will."

"Where is he? I'm surprised he's not here."

I roll my eyes. "He's with Luc somewhere. They've got a bromance to rekindle."

"Alright, get ready." Luc, Ang, Scotch, and I, silent as ninja's, walk across the police station roof in the blaring midday sun. Giggling like a bunch of drunken fools, Luc and I carry a bucket between us, and Scotch and Ang carry another between themselves.

The police station is basically a huge concrete block, so we don't have to worry about creaking roofs or getting caught. We simply tiptoe because we're fools on a happy high. We stop at the front of the roof so cars driving past can see us. We get a couple honking horns, but waving them off, we motion for them to shush, and we set our buckets down just before the wall of the roof begins.

"Remind me why we're doing this?" Scotch mumbles. He's having trouble ambushing his brother. I get it, loyalty and all that, but he's smiling anyway. He wants to do this, he just needs to be told it's okay.

"Because he deserves it after that wedding speech. He's an idiot."

I laugh and pass Luc the first load. In silent agreement like we never spent six months at odds, he nods, but gone is the silly Luc – despite our current activities – and in his place is a shyer version. "Thanks, man."

I take out the second load from the bucket. "You're welcome. Get him good. We only get one shot at this before he turns around and shoots back."

He nods and looks back to the front of the cop shop.

In the last month, not once has Luc kissed my sister in front of me. That's not to say she hasn't kissed him, but I know she does that to piss me off. Never once has he initiated it, so I'm learning to deal. And if I'm being completely honest, I'd acknowledge I've never in my life seen her so happy.

Whether I like it or not, he makes her happy, and I'm not willing to lose her because of something that's not really something.

I'll never ask them their story. I'll never ask how they got to where they are now, and I'll absolutely never ask when it started. I'm just taking Meg's advice and I'm enjoying the *now*. Nothing's worth losing the now.

See. I can be reasonable.

I take my phone from my back pocket and swipe it open to call Alex, but I stop on my text screen.

Meg: I have amazing news for you.

Meg: I love you, baby daddy.

Meg: I bought that paddle. I haven't gone to my 6 week appointment yet, so you can't get laid, but you can watch me spank myself if you want. :D

Meg: ps: Wanna get hitched?

I shake my head and enjoy the feeling of my heart swelling in my chest. It's the most amazing feeling I've ever experienced in my life.

"Macchio?" Scotch throws a discarded bottle cap at my head. "Yo, wake up. You ready?"

"Yeah. Sorry." I reply to Meg quickly: *Yes. To everything. Love you, too.* Then switching screens, I dial Alex's number and wait.

And wait.

And wait.

"What's up, Macchio?"

"Dude!" I turn my voice up with excitement. "Come over to my house, quick. Benny's here and he wants to confess to a crime."

"He– What?"

"Seriously. Benny and Mac smashed up Miss Dixie's lover. He was scared to come into the station. Oh, by the way, don't tell Oz.

It'll piss him off. You gotta hurry, though. He's getting ready to split."

"Don't let him go. It's my turn for payback. Hog tie him if you gotta. Rolling out now."

"Okay, see you in a bit." I hang up and slide my phone into my back pocket, and look up into the faces of the three guys. "He bought it." We all turn back to watch. His cruiser is parked out front today, so with loaded hands, we wait.

And wait. And wait.

And... the sound of the automatic doors whir. Alex sprints out onto the front footpath with Oz close on his tail.

Oops.

Benny's gonna be in trouble.

We wait until we get the go ahead. We've been practicing this. Like a tactical team in a SWAT unit, we wait until Ben steps out from behind a tree with his hands loaded up with water balloons.

Alex skids to a stop so fast that Oz smashes into his back. Ben hesitates when he notices Oz, he wasn't part of our plans, but we're in too deep, now. We can't go back.

It's ride or die time.

I tap Luc on the shoulder and nod silently toward Alex's back thirty feet in front of us. He nods back. Presenting his fist, I bump it and transport us right back to high school.

Yeah, brothers for life. Just like we promised.

I look back to the grass and cup my mouth. "Hey, X!"

He and Oz spin, and it takes them a few extra seconds to think to look up, but when they do, their faces pale. We prepped for today by filling three hundred water balloons and carting those heavy ass buckets up onto the roof. No regrets. "Fire at will, boys!"

...And so Marc and Luc lived happily ever after...

Continue following this family in the next instalment
Pawns In The Bishop's Game

LOOKING TO CONNECT?

Website
Facebook
Newsletter
Email
The Crew

Did you know you can get a FREE book? Go to emiliafinn.com/signup
to get your free copy sent direct to your inbox.

ALSO BY EMILIA FINN

(in reading order)

The Rollin On Series

Finding Home

Finding Victory

Finding Forever

Finding Peace

Finding Redemption

Finding Hope

The Survivor Series

Because of You

Surviving You

Without You

Rewriting You

Always You

Take A Chance On Me

The Checkmate Series

Pawns In The Bishop's Game

Till The Sun Dies

Castling The Rook

Playing For Keeps

Rise Of The King

Sacrifice The Knight

Winner Takes All

Checkmate

Stacked Deck - Rollin On Next Gen

Wildcard

Reshuffle

Game of Hearts

Full House

No Limits

Bluff

Seven Card Stud

Crazy Eights

Eleusis

Dynamite

Busted

Gilded Knights (Rosa Brothers)

Redeeming The Rose

Chasing Fire

Animal Instincts

Inamorata

The Fiera Princess

The Fiera Ruins

The Fiera Reign

Rollin On Novellas

(Do not read before finishing the Rollin On Series)

Begin Again – A Short Story

Written in the Stars – A Short Story

Full Circle – A Short Story

Worth Fighting For – A Bobby & Kit Novella

ACKNOWLEDGMENTS

Thank you!

To the usual suspects,

Tink and Mac, I love you guys so hard.

Siddhi, Debbie, and Jenelle, beta extraordinaires. Thank you all for your hard work. It never goes unappreciated. I promise.

Brandi – Holy Cow! (Ha! See what I did there?) You hustle so hard for me. I love you. I really, really do. Thank you for everything you do for me.

To my Crew, you guys make me laugh. Thank you for loving my boys.

Who's next? I might leave the intriguing hook here for a minute...

insert evil laugh

xo,
Emilia

Made in the USA
Coppell, TX
14 December 2022

89439298R00173